THE PRIVATE MEMOIRS
AND CONFESSIONS
OF A JUSTIFIED SINNER

THE PRIVATE MEMOIRS
AND CONFESSIONS
OF A JUSTIFIED SINNER

James Hogg

edited by
Adrian Hunter

broadview literary texts

National Library of Canada Cataloguing in Publication Data

Hogg, James, 1770-1835
    The private memoirs and confessions of a justified sinner

(Broadview literary texts)
Includes bibliographical references.
ISBN 1-55111-226-4

I. Hunter, Adrian, 1971- . II. Title. III. Series.

PR4791.P7 2001   823'.7   C2001-930378-5

Broadview Press Ltd. is an independent, international publishing house, incorporated in 1985

North America
Post Office Box 1243, Peterborough, Ontario, Canada K9J 7H5
3576 California Road, Orchard Park, NY 14127
Tel: (705) 743-8990; Fax: (705) 743-8353;
e-mail: customerservice@broadviewpress.com

United Kingdom:
Turpin Distribution Services, Ltd., Blackhorse Rd., Letchworth, Hertfordshire SG6 1HN
Tel: (1462) 672555; Fax: (1462) 480947; e-mail: turpin@rsc.org

Australia:
St. Clair Press, P.O. Box 287, Rozelle, NSW 2039
Tel: (02) 818-1942; Fax: (02) 418-1923

www.broadviewpress.com

Broadview Press is grateful to Professors Eugene Benson and L.W. Conolly for advice on editorial matters for the Broadview Literary Texts series.

Broadview Press gratefully acknowledges the financial support of the Book Publishing Industry Development Program, Ministry of Canadian Heritage, Government of Canada.

Typesetting and assembly: True to Type Inc., Mississauga, Canada.
PRINTED IN CANADA
Second Printing, August 2002
Third Printing, August 2003

Contents

September 8. — My first night of trial in this place is overpast! Would that it were the last—that if should ever see in this detested world! Of the horrors of hell are equal to those I have suffered, eternity will be of short duration there, for no created energy can support them for one single month, or week. I have been buffeted as never living creature was. My vitals have all been torn and every faculty and feeling of my soul racked, and tormented into callous infallibility. I was even hung by the locks over a yawning chasm to which I could perceive no bottom, and then — not till then, did I repeat the tremendous prayer! — I was instantly at liberty; and what I now am, the Almighty knows! Amen.

Frontispiece from the original edition, purporting to be an extract from Robert Wringhim's diary, in his own hand. See p. 221 of the present text.

See p. 221 of the present text.

Introduction

On the first page of the *Confessions*, Hogg's fictional Editor records the marriage of George Colwan, Laird of Dalcastle, to his young bride, Rabina. That the union proves disagreeable to both parties is to be explained, the Editor tells us, by reference to movements in Scottish constitutional and religious history: "It is well known, that the Reformation principles had long before that time taken a powerful hold of the hearts and affections of the people of Scotland, although the feeling was by no means general, or in equal degrees; and it so happened that this married couple felt completely at variance on the subject" (49). The novel's dependence on such grand contexts of reference (especially in the early pages) to explain the actions and motives of characters has struck many readers as a flaw: "A clumsy mixture of the politics of the day is forced into the story," laments one early reviewer, "with a view to giving it the circumstantiality of authentic narrative" (Appendix C.4). The fondness for historical paraphrase seems a dereliction of the novelist's duty to convince us, by slow degrees, of an absent, imaginary, other world. Accordingly, the *Confessions* has frequently been dismissed as a crude and unpolished work in which Hogg confused the discourse of history and the art of fiction.

It could be argued, however, that the formal awkwardness of the *Confessions*, especially in the Editor's Narrative, is deliberately produced. The Editor is, after all, as much a character in the text as the Dalcastles and Wringhims, and the story he tells—the history he composes—is as partial and subjective an account as Robert's confession. Just because the Editor claims to be writing disinterestedly does not mean that his text is value-free, that he presents, as it were, a view from nowhere. He may profess the standards of the modern "man of science" (78), the post-Enlightenment rationalist and sceptic who bases his confident reporting of events in the dispassionate values of "nature, utility, and common sense" (57), but these still amount to an ideological position in which certain data and points of view are preferred over others. The Editor's refusal to entertain the widely mooted opinion that Gil-Martin is in fact the devil is an example of this partiality. According to him, we must consider Robert either a "fool" or a "maniac" (232) because belief in demonic possession is found only in popular (unregulated) superstition, and as such does not merit the attention of modern-minded men.

Hogg, it seems, wants us to be sceptical about histories and about those who compose them, yet at the same time his novel depends on our being informed about the past, and in particular about the constitutional and religious conflicts that have conspired to form Scottish national identity. In its peculiar structure, the *Confessions* shows an awareness of history as always an imaginative expression or interpretation of events. What struck early readers as errors and inconsistencies, such as the disagreements between the Editor and Wringhim on several important matters, or the uncertainty over whose body is in fact dug up at the end, can be taken as deliberate underminings by Hogg of the story each wishes to tell. As we read, we become aware of a growing number of discrepant details between the narratives, and of Hogg's refusal to allow any one account to emerge as definitive. What we are left with is an historical novel which threatens the truth-value of history. The past may be vital to our understanding of the story, but the past, as we encounter it, is not necessarily the same as what happened.

As the considerable body of critical commentary surrounding it suggests, the *Confessions* is a beguiling work, and one should make no pretence of mastery over it. However, a better understanding of its complexities can be achieved if we are familiar with the contexts informing the story of Robert Wringhim (what I call here contexts of reference), and the conditions under which the book was written (the contexts of production). In trying to disentangle (rather than decipher) the *Confessions*, it is helpful to consider why Hogg decided to write a novel about early eighteenth-century religious extremism at the time he did—how, in other words, the contexts of reference might relate to the contexts of production. In the course of this introduction, some of these relationships and connections will be elaborated in reference to a range of historical documents printed in the appendices. The intention is to make the various parts of the narrative more readily intelligible to the modern reader. However, it must be acknowledged that the brilliance of Hogg's novel is such that we cannot by these means claim to secure the meaning of the whole.

Contexts of Reference

The Covenanters: history and text
The story of Robert Wringhim takes place, by all accounts, between 1687 and 1712, in the immediate aftermath of bloody religious conflict in Scotland, and in the midst of profound upheaval affecting the

constitutions of Church and state. It is a period troubled by the recent past and uncertain of what lies ahead, a period in which Scottish national identity—as defined in language, politics and faith—is felt to be in crisis. The immediate cause of this crisis can be traced, for convenience sake, to 1660 and the restoration of Charles II to the English throne. Since 1638, the Church in Scotland had been Presbyterian and so had operated free from state interference. Charles sought to regain control of the Kirk by imposing on it an Episcopalian system of government. He rescinded the powers of the General Assembly in Edinburgh and outlawed all forms of public worship not authorized by his appointed bishops. Furthermore, he denounced the National Covenant of 1638 which had declared the Scottish people and their Church "covenanted" to Christ alone, and in its stead devised an oath of allegiance acknowledging the absolute authority of the king. Dissenting Presbyterians, so-called "Covenanters," refused to adhere to Charles' decrees, and for some thirty years afterwards were bloodily persecuted in their own land, their congregations violently dispersed, and their ministers proscribed on pain of death in what came to be known as the "Killing Times."

Presbyterianism was eventually re-established in the Scottish Church following the Glorious Revolution of 1688. However, the martyrdom of the Covenanters remained a bitter example to many of the colonial ambitions of the English and of the fragile hold Scots had over their national sovereignty. What is more, in the early years of the eighteenth-century the Church's authority continued to be tested by, on the one hand, greater toleration of episcopacy under Queen Anne, and on the other, the ever-present threat of a Jacobite restoration. Following the political union of Scotland and England in 1707, the Kirk had furthermore to contend with the new British parliament's in-built Anglican majority and, within its own ranks, the emergence of those who considered 1690 a betrayal of Covenanting ideals.

When conflict breaks out in the *Confessions*, it does so, therefore, in an environment already febrile with political and religious controversy. The enmity between Robert and his brother George is immediately translated into ideological terms as a struggle between vested interests vying for control of the nation's future: "Revolutionaries" war with "Jacobites," "Whigs" with "Tories," the "court-party" with the "country-party," "presbyterians" with "High-Church/Cavaliers." The hostility between the Reverend Wringhim and the old Laird opposes a "flaming predestinarian divine" (50) with one moderately inclined "to the side of the kingly prerogative" (62–63), and this personal animus finds expression in political opposition when the two men attend that "famous session" (63) of the Scottish parliament in 1703. Among other matters debated there was the Act of Security, a bilious piece of legislation designed to limit English influence over Scottish affairs and secure Scotland's right to choose its own monarch. As a landed aristocrat, Tory and royalist, the Laird would have stood against the Act; Wringhim, a Whig and revolutionary Presbyterian, would have championed it as a protection of Christ's covenanted nation against the society of the wicked and unconverted.

In a literal sense, the personal is inseparable from the political in Hogg's novel. To grasp the significance of the action, and the motives of the characters, we need to understand the holy mess of Scotland at the beginning of the eighteenth-century. This is especially important when it comes to reading the central character, Robert Wringhim. Hogg uses the crisis surrounding Scottish religious and cultural identity to define and structure Robert's mentality and provide the stimulus for his murderous career. Throughout his confession, Robert makes frequent appeal to the history of the Covenanters. He sees himself as one destined to struggle and suffer, a martyr to the truth: "My sorrows have all been for a slighted gospel," he writes, "and my vengeance has been wreaked on its adversaries" (117). Consolation comes from a shared sense of purpose with the "great covenanted reformers" (170), those brave "imprisoned saints" (155) who suffered to defend the nation's bond with Christ. At one point he mentions having read a book called *A Cloud of Witnesses* (155), or to give it its full title, *A Cloud of Witnesses, for the Royal Prerogatives of Jesus Christ; or, The Last Speeches and Testimonies of those who have suffered for the Truth, in Scotland, since the Year 1680.* This volume records the final testimonies of Covenanters executed between 1680 and 1685 by, its preface tells us, "a profane wicked Generation of *Malignant Prelatics*, during the reigns of the late King *Charles 2, James 7*" whose ambition was to bring the Scottish people "to a tame Submission and slavish Compliance with the whole Course of their Christ-dethroning, and Land-enslaving Constitutions and Administrations" (Appendix A.3.i–ii). Robert conceives of his own struggles in such terms, as a commission to free Scotland from "the prelatic party [i.e. the Episcopalians], and the preachers up of good works" (125). What he also might fairly be said to have gathered from *A Cloud of Witnesses* is a justification of violence, even of killing, in the name of Christ and the defence of the covenants. Several of the martyrs account for their bloody deeds in ways that remind us of Robert. For instance, James Skeen recounts how he was questioned about the assassination in 1678 of James Sharp, the Archbishop of St Andrews:

> He asked me, thought I it not a sinful Murder, the Killing of the Arch Prelate? I said, I thought it was their duty to kill him, when God gave them Opportunity; for he had been the Author of much Bloodshed. They asked me, why I carried Arms, I told them, I was for self Defence, and the Defence of the Gospel. They asked me, why I poisoned my Ball? I told them, I wished none of them to recover whom I shot ... They asked, if I would think it duty to Kill the King. I said he had stated himself an Enemy to God's interest, and there was War declared against him. (Appendix A.3.v)

Killing is justified for Skeen because it is motivated by religious calling. When urging Robert to the murder of the moderate minister Blanchard, Gil-Martin employs the same logic, arguing that the assassination is warranted in the name of Christ and His true church: "it is better that one fall than that a thousand souls perish" (144). This lust for a purifying violence is evident, too, in Robert's own declarations:

> From that moment, I conceived it decreed, not that I should be a minister of the gospel, but a champion of it, to cut off the enemies of the Lord from the face of the earth; and I rejoiced in the commission, finding it more congenial to my nature to be cutting sinners off with the sword, than to be haranguing them from the pulpit, striving to produce an effect, which God, by his act of absolute predestination, had for ever rendered impracticable. (136)

Robert sublimates his own conduct by appeal to a higher (albeit selectively understood) purpose in the form of the doctrine of absolute predestination. The theological basis of this doctrine will be explored below, but for now it is sufficient to observe the way in which the singularity of Robert's conviction allows him to move from the "pulpit" to the "sword" without any moral misgiving. He does not doubt the rightness of what he believes, therefore he is able to absent himself from considerations of law and morality. He has no need to enter into dialogue or disquisition when he can act decisively upon the manifest destiny his faith has revealed to him.

The placing of Robert's confession within the context of the Covenanting struggle might tempt us to conclude that Hogg is providing some mitigation of his character's deeds. But this is not the case. In fact, Hogg is at pains throughout the book to show that Robert's confidence is the product of his faulty and partial readings of the texts and doctrines he espouses. One must assume, for example, that Robert reflected neither upon himself, nor upon Gil-Martin, nor upon the significance of their deeds, in reading this passage from *A Cloud of Witnesses*, on how the devil can trap his prey by "secret fraud":

> Hence the sacred Scriptures describe him, both as a *Dragon* for *Cruelty*, and a *Serpent* for *Subtlety*: But because he either cannot, or thinks not fit to do this visibly in Person; therefore he does it more invisibly, and so more successfully by his Agents …These he Acts and Animates, as it were so many Machines, to endeavour by *Crafty Seduction*, or *Violent Persecution*, to draw, or drive the *Followers of the Lamb* from their Subjection, Obedience and Loyalty to the *Captain of their Salvation*, that he may *drown them in Perdition and Destruction*. (Appendix A.3.i)

When unable any longer to resist the accusations concerning Gil-Martin's true identity, Robert finally looks to see if his illustrious companion's foot is cloven. He is relieved to discover that it is not. To the attentive reader of *A Cloud of Witnesses*, however, that should provide no comfort. Yet Robert, incurious and impercipient, goes on to pledge himself to his "devoted friend" (221). He has selected from *A Cloud of Witnesses* only those passages that suit his self-fashioning and apparently justify his conduct. Like the Editor, he fails to interrogate the status of his own knowledge. The conviction that he is one of God's chosen people, and therefore above the law of men, rests on nothing more than his undaunted *belief* that it is so. He is in every sense a failed reader: of himself, of scripture, of history. The novel's deep ironic structure consists in allowing us *as readers* to witness these failures in comprehension. Robert's lack of suspicion about Gil-Martin is consistently amazing. Even as he views the body of his own murdered mother we find him marvelling at the strange power of Gil-Martin to turn his heart with pride "towards that which [is] evil, horrible, and disgustful." Yet he remains convinced of his own and Gil-Martin's virtue and of the "counsels of heaven" (199) which protect them. Here, as elsewhere, Hogg challenges us to be better (more critical) readers than the characters in his novel.

The irony perpetrated against Robert has led many critics to argue that the *Confessions* is a satire on Covenanting extremism by the moderate Presbyterian Hogg. Certainly, there is plenty of biographical evidence indicating Hogg's hostility to all forms of religious fanaticism. In a letter of 1832, he describes a sermon heard in London as "the ravings of enthusiastic madness" (Garden 243), and in his lay writings repeatedly expresses his preference for "the mild and humble religion of Jesus" over fervent proclamations of belief: for "[religion] is a dangerous topic, and apt to be productive of more good than evil" (*Lay Sermons* 37). However, it would be wrong to conclude that Hogg's opposition is solely to the kind of disfiguring zeal evident in a particular faction of the Church of Scotland. In the *Lay Sermons*, he condemns megalomania as it occurs in people of all dispositions—the sceptical rationalist as much as the devout believer:

> When a man is astonished at what he knows, it may be a proof that he has stood on the brink of science; but it is also a proof that he has not discovered it to be boundless and unfathomable. The ignorance of such a person makes him loquacious and opinionative, because he has never known what it was to be beyond his depth. ("Good Breeding," *Lay Sermons* 28)

Dogmatic conviction is the mark of a mind unconscious of reality. It is therefore fitting that Robert, assured of his own election and justification, should repeatedly lose his mind to delusion and fantasy. For Hogg, such dangers are especially present to the religious believer. Faith must therefore be based in a recognition of the limits of one's own understanding. As he writes in his sermon on "Deistical Reformers":

> I think it is therefore best, in supporting the doctrines of the Christian religion, always to avoid any attempt to explain mysteries. The necessity and belief of a mystery is one thing, but the explanation another ... [It] is no objection to a truth revealed as essentially necessary to our comfort, that it is above our comprehension. (*Lay Sermons* 110-11)

Hogg's moderate, liberal faith chimes with that of the Reverend Blanchard in the novel who argues against Robert's and Gil-Martin's gross fundamentalism, and who, for his pains, becomes their first victim. For Blanchard, as for Hogg, the true believer is one humbly conscious of the inscrutability of God and the frailty of his own judgement. He is a generous and self-critical reader, suspicious of dogma and violent absolutism. The ironic structure of the novel depends upon our noting the justified sinner's aberration from these positive values of tolerance and reverence.

Calvinism and the Antinomian Heresy
The ideological conflict between extremism and moderatism in the
Scottish Protestant faith arises out of the Church's distinctly Calvinist formation. In Scotland, the secession from Roman Catholicism
was effected in 1560, largely through the efforts of John Knox
(c.1514-72) who had been a student of the Protestant reformer Jean
Calvin (1509-64) in Geneva. Under Knox's guidance, the newly
established Church in Scotland embraced the full rigour of Calvinist theology, the central conviction of which was that mankind was
entirely sinful—totally depraved, in Calvin's terms—outside of
God's redeeming grace. According to Calvin, mankind was divided
into the "elect" (those predestined for salvation) and the "reprobate"
(those eternally damned). Nothing the sinner did by way of good
works or meritorious conduct could begin the process of election
by which God bestowed his grace. Equally—and of crucial importance to Hogg's novel—the elect could not, as a result of their own
actions, come to be damned.

As was the case in all Reformation theology, the writings of St.
Paul provided the scriptural basis of Calvin's thought. In his epistle
to the Romans in particular, Paul established the principles of election, predestination and justification (see Appendix A.1.v). Romans
also offers the clearest statement of the conviction that "a man is
justified by faith without the deeds of the law" (A.1.i). Paul's belief
that this was so emerged partly in opposition to his Judaic upbringing which had taught that the way for the sinner to obtain God's
favour was by strict observance of Old Testament law, especially the
ten commandments. Paul insisted, on the contrary, that righteousness came through faith and that salvation was given by God's free
will and could not be effected by "good works" or obedience:

> For Christ is the end of the law for righteousness to every one that
> believeth. For Moses describeth the righteousness which is of the law,
> That the man which doeth those things shall live by them. But the
> righteousness which is of faith speaketh on this wise, Say not in thine
> heart, Who shall ascend into heaven?... Or, Who shall descend into the
> deep?... But what saith it? The word is nigh thee, *even* in thy mouth,
> and in thy heart: that is, the word of faith, which we preach; That if
> thou shalt confess with thy mouth the Lord Jesus, and shalt believe in
> thine heart that God hath raised him from the dead, thou shalt be
> saved. (A.1.vi)

Paul's purpose was to dispel the heretical notion that mankind had
the power or ability to influence God. However, it is not difficult

to spot the dangers that might arise from a selective or tendentious interpretation of a passage such as this. Paul seems to be suggesting that faith takes the place of law and good works in the elect, and that by extension the justified are above and beyond any moral or legalistic obligation, their salvation having already been decided by God's gracious initiative. As he puts it, "now we are delivered from the law ... we should serve in newness of spirit, and not *in* the oldness of the letter" (A.1.iv).

The danger that the believer might consider himself exempt from any earthly bond lurks in Calvin's writings too. Discussing justification and Christian liberty, Calvin insists that "the faithful, when seeking an assurance of their justification before God, should raise themselves above the law, and forget all the righteousness of the law ..." (Appendix A.2.v). The elect, he goes on to say, "do not observe the law, as being under any legal obligation; but ... being liberated from the yoke of the law, they yield a voluntary obedience to the will of God" (A.2.vi). The difficulty here is that in displacing the idea that good works or obedience can of themselves lead to salvation, Calvin implies that the elect are free from necessity in respect of these virtues. Calvin believed that those in the state of grace would naturally perform good deeds and act morally. Nevertheless, it is an essential tenet of his theology that the elect are so by God's volition, irrespective of their earthly conduct, and, as John Bligh points out, this is a belief which "lends itself with the greatest of ease to an interpretation which is subversive of ... social order" (Bligh 149).

The fundamental division in Calvinist thought between election and reprobation raises serious problems too, because the question of whether one is or is not among the elect is largely a matter of self-assessment. Calvin's own approximate tests for the state of grace are notoriously unreliable: if you conduct yourself in a manner befitting a Christian, can honestly profess your faith, and feel love for the sacraments, then you can be reasonably assured of your election. The arbitrary nature of such tests arguably gives rise to the self-justifying absolutism not only of Robert but of his mother and the Reverend Wringhim as well. "To the wicked, all things are wicked," the minister says, "but to the just, all things are just and right" (58). Lady Dalcastle's response is worth quoting in full:

> "Ah, that is a sweet and comfortable saying, Mr Wringhim! How delightful to think that a justified person can do no wrong! Who would not envy the liberty wherewith we are made free? Go to my

husband, that poor unfortunate, blindfolded person, and open his eyes to his degenerate and sinful state; for well are you fitted to the task." (58)

Lady Dalcastle delights in the brilliant decisiveness of Calvinist logic: the justified person is at liberty from the constraints of law, while the reprobate (in the figure of her estranged husband) dwells in a benighted state. In the same way, Robert believes himself to be following through the natural consequences of Calvinism when he declares his preference for the "sword" over the "pulpit": because God "by his act of absolute predestination" (136) has rendered the reprobate forever beyond redemption, why, asks Robert, should the elect not put them out of their misery, so that the saints can "inherit the earth in peace" (136)?

Of course, these are the sentiments of the of the great reformers "mightily overstrained and deformed" (50). What we witness here, as in Robert's engagement with Covenanting history, are the consequences of a wilfully exploitative and partial reading of religious texts. Both Robert and Lady Dalcastle take the doctrine of predestination to an extreme that Calvin would not have endorsed. Calvin did not state that the elect could "do no wrong;" rather, his point was that mankind had no power by virtue of his own actions to influence God's judgement. As Clark Hutton explains, it was presumed that "anyone receiving the effectual call would either already be morally upright, or would become so soon thereafter. The elect would consider themselves bound by the moral law, not above it" (47).

In theological terms, the Wringhims' conviction that the elect are above the moral law is known as the Antinomian (literally "opposed to law") heresy. Antinomianism has a history as long as that of the Reformation, and, like Calvinism, is based in the teachings of St Paul. In fact, Antinomianism can be considered the logical outcome of piecing together (or reading selectively among) Paul's "polemical utterances" (Bligh 151) concerning election, reprobation and predestination. Acknowledging the doctrinal basis of Antinomianism allows us to understand why it is that Gil-Martin is able to control Robert so effectively. He does so by reasoning on the basis of Robert's own belief in the "infallibility of the elect, and the pre-ordination of all things that come to pass" (138). Robert finds it impossible to refute Gil-Martin because the latter's logic never conflicts with his own understanding that he is justified, and so beyond reproach.

In the early 18th century, when the novel is set, there was a serious outbreak of Antinomianism in Scotland which threatened the established Presbyterian church. The controversy began when two ministers of the Presbytery of Auchterarder—James Hog of Carnock, and Thomas Boston, minister in Hogg's home parish of Ettrick—were charged with Antinomianism in relation to a catechism they had drawn up (Simpson, L. 171). Later, in 1718, Hog (no relation to Hogg the author) provided the preface to the new edition of a work, first published in 1646, entitled *The Marrow of Modern Divinity* by Edward Fisher (Appendix A.4). With the publication of *The Marrow*, the Antinomian controversy came to a head and the book was proscribed by the General Assembly of the Church of Scotland. Nevertheless, *The Marrow* remained in print and was still widely available at the time Hogg was writing the *Confessions*. As Louis Simpson has shown, Hogg would certainly have been aware of the controversy over Antinomianism and Auchterarder. Indeed, in his sketch "Odd Characters," and in the story "The Mysterious Bride," he mentions Thomas Boston and his writings. It is also the case that fear of Antinomianism was still widespread among Presbyterians in Hogg's day. In 1823, Joseph Cottle (friend to the poet Robert Southey, whom Hogg knew personally) published a book called *Strictures on the Plymouth Antinomians*, following an outbreak of the creed there in 1822. That the figure of the self-justifying sinner was a familiar one in Scotland in Hogg's own time is furthermore evidenced by Robert Burns's popular humorous poem "Holy Willie's Prayer," in which a church Elder offers a prayer thanking God for making him one of the "chosen race," and calls down vengeance on the unregenerate (Appendix A.6).

In order that the reader can peruse source statements from the Antinomian controversy, extracts from Fisher's *Marrow* and James Hadow's celebrated response to it have been included as Appendices A.4 and A.5. Taken together, these documents lay out the main tenets of the Antinomian position and show how it extends logically from St Paul and Calvin. In particular, they reveal the selectivity and literalism of Antinomian discourse and its sclerotic effect on the texts it draws from. "[T]his then is perfect Righteousness, to hear nothing, to do nothing of the *Law of Works*," Fisher writes at one point (A.4.i); "Justice hath nothing to do with me, for it judgeth according to the *Law*" (A.4.iii). Of particular interest in relation to the *Confessions* is James Hadow's response to Fisher, in which he puts forward the established Church's definition of Antinomianism. In many points, Hadow's critique resembles that offered by the moderate Reverend Blanchard to Robert in the novel. Hadow writes:

> When we assert the Necessity of Holiness and Good Works, we do not mean that they are the Matter and Ground of our Justification, or that they are meritorious of Salvation, or the procuring cause of the Right and Title to Eternal Life ... [W]e say that they are necessary by the Commandment of God, and as Means to make them meet for the Inheritance of the Saints in Light. *Antinomians* oppose this Doctrine, and the Marrow agrees with them therein. (Appendix A.5.v)

Hadow's statement centres around the defining issue in Antinomianism of the necessity or otherwise of good works, and by extension, of the law. Hadow is careful to point out that while works and the law are not the basis for justification, they are nevertheless commanded by God. Thus he succeeds in repudiating the Antinomian position without violating the Calvinist principle of justification through faith. The Reverend Blanchard's attack on Robert and Gil-Martin works in the same way:

> There is not an error into which a man can fall, which he may not press Scripture into his service as proof of the probity of ... I can easily see that both you and he [Gil-Martin] are carrying your ideas of absolute predestination, and its concomitant appendages, to an extent that overthrows all religion and revelation together; or, at least, jumbles them into a chaos, out of which human capacity can never select what is good. (142)

In condemning Antinomian extremism, Blanchard simultaneously puts forward a defence of his own moderate Presbyterianism. The necessity of mounting this defence is that, like Hadow, Blanchard is being forced to acknowledge that his own Calvinist discourse is susceptible to misrepresentation, and that Antinomian extremism is in many ways the logical outcome of fundamental principles in his own faith. In seeking to remedy this, he must appeal to the idea that there is some essential moral capacity in humankind to know good from bad, and offer that as damning evidence of the abuse of scripture that Robert and his friend are committing.

Clearly, religious discourse is subject to tremendous analytical pressure in the *Confessions*, and I think it is fair to say that in this respect Hogg raises more questions than his novel is capable of answering. Indeed, one reason why the portrait of evil in the book is so enduring is because it is shown to originate, albeit perversely, from good and Godly intentions. Nevertheless, it is clearly Hogg's purpose to satirize fanaticism, and we do not have to appeal to what we know of his own religious beliefs to justify this assertion: the text itself offers plenty of evidence that this is the controlling intention.

One of Robert's earliest convictions is that the elect are in possession of what he calls a "glorious discernment between good and evil, right and wrong" (117). This absolute clarity of vision and ability to discern the world in terms of its rigid binary of good and bad, justified and damned, is the privilege of the chosen, Robert reasons, for why would God allow his people to dwell in uncertainty? The sword, not the pulpit, is thus the fitting instrument of his faith. Robert's belief that he is elect makes him intolerant of contradiction because he is convinced of the infallibility of his judgement. This trait is evident even in his childhood. At school he cannot understand why M'Gill, whom he *knows* to be "a wicked person, and one of the devil's hand-fasted children" (126), consistently out-performs him in Latin. How could it be that God would allow the wicked to be successful? Unable to bear this paradox, he brings about M'Gill's ruin, congratulating himself as he does so for exposing the manifest "guilt" of this "most incorrigible vagabond" (127).

Destroying M'Gill is Robert's way of dissolving a contradiction, of freeing himself from a puzzle that threatens his deepest convictions about himself. By extension, his initial attraction to Gil-Martin is based in the fact that the latter acquiesces in everything he says. He even looks identical to him. As their relationship develops, Robert feels himself to be increasingly "in unison" (157) with Gil-Martin intellectually, and "incorporated" (180) with him in person. Gil-Martin's great service to Robert is to preserve him from "multiplicity" (169) and disunity, to grant closure and security where there is worrisome irresolution: "he had the art of reconciling all, by reverting to my justified and infallible state, which I found to prove a delightful healing salve for every sore" (187). Gil-Martin heals and reconciles the flux and disorder of reality and experience, making the world fit with the rigidities of Robert's Calvinist either/or. Blanchard's accusation against him threatens this logic because it implies that evil can be done in the name of scripture, and done by the elect. Gil-Martin's solution is to eliminate Blanchard. "If the man Blanchard is worthy," he tells Robert, "he is only changing his situation for a better one" (144). As in a witch trial (in which those who survived the test of drowning

[margin handwritten note:] Robert never quests himself

would be burnt as witches), either way the dissident voice is silenced, the doubt eradicated.

Once again, however, Robert's absolutist world-view is the target of Hogg's irony. His determinations and judgements are increasingly plagued by failure, by some leakage in the system of his thought. This is evident in the M'Gill episode where, despite the fact that Robert frees himself from the nuisance of his classmate, M'Gill's incongruity with his scheme of things remains unresolved. Of course, Robert himself does not (or cannot) see this. In the same way, we detect the falsity of the actual moment of election because it does not occur as an inner revelation but is instead decided on Robert's behalf by Wringhim. Robert's reaction on hearing the news that he is a justified person is to seek out a fittingly elevated solitude for himself. This he figures in the soaring supremacy of a bird of prey:

> A exaltation of spirit lifted me, as it were, far above the earth, and the sinful creatures crawling on its surface; and I deemed myself an eagle among the children of men, soaring on high, and looking down with pity and contempt on the grovelling creatures below. (131)

At the moment he envisages this splendid isolation, however, he is confronted by Gil-Martin. The security of his solitude immediately gives way to a confusing doubleness. As he reflects on their meeting, Robert admits that, despite his acquiescent conduct, Gil-Martin nevertheless represents a "puzzle" (131). Furthermore, his shifting identity is bewildering: Robert is unsure if he is his "guardian angel," his brother, or his "second self" (132). As the two begin to discuss points of theology, the breakdown in Robert's newly ordained condition becomes evident. Gil-Martin concurs in every point of faith, yet at the same time he appears to be "advancing blasphemies" (132). Robert feels at once deeply drawn to him, yet is repulsed by "an involuntary inclination to escape his presence" (133). Reflecting back on the meeting, he is forced to conclude that this day of singular conviction for him was in fact entirely without certainty of meaning:

> Whether it behoves me to bless God for the events of that day, or to deplore them, has been hid from my discernment, though I have inquired into it with fear and trembling; and I have now lost all hopes of ever discovering the true import of these events until that day when my accounts are to make up and reckon for in another world. (133–34)

Robert's moment of election has not brought him "glorious discernment" but a "whirlpool" (133) of contradictions. As his confession unfolds, he is increasingly drawn to images of chaos when describing his state of mind. When he speaks, he experiences "a confusion in all [his] words" (159); bewildered by the apparent doubleness in his own personality, he feels himself to be "sojourning in the midst of a chaos of confusion" (180); caught in the weaver's web he finds himself entangled among "looms, treadles, pirns, and confusion without end" (202). Hogg's irony is effective because Robert is unconscious of the significance of what he is admitting to here: he does not sense that this disorder and doubleness in any way undermines his presumption that he is one of the chosen, blessed with certitude and the key to life. Instead it is left to the reader to note the blind spots and failures in his system, the ineradicable doubts, the mysteries and complexities and inextricable webs that elude his brutal Calvinist either/or—indeed, all that is undreamt of in his philosophy.

Contexts of Production

In reading the *Confessions* as a satire on Calvinism, as many critics do, we run the danger of simplifying it and overlooking the novel's ironic treatment of other characters, especially those opposed to Robert. While Hogg is undoubtedly critical of the extremist position, he is also conscious of the forces that form a mind like Robert's, and, as has been suggested, he expects us to be equally critical in our interpretation of the Editor and his tendentious narrative. To appreciate this other side of the story—as the novel's bipartite structure encourages us to—it is necessary to place it in the context of the early nineteenth-century, when Hogg lived and wrote, and consider in what ways it would have been significant to its contemporary readership, particularly in Scotland.

Language and Identity
In his introduction to the Oxford edition of the *Confessions*, John Carey draws a number of seductive parallels between Robert and his creator. In particular, Carey is intrigued by the crises of identity and legitimacy which Wringhim suffers and how these might be said to reflect what Hogg himself was enduring in his public and professional life. The son of a shepherd, sporadically schooled, Hogg had turned to professional writing only in middle age after business failure forced him to abandon farming. He moved to Edinburgh in

1810, and in an extraordinary leap of faith attempted to make a living from his poetry and fiction. Finding acceptance as a serious writer among the mannered, patronizing, fickle *literati* proved difficult, however. He struggled to reconcile the traditions of his Borders upbringing with the requirements of polite lettered society. Throughout his major work we see evidence of this conflict, this "perpetually shifting, ever-imitative desire to find a 'vision' and form acceptable to a polite Edinburgh and British audience" (Gifford 11). The religious fundamentalism and superstition characteristic of Border belief sat at odds with the secularized "rationalism" of post-Enlightenment Edinburgh, causing Hogg to evolve a manner of writing by which he would be able to sustain "both belief and scepticism ... leaving the reader to choose between them" (Gifford 20).

Gifford's account accurately defines the characteristic evasiveness of Hogg's fiction, with its interest in guises, masks, equivocations, and intrigues in the narratorial perspective. In the *Confessions*, he establishes a series of narrating voices—the Editor's, Robert Wringhim's, and the character "James Hogg's"—but refuses to bring these perspectives into alignment. He endorses neither the Editor's historicizing rationalism nor Robert's fanatical confession, while the information given to the Editor in the last section by "James Hogg" proves wholly inaccurate. We can trace this interest in constructing identities to Hogg's involvement with *Blackwood's Magazine*, which he began co-editing with John Gibson Lockhart and John Wilson in 1817. The famous table-talk pieces, "Noctes Ambrosianae," in which Hogg appeared in the guise of the "Ettrick Shepherd," started running in the magazine in 1822. Originally co-authored by Hogg, Lockhart and Wilson (the last under the pseudonym "Christopher North"), the "Noctes" series eventually came under the exclusive control of the two Edinburgh men. Much to Hogg's annoyance, they proceeded to make the Ettrick Shepherd character a buffoonish and reactionary figure, depicting him as a chronic drinker and gormandizer. More damagingly still, articles and opinions began to appear in the magazine attributed to Hogg which he had not authored, while genuine contributions of his were rejected. The contemptuous snobbery and double-dealing of the *Blackwood's* set is well displayed in the reception of Hogg's novel *The Three Perils of Woman*, reviewed by Wilson in October 1823:

> You have no intention to be an immoral writer, and we acquit you of that; but you have an intention to be a most unmannerly writer, and

of that you are found and declared guilty. You think you are shewing your knowledge of human nature, in these your coarse daubings; and that you are another Shakespeare. But consider that a writer may be indelicate, coarse, gross, even beastly, and yet not at all natural. (Strout 255-6)

The terms of Wilson's address here to his friend hardly need remarking, but it is interesting to consider what are the positive critical values underlying his position: manner, morality, delicacy, refinement, culture, *politesse*. These are the standards meant to flatter *Blackwood's's* "middle-brow, middle-class audience" (Noble 141-2). Wilson's comments in many ways reflect the ethos of the magazine and of its proprietor, who also had a private and a public face for Hogg. Concerned that Wilson's *Three Perils* review would enrage the "poor monster" Hogg, Blackwood urged his editor to tone the piece down, in case it so "irritate[d] the creature as to drive him to some beastly personal attack on you" (Strout 253).

Hogg was stung by the review of *The Three Perils of Woman*, yet it should be said that his subsequent estrangement from Wilson and Blackwood was short-lived (Garden 142). In many ways, the author played up to his caricature in polite society, cutting a swathe as the indignant, raffish, Ettrick bard. But he was well aware of the damage he was doing to his reputation by indulging the image promulgated by Wilson and Blackwood, and this may explain why he chose to publish the *Confessions* anonymously, disguising its provenance with a dedication to the Lord Provost of Glasgow. The dedication is yet another of Hogg's masks, yet another splintering of identity in a text already replete with multiple personalities. Hogg's need to protect himself by disclaiming authorship reveals his situation as an outsider in the literary society of his day, and it is this eccentric status which has led several critics to identify him with Robert Wringhim. Denied by his father, subject to rumours about his own legitimacy, excluded from the convivial society of young aristocrats of which his brother is so conspicuously part, the young Robert is a study in oddness. His failures in assimilation have been attributed by the critic Eve Kosovsky Sedgwick to his lacking the essential elements of "male prestige" as embodied in his brother George, whose achievements on the sports field and in the company of women mark him out as the archetypal "British racial ideal" (99). As a devout Calvinist, Robert's values do not accord with those of his sensual, aristocratic father and brother, nor does he find any comfort in the Editor's "bluff masculist" (Sedgwick 103) narrative. As we have noted, the Editor is clearly hostile towards Robert and reveals his sympathies towards the Laird and his elder son on several occasions. Robert is thus, as Hogg was in Edinburgh, excluded by a kind of conspiracy of Toryism in the text.

While Hogg is certainly highly critical of Robert and his revolutionary co-religionists, he is nevertheless careful to ensure that no implicit endorsement of the Dalcastles emerges by default. Reading against the grain of the Editor's narrative, we uncover a number of discrediting aspects to George and his father, and this in turn makes for a more sympathetic understanding of the nature of Robert's "difference." For example, in the Editor's account of the wedding night of the Laird and Robert's mother, the wife is considered to be at fault in her refusal of her husband and her preference for the "writings of the Evangelists" (51). The Editor even goes as far as to imply that she is a "bigot" and a "hypocrite" and mocks her insistence on the virtues of family worship (52). However, we might be inclined to take the Laird's dancing, drinking and demanding intimacy as a boorish and bullying violation of his wife's principles and her person: he is at least as extreme in his sensuality as she is in her probity. When refused assistance by her own father, Rabina is forced to establish herself in a room of her own in order to resist her husband's overbearing designs. The Editor then accuses her of "intermeddling" (56) in her husband's affairs after he takes a mistress. Similar bias is evident in the way in which the Editor depicts the confrontation between the Laird and the Reverend Wringhim. The Laird's humorously exaggerated condemnation of the minister is given in direct speech, for full rhetorical and comic effect, while the response of the "officious sycophant" (60), Wringhim, is omitted, the Editor merely alluding to its notoriety among "certain incendiaries" (60) of the Calvinist hue.

Robert's oddity, as the Editor sees it, is figured in his aberrant effeminacy. He does not play team games, languish in public houses, or frequent brothels. His nose is easily bloodied—"emblem of a specifically female powerlessness" (Sedgwick 101); he is unable to establish commonality with other men through the objectification of women because he loathes that sex; and his relationship with Gil-Martin is conveyed, Sedgwick argues, in "a genuinely erotic language of romantic infatuation" (103). The Editor wants us to accept these characteristics as evidence of Robert's deviance. In his confession, Robert recounts striding up to his brother and kicking him while the latter is involved in a game of tennis (154). In the Editor's Narrative, the blow is dealt while George is offering a hand in sporting reconciliation to his "polluted brother" (67). Similarly, in the confession George is excluded from the company of his fellows because they are terrified of Robert (158). The Editor claims, on the contrary, that they are forced to drop George from their number in the interests of gentlemanly conduct (75). Of course, we are well aware of the likely distortions in Robert's account, but the Editor's shaping hand is just as evident in his narrative. If we resist the Editor's version, and therefore his values, then Robert emerges—as I think Hogg desires—as a complex portrait of the repulsions and motivations that produce dissidence or non-belonging in society. Hogg's own experiences in his professional life with the "bluff masculists" of *Blackwood's*, and his consequent struggles to manage a literary identity for himself, may well be the basis for this interest in the dynamics of exclusion, not to mention the aversion to overbearing Tories.

Not long after the launch of *Blackwood's*, Hogg returned to his native Ettrick, in the Borders, where he would spend the rest of his life, commuting to Edinburgh as business required. It seems appropriate, given his experience with Wilson and the others, that he should have retreated to the periphery in this way, keeping his distance from the metaphorical centre of Scottish cultural life. In the *Confessions*, Robert too seeks refuge in the Borders as his crimes at home come to light. Hogg's choice of this locale for his character is significant, for it is in the border region of any country that ideas of national identity are most problematic, where the presence of the "other" is most keenly felt. A border may represent a resolute line of demarcation between two territories—a decisive either/or—but it is simultaneously the place where identities are least secure, where contamination and incursion, a blurring of cultural boundaries, are most likely to occur. As Geoffrey Bennington puts it, "The frontier does not merely close the nation in on itself, but also, immediately, opens it to an outside, to other nations" (121).

As Robert treads the border, jingling both Scottish and English money in his pocket, the defining presence of the English "other" comes into focus. Bound up inextricably with the religious motivations in the text is, as we have seen, the crucial matter of national identity. The Covenants were intended, at least in part, to mark Scotland's essential "difference" from England, but in the century following the Union the erasure of that difference began to seem inevitable. Hogg writes, then, in the continuation of a period of "prolonged spiritual resistance against being completely assimilated to the South" (Davie xiii). 1707 had guaranteed Scotland her own religious, legal and education systems, but throughout the eighteenth-century the trend was towards domination by an ever more prosperous, powerful and populous England. Taking their national identity for granted was something Scots found it difficult to do. This was particularly the case for Scots writers who, as David Craig describes, were forced to represent a country "with no very extensive recent or classic literature to enrich its sense of itself" (160). Paradoxically, economic improvement after 1780 only made matters worse as industrial and agrarian reform brought pressure for further assimilation of the legal and financial systems of the two countries. By the early nineteenth-century, many, like Hogg's friend Sir Walter Scott, were arguing that it was Scotland's manifest destiny to complete the Union with England (Phillipson 178).

The early nineteenth-century was witness also to a growing crisis of identity in the Scottish Church. The threat to the established Kirk came now not from Episcopalianism but from secessionist churches within the Presbyterian movement itself. In particular, the system of patronage, by which ministers were nominated and elected, was felt by a growing number of people to be a debasement of Covenanting principles, and the means by which the ruling Moderate faction of the Church asserted political control on behalf of the aristocracy. By 1820, dissent had consolidated in the form of the Evangelical movement, which was based largely among the growing industrial middle classes. There was particular concern at the way in which the Evangelicals appealed to Covenanting history to define their radical agenda. The Covenanters provided inspiration for many groups, such as the Scottish Convention of the Friends of the People, agitating for social reform in the early nineteenth-century (Finlay 130). To many in the establishment, the movement represented a dangerous assault on the Presbyterian tradition by a potentially revolutionary constituency.

Hogg's tale of religious enthusiasm would therefore have had a sharp contemporary relevance for his readers, and the references to the Covenanters would have been of more than just historical interest. However, the rise of Evangelicism had another, arguably more significant, effect: by weakening the established Presbyterian Church, it further undermined the concerted institutional resistance in Scotland to English domination. Throughout the eighteenth-century, a delicate protocol between religious and secular interests had acted to resist what Gifford calls "'Anglicising' tendencies in education and cultural values" (*The History of Scottish Literature* 3). By disturbing that protocol, the

Evangelical movement hastened the drift towards assimilation to England.

In all Hogg's work, we find evidence of anxiety over the unionist threat to Scottish identity. Typically this anxiety is expressed (as it was in much Scottish writing of the time) as a linguistic conflict between speakers of standard English and Lowland Scots. Often Hogg will use unexpurgated transcriptions of Scots vernacular to frustrate the dominant sense-making patterns of English speakers. In the *Confessions*, we find several examples of this device, as when Bessy Gillies is questioned by the depute-advocate at the trial of Arabella Calvert:

> "An when you went home, what did you find?"
>
> "What found we? By my sooth, we found a broken lock, an' toom kists."
>
> "Relate some of the particulars, if you please."
>
> "O, sir, the thieves didna stand upon particulars: they were halesale dealers in a' our best wares."
>
> "I mean, what passed between your mistress and you on the occasion?"
>
> "What passed, say ye? O, there wasna muckle: I was in a great passion, but she was dung doitrified a wee. When she gaed to put the key i' the door, up it flew to the fer wa'.—'Bess, ye jaud, what's the meaning o' this?' quo she. 'Ye hae left the door open, ye tawpie!' quo she.
>
> 'The ne'er o' that I did,' quo I, 'or may my shakel bane never turn another key.' When we got the candle lightit, a' the house was in a hoad-road. 'Bessy, my woman,' quo she, 'we are baith ruined and undone creatures.' 'The deil a bit,' quo I; 'that I deny positively. I I'mh! to speak o' a lass o' my age being ruined and undone! I never had muckle except what was within a good jerkin, an' let the thief ruin me there wha can'." (97)

The critic Emma Letley points out that many Scottish novelists in the 1820s sought to give Scots back its voice in the highly anglicized contexts of the courtroom and the Kirk ("Language and Nineteenth-Century Scottish Fiction" 324). Here, Bessy's fastidious translations of the prosecutor's questions into her own idiom are taken by the judge to be deliberately oppositional and evasive. In fact, she is simply asserting the validity of her own language by insisting that it is as much the responsibility of the advocate to make himself understood to her. When asked to "relate some of the particulars," she responds in accordance with her own community's understanding of the word "particulars." The advocate is forced to rephrase his question—to adapt to Bessy's discourse—in order to obtain the information he desires. She, of course, answers him on her own terms by a lengthy retailing of events in direct speech, giving each voice its due weight and refusing to make any rationalizing summary or paraphrase. As the exchange proceeds, the advocate becomes increasingly frustrated in his efforts to edit her information and make it tend towards definite conclusions. Bessy offers an excess of data in a language he cannot satisfactorily translate or bring into line with his own discursive codes.

To Hogg's contemporary Scottish reader, the clash between English and Scots language would have had a powerful cultural significance. Since the Union, Scots wishing to find acceptance in public life had been required to purge their writing of what came to be called "Scotticisms." Using English was not only a mark of gentility but was considered part of a general process of "improvement" for the Scots writer who had at his disposal a plentiful supply of English literary models from which he could learn. Several leading figures of the Scottish Enlightenment, such as Adam Smith, William Barron and Hugh Blair, lectured and published on the subjects of rhetoric and *belles lettres*, undertaking analyses of contemporary English writers in an attempt to provide stylistic models for prose writing. What they succeeded in establishing, as Robert Crawford has explored, was "a canon whose works were, by and large, the literary embodiment of English metropolitan taste" (41). That this canon came to form the basis for judgements about literature is evident from the reviews Hogg received for the *Confessions*, many of which were highly critical of what they saw as his iniquitously "bad English" (see Appendix C).

The disintegration of Scots as a literary language meant that it tended to appear in novels in the direct speech of lower class, unlettered characters, and was paraded by comic juxtaposition with the standard English narrational discourse. Those authors, most notably Burns, who did manage to maintain elements of Scots vernacular in their serious writing, gained acceptance on the basis that they were "natural" or "rustic" talents (Crawford 99). Despite his deep learning, and the highly sophisticated syntheses of English and Scots which he employed in his poetry, Burns nevertheless found it profitable to project the image of himself as the untutored, instinctual "bard," and was celebrated in this guise much as Hogg was in his rustic persona of the "Ettrick Shepherd."

Several linguistic identities are in evidence in the *Confessions*. Principal among these are the Editor's Narrative, Robert Wringhim's confession, and the letter from the character "James Hogg" which appears in the final section of the book. The "Hogg" figure is particularly interesting because there the real Hogg, who actually did publish the reproduced letter in *Blackwood's* the year before, reconstructs the surly, fictional "Ettrick Shepherd" version of himself familiar to readers of the *Noctes*. The "James Hogg" whom the Editor encounters is characterized, as Bessy Gillies is, by his linguistic contrariety:

> We soon found Hogg, standing near the foot of the market, as he called it, beside a great drove of paulies, a species of stock that I never heard of before. They were small sheep, striped on the backs with red chalk. Mr. L——t introduced me to him as a great wool-stapler, come to raise the price of that article; but he eyed me with distrust, and turning his back on us, answered, "I hae sell'd mine."
>
> I followed, and shewing him the above-quoted letter, said I was exceedingly curious to have a look of these singular remains he had so ingeniously described; but he only answered me with the remark, that "It was a queer fancy for a woo-stapler to tak."
>
> His two friends then requested him to accompany us to the spot, and to take some of his shepherds with us to assist in raising the body; but he spurned at the idea, saying, "Od bless ye, lad! I hae ither matters to mind. I hae a' thae paulies to sell, an' a' yon Highland stotts down on the green every ane; an' then I hae ten scores o' yowes to buy after, an' if I canna first sell my ain stock, I canna buy nae ither body's. I hae mair ado than I can manage the day, foreby ganging to houk up hunder-year-auld banes." (226–27)

This passage works by imposing an ironic distance between the Editor and the Scots-speaking "Hogg." As with the advocate in his interrogation of Bessy, the Editor is forced to carry out unsatisfactory translations into standard English of "Hogg's" utterances. The Editor places "Hogg's" responses in direct speech in order to display their oddity: "he only answered me with the remark, that 'It was a queer fancy for a woo-stapler to tak.'" Emma Letley points out that the original letter to *Blackwood's* was written in standard English, and that the reversion to Scots by "Hogg" when confronted by the Editor signals his resistance to the Editor's authority ("Some Literary Uses of Scots" 32-3). This is an important point and raises another doubt over the Editor's reliability. As Letley goes on to observe, Scots language exchanges occur on several occasions in Robert's confession but are largely absent from the Editor's Narrative. Indeed, the Editor admits at one point that the "shackles of modern decorum" (60) control what he feels able to include in his account, and this would appear to involve purging (or at least ignoring) oral accounts in Scots in favour of written English-language judicial records.

When we encounter the Scots-speaking Samuel Scrape in the confession, we find that alternative, and differently articulated, explanations for Robert's career emerge. Scrape, in his tale of Auchtermuchty (188–95), gives voice to the belief among the "auld crazy kimmers" of the parish that Robert's strange ability to be in two places at once is proof that he is possessed, most probably by the Devil himself: "Gin ever he observes a proud professor, wha has mae than ordinary pretensions to a divine calling ... *that's* the man Auld Simmie fixes on to mak a dishclout o'" (190). Popular opinion in the Scots-speaking community is that supernatural forces are at work in Wringhim. This is directly at odds with the account the Editor wishes to promote. He says that we must consider Wringhim to be either a great fool or a religious maniac, for "in this day, and with the present generation, it will not go down, that a man should be daily tempted by the devil, in the semblance of a fellow-creature" (232). The Editor's privileging of his own scrupulously rational, anglicized version of events here reveals his contemptuous dismissal of the alternative, non-standard narrative signalled by the Scots community. It is not just that he assumes superiority over Scots oral culture and faith, but that he does so through his role as editor, exercising his linguistic prejudice.

As a writer and a Scots speaker, Hogg was doubly conscious of how language can work both expressively and repressively, in the individual mind, the writing project, and the history of culture and nation. In reading the *Confessions*, therefore, we must be determined not just to sound out every voice in the novel, but to value them equally too.

Literary Antecedents
One area of Hogg studies where further work needs to be done concerns the relationship between the *Confessions* and other literature of the period. Unfortunately, we know relatively little about Hogg's reading, and so much of the evidence we can cite in this connection is circumstantial. However, it is still useful to explore the novel in relation to its probable source texts and, more generally, to significant literary trends in Hogg's day.

David Groves suggests that Robert's claims to divine inspiration, his confessional passion, and the spontaneous method of composition in his diary, take to an obvious extreme "Romantic modes of thinking or writing" ("James Hogg as a Romantic Writer" 3–4).

Groves has in mind here such descriptions and formulations of poetic creativity as we find in Blake, Wordsworth, and Shelley, where the poet figures as one endowed with a more "comprehensive soul," and composition is the product of a "spontaneous overflow of powerful feelings." Hogg's attitude to such high-flown thought was ambivalent, and in several of his writings—most obviously *The Poetic Mirror*, with its parodies of Wordsworth, Coleridge and Byron—he signalled his scepticism concerning Romantic claims about poetic selfhood and superlative nonconformity. The *Confessions* has been read in this context as a demonstration of the dangers of a self-empowering, anti-social individualism, in which the central character ends his days in the despair of isolation, unable to assimilate to any of the communities he encounters, be it the weaver and his wife, the workers in the print house, or the society of shepherds. In the mould of the great Romantic revolutionary outsiders, such as Byron's Manfred and Shelley's Prometheus, Robert sees himself as a pilgrim—solitary, misunderstood, heroic—comforted only in the "certainty, that the believer's progress through life is one of warfare and suffering" (212), yet destined in his own judgement to "astonish mankind, and confound their self wisdom" (208).

The dangers of predatory individualism are a central concern, too, of the Gothic novel, a genre with which Hogg was clearly familiar. Indeed, one reason for the novel's poor reception among early reviewers was that the Gothic was, by 1824, felt to be an exhausted and outmoded form. In fact, the *Confessions* differs in important ways from the earlier central Gothic texts, such as Ann Radcliffe's *The Mysteries of Udolpho* (1794) and *The Italian* (1797), and M.G. Lewis's *The Monk* (1796), in that it is set within a precise and recognizable history and locale. The settings of the earlier Gothic novels—usually in an exotic Catholic Europe—were not specific or accurately detailed but were intended to heighten the reader's sense of estrangement and other-worldliness, intensifying the fantasy by evoking a reality "released from the rules of the here and now" (Day 32). Hogg's text, as we have seen, is crucially precise about history and environment. However, the *Confessions* does have some strong affinities with the Gothic. It is interested in subjectivity and psychological states of fear and division, in the externalization of mental conflicts through acts of murder and violence, and in the presentation of paranoia as a product of religious obsessiveness. It also contains an ambivalent supernaturalism and shows a fascination with material resurrected from the past. Perhaps most importantly of all, the interest in doubles, alter-egos, *doppelgängers* is characteristically Gothic. William Patrick Day has described how in Gothic fantasy, ranging from Horace Walpole's *The Castle of Otranto* (1764), through Godwin's *Caleb Williams* (1794) and Stevenson's *Jekyll and Hyde* (1886), to Wilde's *The Picture of Dorian Gray* (1890), the identity of the central character is frequently subject to fracture and doubling, either through psychological disintegration or through the manifestation of an "other" who pursues the protagonist and whose actions and identity may become coterminous with his. Some possible psychoanalytic sources for Hogg's treatment of the "doubling" theme will be explored in detail in the next section, but here we can consider a likely literary basis in a text which has many important similarities to the *Confessions*: E.T.A. Hoffmann's *The Devil's Elixir* (*Die Elixiere des Teufels*, 1824).

It is probable that Hogg became familiar with *The Devil's Elixir* through his close friend R.P. Gillies, who translated the novel into English for *Blackwood's*. Like the *Confessions,* it is narrated in the first person, and in confessional style, by Medardus, a Capuchin monk. Early in his life, Medardus becomes convinced of his religious calling, but like Robert, the actual moment of his conversion is dubious. Medardus describes how, having been rejected by the young woman of his affections, he realizes his true destiny and takes the vows of the order. In so doing, he is forced to lie about his motivations to the Prior (Appendix B.1.i). In Hogg's text, the moment of election for Robert is similarly suspect as it does not arise out of pious meditation but is instead granted by Wringhim, who claims to have wrestled with the Almighty in order to secure it. In both novels it is implied that the subsequent murderous careers of the protagonists are based in the faulty first principles of their faith. Once ordained, Medardus begins to differentiate the superior nature of his own calling from that of his fellow monks:

> Almost unconsciously, I began to look upon myself as the *one elect,*— the preeminently *chosen* of Heaven ... [All] seemed to indicate that my lofty spirit, in immediate commerce with supernatural beings, belonged not properly to earth, but to Heaven, and was suffered, for a space, to wander here, for the benefit and consolation of mortals! (B.1.iii)

Medardus, like Robert, considers his earthly progress a pilgrimage, a necessary defilement among the fallen to be suffered by one whose higher destiny is assured; and as with Robert his contempt extends even to his co-religionists, whom he believes ought to recognize his special status as "one of the specially elect of Heaven [who] had been sent for a space to wander in sublunary regions" (B.1.iii).

Medardus's fall into criminality occurs once he has drunk of the elixir supposedly given to St Anthony by the Devil. From then on he is pursued by a mysterious "double." Several central dramatic episodes involving the *doppelgänger* prefigure in quite obvious ways the *Confessions*. There is, for instance, Medardus's first encounter with his brother Victorin on the verge of a high precipice (B.1.iv), reminiscent of Robert and George's meeting on Arthur's Seat (78–82). More striking still are the moments when Medardus's identity conflates with that of his brother: "Methought it was not *I*, but *he*, that had spoken the words in which I thought to triumph" (B.1.v). In Hogg's text, Robert experiences a similar ontological uncertainty: lying in bed he believes he has a "second self," yet at the same time he does not conceive himself to be either of the two persons of which he is conscious (159); and like Medardus, he frequently finds himself speaking and answering for the actions of another man "in the character of another man" (159). They both also experience lapses in consciousness: Robert finds himself unable to account for large periods of time in which his most heinous acts were committed, while Medardus is unable to say distinctly how long he has been "persecuted by [his] relentless double" (B.1.vii).

Comparing the two texts, however, we also find informative differences between them, especially in the consistency of the psychological portraiture. Medardus is prompted to criminality by having drunk of the Satanic potion. The cause of his evil actions is therefore unambiguously diabolical, the result of an external force working upon him. Robert's crimes, on the other hand, arise from the delusions of his faith. Hogg produces his "devil" from Robert's mentality, and, crucially, he remains ambivalent about the identity of Gil-Martin. Despite the enigmas that proliferate as Medardus tells his story, all issues of identity and motive are clearly resolved at the end in Medardus's mature reflections, from the quietude of a Capuchin cloister, on his life of crime and temptation by the Devil (B.1.viii). Hogg, by contrast, does not put beyond doubt the reality or otherwise of Gil-Martin; in fact, enigmas multiply in the final pages of his text. Nor is Robert permitted any rational vantage point from which to view his delusional condition. It is important for the sake of psychological continuity that he is prevented from achieving self-knowledge. Given his conviction that he is chosen, there would be no meaning for Robert in self-doubt. To allow him to escape the circularity of his own thought, as Hoffmann does Medardus, would be to compromise the integrity of characterization for the sake of formal closure.

Hogg was clearly a perceptive and critical reader of Hoffmann and understood how he could use the *doppelgänger* device to more powerful effect by maintaining the impercipience of his central character. The matter of self-knowledge is also crucial in another text considered by many critics to have been a likely influence on Hogg's novel: *The Confession of Nicol Muschet of Boghall* (1721) (Appendix B.2). Re-published in 1818, this was the true testimony of an Edinburgh man executed for murdering his wife in the park below Arthur's Seat. Muschet claimed he was encouraged to commit his crime by an associate, one James Campbell of Burnbank, who convinced him that murder was the only means by which he could free himself from a shameful marriage. "Burnbank in a little time perfectly well understanding my failing, daily made it his business to assault me by flatteries," Muschet writes, claiming that he "was the only vicegerent of the devil to prompt me up to be guilty of all the following wickedness" (B.2.i). Throughout his text, Muschet casts himself as a victim of diabolical temptation, and like Robert he gives the impression of himself as a pilgrim suffering in a "vain and transitory world" (B.2.iv).

But of deeper interest as regards Hogg's novel is the inference one inevitably draws that Muschet is a religious fanatic. Even amid the direst confessions of his crimes, and on the eve of his execution, Muschet cannot humble himself before his God: he is convinced of his salvation, and even implies that others may have been responsible for his actions. He questions the priest who consecrated his marriage in the first place within "the sinful superstitions of the church of England, contrary to my baptismal and national vows"; and he suggests that his wife may have in some sense conspired in her own death by being someone of questionable piety and virtue (B.2.ii). He even convinces himself that her murder may have been the result of some divinely instituted plan, as the means of killing her were presented to him after his hearing a sermon on the sin of shedding innocent blood. Muschet reflects that, through God's righteousness, "those very means, which tend to the deterring of others from sin, had quite the contrary effect on me" (B.2.iii).

Muschet considers his confession a pious and soul-searching work, but in the midst of the self-abasement and declarations of humility we detect, as we do in Robert's final pages, a man still convinced of his righteousness and of the sublime significance of the deeds he has done:

> I say, in the faith of what I have said, I willingly and cheerfully resign my spirit to Him who gave it, who is one in three and three in one: for dust we are, and to dust we must return: and blessed be God in lovely Jesus, that I am now enabled by faith to look upon all sublunary things as dung in comparison of the excellency of Christ. (B.2. iv)

Hogg, as we know from his letters and *Lay Sermons*, was sensitive to the self-deluding discourse of the fanatic and in the *Confessions* blights Robert with the same impercipience. Both confessions are powerful (Hogg's designedly so) because they are trapped within the subjectivities of the confessors. Both texts convince us of the "fallacy of autobiographical completeness" (Levin 6) by exposing the blind spots in any account of the self.

Abnormal Psychology

It was not only Romantic writers who were interested in the hidden aspects of the mind in Hogg's day. The medical profession was at this time developing its own descriptive vocabulary and exploring new ways of diagnosing and treating mental disturbance. Allan Beveridge has discovered that Hogg was acquainted with Dr Andrew Duncan, a prominent Edinburgh physician who was instrumental in establishing the capital's first asylum in 1813, and suggests that the two may well have visited that institution together ("James Hogg and Abnormal Psychology" 92). Hogg mentions asylums in some of his fiction, but these references aside, we have no evidence of the extent of his knowledge or interest in mental illness. However, this has not stopped critics from discussing the *Confessions* in terms of abnormal psychology or from pursuing sources for it among medical case studies of the time.

Beveridge (himself a consultant psychiatrist) has "diagnosed" Robert as suffering from various psychopathological conditions. For example, his experience of seeing himself standing "about three paces off me towards my left side" (159), and then his later conviction that a "second self" commits actions in his likeness, is described by Beveridge as an instance of "autoscopic delusion" in which "the subject has a fixed delusional belief in his separate concrete existence but no complementary perceptual experience." Similarly, Robert's claim that Gil-Martin can change identity is indicative of Frégoli syndrome, in which "the patient feels that his persecutor can change faces." Beveridge's conclusion is that Robert is suffering from a "fundamental disturbance of identity" and that his condition closely resembles that of schizophrenia ("The confessions" 345).

In her full-blooded psychoanalytic readings of the novel, Barbara Bloedé has sought to account for Robert's "madness in the light of modern understanding of the etiology of mental illness" ("The Paranoiac Nucleus" 15). Bloedé investigates Robert's upbringing, his illegitimacy, his anxious and solitary childhood, and concludes that he suffers from "paraphrenia"—a chronic psychotic condition tending towards schizophrenia and characterized by "hallucination and fabulation" (17). In Bloedé's account, Gil-Martin is a projection of Robert's mind. Anxious about his own salvation, tormented by hateful thoughts towards his father and the spectre of illegitimacy, Robert projects all this evil onto his Double. Producing Gil-Martin is a self-defence mechanism for Robert, in which he "dissociates himself from that part of his ego of which his conscious thoughts disapprove and from which he is trying to escape" (19). It is obvious how Bloedé's theory would permit a radical interpretation of the text, and this is what she gives us when she argues that Robert may not have murdered Blanchard. After all, Robert is our only witness to the attack and, as Bloedé suggests, given the threat Blanchard poses to his relations with Gil-Martin, it is not inconceivable that he should attribute the murder to himself, constructing it as a righteous calling. Can we really trust the account Robert gives, considering his propensity for lying, his megalomania, and his delusory state of mind in which golden weapons are lowered from heaven for the task?

The same doubts over reliability pertain to the death of George. In his recollection of the murder, Robert admits that he is unsure about precisely what happened on the drying green, and that his "own immediate impressions" (171) conflict with the version he gets from Gil-Martin. Now, it might be argued that Robert's confusion is irrelevant because there were external witnesses to the crime in the shape of Bell Calvert and Mrs Logan. But we need to remember where we find their testimonies—in the Editor's Narrative, which, as we have already seen, is neither impartial nor complete. Moreover, the women themselves are unsure of precisely what they saw. "We have nothing on earth but our senses to depend upon," Bell says; "if these deceive us, what are we to do" (107). But it is their senses which fail them when they attempt to identify Robert's co-conspirator:

"It *is* he!" cried Mrs Logan, hysterically.

"Yes, yes, it is he!" cried the landlady in unison.

"It is who?" said Mrs Calvert; "whom do you mean, mistress?"

"Oh, I don't know! I don't know! I was affrighted."

"Hold you peace then till you recover your senses, and tell me, if you can, who that young gentleman is, who keeps company with the new Laird of Dalcastle?"

"Oh, it is he! it is he!" screamed Mrs Logan, wringing her hands.

"Oh, it is he! it is he!" cried the landlady, wringing hers.

Mrs Calvert turned the latter gently and civilly out of the apartment, observing that there seemed to be some infection in the air of the room, and she would be wise for herself to keep out of it.

The two dames had a restless and hideous night. Sleep came not to their relief; for their conversation was wholly about the dead, who seemed to be alive, and their minds were wandering and groping in a chaos of mystery. (110)

The confusion of identities recalls the mayhem following the riot at the Black Bull in which Whigs, Tories, Cameronians and royalists became indistinguishable from one another. Later, the two women boast of their observational powers while at the same time preparing disguises meant to frustrate observation. Our doubts about their testimony increase when we compare the surgeon's account of George's injuries. Bell claims she saw George stabbed twice in the back and that each thrust "pierced through his body" (106), but the surgeon says that the first wound was a "slight one" below the left arm (89). As Douglas Gifford reminds us, at the time of the incident Bell was under great stress having recently been abandoned by a scoundrel, having had a drink, and being much taken with Drummond. When we add to this that is was dark outside, "the total of what she tells that would be acceptable to a court of law is that Drummond did not kill George, and that Robert had an accomplice" (*James Hogg* 150).

The psychological readings undertaken by Gide, Beveridge, Bloedé and Lee, among others, are plausible because of the novel's studied refusal to secure evidence concerning the identity, or even the existence, of Gil-Martin. Indeed, Robert himself notes how the various accounts of his companion given to his parents "all described him differently" (140). The opinion that Gil-Martin is the Devil emerges from inference; no one ever identifies him as such. Allowing that he might indeed be a projection of Robert's damaged mind has prompted an enquiry into what Hogg himself knew of abnormal psychology and whether his extraordinary treatment of the "double" theme has its basis in other than literary sources. Cases of so-called "double personality" or "double consciousness" were reported in medical journals as well as the popular press in Hogg's lifetime. The most widely known of these concerned a young Pennsylvania woman, Mary Reynolds, whose case notes were written up by Samuel Lathan Mitchill, a New York physician and acquaintance of Francis Jeffrey, editor of the *Edinburgh Review* (see Bloedé, "A Nineteenth-Century Case of Double Personality"). Mitchill's account of Reynolds' illness appeared in the *Edinburgh Weekly Journal* in 1816 (Appendix B.3) and was widely remarked at the time. Particularly striking for readers of the *Confessions* is the way in which the alternation between the "two distinct persons" which apparently inhabit Mary's mind are always "consequent upon a long and sound sleep." Robert's first experience of having a "second self" coincides with an episode of somnolence and amnesia. He believes he has been confined to bed for a month, but others attest that during this time he has "persecuted" his brother "day and night" (159). As in the case of Mary Reynolds, the two aspects of Robert's personality remain discrete and he is unconscious of having committed the crimes with which he is charged. He makes several attempts at accounting for his condition but each time finds that it escapes definition:

> Either I had a second self, who transacted business in my likeness, or else my body was at times possessed by a spirit over which it had no controul, and of whose actions my own soul was wholly unconscious. This was an anomaly not to be accounted for by any philosophy of mine, and I was many times, in contemplating it, excited to terrors and mental torments hardly describable. To be in a state of consciousness and unconsciousness, at the same time, in the same body and same spirit, was impossible. (179)

Robert tries and fails to subject his own mind to his "philosophy," his either/or. But in the novel's most profound act of "doubling," the "anomaly" refuses to be contained in this crude binary. His belief in his ability to define and act upon moral absolutes finally founders on the inscrutable puzzle of his own personality. Robert finds it impossible that anyone might simultaneously be in a state of consciousness and unconsciousness: that is, quite literally, unthinkable to him. But psychology in Hogg's day reported otherwise. In another case presented to the Royal Society of Edinburgh in 1823 (Appendix B.4), even that most fundamental of oppositions between wake and sleep was being revised to admit of greater complexities:

> Such facts [as sleepwalking] evince a strange mixture of accurate perception and self-management with the absence of general recollection and self-knowledge: and it is remarkable that the accurate perceptions which persons in this situation retain, and which may in some measure be the effect of habit on the faculties, are so completely dissevered from the immediate influence of general sensation. (B.4)

Here is scientific enquiry, but conducted in a spirit of mystified amazement. The phenomena of the mind are indeed "remarkable," and remarking upon them may be the limit of what is possible for science. Placing Robert's state of mind outside of his own methods of comprehension is Hogg's most startling act in the *Confessions*. But recognizing this mystery of Robert to himself should induce doubt and circumspection in the reader, not a feeling of superiority or confidence. The Editor fails this test when, in his concluding narrative, he summarizes Robert's confession as "either dreaming or madness" (232). In this limited appraisal, this either/or, he resembles his subject more than he knows: he too fails to read his own act of reading, to escape the confines of his own perspective. For Hogg, this is a failure of imagination, a failure to discover the world, as he puts it in the *Lay Sermons*, to be "boundless and unfathomable." Above all else, the *Confessions* demands that we be generous readers of history, science, faith, and the mind. For such readers as we are, this is a book of many mysteries.

James Hogg: A Brief Chronology

1770   James Hogg born, probably in November, at Ettrickhall Farm, Selkirkshire, Scotland, to Robert and Margaret Hogg, the second of four sons

1777   Leaves school following father's bankruptcy

1778   Begins work as cow-herd and menial labourer

1788   Employed as shepherd by Mr Laidlaw of Willenslee

1790   Begins shepherding for Mr Laidlaw of Blackhouse

1794   Contributes poem to *Scots Magazine*

1800   Recruiting-song "Donald M'Donald" achieves widespread popularity throughout Scotland

1801   *Scottish Pastorals* (poems) published. Collects ballads for Walter Scott.

1802   Meets Walter Scott

1807   *The Mountain Bard* (poems) and *The Shepherd's Guide* (on the management of sheep-diseases) published

1810   Moves to Edinburgh to pursue a career in writing. Publishes songs, *The Forest Minstrel*; edits and largely composes weekly journal, *The Spy*

1813   *The Queen's Wake* (narrative poem) published

1814   Becomes acquainted with William Wordsworth, Thomas De Quincey, and Robert Southey

1815   Gifted Moss End Farm at Altrive Lake by the Duke of Buccleuch. Publishes visionary poem, *The Pilgrims of the Sun*

1816   Publishes narrative poem, *Mador of the Moor*, and a volume of parodies, *The Poetic Mirror*

1817   Association with *Blackwood's Magazine* begins. *Chaldee Manuscript* (satire), co-authored with Wilson and Lockhart, published in first number, provoking considerable controversy

1818   Publishes *The Brownie of Bodsbeck* (novel)

1819   Publishes *Jacobite Relics of Scotland, First Series*

1820   Marries Margaret Phillips. Publishes *Winter Evening Tales*

1821   Commences nine-year lease of Mount-Benger Farm, which proves financially disastrous. *Jacobite Relics, Second Series* published

1822   Four-volume *Poetical Works* and *The Three Perils of Man* (novel) published. 'Noctes Ambrosianae' series begins in *Blackwood's*

1823   Publishes *The Three Perils of Woman*

1824   Publishes *The Private Memoirs and Confessions of a Justified Sinner*

1825   Epic poem *Queen Hynde* published

1829   *The Shepherd's Calendar* (short stories) published

1831   *Songs, by the Ettrick Shepherd* published. Goes to London

1832   *Altrive Tales* (volume 1) and *A Queer Book* published. Death of Scott

1834   Publishes *Familiar Anecdotes of Sir Walter Scott* in New York; *The Domestic Manners and Private Life of Sir Walter Scott* in London. Collection *Lay Sermons published*

1835   *Tales of the Wars of Montrose* published. Bankrupt. Dies November 21.

A Note on the Text

The present text follows the 1824 first edition of the novel published by Longman, correcting these misprints:

"with which she had to deal" for "with which she had to deal with" (p. 95, line 22)
close speech marks after "wear" (p. 98, line 33)
"least" for "lest" (p. 129, line 4)
"there" for "their" (p. 147, line 4)
"dost not know" for "dost not not know" (p. 158, line 8)
close speech marks after "able" (p. 198, line 22)
"effort" for "effect" (p. 204, line 23)
"His answer was," for "His answer was." (p. 207, line 12)

Readers unfamiliar with the Scots language are referred to the glossary on page 313.

THE PRIVATE MEMOIRS

AND CONFESSIONS

OF A JUSTIFIED SINNER:

WRITTEN BY HIMSELF:

WITH A DETAIL OF CURIOUS TRADITIONARY FACTS, AND
OTHER EVIDENCE, BY THE EDITOR.

LONDON:

PRINTED FOR LONGMAN, HURST, REES, ORME, BROWN,
AND GREEN, PATERNOSTER ROW.

MDCCCXXIV.

1824 title page

To
The Hon. William Smith
Lord Provost of Glasgow[1]
&c. &c. &c.
This work is respectfully inscribed,
as a small mark of
The Editor's
esteem for him as a man, and respect for him as a magistrate

---

1   from 1822–24

IT appears from tradition, as well as some parish registers still extant, that the lands of Dalcastle (or Dalchastel, as it is often spelled) were possessed by a family of the name of Colwan, about one hundred and fifty years ago, and for at least a century previous to that period. That family was supposed to have been a branch of the ancient family of Colquhoun, and it is certain that from it spring the Cowans that spread towards the Border. I find, that in the year 1687, George Colwan succeeded his uncle of the same name, in the lands of Dalchastel and Balgrennan; and this being all I can gather of the family from history, to tradition I must appeal *oral* for the remainder of the motley adventures of that house. But of *tradition— folklore* the matter furnished by the latter of these powerful monitors, I have no reason to complain: It has been handed down to the world in unlimited abundance; and I am certain, that in recording the hideous events which follow, I am only relating to the greater part of the inhabitants of at least four counties of Scotland, matters of which they were before perfectly well informed.

This George was a rich man, or supposed to be so, and was married, when considerably advanced in life, to the sole heiress and reputed daughter of a Baillie Orde, of Glasgow. This proved a conjunction any thing but agreeable to the parties contracting. It is well known, that the Reformation principles had long before that time taken a powerful hold of the hearts and affections of the people of Scotland, although the feeling was by no means general, or in equal degrees; and it so happened that this married couple felt completely at variance on the subject. Granting it to have been so, one would have thought that the laird, owing to his retired situation, would have been the one that inclined to the stern doctrines of the reformers; and that the young and gay dame from the city would have adhered to the free principles cherished by the court party, and indulged in rather to extremity, in opposition to their severe and carping contemporaries.

The contrary, however, happened to be the case. The laird was what his country neighbours called "a droll, careless chap," with a very limited proportion of the fear of God in his heart, and very nearly as little of the fear of man. The laird had not intentionally wronged or offended either of the parties, and perceived not the necessity of deprecating their vengeance. He had hitherto believed that he was living in most cordial terms with the greater part of the inhabitants of the earth, and with the powers above in particular: but woe be unto him if he was not soon convinced of the fallacy of such damning security! for his lady was the most severe and gloomy of all bigots to the principles of the Reformation. Hers were not the tenets of the great reformers, but theirs mightily over-strained and deformed. Theirs was an unguent hard to be swallowed; but hers was that unguent embittered and overheated until nature could not longer bear it. She had imbibed her ideas from the doctrines of one flaming predestinarian divine alone; and these were so rigid, that they became a stumbling-block to many of his brethren, and a mighty handle for the enemies of his party to turn the machine of the state against them.

The wedding festivities at Dalcastle partook of all the gaiety, not of that stern age, but of one previous to it. There was feasting, dancing, piping, and singing: the liquors were handed around in great fulness, the ale in large wooden bickers, and the brandy in capacious horns of oxen. The laird gave full scope to his homely glee. He danced,—he snapped his fingers to the music,—clapped his hands and shouted at the turn of the tune. He saluted every girl in the hall whose appearance was any thing tolerable, and requested of their sweethearts to take the same freedom with his bride, by way of retaliation. But there she sat at the head of the hall in still and blooming beauty, absolutely refusing to tread a single measure with any gentleman there. The only enjoyment in which she appeared to partake, was in now and then stealing a word of sweet conversation with her favourite pastor about divine things; for he had accompanied her home after marrying her to her husband, to see her fairly settled in her new dwelling. He addressed her several times by her new name, Mrs. Colwan; but she turned away her head disgusted, and looked with pity and contempt towards the old inadvertent sinner, capering away in the height of his unregenerated mirth. The minister perceived the workings of her pious mind, and thenceforward addressed her by the courteous title of Lady Dalcastle, which sounded somewhat better, as not coupling her name with one of the wicked: and there is too great reason to believe, that for all the solemn vows she had come under, and these were of no ordinary binding, par-ticularly on the laird's part, she at that time despised, if not abhorred him, in her heart.

The good parson again blessed her, and went away. She took leave of him with tears in her eyes, entreating him often to visit her in that heathen land of the Amorite, the Hittite, and the Gir-gashite[1]: to which he assented, on many solemn and qualifying conditions,—and then the comely bride retired to her chamber to pray.

It was customary, in those days, for the bride's-man and maiden, and a few select friends, to visit the new married couple after they had retired to rest, and drink a cup to their healths, their happiness, and a numerous posterity. But the laird delighted not in this: he wished to have his jewel to himself; and, slipping away quietly from his jovial party, he retired to his chamber to his beloved, and bolt-ed the door. He found her engaged with the writings of the Evan-gelists, and terribly demure. The laird went up to caress her; but she turned away her head, and spoke of the follies of aged men, and something of the broad way that leadeth to destruction. The laird did not thoroughly comprehend this allusion; but being con-siderably flustered by drinking, and disposed to take all in good part, he only remarked, as he took off his shoes and stockings, "that whether the way was broad or narrow, it was time that they were in their bed."

"Sure, Mr. Colwan, you won't go to bed to-night, at such an important period of your life, without first saying prayers for your-self and me."

When she said this, the laird had his head down almost to the ground, loosing his shoe-buckle; but when he heard of *prayers*, on such a night, he raised his face suddenly up, which was all over as flushed and red as a rose, and answered,—

"Prayers, Mistress! Lord help your crazed head, is this a night for prayers?"

He had better have held his peace. There was such a torrent of profound divinity poured out upon him, that the laird became ashamed, both of himself and his new-made spouse, and wist not what to say: but the brandy helped him out.

"It strikes me, my dear, that religious devotion would be some-what out of place to-night," said he. "Allowing that it is ever so beautiful, and ever so beneficial, were we to ride on the rigging of it at all times, would we not be constantly making a farce of it: It would be like reading the Bible and the jest-book, verse about, and would render the life of man a medley of absurdity and confusion."

---

1 Old Testament tribes and enemies of Israel, expelled from Canaan by Moses.

But against the cant of the bigot or the hypocrite, no reasoning can aught avail. If you would argue until the end of life, the infallible creature must alone be right. So it proved with the laird. One Scripture text followed another, not in the least connected, and one sentence of the profound Mr. Wringhim's sermons after another, proving the duty of family worship, till the laird lost patience, and, tossing himself into bed, said, carelessly, that he would leave that duty upon her shoulders for one night.

The meek mind of Lady Dalcastle was somewhat disarranged by this sudden evolution. She felt that she was left rather in an awkward situation. However, to show her unconscionable spouse that she was resolved to hold fast her integrity, she kneeled down and prayed in terms so potent, that she deemed she was sure of making an impression on him. She did so; for in a short time the laird began to utter a response so fervent, that she was utterly astounded, and fairly driven from the chain of her orisons. He began, in truth, to sound a nasal bugle of no ordinary calibre,— the notes being little inferior to those of a military trumpet. The lady tried to proceed, but every returning note from the bed burst on her ear with a louder twang, and a longer peal, till the concord of sweet sounds became so truly pathetic, that the meek spirit of the dame was quite overcome; and after shedding a flood of tears, she arose from her knees, and retired to the chimney-corner with her Bible in her lap, there to spend the hours in holy meditation till such time as the inebriated trumpeter should awaken to a sense of propriety.

The laird did not awake in any reasonable time; for, he being overcome with fatigue and wassail, his sleep became sounder, and his Morphean[1] measures more intense. These varied a little in their structure; but the general run of the bars sounded something in this way,—"Hic- hoc-wheew!" It was most profoundly ludicrous; and could not have missed exciting risibility in any one, save a pious, a disappointed, and humbled bride.

The good dame wept bitterly. She could not for her life go and awaken the monster, and request him to make room for her: but she retired somewhere; for the laird, on awaking next morning, found that he was still lying alone. His sleep had been of the deepest and most genuine sort; and all the time that it lasted, he had

---

1 Morpheus was the Roman god of dreams.

never once thought of either wives, children, or sweethearts, save in the way of dreaming about them; but as his spirit began again by slow degrees to verge towards the boundaries of reason, it became lighter and more buoyant from the effects of deep repose, and his dreams partook of that buoyancy, yea, to a degree hardly expressible. He dreamed of the reel, the jig, the strathspey, and the corant; and the elasticity of his frame was such, that he was bounding over the heads of the maidens, and making his feet skimmer against the ceiling, enjoying, the while, the most extatic emotions. These grew too fervent for the shackles of the drowsy god to restrain. The nasal bugle ceased its prolonged sounds in one moment, and a sort of hectic laugh took its place. "Keep it going,—play up, you devils!" cried the laird, without changing his position on the pillow. But this exertion to hold the fiddlers at their work, fairly awakened the delighted dreamer; and though he could not refrain from continuing his laugh, he at length, by tracing out a regular chain of facts, came to be sensible of his real situation. "Rabina, where are you? What's become of you, my dear?" cried the laird. But there was no voice, nor any one that answered or regarded. He flung open the curtains, thinking to find her still on her knees, as he had seen her; but she was not there, either sleeping or waking. "Rabina! Mrs. Colwan!" shouted he, as loud as he could call, and then added, in the same breath, "God save the king,—I have lost my wife!"

He sprung up and opened the casement: the day-light was beginning to streak the east, for it was spring, and the nights were short, and the mornings very long. The laird half dressed himself in an instant, and strode through every room in the house, opening the windows as he went, and scrutinizing every bed and every corner. He came into the hall where the wedding festival had held; and, as he opened the various window-boards, loving couples flew off like hares surprised too late in the morning among the early braird. "Hoo-boo! Fie, be frightened!" cried the laird. "Fie, rin like fools, as if ye were caught in an ill turn!"—His bride was not among them; so he was obliged to betake himself to farther search. "She will be praying in some corner, poor woman," said he to himself. "It is an unlucky thing this praying. But, for my part, I fear I have behaved very ill; and I must endeavour to make amends."

The laird continued his search, and at length found his beloved in the same bed with her Glasgow cousin, who had acted as bride's-maid. "You sly and malevolent imp," said the laird; "you have played me such a trick when I was fast asleep! I have not known a frolic so clever, and, at the same time, so severe. Come along, you baggage you!"

"Sir, I will let you know, that I detest your principles and your person alike," said she. "It shall never be said, Sir, that my person was at the controul of a heathenish man of Belial,[1]—a dangler among the daughters of women,—a promiscuous dancer,—and a player at unlawful games. Forego your rudeness, Sir, I say, and depart away from my presence and that of my kinswoman."

"Come along, I say, my charming Rab. If you were the pink of all puritans, and the saint of all saints, you are my wife, and must do as I command you."

"Sir, I will sooner lay down my life than be subjected to your godless will; therefore, I say, desist, and begone with you."

But the laird regarded none of these testy sayings: he rolled her in a blanket, and bore her triumphantly away to his chamber, taking care to keep a fold or two of the blanket always rather near to her mouth, in case of any outrageous forthcoming of noise. The next day at breakfast the bride was long in making her appearance. Her maid asked to see her; but George did not choose that any body should see her but himself: he paid her several visits, and always turned the key as he came out. At length breakfast was served; and during the time of refreshment the laird tried to break several jokes; but it was remarked, that they wanted their accustomed brilliancy, and that his nose was particularly red at the top.

Matters, without all doubt, had been very bad between the new-married couple; for in the course of the day the lady deserted her quarters, and returned to her father's house in Glasgow, after having been a night on the road; stage-coaches and steam-boats having then no existence in that quarter. Though Baillie Orde had acquiesced in his wife's asseveration regarding the likeness of their only daughter to her father, he never loved or admired her greatly; therefore this behaviour nothing astounded him. He questioned her strictly as to the grievous offence committed against her; and could discover nothing that warranted a procedure so fraught with disagreeable consequences. So, after mature deliberation, the baillie addressed her as follows:—

---

1 Satan, the Devil; literally the Hebrew means "worthlessness."

"Ay, ay, Raby! An' sae I find that Dalcastle has actually refused to say prayers with you when you ordered him; an' has guidit you in a rude indelicate manner, outstepping the respect due to my daughter,—as my daughter. But wi' regard to what is due to his own wife, of that he's a better judge nor me. However, since he has behaved in that manner to *my daughter*, I shall be revenged on him for aince; for I shall return the obligation to ane nearer to him: that is, I shall take pennyworths of his wife,—an' let him lick at that."

"What do you mean, Sir?" said the astonished damsel.

"I mean to be revenged on that villain Dalcastle," said he, "for what he has done to my daughter. Come hither, Mrs. Colwan, you shall pay for this."

So saying, the baillie began to inflict corporal punishment on the runaway wife. His strokes were not indeed very deadly, but he made a mighty flourish in the infliction, pretending to be in a great rage only at the Laird of Dalcastle. "Villain that he is!" exclaimed he, "I shall teach him to behave in such a manner to a child of mine, be she as she may; since I cannot get at himself, I shall lounder her that is nearest to him in life. Take you that, and that, Mrs. Colwan, for your husband's impertinence!"

The poor afflicted woman wept and prayed, but the baillie would not abate aught of his severity. After fuming, and beating her with many stripes, far drawn, and lightly laid down, he took her up to her chamber, five stories high, locked her in, and there he fed her on bread and water, all to be revenged on the presumptuous Laird of Dalcastle; but ever and anon, as the baillie came down the stair from carrying his daughter's meal, he said to himself, "I shall make the sight of the laird the blithest she ever saw in her life."

Lady Dalcastle got plenty of time to read, and pray, and meditate; but she was at a great loss for one to dispute with about religious tenets; for she found, that without this advantage, about which there was a perfect rage at that time, her reading, and learning of Scripture texts, and sentences of intricate doctrine, availed her nought; so she was often driven to sit at her casement and look out for the approach of the heathenish Laird of Dalcastle.

That hero, after a considerable lapse of time, at length made his appearance. Matters were not hard to adjust; for his lady found that there was no refuge for her in her father's house; and so, after some sighs and tears, she accompanied her husband home. For all that had passed, things went on no better. She *would* convert the laird in spite of his teeth: The laird would not be converted. She *would* have the laird to say family prayers, both morning and evening: The laird would neither pray morning nor evening. He would not even sing psalms, and kneel beside her, while she performed the exercise; neither would he converse at all times, and in all places, about the sacred mysteries of religion, although his lady took occasion to contradict flatly every assertion that he made, in order that she might spiritualize him by drawing him into argument.

The laird kept his temper a long while, but at length his patience wore out; he cut her short in all her futile attempts at spiritualization, and mocked at her wire-drawn degrees of faith, hope, and repentance. He also dared to doubt of the great standard doctrine of absolute predestination,[1] which put the crown on the lady's christian resentment. She declared her helpmate to be a limb of Antichrist, and one with whom no regenerated person could associate. She therefore bespoke a separate establishment, and before the expiry of the first six months, the arrangements of the separation were amicably adjusted. The upper, or third story of the old mansion-house, was awarded to the lady for her residence. She had a separate door, a separate stair, a separate garden, and walks that in no instance intersected the laird's; so that one would have thought the separation complete. They had each their own parties, selected from their own sort of people; and though the laird never once chafed himself about the lady's companies, it was not long before she began to intermeddle about some of his.

"Who is that fat bouncing dame that visits the laird so often, and always by herself?" said she to her maid Martha one day.

"O dear, mem, how can I ken? We're banished frae our acquaintances here, as weel as frae the sweet gospel ordinances."

"Find me out who that jolly dame is, Martha. You, who hold communion with the household of this ungodly man, can be at no loss to attain this information. I observe that she always casts her eye up toward our windows, both in coming and going; and I suspect that she seldom departs from the house empty-handed."

That same evening Martha came with the information, that this august visitor was a Miss Logan, an old and intimate acquaintance of the laird's, and a very worthy respectable lady, of good connections, whose parents had lost their patrimony in the civil wars.

---

1 See introduction (14ff.), and Appendix A.

"Ha! very well!" said the lady; "very well, Martha! But, never-theless, go thou and watch this respectable lady's motions and behaviour the next time she comes to visit the laird,—and the next after that. You will not, I see, lack opportunities."

Martha's information turned out of that nature, that prayers were said in the uppermost story of Dalcastle-house against the Canaanitish woman, every night and every morning; and great dis-content prevailed there, even to anathemas and tears. Letter after letter was dispatched to Glasgow; and at length, to the lady's great consolation, the Rev. Mr. Wringhim arrived safely and devoutly in her elevated sanctuary. Marvellous was the conversation between these gifted people. Wringhim had held in his doctrines that there were eight different kinds of FAITH, all perfectly distinct in their operations and effects. But the lady, in her secluded state, had dis-covered other five,—making twelve in all: the adjusting of the existence or fallacy of these five faiths served for a most enlight-ened discussion of nearly seventeen hours; in the course of which the two got warm in their arguments, always in proportion as they receded from nature, utility, and common sense. Wringhim at length got into unwonted fervour about some disputed point between one of these faiths and TRUST; when the lady, fearing that zeal was getting beyond its wonted barrier, broke in on his vehement asseverations with the following abrupt discomfiture:—"But, Sir, as long as I remember, what is to be done with this case of open and avowed iniquity?"

The minister was struck dumb. He leaned him back on his chair, stroked his beard, hemmed—considered, and hemmed again; and then said, in an altered and softened tone,—"Why, that is a sec-ondary consideration; you mean the case between your husband and Miss Logan?"

"The same, Sir. I am scandalised at such intimacies going on under my nose. The sufferance of it is a great and crying evil."

"Evil, madam, may be either operative, or passive. To them it is an evil, but to us none. We have no more to do with the sins of the wicked and unconverted here, than with those of an infidel Turk; for all earthly bonds and fellowships are absorbed and swallowed up in the holy community of the Reformed Church.[1] However,

---

1 Any Church accepting the principles of the Reformation, but in particu-lar here a Calvinist Church.

if it is your wish, I shall take him to task, and reprimand and humble him in such a manner, that *he* shall be ashamed of his doings, and renounce such deeds for ever, out of mere self-respect, though all unsanctified the heart, as well as the deed, may be. To the wicked, all things are wicked; but to the just, all things are just and right."

"Ah, that is a sweet and comfortable saying, Mr. Wringhim! How delightful to think that a justified person can do no wrong! Who would not envy the liberty wherewith we are made free? Go to my husband, that poor unfortunate, blindfolded person, and open his eyes to his degenerate and sinful state; for well are you fitted to the task."

"Yea, I will go in unto him, and confound him. I will lay the strong holds of sin and Satan as flat before my face, as the dung that is spread out to fatten the land."

"Master, there's a gentleman at the fore-door wants a private word o' ye."

"Tell him I'm engaged: I can't see any gentleman to-night. But I shall attend on him to-morrow as soon as he pleases."

"He's coming straight in, Sir.——Stop a wee bit, Sir, my master is engaged. He cannot see you at present, Sir."

"Stand aside, thou Moabite![1] my mission admits of no delay. I come to save him from the jaws of destruction."

"An that be the case, Sir, it maks a wide difference; an', as the danger may threaten us a', I fancy I may as weel let ye gang by as fight wi' ye, sin' ye seem sae intent on't.——The man says he's comin' to save ye, an' canna stop, Sir.—Here he is."

The laird was going to break out into a volley of wrath against Waters, his servant; but before he got a word pronounced, the Rev. Mr. Wringhim had stepped inside the room, and Waters had retired, shutting the door behind him.

No introduction could be more *mal-a-propos*: it is impossible; for at that very moment the laird and Arabella Logan were both sitting on one seat, and both looking on one book, when the door opened. "What is it, Sir?" said the laird fiercely.

"A message of the greatest importance, Sir," said the divine, striding unceremoniously up to the chimney,—turning his back to

---

1   Old Testament inhabitant of the Kingdom of Moab, and therefore enemy to the Israelites.

the fire, and his face to the culprits.—"I think you should know me, Sir?" continued he, looking displeasedly at the laird, with his face half turned round.

"I think I should," returned the laird. "You are a Mr. How's-tey-ca'-him, of Glasgow, who did me the worst turn ever I got done to me in my life. You gentry are always ready to do a man such a turn. Pray, Sir, did you ever do a good job for any one to counterbalance that? for, if you have not, you ought to be—."

"Hold, Sir, I say! None of your profanity before me. If I do evil to any one on such occasions, it is because he will have it so; therefore, the evil is not of my doing. I ask you, Sir,—before God and this witness, I ask you, have you kept solemnly and inviolate the vows which I laid upon you that day? Answer me?"

"Has the partner whom you bound me to, kept hers inviolate? Answer me that, Sir? None can better do so than you, Mr. How's-tey-ca'-you."

"So, then, you confess your backslidings, and avow the profligacy of your life. And this person here, is, I suppose, the partner of your iniquity,—she whose beauty hath caused you to err! Stand up, both of you, till I rebuke you, and show you what you are in the eyes of God and man."

"In the first place, stand you still there, till I tell you what *you* are in the eyes of God and man: You are, Sir, a presumptuous, self-conceited pedagogue, a stirrer up of strife and commotion in church, in state, in families, and communities. You are one, Sir, whose righteousness consists in splitting the doctrines of Calvin[1] into thousands of undistinguishable films, and in setting up a system of justifying-grace against all breaches of all laws, moral or divine. In short, Sir, you are a mildew,—a canker-worm in the bosom of the Reformed Church, generating a disease of which she will never be purged, but by the shedding of blood. Go thou in peace, and do these abominations no more; but humble thyself, lest a worse reproof come upon thee."

Wringhim heard all this without flinching. He now and then twisted his mouth in disdain, treasuring up, mean time, his vengeance against the two aggressors; for he felt that he had them on the hip, and resolved to pour out his vengeance and indignation

---

1 Jean Calvin (1509-1564), French theologian and Protestant Reformer. See introduction (14ff.) and Appendix A2.

upon them. Sorry am I, that the shackles of modern decorum restrain me from penning that famous rebuke; fragments of which have been attributed to every divine of old notoriety throughout Scotland. But I have it by heart; and a glorious morsel it is to put into the hands of certain incendiaries. The metaphors were so strong, and so appalling, that Miss Logan could only stand them a very short time: she was obliged to withdraw in confusion. The laird stood his ground with much ado, though his face was often crimsoned over with the hues of shame and anger. Several times he was on the point of turning the officious sycophant to the door; but good manners, and an inherent respect that he entertained for the clergy, as the immediate servants of the Supreme Being, restrained him.

Wringhim, perceiving these symptoms of resentment, took them for marks of shame and contrition, and pushed his reproaches farther than ever divine ventured to do in a similar case. When he had finished, to prevent further discussion, he walked slowly and majestically out of the apartment, making his robes to swing behind him in a most magisterial manner; he being, without doubt, elated with his high conquest. He went to the upper story, and related to his metaphysical associate his wonderful success; how he had driven the dame from the house in tears and deep confusion, and left the backsliding laird in such a quandary of shame and repentance, that he could neither articulate a word, nor lift up his countenance. The dame thanked him most cordially, lauding his friendly zeal and powerful eloquence; and then the two again set keenly to the splitting of hairs, and making distinctions in religion where none existed.

They being both children of adoption, and secured from falling into snares, or any way under the power of the wicked one, it was their custom, on each visit, to sit up a night in the same apartment, for the sake of sweet spiritual converse; but that time, in the course of the night, they differed so materially on a small point, somewhere between justification and final election, that the minister, in the heat of his zeal, sprung from his seat, paced the floor, and maintained his point with such ardour, that Martha was alarmed, and, thinking they were going to fight, and that the minister would be a hard match for her mistress, she put on some clothes, and twice left her bed and stood listening at the back of the door, ready to burst in should need require it. Should any one think this picture over-strained, I can assure him that it is taken from nature and from truth; but I will not likewise aver, that the theologist was neither crazed nor inebriated. If the listener's words were to be relied on, there was no love, no accommodating principle manifested between the two, but a fiery burning zeal, relating to points of such minor importance, that a true Christian would blush to hear them mentioned, and the infidel and profane make a handle of them to turn our religion to scorn.

Great was the dame's exultation at the triumph of her beloved pastor over her sinful neighbours in the lower parts of the house; and she boasted of it to Martha in high-sounding terms. But it was of short duration; for, in five weeks after that, Arabella Logan came to reside with the laird as his house-keeper, sitting at his table, and carrying the keys as mistress-substitute of the mansion. The lady's grief and indignation were now raised to a higher pitch than ever; and she set every agent to work, with whom she had any power, to effect a separation between these two suspected ones. Remonstrance was of no avail: George laughed at them who tried such a course, and retained his house-keeper, while the lady gave herself up to utter despair; for though she would not consort with her husband herself, she could not endure that any other should do so.

But, to countervail this grievous offence, our saintly and afflicted dame, in due time, was safely delivered of a fine boy, whom the laird acknowledged as his son and heir, and had him christened by his own name, and nursed in his own premises. He gave the nurse permission to take the boy to his mother's presence if ever she should desire to see him; but, strange as it may appear, she never once desired to see him from the day that he was born. The boy grew up, and was a healthful and happy child; and, in the course of another year, the lady presented him with a brother. A brother he certainly was, in the eye of the law, and it is more than probable that he was his brother in reality. But the laird thought otherwise; and, though he knew and acknowledged that he was obliged to support and provide for him, he refused to acknowledge him in other respects. He neither would countenance the banquet, nor take the baptismal vows on him in the child's name; of course, the poor boy had to live and remain an alien from the visible church for a year and a day; at which time, Mr. Wringhim, out of pity and kindness, took the lady herself as sponsor for the boy, and baptized him by the name of Robert Wringhim,—that being the noted divine's own name.

George was brought up with his father, and educated partly at the parish-school, and partly at home, by a tutor hired for the purpose. He was a generous and kind-hearted youth; always ready to oblige, and hardly ever dissatisfied with any body. Robert was brought up with Mr. Wringhim, the laird paying a certain allowance for him yearly; and there the boy was early inured to all the sternness and severity of his pastor's arbitrary and unyielding creed. He was taught to pray twice every day, and seven times on Sabbath days; but he was only to pray for the elect, and, like David of old,[1] doom all that were aliens from God to destruction. He had never, in that family into which he had been as it were adopted, heard ought but evil spoken of his reputed father and brother; consequently he held them in utter abhorrence, and prayed against them every day, often "that the old hoary sinner might be cut off in the full flush of his iniquity, and be carried quick into hell; and that the young stem of the corrupt trunk might also be taken from a world that he disgraced, but that his sins might be pardoned, because he knew no better."

Such were the tenets in which it would appear young Robert was bred. He was an acute boy, an excellent learner, had ardent and ungovernable passions, and withal, a sternness of demeanour from which other boys shrunk. He was the best grammarian, the best reader, writer, and accountant in the various classes that he attended, and was fond of writing essays on controverted points of theology, for which he got prizes, and great praise from his guardian and mother. George was much behind him in scholastic acquirements, but greatly his superior in personal prowess, form, feature, and all that constitutes gentility in deportment and appearance. The laird had often manifested to Miss Logan an earnest wish that the two young men should never meet, or at all events that they should be as little conversant as possible; and Miss Logan, who was as much attached to George as if he had been her own son, took every precaution, while he was a boy, that he should never meet with his brother; but as they advanced towards manhood, this became impracticable. The lady was removed from her apartments in her husband's house to Glasgow, to her great content; and all to prevent the young laird being tainted with the company of her and her second son; for the laird had felt the effects of the principles they professed, and dreaded them more than persecution, fire, and sword. During all the dreadful times that had overpast, though the laird had been a moderate man, he had still leaned to the side of

---

1 David, King of Israel c.1000–962BC. He defeated the Philistines and united the tribes of Israel.

the kingly prerogative, and had escaped confiscation and fines, without ever taking any active hand in suppressing the Covenanters.[1] But after experiencing a specimen of their tenets and manner in his wife, from a secret favourer of them and their doctrines, he grew alarmed at the prevalence of such stern and factious principles, now that there was no check nor restraint upon them; and from that time he began to set himself against them, joining with the cavalier party[2] of that day in all their proceedings.

It so happened, that, under the influence of the Earls of Seafield and Tullibardine[3], he was returned for a Member of Parliament in the famous session that sat at Edinburgh, when the Duke of Queensberry was commissioner, and in which party spirit ran to such an extremity.[4] The young laird went with his father to the court, and remained in town all the time that the session lasted; and as all interested people of both factions flocked to the town at that period, so the important Mr. Wringhim was there among the rest, during the greater part of the time, blowing the coal of revolutionary principles with all his might, in every society to which he could obtain admission. He was a great favourite with some of the west country gentlemen of that faction, by reason of his unbending impudence. No opposition could for a moment cause him either to blush, or retract one item that he had advanced. Therefore the Duke of Argyle[5] and his friends made such use of him as

---

1   Adherents of the National Covenant of the Solemn League and Covenant in Scotland, defending and promoting Presbyteriansim in the Church of Scotland. See introduction (8ff.).

2   i.e. Jacobites—supporters of exiled Stuart King James II of England and VII of Scotland (1633-1701) who had been deposed in the Glorious Revolution of 1688.

3   A committed unionist, the Earl of Seafield (James Ogilvy, 1633-1730) was appointed Lord High Chancellor of Scotland in 1702. Although originally a Whig, the Earl of Tullibardine (John Murray, 1660-1724) converted to the Jacobite cause, becoming Duke of Atholl in 1703.

4   The "famous session" of the Scottish Parliament (May-September 1703) passed, among other legislation, the Act of Security of the Kingdom, reserving the right for Scotland to choose its own monarch. Despite the proviso that the monarch must be a Protestant, many felt that by opposing the will of the English Parliament the Act allowed for the restoration of the Stuarts in Scotland.

5   Archibald Campbell (c.1652-1703), the first Duke, from 1701-3.

sportsmen often do of terriers, to start the game, and make a great yelping noise to let them know whither the chace is proceeding. They often did this out of sport, in order to teaze their opponent; for of all pesterers that ever fastened on man he was the most insufferable: knowing that his coat protected him from manual chastisement, he spared no acrimony, and delighted in the chagrin and anger of those with whom he contended. But he was sometimes likewise *of real use* to the heads of the presbyterian faction, and therefore was admitted to their tables, and of course conceived himself a very great man.

His ward accompanied him; and very shortly after their arrival in Edinburgh, Robert, for the first time, met with the young laird his brother, in a match at tennis. The prowess and agility of the young squire drew forth the loudest plaudits of approval from his associates, and his own exertion alone carried the game every time on the one side, and that so far as all along to count three for their one. The hero's name soon ran round the circle, and when his brother Robert, who was an onlooker, learned who it was that was gaining so much applause, he came and stood close beside him all the time that the game lasted, always now and then putting in a cutting remark by way of mockery.

George could not help perceiving him, not only on account of his impertinent remarks, but he, moreover, stood so near him that he several times impeded him in his rapid evolutions, and of course got himself shoved aside in no very ceremonious way. Instead of making him keep his distance, these rude shocks and pushes, accompanied sometimes with hasty curses, only made him cling the closer to this king of the game. He seemed determined to maintain his right to his place as an onlooker, as well as any of those engaged in the game, and if they had tried him at an argument, he would have carried his point: or perhaps he wished to quarrel with this spark of his jealousy and aversion, and draw the attention of the gay crowd to himself by these means; for, like his guardian, he knew no other pleasure but what consisted in opposition. George took him for some impertinent student of divinity, rather set upon a joke than any thing else. He perceived a lad with black clothes, and a methodistical face, whose countenance and eye he disliked exceedingly, several times in his way, and that was all the notice he took of him the first time they two met. But the next day, and every succeeding one, the same devilish-looking youth attended him as constantly as his shadow; was always in his way as with intention to impede him, and ever and anon his deep and malignant eye met those of his elder brother with a glance so fierce that it sometimes startled him.

The very next time that George was engaged at tennis, he had not struck the ball above twice till the same intrusive being was again in his way. The party played for considerable stakes that day, namely, a dinner and wine at the Black Bull tavern; and George, as the hero and head of his party, was much interested in its honour; consequently, the sight of this moody and hellish-looking student affected him in no very pleasant manner. "Pray, Sir, be so good as keep without the range of the ball," said he.

"Is there any law or enactment that can compel me to do so?" said the other, biting his lip with scorn.

"If there is not, they are here that shall compel you," returned George: "so, friend, I rede you to be on your guard."

As he said this, a flush of anger glowed in his handsome face, and flashed from his sparkling blue eye; but it was a stranger to both, and momently took its departure. The black-coated youth set up his cap before, brought his heavy brows over his deep dark eyes, put his hands in the pockets of his black plush breeches, and stepped a little farther into the semi-circle, immediately on his brother's right hand, than he had ever ventured to do before. There he set himself firm on his legs, and, with a face as demure as death, seemed determined to keep his ground. He pretended to be following the ball with his eyes; but every moment they were glancing aside at George. One of the competitors chanced to say rashly, in the moment of exultation, "That's a d——d fine blow, George!" On which the intruder took up the word, as character-istic of the competitors, and repeated it every stroke that was given, making such a ludicrous use of it, that several of the on-lookers were compelled to laugh immoderately; but the play-ers were terribly nettled at it, as he really contrived, by dint of sliding in some canonical terms, to render the competitors and their game ridiculous.

But matters at length came to a crisis that put them beyond sport. George, in flying backward to gain the point at which the ball was going to light, came inadvertently so rudely in contact with this obstreperous interloper, that he not only overthrew him, but also got a grievous fall over his legs; and, as he arose, the other made a spurn at him with his foot, which, if it had hit to its aim, would undoubtedly have finished the course of the young laird of Dalcastle and Balgrennan. George, being irritated beyond measure, as may well be conceived, especially at the deadly stroke aimed at him, struck the assailant with his racket, rather slightly, but so that his mouth and nose gushed out blood; and, at the same time, he said, turning to his cronies,—"Does any of you know who the infernal puppy is?"

"Do you not know, Sir?" said one of the onlookers, a stranger: "The gentleman is your own brother, Sir—Mr. Robert Wringhim Colwan!"

"No, not Colwan, Sir," said Robert, putting his hands in his pockets, and setting himself still farther forward than before,—"not a Colwan, Sir; henceforth I disclaim the name."

"No, certainly not," repeated George: "My mother's son you may be,—but *not a Colwan!* There you are right." Then turning round to his informer, he said, "Mercy be about us, Sir! is this the crazy minister's son from Glasgow?"

This question was put in the irritation of the moment; but it was too rude, and too far out of place, and no one deigned any answer to it. He felt the reproof, and felt it deeply; seeming anxious for some opportunity to make an acknowledgment, or some reparation.

In the meantime, young Wringhim was an object to all of the uttermost disgust. The blood flowing from his mouth and nose he took no pains to stem, neither did he so much as wipe it away; so that it spread over all his cheeks, and breast, even off at his toes. In that state did he take up his station in the middle of the competitors; and he did not now keep his place, but ran about, impeding every one who attempted to make at the ball. They loaded him with execrations, but it availed nothing; he seemed courting persecution and buffetings, keeping stedfastly to his old joke of damnation, and marring the game so completely, that, in spite of every effort on the part of the players, he forced them to stop their game, and give it up. He was such a rueful-looking object, covered with blood, that none of them had the heart to kick him, although it appeared the only thing he wanted; and as for George, he said not another word to him, either in anger or reproof.

When the game was fairly given up, and the party were washing their hands in the stone fount, some of them besought Robert Wringhim to wash himself; but he mocked at them, and said, he was much better as he was. George, at length, came forward abashedly toward him, and said,—"I have been greatly to blame, Robert, and am very sorry for what I have done. But, in the first instance, I erred through ignorance, not knowing you were my brother, which you certainly are; and, in the second, through a

momentary irritation, for which I am ashamed. I pray you, therefore, to pardon me, and give me your hand."

As he said this, he held out his hand toward his polluted brother; but the froward predestinarian took not his from his breeches
pocket, but lifting his foot, he gave his brother's hand a kick. "I'll
give you what will suit such a hand better than mine," said he, with
a sneer. And then, turning lightly about, he added,—"Are there to
be no more of these d——d fine blows, gentlemen? For shame, to
give up such a profitable and edifying game!"

"This is too bad," said George. "But, since it is thus, I have the
less to regret." And, having made this general remark, he took no
more note of the uncouth aggressor. But the persecution of the
latter terminated not on the play-ground: he ranked up among
them, bloody and disgusting as he was, and, keeping close by his
brother's side, he marched along with the party all the way to the
Black Bull. Before they got there, a great number of boys and idle
people had surrounded them, hooting and incommoding them
exceedingly, so that they were glad to get into the inn; and the
unaccountable monster actually tried to get in alongst with them,
to make one of the party at dinner. But the innkeeper and his men,
getting the hint, by force prevented him from entering, although
he attempted it again and again, both by telling lies and offering a
bribe. Finding he could not prevail, he set to exciting the mob at
the door to acts of violence; in which he had like to have succeeded. The landlord had no other shift, at last, but to send privately for two officers, and have him carried to the guard-house;
and the hilarity and joy of the party of young gentlemen, for the
evening, was quite spoiled, by the inauspicious termination of their
game.

The Rev. Robert Wringham was now to send for, to release his
beloved ward. The messenger found him at table, with a number
of the leaders of the Whig faction,[1] the Marquis of Annandale[2]
being in the chair; and the prisoner's note being produced,
Wringhim read it aloud, accompanying it with some explanatory

---

1   Broadly, the anti-Royalist faction. At this time Whigs represented the
    interests of landowning families and the affluent middle class and support-
    ed religious toleration.
2   William Johnstone (1672-1721), Lord President of the Privy Council
    1702-6.

remarks. The circumstances of the case being thus magnified and distorted, it excited the utmost abhorrence, both of the deed and the perpetrators, among the assembled faction. They declaimed against the act as an unnatural attempt on the character, and even the life, of an unfortunate brother, who had been expelled from his father's house. And, as party spirit was the order of the day, an attempt was made to lay the burden of it to that account. In short, the young culprit got some of the best blood of the land to enter as his securities, and was set at liberty. But when Wringhim perceived the plight that he was in, he took him, as he was, and presented him to his honourable patrons. This raised the indignation against the young laird and his associates a thousand fold, which actually roused the party to temporary madness. They were, perhaps, a little excited by the wine and spirits they had swallowed; else a casual quarrel between two young men, at tennis, could not have driven them to such extremes. But certain it is, that from one at first arising to address the party on the atrocity of the offence, both in a moral and political point of view, on a sudden there were six on their feet, at the same time, expatiating on it; and, in a very short time thereafter, every one in the room was up, talking with the utmost vociferation, all on the same subject, and all taking the same side in the debate.

In the midst of this confusion, some one or other issued from the house, which was at the back of the Canongate, calling out,— "A plot, a plot! Treason, treason! Down with the bloody incendiaries at the Black Bull!"

The concourse of people that were assembled in Edinburgh at that time was prodigious; and as they were all actuated by political motives, they wanted only a ready-blown coal to set the mountain on fire. The evening being fine, and the streets thronged, the cry ran from mouth to mouth through the whole city. More than that, the mob that had of late been gathered to the door of the Black Bull, had, by degrees, dispersed; but, they being young men, and idle vagrants, they had only spread themselves over the rest of the street to lounge in search of farther amusement: consequently, a word was sufficient to send them back to their late rendezvous, where they had previously witnessed something they did not much approve of.

The master of the tavern was astonished at seeing the mob again assembling; and that with such hurry and noise. But his inmates being all of the highest respectability, he judged himself sure of protection, or, at least, of indemnity. He had two large parties in his house at the time; the largest of which was of the Revolutionist faction. The other consisted of our young tennis-players, and their associates, who were all of the Jacobite order; or, at all events, leaned to the Episcopal side. The largest party were in a front-room; and the attack of the mob fell first on their windows, though rather with fear and caution. Jingle went one pane; then a loud hurra; and that again was followed by a number of voices, endeavouring to restrain the indignation from venting itself in destroying the windows, and to turn it on the inmates. The Whigs, calling the landlord, inquired what the assault meant: he cunningly answered, that he suspected it was some of the youths of the Cavalier, or High-Church party, exciting the mob against them. The party consisted mostly of young gentlemen, by that time in a key to engage in any row; and, at all events, to suffer nothing from the other party, against whom their passions were mightily inflamed.

The landlord, therefore, had no sooner given them the spirit-rousing intelligence, than every one, as by instinct, swore his own natural oath, and grasped his own natural weapon. A few of those of the highest rank were armed with swords, which they boldly drew; those of the subordinate orders immediately flew to such weapons as the room, kitchen, and scullery afforded;—such as tongs, pokers, spits, racks, and shovels; and breathing vengeance on the prelatic party, the children of Antichrist and the heirs of d—n—t—n! the barterers of the liberties of their country, and betrayers of the most sacred trust,—thus elevated, and thus armed, in the cause of right, justice, and liberty, our heroes rushed to the street, and attacked the mob with such violence, that they broke the mass in a moment, and dispersed their thousands like chaff before the wind. The other party of young Jacobites, who sat in a room farther from the front, and were those against whom the fury of the mob was meant to have been directed, knew nothing of this second uproar, till the noise of the sally made by the Whigs assailed their ears; being then informed that the mob had attacked the house on account of the treatment they themselves had given to a young gentleman of the adverse faction, and that another jovial party had issued from the house in their defence, and was now engaged in an unequal combat, the sparks likewise flew to the field to back their defenders with all their prowess, without troubling their heads about who they were.

A mob is like a spring-tide in an eastern storm, that retires only to return with more overwhelming fury. The crowd was taken by surprise, when such a strong and well-armed party issued from the

house with so great fury, laying all prostrate that came in their way.
Those who were next to the door, and were, of course, the first
whom the imminent danger assailed, rushed backward among the
crowd with their whole force. The Black Bull standing in a small
square half way between the High Street and the Cowgate, and the
entrance to it being by two closes, into these the pressure outward
was simultaneous, and thousands were moved to an involuntary
flight they knew not why.

But the High Street of Edinburgh, which they soon reached, is
a dangerous place in which to make an open attack upon a mob.
And it appears that the entrances to the tavern had been somewhere near to the Cross, on the south side of the street; for the
crowd fled with great expedition, both to the east and west, and the
conquerors, separating themselves as chance directed, pursued impetuously, wounding and maiming as they flew. But, it so chanced,
that before either of the wings had followed the flying squadrons
of their enemies for the space of a hundred yards each way, the
devil an enemy they had to pursue! the multitude had vanished
like so many thousands of phantoms! What could our heroes do?—
Why, they faced about to return toward their citadel, the Black
Bull. But that feat was not so easily, nor so readily accomplished, as
they divined. The unnumbered alleys on each side of the street had
swallowed up the multitude in a few seconds; but from these they
were busy reconnoitring; and, perceiving the deficiency in the
number of their assailants, the rush from both sides of the street was
as rapid, and as wonderful, as the disappearance of the crowd had
been a few minutes before. Each close vomited out its levies, and
these better armed with missiles than when they sought it for a
temporary retreat. Woe then to our two columns of victorious
Whigs! The mob actually closed around them as they would have
swallowed them up; and, in the meanwhile, shower after shower of
the most abominable weapons of offence were rained in upon
them. If the gentlemen were irritated before, this inflamed them
still farther; but their danger was now so apparent, they could not
shut their eyes on it, therefore, both parties, as if actuated by the
same spirit, made a desperate effort to join, and the greater part
effected it; but some were knocked down, and others were separated from their friends, and blithe to become silent members of
the mob.

The battle now raged immediately in front of the closes leading
to the Black Bull; the small body of Whig gentlemen was hardly
bested, and it is likely would have been overcome and trampled

down every man, had they not been then and there joined by the young Cavaliers; who, fresh to arms, broke from the wynd, opened the head of the passage, laid about them manfully, and thus kept up the spirits of the exasperated Whigs, who were the men in fact that wrought the most deray among the populace.

The town-guard was now on the alert; and two companies of the Cameronian regiment, with the Hon. Captain Douglas, rushed down from the Castle to the scene of action; but, for all the noise and hubbub that these caused in the street, the combat had become so close and inveterate, that numbers of both sides were taken prisoners fighting hand to hand, and could scarcely be separated when the guardsmen and soldiers had them by the necks.

Great was the alarm and confusion that night in Edinburgh; for every one concluded that it was a party scuffle, and, the two parties being so equal in power, the most serious consequences were anticipated. The agitation was so prevailing, that every party in the town, great and small, was broken up; and the lord-commissioner thought proper to go to the council-chamber himself, even at that late hour, accompanied by the sheriffs of Edinburgh and Linlithgow,[1] with sundry noblemen besides, in order to learn something of the origin of the affray.

For a long time the court was completely puzzled. Every gentleman brought in exclaimed against the treatment he had received, in most bitter terms, blaming a mob set on him and his friends by the adverse party, and matters looked extremely ill, until at length they began to perceive that they were examining gentlemen of both parties, and that they had been doing so from the beginning, almost alternately, so equally had the prisoners been taken from both parties. Finally, it turned out, that a few gentlemen, two-thirds of whom were strenuous Whigs themselves, had joined in mauling the whole Whig population of Edinburgh. The investigation disclosed nothing the effect of which was not ludicrous; and the Duke of Queensberry,[2] whose aim was at that time to conciliate the two factions, tried all that he could to turn the whole *fracas* into a joke—an unlucky frolic, where no ill was meant on either side, and which yet had been productive of a great deal.

---

1 A town near Edinburgh.
2 James Douglas (1662-1711), who became Duke in 1695.

The greater part of the people went home satisfied; but not so the Rev. Robert Wringhim. He did all that he could to inflame both judges and populace against the young Cavaliers, especially against the young Laird of Dalcastle, whom he represented as an incendiary, set on by an unnatural parent to slander his mother, and make away with a hapless and only brother; and, in truth, that declaimer against all human merit had that sort of powerful, homely, and bitter eloquence, which seldom missed affecting his hearers: the consequence at that time was, that he made the unfortunate affair between the two brothers appear in extremely bad colours, and the populace retired to their homes impressed with no very favourable opinion of either the Laird of Dalcastle or his son George, neither of whom were there present to speak for themselves.

As for Wringhim himself, he went home to his lodgings, filled with gall and with spite against the young laird, whom he was made to believe the aggressor, and that intentionally. But most of all was he filled with indignation against the father, whom he held in abhorrence at all times, and blamed solely for this unmannerly attack made on his favourite ward, namesake, and adopted son; and for the public imputation of a crime to his own reverence, in calling the lad *his* son, and thus charging him with a sin against which he was well known to have levelled all the arrows of church censure with unsparing might.

But, filled as his heart was with some portion of these bad feelings, to which all flesh is subject, he kept, nevertheless, the fear of the Lord always before his eyes so far as never to omit any of the external duties of religion, and farther than that, man hath no power to pry. He lodged with the family of a Mr. Miller, whose lady was originally from Glasgow, and had been a hearer, and, of course, a great admirer of Mr. Wringhim. In that family he made public worship every evening; and that night, in his petitions at a throne of grace, he prayed for so many vials of wrath to be poured on the head of some particular sinner, that the hearers trembled, and stopped their ears. But that he might not proceed with so violent a measure, amounting to excommunication, without due scripture warrant, he began the exercise of the evening by singing the following verses,[1] which it is a pity should ever have been admitted into a Christian psalmody, being so adverse to all its mild and benevolent principles:—

---

1   From metrical Psalm 109, verses 6-9, 14, 17-18.

Set thou the wicked over him,
And upon his right hand
Give thou his greatest enemy,
Even Satan, leave to stand.
And when by thee he shall be judged,
Let him remembered be;
And let his prayer be turned to sin,
When he shall call on thee.
Few be his days; and in his room
His charge another take;
His children let be fatherless;
His wife a widow make:
Let God his father's wickedness
Still to remembrance call;
And never let his mother's sin
Be blotted out at all.
As he in cursing pleasure took,
So let it to him fall;
As he delighted not to bless,
So bless him not at all.
As cursing he like clothes put on,
Into his bowels so,
Like water, and into his bones
Like oil, down let it go.

Young Wringhim only knew the full purport of this spiritual song; and went to his bed better satisfied than ever, that his father and brother were cast-aways, reprobates, aliens from the church and the true faith, and cursed in time and eternity.

The next day George and his companions met as usual,—all who were not seriously wounded of them. But as they strolled about the city, the rancorous eye and the finger of scorn was pointed against them. None of them was at first aware of the reason; but it threw a damp over their spirits and enjoyments, which they could not master. They went to take a forenoon game at their old play of tennis, not on a match, but by way of improving themselves; but they had not well taken their places till young Wringhim appeared in his old station, at his brother's right hand, with looks more demure and determined than ever. His lips were primmed so close that his mouth was hardly discernible, and his dark deep eye flashed gleams of holy indignation on the godless set, but particularly on his brother. His presence acted as a mildew on all social intercourse or enjoyment; the game was marred, and ended ere ever it was well begun. There were whisperings apart—the party separated; and, in order to shake off the blighting influence of this dogged persecutor, they entered sundry houses of their acquaintances, with an understanding that they were to meet on the Links for a game at cricket.

They did so; and, stripping off part of their clothes, they began that violent and spirited game. They had not played five minutes, till Wringhim was stalking in the midst of them, and totally impeding the play. A cry arose from all corners of "O, this will never do. Kick him out of the playground! Knock down the scoundrel; or bind him, and let him lie in peace."

"By no means," cried George: "it is evident he wants nothing else. Pray do not humour him so much as to touch him with either foot or finger." Then turning to a friend, he said in a whisper, "Speak to him, Gordon; he surely will not refuse to let us have the ground to ourselves, if you request it of him."

Gordon went up to him, and requested of him, civilly, but ardently, "to retire to a certain distance, else none of them could or would be answerable, however sore he might be hurt."

He turned disdainfully on his heel, uttered a kind of pulpit hem! and then added, "I will take my chance of that; hurt me, any of you, at your peril."

The young gentlemen smiled, through spite and disdain of the dogged animal. Gordon followed him up, and tried to remonstrate with him; but he let him know that "it was his pleasure to be there at that time; and, unless he could demonstrate to him what superior right he and his party had to that ground, in preference to him, and to the exclusion of all others, he was determined to assert his right, and the rights of his fellow-citizens, by keeping possession of whatsoever part of that common field he chose."

"You are no gentleman, Sir," said Gordon.

"Are you one, Sir?" said the other.

"Yes, Sir, I will let you know that I am, by G——!"

"Then, thanks be to Him whose name you have profaned, I am none. If *one* of the party be a gentleman, *I do hope in God I am not!*"

It was now apparent to them all that he was courting obloquy and manual chastisement from their hands, if by any means he could provoke them to the deed; and, apprehensive that he had some sinister and deep-laid design in hunting after such a singular favour, they wisely restrained one another from inflicting the pun-

Robert claims to be religious, but in tempting another toward sin, acts as Satan

ishment that each of them yearned to bestow, personally, and which he so well deserved.

But the unpopularity of the Younger George Colwan could no longer be concealed from his associates. It was manifested wherever the populace were assembled; and his young and intimate friend, Adam Gordon, was obliged to warn him of the circumstance, that he might not be surprised at the gentlemen of their acquaintance withdrawing themselves from his society, as they could not be seen with him without being insulted. George thanked him; and it was agreed between them, that the former should keep himself retired during the daytime while he remained in Edinburgh, and that at night they should always meet together, along with such of their companions as were disengaged.

George found it every day more and more necessary to adhere to this system of seclusion; for it was not alone the hisses of the boys and populace that pursued him,—a fiend of more malignant aspect was ever at his elbow, in the form of his brother. To whatever place of amusement he betook himself, and however well he concealed his intentions of going there from all flesh living, there was his brother Wringhim also, and always within a few yards of him, generally about the same distance, and ever and anon darting looks at him that chilled his very soul. They were looks that cannot be described; but they were felt piercing to the bosom's deepest core. They affected even the on-lookers in a very particular manner, for all whose eyes caught a glimpse of these hideous glances followed them to the object toward which they were darted: the gentlemanly and mild demeanour of that object generally calmed their startled apprehensions; for no one ever yet noted the glances of the young man's eye in the black coat, at the face of his brother, who did not at first manifest strong symptoms of alarm.

George became utterly confounded; not only at the import of this persecution, but how in the world it came to pass that this unaccountable being knew all his motions, and every intention of his heart, as it were intuitively. On consulting his own previous feelings and resolutions, he found that the circumstances of his going to such and such a place were often the most casual incidents in nature—the caprice of a moment had carried him there, and yet he had never sat or stood many minutes till there was the self-same being, always in the same position with regard to himself, as regularly as the shadow is cast from the substance, or the ray of light from the opposing denser medium.

For instance, he remembered one day of setting out with the intention of going to attend divine worship in the High Church,[1] and when within a short space of its door, he was overtaken by young Kilpatrick of Closeburn, who was bound to the Grey-Friars[2] to see his sweetheart, as he said; "and if you will go with me, Colwan," said he, "I will let you see her too, and then you will be just as far forward as I am."

George assented at once, and went; and after taking his seat, he leaned his head forward on the pew to repeat over to himself a short ejaculatory prayer, as had always been his custom on entering the house of God. When he had done, he lifted his eyes naturally toward that point on his right hand where the fierce apparition of his brother had been wont to meet his view: there he was, in the same habit, form, demeanour, and precise point of distance, as usual! George again laid down his head, and his mind was so astounded, that he had nearly fallen into a swoon. He tried shortly after to muster up courage to look at the speaker, at the congregation, and at Captain Kilpatrick's sweetheart in particular; but the fiendish glances of the young man in the black clothes were too appalling to be withstood,—his eye caught them whether he was looking that way or not: at length his courage was fairly mastered, and he was obliged to look down during the remainder of the service.

By night or by day it was the same. In the gallery of the Parliament House, in the boxes of the play-house, in the church, in the assembly, in the streets, suburbs, and the fields; and every day, and every hour, from the first rencounter of the two, the attendance became more and more constant, more inexplicable, and altogether more alarming and insufferable, until at last George was fairly driven from society, and forced to spend his days in his own and his father's lodgings with closed doors. Even there, he was constantly harassed with the idea, that the next time he lifted his eyes, he would to a certainty see that face, the most repulsive to all his feelings of aught the earth contained. The attendance of that brother was now become like the attendance of a demon on some devoted being that had sold himself to destruction; his approaches as undiscerned, and his looks as fraught with hideous malignity. It was sel-

---

1   The High Kirk of St Giles, Parliament Square, on Edinburgh's High Street.
2   Greyfriars Church, the first to be built in Edinburgh following the Reformation. The National Covenant was signed there in 1638.

dom that he saw him either following him in the streets, or entering any house or church after him; he only appeared in his place, George wist not how, or whence; and, having sped so ill in his first friendly approaches, he had never spoken to his equivocal attendant a second time.

It came at length into George's head, as he was pondering, by himself, on the circumstances of this extraordinary attendance, that perhaps his brother had relented, and, though of so sullen and unaccommodating a temper that he would not acknowledge it, or beg a reconciliation, it might be for that very purpose that he followed his steps night and day in that extraordinary manner. "I cannot for my life see for what other purpose it can be," thought he. "He never offers to attempt my life; nor dares he, if he had the inclination; therefore, although his manner is peculiarly repulsive to me, I shall not have my mind burdened with the reflection, that my own mother's son yearned for a reconciliation with me, and was repulsed by my haughty and insolent behaviour. The next time he comes to my hand, I am resolved that I will accost him as one brother ought to address another, whatever it may cost me; and, if I am still flouted with disdain, then shall the blame rest with him." *George still model of Christian charity & forgiveness*

After this generous resolution, it was a good while before his gratuitous attendant appeared at his side again; and George began to think that his visits were discontinued. The hope was a relief that could not be calculated; but still George had a feeling that it was too supreme to last. His enemy had been too pertinacious to abandon his design, whatever it was. He, however, began to indulge in a little more liberty, and for several days he enjoyed it with impunity.

George was, from infancy, of a stirring active disposition, and could not endure confinement; and, having been of late much restrained in his youthful exercises by this singular persecutor, he grew uneasy under such restraint, and, one morning, chancing to awaken very early, he arose to make an excursion to the top of Arthur's Seat,[1] to breathe the breeze of the dawning, and see the sun arise out of the eastern ocean. The morning was calm and serene; and as he walked down the south back of the Canongate, toward the Palace,[2] the haze was so close around him that he could

---

1 A 250m high upthrust of lava, located in Holyrood Park, affording dramatic views of the city and the Forth estuary.
2 Holyrood Palace, on the Royal Mile: official residence of the sovereign in Scotland.

not see the houses on the opposite side of the way. As he passed the lord-commissioner's house, the guards were in attendance, who cautioned him not to go by the Palace, as all the gates would be shut and guarded for an hour to come, on which he went by the back of St. Anthony's gardens, and found his way into that little romantic glade adjoining to the Saint's chapel and well. He was still involved in a blue haze, like a dense smoke, but yet in the midst of it the respiration was the most refreshing and delicious. The grass and the flowers were loaden with dew; and, on taking off his hat to wipe his forehead, he perceived that the black glossy fur of which his chaperon was wrought, was all covered with a tissue of the most delicate silver—a fairy web, composed of little spheres, so minute that no eye could discern any one of them; yet there they were shining in lovely millions. Afraid of defacing so beautiful and so delicate a garnish, he replaced his hat with the greatest caution, and went on his way light of heart.

As he approached the swire at the head of the dell,—that little delightful verge from which in one moment the eastern limits and shores of Lothian[1] arise on the view,—as he approached it, I say, and a little space from the height, he beheld, to his astonishment, a bright halo in the cloud of haze, that rose in a semi-circle over his head like a pale rainbow. He was struck motionless at the view of the lovely vision; for it so chanced that he had never seen the same appearance before, though common at early morn. But he soon perceived the cause of the phenomenon, and that it proceeded from the rays of the sun from a pure unclouded morning sky striking upon this dense vapour which refracted them. But the better all the works of nature are understood, the more they will be ever admired. That was a scene that would have entranced the man of science with delight, but which the uninitiated and sordid man would have regarded less than the mole rearing up his hill in silence and in darkness.

George did admire this halo of glory, which still grew wider, and less defined, as he approached the surface of the cloud. But, to his utter amazement and supreme delight, he found, on reaching the top of Arthur's Seat, that this sublunary rainbow, this terrestrial glory, was spread in its most vivid hues beneath his feet. Still he could not perceive the body of the sun, although the light behind

---

1 Eastern region of Scotland in which Edinburgh is located.

him was dazzling; but the cloud of haze lying dense in that deep dell that separates the hill from the rocks of Salisbury, and the dull shadow of the hill mingling with that cloud, made the dell a pit of darkness. On that shadowy cloud was the lovely rainbow formed, spreading itself on a horizontal plain, and having a slight and brilliant shade of all the colours of the heavenly bow, but all of them paler and less defined. But this terrestrial phenomenon of the early morn cannot be better delineated than by the name given of it by the shepherd boys, "The little wee ghost of the rainbow." so loving in its familiarity

Such was the description of the morning, and the wild shades of the hill, that George gave to his father and Mr. Adam Gordon that same day on which he had witnessed them; and it is necessary that the reader should comprehend something of their nature, to understand what follows.

He seated himself on the pinnacle of the rocky precipice, a little within the top of the hill to the westward, and, with a light and buoyant heart, viewed the beauties of the morning, and inhaled its salubrious breeze. "Here," thought he, "I can converse with nature without disturbance, and without being intruded on by any appalling or obnoxious visitor." The idea of his brother's dark and malevolent looks coming at that moment across his mind, he turned his eyes instinctively to the right, to the point where that unwelcome guest was wont to make his appearance. Gracious Heaven! What an apparition was there presented to his view! He saw, delineated in the cloud, the shoulders, arms, and features of a human being of the most dreadful aspect. The face was the face of his brother, but dilated to twenty times the natural size. Its dark eyes gleamed on him through the mist, while every furrow of its hideous brow frowned deep as the ravines on the brow of the hill. George started, and his hair stood up in bristles as he gazed on this horrible monster. He saw every feature, and every line of the face, distinctly, as it gazed on him with an intensity that was hardly brookable. Its eyes were fixed on him, in the same manner as those of some carnivorous animal fixed on its prey; and yet there was fear and trembling, in these unearthly features, as plainly depicted as murderous malice. The giant apparition seemed sometimes to be cowering down as in terror, so that nothing but its brow and eyes were seen; still these never turned one moment from their object—again it rose imperceptibly up, and began to approach with great caution; and as it neared, the dimensions of its form lessened, still continuing, however, far above the natural size.

George conceived it to be a spirit. He could conceive it to be nothing else; and he took it for some horrid demon by which he was haunted, that had assumed the features of his brother in every lineament, but in taking on itself the human form, had miscalculated dreadfully on the size, and presented itself thus to him in a blown-up, dilated frame of embodied air, exhaled from the caverns of death or the regions of devouring fire. He was farther confirmed in the belief that it was a malignant spirit, on perceiving that it approached him across the front of a precipice, where there was not footing for thing of mortal frame. Still, what with terror and astonishment, he continued rivetted to the spot, till it approached, as he deemed, to within two yards of him; and then, perceiving that it was setting itself to make a violent spring on him, he started to his feet and fled distractedly in the opposite direction, keeping his eye cast behind him lest he had been seized in that dangerous place. But the very first bolt that he made in his flight he came in contact with a *real* body of flesh and blood, and that with such violence that both went down among some scragged rocks, and George rolled over the other. The being called out "Murder;" and, rising, fled precipitately. George then perceived that it was his brother; and, being confounded between the shadow and the substance, he knew not what he was doing or what he had done; and there being only one natural way of retreat from the brink of the rock, he likewise arose and pursued the affrighted culprit with all his speed towards the top of the hill. Wringhim was braying out "Murder! murder!" at which George being disgusted, and his spirits all in a ferment from some hurried idea of intended harm, the moment he came up with the craven he seized him rudely by the shoulder, and clapped his hand on his mouth. "Murder, you beast!" said he; "what do you mean by roaring out murder in that way? Who the devil is murdering you, or offering to murder you?"

Wringhim forced his mouth from under his brother's hand, and roared with redoubled energy, "Eh! Egh! murder! murder!" &c. George had felt resolute to put down this shocking alarm, lest some one might hear it and fly to the spot, or draw inferences widely different from the truth; and, perceiving the terror of this elect youth to be so great that expostulation was vain, he seized him by the mouth and nose with his left hand, so strenuously, that he sunk his fingers into his cheeks. But the poltroon still attempting to bray out, George gave him such a stunning blow with his fist on the left temple, that he crumbled, as it were, to the ground, but more from the effects of terror than those of the blow. His nose, however, again gushed out blood, a system of defence which seemed as natural to him as that resorted to by the race of stinkards. He then raised himself on his knees and hams, and raising up his ghastly face, while the blood streamed over both ears, he besought his life of his brother, in the most abject whining manner, gaping and blubbering most piteously.

"Tell me then, Sir," said George, resolved to make the most of the wretch's terror—"tell me for what purpose it is that you thus haunt my steps? Tell me plainly, and instantly, else I will throw you from the verge of that precipice."

"Oh, I will never do it again! I will never do it again! Spare my life, dear, good brother! Spare my life! Sure I never did you any hurt?"

"Swear to me, then, by the God that made you, that you will never henceforth follow after me to torment me with your hellish threatening looks; swear that you will never again come into my presence without being invited. Will you take an oath to this effect?"

"O yes! I will, I will!"

"But this is not all: you must tell me for what purpose you sought me out here this morning?"

"Oh, brother! for nothing but your good. I had nothing at heart but your unspeakable profit, and great and endless good."

"So then, you indeed knew that I was here?"

"I was told so by a friend, but I did not believe him; a—a—at least I did not know it was true till I saw you."

"Tell me this one thing, then, Robert, and all shall be forgotten and forgiven,—Who was that friend?"

"You do not know him."

"How then does he know me?"

"I cannot tell."

"Was he here present with you to-day?"

"Yes; he was not far distant. He came to this hill with me."

"Where then is he now?"

"I cannot tell."

"Then, wretch, confess that the devil was that friend who told you I was here, and who came here with you? None else could possibly know of my being here."

"Ah! how little you know of him! Would you argue that there is neither man nor spirit endowed with so much foresight as to deduce natural conclusions from previous actions and incidents

↖ Robert introduces that all phenomena have logical

but the devil? Alas, brother! But why should I wonder at such abandoned notions and principles? It was fore-ordained that you should cherish them, and that they should be the ruin of your soul and body, before the world was framed. Be assured of this, however, that I had no aim in seeking you *but your good!*"

"Well, Robert, I will believe it. I am disposed to be hasty and passionate: it is a fault in my nature; but I never meant, or wished you evil; and God is my witness that I would as soon stretch out my hand to my own life, or my father's, as to yours."——— At these words, Wringhim uttered a hollow exulting laugh, put his hands in his pockets, and withdrew a space to his accustomed distance. George continued: "And now, once for all, I request that we may exchange forgiveness, and that we may part and remain friends."

"Would such a thing be expedient, think you? Or consistent with the glory of God? I doubt it."

"I can think of nothing that would be more so. Is it not consistent with every precept of the Gospel? Come, brother, say that our reconciliation is complete."

"O yes, certainly! I tell you, brother, according to the flesh: it is just as complete as the lark's is with the adder; no more so, nor ever can. Reconciled, forsooth! To what would I be reconciled?"

As he said this, he strode indignantly away. From the moment that he heard his life was safe, he assumed his former insolence and revengeful looks—and never were they more dreadful than on parting with his brother that morning on the top of the hill. "Well, go thy ways," said George; "some would despise, but I pity thee. If thou art not a limb of Satan, I never saw one."

The sun had now dispelled the vapours; and the morning being lovely beyond description, George sat himself down on the top of the hill, and pondered deeply on the unaccountable incident that had befallen to him that morning. He could in nowise comprehend it; but, taking it with other previous circumstances, he could not get quit of a conviction that he was haunted by some evil genius in the shape of his brother, as well as by that dark and mysterious wretch himself. In no other way could he account for the apparition he saw that morning on the face of the rock, nor for several sudden appearances of the same being, in places where there was no possibility of any foreknowledge that he himself was to be there, and as little that the same being, if he were flesh and blood like other men, could always start up in the same position with regard to him. He determined, therefore, on reaching home, to relate all that had happened, from beginning to end, to his father, asking his counsel and his assistance, although he knew full well that his father was not the fittest man in the world to solve such a problem. He was now involved in party politics, over head and ears; and, moreover, he could never hear the names of either of the Wringhims mentioned without getting into a quandary of disgust and anger; and all that he would deign to say of them was, to call them by all the opprobrious names he could invent.

It turned out as the young man from the first suggested: old Dalcastle would listen to nothing concerning them with any patience. George complained that his brother harassed him with his presence at all times, and in all places. Old Dal asked why he did not kick the dog out of his presence, whenever he felt him disagreeable? George said, he seemed to have some demon for a familiar. Dal answered, that he did not wonder a bit at that, for the young spark was the third in a direct line who had all been children of adultery; and it was well known that all such were born half deils themselves, and nothing was more likely than that they should hold intercourse with their fellows. In the same style did he sympathise with all his son's late sufferings and perplexities.

In Mr. Adam Gordon, however, George found a friend who entered into all his feelings, and had seen and knew every thing about the matter. He tried to convince him, that at all events there could be nothing supernatural in the circumstances; and that the vision he had seen on the rock, among the thick mist, was the shadow of his brother approaching behind him. George could not swallow this, for he had seen his own shadow on the cloud, and, instead of approaching to aught like his own figure, he perceived nothing but a halo of glory round a point of the cloud, that was whiter and purer than the rest. Gordon said, if he would go with him to a mountain of his father's, which he named, in Aberdeenshire, he would show him a giant spirit of the same dimensions, any morning at the rising of the sun, provided he shone on that spot. This statement excited George's curiosity exceedingly; and, being disgusted with some things about Edinburgh, and glad to get out of the way, he consented to go with Gordon to the Highlands for a space. The day was accordingly set for their departure, the old laird's assent obtained; and the two young sparks parted in a state of great impatience for their excursion.

One of them found out another engagement, however, the instant after this last was determined on. Young Wringhim went off the hill that morning, and home to his upright guardian again, without washing the blood from his face and neck; and there he told a most woful story indeed: How he had gone out to take a morning's walk on the hill, where he had encountered with his reprobate brother among the mist, who had knocked him down and very near murdered him; threatening dreadfully, and with horrid oaths, to throw him from the top of the cliff.

The wrath of the great divine was kindled beyond measure. He cursed the aggressor in the name of the Most High; and bound himself, by an oath, to cause that wicked one's transgressions return upon his own head sevenfold. But before he engaged farther in the business of vengeance, he kneeled with his adopted son, and committed the whole cause unto the Lord, whom he addressed as one coming breathing burning coals of juniper, and casting his lightnings before him, to destroy and root out all who had moved hand or tongue against the children of the promise. Thus did he arise confirmed, and go forth to certain conquest.

We cannot enter into the detail of the events that now occurred, without forestalling a part of the narrative of one who knew all the circumstances—was deeply interested in them, and whose relation is of higher value than any thing that can be retailed out of the stores of tradition and old registers; but, his narrative being different from these, it was judged expedient to give the account as thus publicly handed down to us. Suffice it, that, before evening, George was apprehended, and lodged in jail, on a criminal charge of an assault and battery, to the shedding of blood, with the intent of committing fratricide. Then was the old laird in great consternation, and blamed himself for treating the thing so lightly, which seemed to have been gone about, from the beginning, so systematically, and with an intent which the villains were now going to realize, namely, to get the young laird disposed of, and then his brother, in spite of the old gentleman's teeth, would be laird himself.

Old Dal now set his whole interest to work among the noblemen and lawyers of his party. His son's case looked exceedingly ill, owing to the former assault before witnesses, and the unbecoming expressions made use of by him on that occasion, as well as from the present assault, which George did not deny, and for which no moving cause or motive could be made to appear.

On his first declaration before the sheriff, matters looked no better: but then the sheriff was a Whig. It is well known how differently the people of the present day, in Scotland, view the cases of their own party-men, and those of opposite political principles.

But this day is nothing to that in such matters, although, God knows, they are still sometimes barefaced enough. It appeared, from all the witnesses in the first case, that the complainant was the first aggressor—that he refused to stand out of the way, though apprised of his danger; and when his brother came against him inadvertently, he had aimed a blow at him with his foot, which, if it had taken effect, would have killed him. But as to the story of the apparition in fair day-light—the flying from the face of it—the running foul of his brother—pursuing him, and knocking him down, why the judge smiled at the relation; and saying, "It was a very extraordinary story," he remanded George to prison, leaving the matter to the High Court of Justiciary.

When the case came before that court, matters took a different turn. The constant and sullen attendance of the one brother upon the other excited suspicions; and these were in some manner, confirmed, when the guards at Queensberry-house deponed, that the prisoner went by them on his way to the hill that morning, about twenty minutes before the complainant, and when the latter passed, he asked if such a young man had passed before him, describing the prisoner's appearance to them; and that, on being answered in the affirmative, he mended his pace and fell a-running.

The Lord Justice,[1] on hearing this, asked the prisoner if he had any suspicions that his brother had a design on his life.

He answered, that all along, from the time of their first unfortunate meeting, his brother had dogged his steps so constantly, and so unaccountably, that he was convinced it was with some intent out of the ordinary course of events; and that if, as his lordship supposed, it was indeed his shadow that he had seen approaching him through the mist, then, from the cowering and cautious manner that it advanced, there was too little doubt that his brother's design had been to push him headlong from the cliff that morning.

A conversation then took place between the Judge and the Lord Advocate;[2] and, in the mean time, a bustle was seen in the hall; on which the doors were ordered to be guarded,—and, behold, the precious Mr. R. Wringhim was taken into custody, trying to make

---

1   President of the High Court of Judiciary in Scotland.
2   The principal law officer in Scotland.

his escape out of court. Finally it turned out, that George was honourably acquitted, and young Wringhim bound over to keep the peace, with heavy penalties and securities.

That was a day of high exultation to George and his youthful associates, all of whom abhorred Wringhim; and the evening being spent in great glee, it was agreed between Mr. Adam Gordon and George, that their visit to the Highlands, though thus long delayed, was not to be abandoned; and though they had, through the machinations of an incendiary, lost the season of delight, they would still find plenty of sport in deer-shooting. Accordingly, the day was set a second time for their departure; and, on the day preceding that, all the party were invited by George to dine with him once more at the sign of the Black Bull of Norway. Every one promised to attend, anticipating nothing but festivity and joy. Alas, what short-sighted improvident creatures we are, all of us; and how often does the evening cup of joy lead to sorrow in the morning!

The day arrived—the party of young noblemen and gentlemen met, and were as happy and jovial as men could be. George was never seen so brilliant, or so full of spirits; and exulting to see so many gallant young chiefs and gentlemen about him, who all gloried in the same principles of loyalty, (perhaps this word should have been written *disloyalty*,) he made speeches, gave toasts, and sung songs, all leaning slily to the same side, until a very late hour. By that time he had pushed the bottle so long and so freely, that its fumes had taken possession of every brain to such a degree, that they held Dame Reason rather at the staff's end, overbearing all her counsels and expostulations; and it was imprudently proposed by a wild inebriated spark, and carried by a majority of voices, that the whole party should adjourn to a bagnio[1] for the remainder of the night.

They did so; and it appears from what follows, that the house to which they retired, must have been somewhere on the opposite side of the street to the Black Bull Inn, a little farther to the eastward. They had not been an hour in that house, till some altercation chanced to arise between George Colwan and a Mr. Drummond, the younger son of a nobleman of distinction. It was perfectly casual, and no one thenceforward, to this day, could ever tell what it was about, if it was not about the misunderstanding of

---

1 Literally a Turkish bathing house, but here a brothel.

some word, or term, that the one had uttered. However it was, some high words passed between them; these were followed by threats; and in less than two minutes from the commencement of the quarrel, Drummond left the house in apparent displeasure, hinting to the other that they two should settle that in a more convenient place.

The company looked at one another, for all was over before any of them knew such a thing was begun. "What the devil is the matter?" cried one. "What ails Drummond?" cried another. "Who has he quarrelled with?" asked a third.

"Don't know."—"Can't tell, on my life."—"He has quarrelled with his wine, I suppose, and is going to send it a challenge."

Such were the questions, and such the answers that passed in the jovial party, and the matter was no more thought of.

But in the course of a very short space, about the length of which the ideas of the company were the next day at great variance, a sharp rap came to the door: It was opened by a female; but there being a chain inside, she only saw one side of the person at the door. He appeared to be a young gentleman, in appearance like him who had lately left the house, and asked, in a low whispering voice, "if young Dalcastle was still in the house?" The woman did not know,—"If he is," added he, "pray tell him to speak with me for a few minutes." The woman delivered the message before all the party, among whom there were then sundry courteous ladies of notable distinction, and George, on receiving it, instantly rose from the side of one of them, and said, in the hearing of them all, "I will bet a hundred merks that is Drummond."—"Don't go to quarrel with him, George," said one.—"Bring him in with you," said another. George stepped out; the door was again bolted, the chain drawn across, and the inadvertent party, left within, thought no more of the circumstance till the next morning, that the report had spread over the city, that a young gentleman had been slain, on a little washing-green at the side of the North Loch, and at the very bottom of the close where this thoughtless party had been assembled.

Several of them, on first hearing the report, hasted to the dead-room in the old Guard-house, where the corpse had been deposited, and soon discovered the body to be that of their friend and late entertainer, George Colwan. Great were the consternation and grief of all concerned, and, in particular, of his old father and Miss Logan; for George had always been the sole hope and darling of both, and the news of the event paralysed them so as to render them incapable of all thought or exertion. The spirit of the old laird was broken by the blow, and he descended at once from a jolly, good-natured, and active man, to a mere driveller, weeping over the body of his son, kissing his wound, his lips, and his cold brow alternately; denouncing vengeance on his murderers, and lamenting that he himself had not met the cruel doom, so that the hope of his race might have been preserved. In short, finding that all further motive of action and object of concern or of love, here below, were for ever removed from him, he abandoned himself to despair, and threatened to go down to the grave with his son.

But although he made no attempt to discover the murderers, the arm of justice was not idle; and it being evident to all, that the crime must infallibly be brought home to young Drummond, some of his friends sought him out, and compelled him, sorely against his will, to retire into concealment till the issue of the proof that should be led was made known. At the same time, he denied all knowledge of the incident with a resolution that astonished his intimate friends and relations, who to a man suspected him guilty. His father was not in Scotland, for I think it was said to me that this young man was second son to a John, Duke of Melfort,[1] who lived abroad with the royal family of the Stuarts; but this young gentleman lived with the relations of his mother, one of whom, an uncle, was a Lord of Session:[2] these having thoroughly effected his concealment, went away, and listened to the evidence; and the examination of every new witness convinced them that their noble young relative was the slayer of his friend.

All the young gentlemen of the party were examined, save Drummond, who, when sent for, could not be found, which circumstance sorely confirmed the suspicions against him in the minds of judges and jurors, friends and enemies; and there is little doubt, that the care of his relations in concealing him, injured his character, and his cause. The young gentlemen, of whom the party was composed, varied considerably, with respect to the quarrel between him and the deceased. Some of them had neither heard nor noted it; others had, but not one of them could tell how it began. Some of them had heard the threat uttered by Drummond on leaving the house, and one only had noted him lay his hand on

---

1 John Drummond (1649-1714), titular Duke of Melfort, was a Catholic and Jacobite sympathizer.
2 A Lord of the Court of Session, the supreme civil court in Scotland.

his sword. Not one of them could swear that it was Drummond who came to the door, and desired to speak with the deceased, but the general impression on the minds of them all, was to that effect; and one of the women swore that she heard the voice distinctly at the door, and every word that voice pronounced; and at the same time heard the deceased say, that it was Drummond's.

On the other hand, there were some evidences on Drummond's part, which Lord Craigie, his uncle, had taken care to collect. He produced the sword which his nephew had worn that night, on which there was neither blood nor blemish; and above all, he insisted on the evidence of a number of surgeons, who declared that both the wounds which the deceased had received, had been given behind. One of these was below the left arm, and a slight one; the other was quite through the body, and both evidently inflicted with the same weapon, a two-edged sword, of the same dimensions as that worn by Drummond.

Upon the whole, there was a division in the court, but a majority decided it. Drummond was pronounced guilty of the murder; outlawed for not appearing, and a high reward offered for his apprehension. It was with the greatest difficulty that he escaped on board of a small trading vessel, which landed him in Holland, and from thence, flying into Germany, he entered into the service of the Emperor Charles VI.[1] Many regretted that he was not taken, and made to suffer the penalty due for such a crime, and the melancholy incident became a pulpit theme over a great part of Scotland, being held up as a proper warning to youth to beware of such haunts of vice and depravity, the nurses of all that is precipitate, immoral, and base, among mankind.

After the funeral of this promising and excellent young man, his father never more held up his head. Miss Logan, with all her art, could not get him to attend to any worldly thing, or to make any settlement whatsoever of his affairs, save making her over a present of what disposable funds he had about him. As to his estates, when they were mentioned to him, he wished them all in the bottom of the sea, and himself along with them. But whenever she mentioned the circumstance of Thomas Drummond having been the murderer of his son, he shook his head, and once made the remark, that "It was all a mistake, a gross and fatal error; but that God, who

---

1   Charles VI of Austria (1685-1740), Holy Roman Emperor 1711-40.

had permitted such a flagrant deed, would bring it to light in his own time and way." In a few weeks he followed his son to the grave, and the notorious Robert Wringhim took possession of his estates as the lawful son of the late laird, born in wedlock, and under his father's roof. The investiture was celebrated by prayer, singing of psalms, and religious disputation. The late guardian and adopted father, and the mother of the new laird, presided on the grand occasion, making a conspicuous figure in all the work of the day; and though the youth himself indulged rather more freely in the bottle, than he had ever been seen to do before, it was agreed by all present, that there had never been a festivity so sanctified within the great hall of Dalcastle. Then, after due thanks returned, they parted rejoicing in spirit; which thanks, by the by, consisted wholly in telling the Almighty what he was; and informing him, with very particular precision, what *they* were who addressed him; for Wringhim's whole system of popular declamation consisted it seems in this,—to denounce all men and women to destruction, and then hold out hopes to his adherents that they were the chosen few, included in the promises, and who could never fall away. It would appear that this pharisaical doctrine is a very delicious one, and the most grateful of all others to the worst characters.

But the ways of heaven are altogether inscrutable, and soar as far above and beyond the works and the comprehensions of man, as the sun, flaming in majesty, is above the tiny boy's evening rocket. It is the controller of Nature alone, that can bring light out of darkness, and order out of confusion. Who is he that causeth the mole, from his secret path of darkness, to throw up the gem, the gold, and the precious ore? The same, that from the mouths of babes and sucklings can extract the perfection of praise, and who can make the most abject of his creatures instrumental in bringing the most hidden truths to light.

Miss Logan had never lost the thought of her late master's prediction, that Heaven would bring to light the truth concerning the untimely death of his son. She perceived that some strange conviction, too horrible for expression, preyed on his mind from the moment that the fatal news reached him, to the last of his existence; and in his last ravings, he uttered some incoherent words about justification by faith alone, and absolute and eternal predestination having been the ruin of his house. These, to be sure, were the words of superannuation, and of the last and severest kind of it; but for all that, they sunk deep into Miss Logan's soul, and at last she began to think with herself, "Is it possible the Wringhims, and the sophisticating wretch who is in conjunction with them, the mother of my late beautiful and amiable young master, can have effected his destruction? if so, I will spend my days, and my little patrimony, in endeavours to rake up and expose the unnatural deed."

In all her outgoings and incomings, Mrs. Logan (as she was now styled) never lost sight of this one object. Every new disappointment only whetted her desire to fish up some particulars concerning it; for she thought so long, and so ardently upon it, that by degrees it became settled in her mind as a sealed truth. And as woman is always most jealous of her own sex in such matters, her suspicions were fixed on her greatest enemy, Mrs. Colwan, now the Lady Dowager of Dalcastle. All was wrapt in a chaos of confusion and darkness; but at last by dint of a thousand sly and secret inquiries, Mrs. Logan found out where Lady Dalcastle had been, on the night that the murder happened, and likewise what company she had kept, as well as some of the comers and goers; and she had hopes of having discovered a cue, which, if she could keep hold of the thread, would lead her through darkness to the light of truth.

Returning very late one evening from a convocation of family servants, which she had drawn together in order to fish something out of them, her maid having been in attendance on her all the evening, they found on going home, that the house had been broken, and a number of valuable articles stolen therefrom. Mrs. Logan had grown quite heartless before this stroke, having been altogether unsuccessful in her inquiries, and now she began to entertain some resolutions of giving up the fruitless search.

In a few days thereafter, she received intelligence that her clothes and plate were mostly recovered, and that she for one was bound over to prosecute the depredator, provided the articles turned out to be hers, as libelled in the indictment, and as a king's evidence had given out. She was likewise summoned, or requested, I know not which, being ignorant of these matters, to go as far as the town of Peebles[1] on Tweedside, in order to survey these articles on such a day, and make affidavit to their identity before the Sheriff. She went accordingly; but on entering the town by the North Gate, she was accosted by a poor girl in tattered apparel, who with great

---

1 A town in the Scottish Borders, close to Ettrick forest.

earnestness inquired if her name was not Mrs. Logan? On being answered in the affirmative, she said that the unfortunate prisoner in the tolbooth requested her, as she valued all that was dear to her in life, to go and see her before she appeared in court, at the hour of cause, as she (the prisoner) had something of the greatest moment to impart to her. Mrs. Logan's curiosity was excited, and she followed the girl straight to the tolbooth, who by the way said to her, that she would find in the prisoner a woman of a superior mind, who had gone through all the vicissitudes of life. "She has been very unfortunate, and I fear very wicked," added the poor thing, "but she is my mother, and God knows, with all her faults and failings, she has never been unkind to me. You, madam, have it in your power to save her; but she has wronged you, and therefore if you will not do it for her sake, do it for mine, and the God of the fatherless will reward you."

Mrs. Logan answered her with a cast of the head, and a hem! and only remarked, that "the guilty must not always be suffered to escape, or what a world must we be doomed to live in!"

She was admitted to the prison, and found a tall emaciated figure, who appeared to have once possessed a sort of masculine beauty in no ordinary degree, but was now considerably advanced in years. She viewed Mrs. Logan with a stern, steady gaze, as if reading her features as a margin to her intellect; and when she addressed her it was not with that humility, and agonized fervor, which are natural for one in such circumstances to address to another, who has the power of her life and death in her hands.

"I am deeply indebted to you, for this timely visit, Mrs. Logan," said she. "It is not that I value life, or because I fear death, that I have sent for you so expressly. But the manner of the death that awaits me, has something peculiarly revolting in it to a female mind. Good God! when I think of being hung up, a spectacle to a gazing, gaping multitude, with numbers of which I have had intimacies and connections, that would render the moment of parting so hideous, that, believe me, it rends to flinders a soul born for another sphere than that in which it has moved, had not the vile selfishness of a lordly fiend ruined all my prospects, and all my hopes. Hear me then; for I do not ask your pity: I only ask of you to look to yourself, and behave with womanly prudence. If you deny this day, that these goods are yours, there is no other evidence whatever against my life, and it is safe for the present. For as for the word of the wretch who has betrayed me, it is of no avail; he has prevaricated so notoriously to save himself. If you deny them, you shall have them all again to the value of a mite, and more to the bargain. If you swear to the identity of them, the process will, one way and another, cost you the half of what they are worth."

"And what security have I for that?" said Mrs. Logan.

"You have none but *my word*," said the other proudly, "and that never yet was violated. If you cannot take that, I know the worst you can do—But I had forgot—I have a poor helpless child without, waiting, and starving about the prison door—Surely it was of her that I wished to speak. This shameful death of mine will leave her in a deplorable state."

"The girl seems to have candour and strong affections," said Mrs. Logan; "I grievously mistake if such a child would not be a thousand times better without such a guardian and director."

"Then will you be so kind as come to the Grass Market,[1] and see me put down?" said the prisoner. "I thought a woman would estimate a woman's and a mother's feelings, when such a dreadful throw was at stake, at least in part. But you are callous, and have never known any feelings but those of subordination to your old unnatural master. Alas, I have no cause of offence! I have wronged you; and justice must take its course. Will you forgive me before we part?"

Mrs. Logan hesitated, for her mind ran on something else: On which the other subjoined, "No, you will not forgive me, I see. But you will pray to God to forgive me? I know you will *do that*."

Mrs. Logan heard not this jeer, but looking at the prisoner with an absent and stupid stare, she said, "Did you know my late master?"

"Ay, that I did, and never for any good," said she. "I knew the old and the young spark both, and was by when the latter was slain."

This careless sentence affected Mrs. Logan in a most peculiar manner. A shower of tears burst from her eyes ere it was done, and when it was, she appeared like one bereaved of her mind. She first turned one way and then another, as if looking for something she had dropped. She seemed to think she had lost her eyes, instead of her tears, and at length, as by instinct, she tottered close up to the prisoner's face, and looking wistfully and joyfully in it, said, with breathless earnestness, "Pray, mistress, what is your name?"

---

1   A market place situated beneath Edinburgh Castle Rock.

"My name is Arabella Calvert," said the other: "Miss, mistress, or widow, as you chuse, for I have been all the three, and that not once nor twice only—Ay, and something beyond all these. But as for you, you have never been any thing!"

"Ay, ay! and so you are Bell Calvert? Well, I thought so—I thought so," said Mrs. Logan; and helping herself to a seat, she came and sat down close by the prisoner's knee. "So you are indeed Bell Calvert, so called once. Well, of all the world you are the woman whom I have longed and travailed the most to see. But you were invisible; a being to be heard of, not seen."

"There have been days, madam," returned she, "when I *was* to be seen, and when there were few to be seen like me. But since that time there have indeed been days on which I was not to be seen. My crimes have been great, but my sufferings have been greater. So great, that neither you nor the world can ever either know or conceive them. I hope they will be taken into account by the Most High. Mine have been crimes of utter desperation. But whom am I speaking to? You had better leave me to myself, mistress."

"Leave you to yourself? That I will be loth to do, till you tell me where you were that night my young master was murdered?"

"Where the devil would, I was! Will that suffice you? Ah, it was a vile action! A night to be remembered that was! Won't you be going? I want to trust my daughter with a commission."

"No, Mrs. Calvert, you and I part not, till you have divulged that mystery to me."

"You must accompany me to the other world, then, for you shall not have it in this."

"If you refuse to answer me, I can have you before a tribunal, where you shall be sifted to the soul."

"Such miserable inanity. What care I for your threatenings of a tribunal? I who must so soon stand before my last earthly one? What could the word of such a culprit avail? Or if it could, where is the judge that could enforce it?"

"Did you not say that there was some mode of accommodating matters on that score?"

"Yes, I prayed you to grant me my life, which is in your power. The saving of it would not have cost you a plack, yet you refused to do it. The taking of it will cost you a great deal, and yet to that purpose you adhere. I can have no parley with such a spirit. I would not have my life in a present from its motions, nor would I exchange courtesies with its possessor."

"Indeed, Mrs. Calvert, since ever we met, I have been so busy thinking about who you might be, that I know not what you have been proposing. I believe, I meant to do what I could to save you. But once for all, tell me every thing that you know concerning that amiable young gentleman's death, and here is my hand there shall be nothing wanting that I can effect for you."

"No, I despise all barter with such mean and selfish curiosity; and, as I believe *that* passion is stronger with you, than fear is with me, we part on equal terms. Do your worst; and my secret shall go to the gallows and the grave with me."

Mrs. Logan was now greatly confounded, and after proffering in vain to concede every thing she could ask in exchange, for the particulars relating to the murder, she became the suppliant in her turn. But the unaccountable culprit, exulting in her advantage, laughed her to scorn; and finally, in a paroxysm of pride and impatience, called in the jailor and had her expelled, ordering him in her hearing not to grant her admittance a second time, on any pretence.

Mrs. Logan was now hard put to it, and again driven almost to despair. She might have succeeded in the attainment of that she thirsted for most in life so easily, had she known the character with which she had to deal—Had she known to have soothed her high and afflicted spirit: but that opportunity was past, and the hour of examination at hand. She once thought of going and claiming her articles, as she at first intended; but then, when she thought again of the Wringhims swaying it at Dalcastle, where she had been wont to hear them held in such contempt, if not abhorrence, and perhaps of holding it by the most diabolical means, she was withheld from marring the only chance that remained of having a glimpse into that mysterious affair.

Finally, she resolved not to answer to her name in the court, rather than to appear and assert a falsehood, which she might be called on to certify by oath. She did so; and heard the Sheriff give orders to the officers to make inquiry for Miss Logan from Edinburgh, at the various places of entertainment in town, and to expedite her arrival in court, as things of great value were in dependence. She also heard the man who had turned king's evidence against the prisoner, examined for the second time, and sifted most cunningly. His answers gave any thing but satisfaction to the Sheriff, though Mrs. Logan believed them to be mainly truth. But there were a few questions and answers that struck her above all others.

"How long is it since Mrs. Calvert and you became acquainted?"

"About a year and a half."

"State the precise time, if you please; the day, or night, according to your remembrance."

"It was on the morning of the 28th of February, 1705."

"What time of the morning?"

"Perhaps about one."

"So early as that? At what place did you meet then?"

"It was at the foot of one of the north wynds of Edinburgh."

"Was it by appointment that you met?"

"No, it was not."

"For what purpose was it then?"

"For no purpose."

"How is it that you chance to remember the day and hour so minutely, if you met that woman, whom you have accused, merely by chance, and for no manner of purpose, as you must have met others that night, perhaps to the amount of hundreds, in the same way?"

"I have good cause to remember it, my lord."

"What was that cause?—No answer?—You don't choose to say what that cause was?"

"I am not at liberty to tell."

The Sheriff then descended to other particulars, all of which tended to prove that the fellow was an accomplished villain, and that the principal share of the atrocities had been committed by him. Indeed the Sheriff hinted, that he suspected the only share Mrs. Calvert had in them, was in being too much in his company, and too true to him. The case was remitted to the Court of Justiciary; but Mrs. Logan had heard enough to convince her that the culprits first met at the very spot, and the very hour, on which George Colwan was slain; and she had no doubt that they were incendiaries set on by his mother, to forward her own and her darling son's way to opulence. Mrs. Logan was wrong, as will appear in the sequel; but her antipathy to Mrs. Colwan made her watch the event with all care. She never quitted Peebles as long as Bell Calvert remained there, and when she was removed to Edinburgh, the other followed. When the trial came on, Mrs. Logan and her maid were again summoned as witnesses before the jury, and compelled by the prosecutor for the Crown to appear.

The maid was first called; and when she came into the witnesses' box, the anxious and hopeless looks of the prisoner were manifest to all: But the girl, whose name, she said, was Bessy

Gillies, answered in so flippant and fearless a way, that the audi-
tors were much amused. After a number of routine questions,
the depute-advocate asked her if she was at home on the morning of the fifth of September last, when her mistress's house was
robbed?

"Was I at hame, say ye? Na, faith-ye, lad! An I had been at hame,
there had been mair to dee. I wad hae raised sic a yelloch!"

"Where were you that morning?"

"Where was I, say you? I was in the house where my mistress
was, sitting dozing an' half sleeping in the kitchen. I thought aye
she would be setting out every minute, for twa hours."

"And when you went home, what did you find?"

"What found we? Be my sooth, we found a broken lock, an'
toom kists.

"Relate some of the particulars, if you please."

"O, sir, the thieves didna stand upon particulars: they were hale-
sale dealers in a' our best wares."

"I mean, what passed between your mistress and you on the
occasion?"

"What passed, say ye? O, there wasna muckle: I was in a great
passion, but she was dung doitrified a wee. When she gaed to put
the key i' the door, up it flew to the fer wa'.—'Bess, ye jaud, what's
the meaning o' this?' quo she. 'Ye hae left the door open, ye taw-
pie!' quo she.

'The ne'er o' that I did,' quo I, 'or may my shakel bane never
turn another key.' When we got the candle lightit, a' the house was
in a hoad-road. 'Bessy, my woman,' quo she, 'we are baith ruined
and undone creatures.' 'The deil a bit,' quo I; 'that I deny positively. H'mh! to speak o' a lass o' my age being ruined and undone! I
never had muckle except what was within a good jerkin, an' let the
thief ruin me there wha can.'"

"Do you remember ought else that your mistress said on the
occasion? Did you hear her blame any person?"

"O, she made a great deal o' grumphing an' groaning about the
misfortune, as she ca'd it, an' I think she said it was a part o' the ruin
wrought by the Ringans, or some sic name,—'they'll hae't a'!
they'll hae't a'!' cried she, wringing her hands; 'they'll hae't a', an'
hell wi't, an' they'll get them baith.' 'Aweel, that's aye some satisfaction,' quo I."

"Whom did she mean by the Ringans, do you know?"

"I fancy they are some creatures that she has dreamed about, for
I think there canna be as ill folks living as she ca's them."

"Did you never hear her say that the prisoner at the bar there, Mrs. Calvert, or Bell Calvert, was the robber of her house; or that she was one of the Ringans?"

"Never. Somebody tauld her lately, that ane Bell Calvert robbed her house, but she disna believe it. Neither do I."

"What reasons have you for doubting it?"

"Because it was nae woman's fingers that broke up the bolts an' the locks that were torn open that night."

"Very pertinent, Bessy. Come then within the bar, and look at these articles on the table. Did you ever see these silver spoons before?"

"I hae seen some very like them, and whaever has seen siller spoons, has done the same."

"Can you swear you never saw them before?"

"Na, na, I wadna swear to ony siller spoons that ever war made, unless I had put a private mark on them wi' my ain hand, an' that's what I never did to ane."

"See, they are all marked with a C."

"Sae are a' the spoons in Argyle, an' the half o' them in Edinburgh I think. A C is a very common letter, an' so are a' the names that begin wi't. Lay them by, lay them by, an' gie the poor woman her spoons again. They are marked wi' her ain name, an' I hae little doubt they are hers, an' that she has seen better days."

"Ah, God bless her heart!" sighed the prisoner; and that blessing was echoed in the breathings of many a feeling breast.

"Did you ever see this gown before, think you?"

"I hae seen ane very like it."

"Could you not swear that gown was your mistress's once?"

"No, unless I saw her hae't on, an' kend that she had paid for't. I am very scrupulous about an oath. *Like* is an ill mark. Sae ill indeed, that I wad hardly swear to ony thing."

"But you say that gown is *very like* one your mistress used to wear."

"I never said sic a thing. It is like one I hae seen her hae out airing on the hay raip i' the back green. It is very like ane I hae seen Mrs. Butler in the Grass Market wearing too; I rather think it is the same. Bless you, sir, I wadna swear to my ain fore finger, if it had been as lang out o' my sight, an' brought in an' laid on that table."

"Perhaps you are not aware, girl, that this scrupulousness of yours is likely to thwart the purposes of justice, and bereave your mistress of property to the amount of a thousand merks?" *(From the Judge.)*

"I canna help that, my lord: that's her lookout. For my part, I am resolved to keep a clear conscience, till I be married, at any rate."

"Look over these things and see if there is any one article among them which you can fix on as the property of your mistress."

"No ane o' them, sir, no ane o' them. An oath is an awfu' thing, especially when it is for life or death. Gie the poor woman her things again, an' let my mistress pick up the next she finds: that's my advice."

When Mrs. Logan came into the box, the prisoner groaned, and laid down her head. But how she was astonished when she heard her deliver herself something to the following purport!—That whatever penalties she was doomed to abide, she was determined she would not bear witness against a woman's life, from a certain conviction that it could not be a woman who broke her house. "I have no doubt that I may find some of my own things there," added she, "but if they were found in her possession, she has been made a tool, or the dupe, of an infernal set, who shall be nameless here. I believe she *did not* rob me, and for that reason I will have no hand in her condemnation."

The Judge. "This is the most singular perversion I have ever witnessed. Mrs. Logan, I entertain strong suspicions that the prisoner, or her agents, have made some agreement with you on this matter, to prevent the course of justice."

"So far from that, my lord, I went into the jail at Peebles to this woman, whom I had never seen before, and proffered to withdraw my part in the prosecution, as well as my evidence, provided she would tell me a few simple facts; but she spurned at my offer, and had me turned insolently out of the prison, with orders to the jailor never to admit me again on any pretence."

The prisoner's counsel, taking hold of this evidence, addressed the jury with great fluency; and finally, the prosecution was withdrawn, and the prisoner dismissed from the bar, with a severe reprimand for her past conduct, and an exhortation to keep better company.

It was not many days till a caddy came with a large parcel to Mrs. Logan's house, which parcel he delivered into her hands, accompanied with a sealed note, containing an inventory of the articles, and a request to know if the unfortunate Arabella Calvert would be admitted to converse with Mrs. Logan.

Never was there a woman so much overjoyed as Mrs. Logan was at this message. She returned compliments: Would be most happy to see her; and no article of the parcel should be looked at, or touched, till her arrival.—It was not long till she made her appearance, dressed in somewhat better style than she had yet seen her; delivered her over the greater part of the stolen property, besides many things that either never had belonged to Mrs. Logan, or that she thought proper to deny, in order that the other might retain them.

The tale that she told of her misfortunes was of the most distressing nature, and was enough to stir up all the tender, as well as abhorrent feelings in the bosom of humanity. She had suffered every deprivation in fame, fortune, and person. She had been imprisoned; she had been scourged, and branded as an impostor; and all on account of her resolute and unmoving fidelity and truth to *several* of the very worst of men, every one of whom had abandoned her to utter destitution and shame. But this story we cannot enter on at present, as it would perhaps mar the thread of our story, as much as it did the anxious anticipations of Mrs. Logan, who sat pining and longing for the relation that follows.

"Now I know, Mrs. Logan, that you are expecting a detail of the circumstances relating to the death of Mr. George Colwan; and in gratitude for your unbounded generosity, and disinterestedness, I will tell you all that I know, although, for causes that will appear obvious to you, I had determined never in life to divulge one circumstance of it. I can tell you, however, that you will be disappointed, for it was not the gentleman who was accused, found guilty, and would have suffered the utmost penalty of the law, had he not made his escape. *It was not he*, I say, who slew your young master, nor had he any hand in it."

"I never thought he had. But, pray, how do you come to know this?"

"You shall hear. I had been abandoned in York, by an artful and consummate fiend; found guilty of being art and part concerned in the most heinous atrocities, and, in his place, suffered what I yet shudder to think of. I was banished the county—begged my way with my poor outcast child up to Edinburgh, and was there obliged, for the second time in my life, to betake myself to the most degrading of all means to support two wretched lives. I hired a dress, and betook me, shivering, to the High Street, too well aware that my form and appearance would soon draw me suitors enow at that throng and intemperate time of the parliament. On my very first stepping out to the street, a party of young gentlemen was passing. I heard by the noise they made, and the tenor of their speech, that they were more than mellow, and so I resolved to keep near them, in order, if possible, to make some of them my prey. But just as one of them began to eye me, I was rudely thrust into a narrow close by one of the guardsmen. I had heard to what house the party was bound, for the men were talking exceedingly loud, and making no secret of it: so I hasted down the close, and round below to the one where their rendezvous was to be; but I was too late, they were all housed and the door bolted. I resolved to wait, thinking they could not all stay long; but I was perishing with famine, and was like to fall down. The moon shone as bright as day, and I perceived, by a sign at the bottom of the close, that there was a small tavern of a certain description up two stairs there. I went up and called, telling the mistress of the house my plan. She approved of it mainly, and offered me her best apartment, provided I could get one of these noble mates to accompany me. She abused Lucky Sudds, as she called her, at the inn where the party was, envying her huge profits, no doubt, and giving me afterward something to drink, for which I really felt exceedingly grateful in my need. I stepped down stairs in order to be on the alert. The moment that I reached the ground, the door of Lucky Sudds' house opened and shut, and down came the Honourable Thomas Drummond, with hasty and impassioned strides, his sword rattling at his heel. I accosted him in a soft and soothing tone. He was taken with my address; for he instantly stood still and gazed intently at me, then at the place, and then at me again. I beckoned him to follow me, which he did without farther ceremony, and we soon found ourselves together in the best room of a house where every thing was wretched. He still looked about him, and at me; but all this while he had never spoken a word. At length, I asked if he would take any refreshment? 'If you please,' said he. I asked what he would have? but he only answered, 'Whatever you choose, madam.' If he was taken with my address, I was much more taken with his; for he was a complete gentleman, and a gentleman will ever act as one. At length, he began as follows:

"'I am utterly at a loss to account for this adventure, madam. It seems to me like enchantment, and I can hardly believe my senses. An English lady, I judge, and one, who from her manner and address should belong to the first class of society, in such a place as this, is indeed matter of wonder to me. At the foot of a close in Edinburgh! and at this time of the night! Surely it must have been no common reverse of fortune that reduced you to this?' I wept, or pretended to do so; on which he added. 'Pray, madam, take heart. Tell me what has befallen you; and if I can do any thing for you, in restoring you to your country or your friends, you shall command my interest.'

"I had great need of a friend then, and I thought now was the time to secure one. So I began and told him the moving tale I have told you. But I soon perceived that I had kept by the naked truth too unvarnishedly, and thereby quite overshot my mark. When he learned that he was sitting in a wretched corner of an irregular house, with a felon, who had so lately been scourged, and banished as a swindler and impostor, his modest nature took the alarm, and he was shocked, instead of being moved with pity. His eye fixed on some of the casual stripes on my arm, and from that moment he became restless and impatient to be gone. I tried some gentle arts to retain him, but in vain; so, after paying both the landlady and me for pleasures he had neither tasted nor asked, he took his leave.

"I showed him down stairs; and just as he turned the corner of the next land, a man came rushing violently by him; exchanged looks with him, and came running up to me. He appeared in great agitation, and was quite out of breath; and, taking my hand in his, we ran up stairs together without speaking, and were instantly in the apartment I had left, where a stoup of wine still stood untasted. 'Ah, this is fortunate!' said my new spark, and helped himself. In the mean while, as our apartment was a corner one, and looked both east and north, I ran to the easter casement to look after Drummond. Now, note me well: I saw him going eastward in his tartans and bonnet, and the gilded hilt of his claymore[1] glittering in the moon; and, at the very same time, I saw two men, the one in black, and the other likewise in tartans, coming toward the steps from the opposite bank, by the foot of the loch; and I saw Drummond and they eying each other as they passed. I kept view of *him* till he vanished towards Leith Wynd, and by that time the two strangers had come close up under our window. This is what I wish you to pay particular attention to. I had only lost sight of Drummond, (who had given me his name and address,) for the short space of time that we took in running up one pair of short stairs; and during that space he had halted a moment, for, when I got my eye on him again, he had not crossed the mouth of the next entry, nor proceeded above ten or twelve paces, and, *at the same time*, I saw the two men coming down the bank on the opposite side of the loch,

---

1 A large two-edged sword.

at about three hundred paces distance. Both he and they were distinctly in my view, and never within speech of each other, until he vanished into one of the wynds leading toward the bottom of the High Street, at which precise time the two strangers came below my window; so that it was quite clear he neither could be one of them, nor have any communication with them.

"Yet, mark me again; for of all things I have ever seen, this was the most singular. When I looked down at the two strangers, *one of them was extremely like Drummond*. So like was he, that there was not one item in dress, form, feature, nor voice, by which I could distinguish the one from the other. I was certain it was not he, because I had seen the one going and the other approaching at the same time, and my impression at the moment was, that I looked upon some spirit, or demon, in his likeness. I felt a chillness creep all round my heart, my knees tottered, and, withdrawing my head from the open casement that lay in the dark shade, I said to the man who was with me, 'Good God, what is this!'

"'What is it, my dear?' said he, as much alarmed as I was.

"'As I live, there stands an apparition!' said I.

"He was not so much afraid when he heard me say so, and peeping cautiously out, he looked and listened a-while, and then drawing back, he said in a whisper, 'They are both living men, and one of them is he I passed at the corner.'

"'That he is not,' said I, emphatically. 'To that I will make oath.'

"He smiled and shook his head, and then added, 'I never then saw a man before, whom I could not know again, particularly if he was the very last I had seen. But what matters it whether it be or not? As it is no concern of ours, let us sit down and enjoy ourselves.'

"'But it *does* matter a very great deal with me, sir,' said I.—'Bless me, my head is giddy—my breath quite gone, and I feel as if I were surrounded with fiends. Who are you, sir?'

"'You shall know that ere we two part, my love,' said he: 'I cannot conceive why the return of this young gentleman to the spot he so lately left, should discompose you? I suppose he got a glance of you as he passed, and has returned to look after you, and that is the whole secret of the matter.'

"'If you will be so civil as to walk out and join him then, it will oblige me hugely,' said I, 'for I never in my life experienced such boding apprehensions of evil company. I cannot conceive how you should come up here without asking my permission? Will it please you to begone, sir?'—I was within an ace of prevailing. He took out his purse—I need not say more—I was bribed to let him remain. Ah, had I kept by my frail resolution of dismissing him at that moment, what a world of shame and misery had been evited! But that, though uppermost still in my mind, has nothing ado here.

"When I peeped over again, the two men were disputing in a whisper, the one of them in violent agitation and terror, and the other upbraiding him, and urging him on to some desperate act. At length I heard the young man in the Highland garb say indignantly, 'Hush, recreant! It is God's work which you are commissioned to execute, and it must be done. But if you positively decline it, I will do it myself, and do you beware of the consequences.'

"'Oh, I will, I will!' cried the other in black clothes, in a wretched beseeching tone. 'You shall instruct me in this, as in all things else.'

"I thought all this while I was closely concealed from them, and wondered not a little when he in tartans gave me a sly nod, as much as to say, 'What do you think of this?' or, 'Take note of what you see,' or something to that effect, from which I perceived, that whatever he was about, he did not wish it to be kept a secret. For all that, I was impressed with a terror and anxiety that I could not overcome, but it only made me mark every event with the more intense curiosity. The Highlander, whom I still could not help regarding as the evil genius of Thomas Drummond, performed every action, as with the quickness of thought. He concealed the youth in black in a narrow entry, a little to the westward of my windows, and as he was leading him across the moonlight green by the shoulder, I perceived, for the first time, that both of them were armed with rapiers. He pushed him without resistance into the dark shaded close, made another signal to me, and hasted up the close to Lucky Sudds' door. The city and the morning were so still, that I heard every word that was uttered, on putting my head out a little. He knocked at the door sharply, and after waiting a considerable space, the bolt was drawn, and the door, as I conceived, edged up as far as the massy chain would let it. 'Is young Dalcastle still in the house?' said he sharply.

"I did not hear the answer, but I heard him say, shortly after, 'If he is, pray tell him to speak with me for a few minutes.' He then withdrew from the door, and came slowly down the close, in a lingering manner, looking oft behind him. Dalcastle came out; advanced a few steps after him, and then stood still, as if hesitating whether or not he should call out a friend to accompany him; and that instant the door behind him was closed, chained, and the iron bolt drawn; on hearing of which, he followed his adversary without farther hesitation.

As he passed below my window, I heard him say, 'I beseech you, Tom, let us do nothing in this matter rashly;' but I could not hear the answer of the other, who had turned the corner.

"I roused up my drowsy companion, who was leaning on the bed, and we both looked together from the north window. We were in the shade, but the moon shone full on the two young gentlemen. Young Dalcastle was visibly the worse of liquor, and his back being turned toward us, he said something to the other which I could not make out, although he spoke a considerable time, and, from his tones and gestures, appeared to be reasoning. When he had done, the tall young man in the tartans drew his sword, and his face being straight to us, we heard him say distinctly, 'No more words about it, George, if you please; but if you be a man, as I take you to be, draw your sword, and let us settle it here.'

"Dalcastle drew his sword, without changing his attitude; but he spoke with more warmth, for we heard his words, 'Think you that I fear you, Tom? Be assured, sir, I would not fear ten of the best of your name, at each other's backs: all that I want is to have friends with us to see fair play, for if you close with me, you are a dead man.'

"The other stormed at these words. 'You are a braggart, sir,' cried he, 'a wretch—a blot on the cheek of nature a blight on the Christian world—a reprobate— I'll have your soul, sir—You must play at tennis, and put down elect brethren in another world to-morrow.' As he said this, he brandished his rapier, exciting Dalcastle to offence. He gained his point: The latter, who had previously drawn, advanced in upon his vapouring and licentious antagonist, and a fierce combat ensued. My companion was delighted beyond measure, and I could not keep him from exclaiming, loud enough to have been heard, 'that's grand! that's excellent!' For me, my heart quaked like an aspen. Young Dalcastle either had a decided advantage over his adversary, or else the other thought proper to let him have it; for he shifted, and wore, and flitted from Dalcastle's thrusts like a shadow, uttering ofttimes a sarcastic laugh, that seemed to provoke the other beyond all bearing. At one time, he would spring away to a great distance, then advance again on young Dalcastle with the swiftness of lightning. But that young hero always stood his ground, and repelled the attack: he never gave way, although they fought nearly twice round the bleaching green,[1]

---

1 An area for drying clothes.

which you know is not a very small one. At length they fought close up to the mouth of the dark entry, where the fellow in black stood all this while concealed, and then the combatant in tartans closed with his antagonist, or pretended to do so; but the moment they began to grapple, he wheeled about, turning Colwan's back towards the entry, and then cried out, 'Ah, hell has it! My friend, my friend!'

"That moment the fellow in black rushed from his cover with his drawn rapier, and gave the brave young Dalcastle two deadly wounds in the back, as quick as arm could thrust, both of which I thought pierced through his body. He fell, and rolling himself on his back, he perceived who it was that had slain him thus foully, and said, with a dying emphasis, which I never heard equalled, 'Oh, dog of hell, is it you who has done this!'

"He articulated some more, which I could not hear for other sounds; for the moment that the man in black inflicted the deadly wound, my companion called out, 'That's unfair, you rip! That's damnable! to strike a brave fellow behind! One at a time, you cowards! &c.' to all which the unnatural fiend in the tartans answered with a loud exulting laugh; and then, taking the poor paralysed murderer by the bow of the arm, he hurried him into the dark entry once more, where I lost sight of them for ever."

Before this time, Mrs. Logan had risen up; and when the narrator had finished, she was standing with her arms stretched upward at their full length, and her visage turned down, on which were pourtrayed the lines of the most absolute horror. "The dark suspicions of my late benefactor have been just, and his last prediction is fulfilled," cried she. "The murderer of the accomplished George Colwan has been his own brother, set on, there is little doubt, by her who bare them both, and her directing angel, the self-justified bigot. Aye, and yonder they sit, enjoying the luxuries so dearly purchased, with perfect impunity! If the Almighty do not hurl them down, blasted with shame and confusion, there is no hope of retribution in this life. And, by his might, I will be the agent to accomplish it! Why did the man not pursue the foul murderers? Why did he not raise the alarm, and call the watch?"

"He? The wretch! He durst not move from the shelter he had obtained,—no, not for the soul of him. He was pursued for his life, at the moment when he first flew into my arms. But I did not know it; no, I did not *then* know him. May the curse of heaven, and the blight of hell, settle on the detestable wretch! He pursue for the sake of justice! No; his efforts have all been for evil, but never for good. But *I* raised the alarm; miserable and degraded as I was, I pursued and raised the watch myself. Have you not heard the name of Bell Calvert coupled with that hideous and mysterious affair?"

"Yes, I have. In secret often I have heard it. But how came it that you could never be found? How came it that you never appeared in defence of the Honourable Thomas Drummond; you, the only person who could have justified him?"

"I could not, for I then fell under the power and guidance of a wretch, who durst not for the soul of him be brought forward in the affair. And what was worse, his evidence would have overborne mine, for he would have sworn, that the man who called out and fought Colwan, was the same he met leaving my apartment, and there was an end of it. And moreover, it is well known, that this same man,—this wretch of whom I speak, never mistook one man for another in his life, which makes the mystery of the likeness between this incendiary and Drummond the more extraordinary."

"If it was Drummond, after all that you have asserted, then are my surmises still wrong."

"There is nothing of which I can be more certain, than that it was not Drummond. We have nothing on earth but our senses to depend upon: if these deceive us, what are we to do. I own I cannot account for it; nor ever shall be able to account for it as long as I live."

"Could you know the man in black, if you saw him again?"

"I think I could, if I saw him walk or run: his gait was very particular: He walked as if he had been flat-soled, and his legs made of steel, without any joints in his feet or ancles."

"The very same! The very same! The very same! Pray will you take a few days' journey into the country with me, to look at such a man?"

"You have preserved my life, and for you I will do any thing. I will accompany you with pleasure: and I think I can say that I will know him, for his form left an impression on my heart not soon to be effaced. But of this I am sure, that my unworthy companion *will* recognize him, and that he will be able to swear to his identity every day as long as he lives."

"Where is he? Where is he! O! Mrs. Calvert, where is he?"

"Where is he? He is the wretch whom you heard giving me up to the death; who, after experiencing every mark of affection that a poor ruined being could confer, and after committing a thousand atrocities of which she was ignorant, became an informer to save his diabolical life, and attempted to offer up mine as a sacrifice for all. We will go by ourselves first, and I will tell you if it is necessary to send any farther."

The two dames, the very next morning, dressed themselves like country goodwives; and, hiring two stout ponies furnished with pillions, they took their journey westward, and the second evening after leaving Edinburgh they arrived at the village about two miles below Dalcastle, where they alighted. But Mrs. Logan, being anxious to have Mrs. Calvert's judgment, without either hint or preparation, took care not to mention that they were so near to the end of their journey. In conformity with this plan, she said, after they had sat a while, "Heigh-ho, but I am weary! What suppose we should rest a day here before we proceed farther on our journey?"

Mrs. Calvert was leaning on the casement, and looking out when her companion addressed these words to her, and by far too much engaged to return any answer, for her eyes were riveted on two young men who approached from the farther end of the village; and at length, turning round her head, she said, with the most intense interest, "Proceed farther on our journey, did you say? That we need not do; for, as I live, here comes the very man!"

Mrs. Logan ran to the window, and behold, there was indeed Robert Wringhim Colwan (now the Laird of Dalcastle) coming forward almost below their window, walking arm in arm with another young man; and as the two passed, the latter looked up and made a sly signal to the two dames, biting his lip, winking with his left eye, and nodding his head. Mrs. Calvert was astonished at this recognizance, the young man's former companion having made exactly such another signal on the night of the duel, by the light of the moon; and it struck her, moreover, that she had somewhere seen this young man's face before. She looked after him, and he winked over his shoulder to her; but she was prevented from returning his salute by her companion, who uttered a loud cry, between a groan and shriek, and fell down on the floor with a rumble like a wall that had suddenly been undermined. She had fainted quite away, and required all her companion's attention during the remainder of the evening, for she had scarcely ever well recovered out of one fit before she fell into another, and in the short intervals she raved like one distracted, or in a dream. After falling into a sound sleep by night, she recovered her equanimity, and the two began to converse seriously on what they had seen. Mrs. Calvert averred that the young man who passed next to the window, *was* the very man who stabbed George Colwan in the back, and she said she was willing to take her oath on it at any time when required, and was certain if the wretch Ridsley saw him, that he would make oath to the same purport, for that his walk was so peculiar, no one of common discernment could mistake it.

Mrs. Logan was in great agitation, and said, "It is what I have suspected all along, and what I am sure my late master and benefactor was persuaded of, and the horror of such an idea cut short his days. That wretch, Mrs. Calvert, is the born brother of him he murdered, sons of the same mother they were, whether or not of the same father, the Lord only knows. But, O Mrs. Calvert, that is not the main thing that has discomposed me, and shaken my nerves to pieces at this time. Who do you think the young man was who walked in his company to night?"

"I cannot for my life recollect, but am convinced I have seen the same fine form and face before."

"And did not he seem to know us, Mrs. Calvert? You who are able to recollect things as they happened, did he not seem to recollect us, and make signs to that effect?"

"He did, indeed, and apparently with great good humour."

"O, Mrs. Calvert, hold me, else I shall fall into hysterics again! Who is he? Who is he? Tell me who you suppose he is, for I cannot say my own thought."

"On my life, I cannot remember."

"Did you note the appearance of the young gentleman you saw slain that night? Do you recollect aught of the appearance of my young master, George Colwan?"

Mrs. Calvert sat silent, and stared the other mildly in the face. Their looks encountered, and there was an unearthly amazement that gleamed from each, which, meeting together, caught real fire, and returned the flame to their heated imaginations, till the two associates became like two statues, with their hands spread, their eyes fixed, and their chops fallen down upon their bosoms. An old woman who kept the lodging-house, having been called in before when Mrs. Logan was faintish, chanced to enter at this crisis with some cordial; and, seeing the state of her lodgers, she caught the infection, and fell into the same rigid and statue-like appearance. No scene more striking was ever exhibited; and if Mrs. Calvert had not resumed strength of mind to speak, and break the spell, it is impossible to say how long it might have continued. "It is he, I believe," said she, uttering the words as it were inwardly. "It can be none other but he. But, no, it is impossible! I saw him stabbed through and through the heart; I saw him roll backward on the green in his own blood, utter his last words, and groan away his soul. Yet, if it is not he, who can it be?"

"It *is* he!" cried Mrs. Logan, hysterically.

"Yes, yes, it *is* he!" cried the landlady, in unison.

"It is who?" said Mrs. Calvert; "whom do you mean, mistress?"

"Oh, I don't know! I don't know! I was affrighted."

"Hold your peace then till you recover your senses, and tell me, if you can, who that young gentleman is, who keeps company with the new Laird of Dalcastle?"

"Oh, it is he! it is he!" screamed Mrs. Logan, wringing her hands.

"Oh, it is he! it is he!" cried the landlady, wringing hers.

Mrs. Calvert turned the latter gently and civilly out of the apartment, observing that there seemed to be some infection in the air of the room, and she would be wise for herself to keep out of it.

The two dames had a restless and hideous night. Sleep came not to their relief; for their conversation was wholly about the dead, who seemed to be alive, and their minds were wandering and groping in a chaos of mystery. "Did you attend to his corpse, and know that he positively died and was buried?" said Mrs. Calvert.

"O, yes, from the moment that his fair but mangled corpse was brought home, I attended it till that when it was screwed in the coffin. I washed the long stripes of blood from his lifeless form, on both sides of the body—I bathed the livid wound that passed through his generous and gentle heart. There was one through the flesh of his left side too, which had bled most outwardly of them all. I bathed them, and bandaged them up with wax and perfumed ointment, but still the blood oozed through all, so that when he was laid in the coffin he was like one newly murdered. My brave, my generous young master! he was always as a son to me, and no son was ever more kind or more respectful to a mother. But he was butchered—he was cut off from the earth ere he had well reached to manhood—most barbarously and unfairly slain. And how is it, how can it be, that we again see him here, walking arm in arm with his murderer?"

"The thing cannot be, Mrs. Logan. It is a phantasy of our disturbed imaginations, therefore let us compose ourselves till we investigate this matter farther."

"It cannot be in nature, that is quite clear," said Mrs. Logan; "yet how it should be that I should *think* so—I who knew and nursed him from his infancy—there lies the paradox. As you said once before, we have nothing but our senses to depend on, and if you and I believe that we see a person, why, we do see him. Whose word, or whose reasoning can convince us against our own senses? We will disguise ourselves, as poor women selling a few country wares, and we will go up to the Hall, and see what is to see, and hear what we can hear, for this is a weighty business in which we are engaged, namely, to turn the vengeance of the law upon an unnatural monster; and we will farther learn, if we can, who this is that accompanies him."

Mrs. Calvert acquiesced, and the two dames took their way to Dalcastle, with baskets well furnished with trifles. They did not take the common path from the village, but went about, and approached the mansion by a different way. But it seemed as if some overruling power ordered it, that they should miss no chance of attaining the information they wanted. For ere ever they came within half a mile of Dalcastle, they perceived the two youths coming, as to meet them, on the same path. The road leading from Dalcastle toward the north-east, as all the country knows, goes along a dark bank of brushwood called the Bogle-heuch. It was by this track that the two women were going; and when they perceived the two gentlemen meeting them, they turned back, and the moment they were out of their sight, they concealed themselves in a thicket close by the road. They did this because Mrs. Logan was terrified for being discovered, and because they wished to reconnoitre without being seen. Mrs. Calvert now charged her, whatever she saw, or whatever she heard, to put on a resolution, and support it, for if she fainted there and was discovered, what was to become of her!

The two young men came on, in earnest and vehement conversation; but the subject they were on was a terrible one, and hardly fit to be repeated in the face of a Christian community. Wringhim was disputing the boundlessness of the true Christian's freedom, and expressing doubts, that, chosen as he knew he was from all eternity, still it might be possible for him to commit acts that would exclude him from the limits of the covenant. The other argued, with mighty fluency, that the thing was utterly impossible, and altogether inconsistent with eternal predestination. The arguments of the latter prevailed, and the laird was driven to sullen silence. But, to the women's utter surprise, as the conquering disputant passed, he made a signal of recognizance through the brambles to them, as formerly, and that he might expose his associate fully, and in his true colours, he led him backward and forward by the women more than twenty times, making him to confess both the crimes that he had done, and those he had in contemplation.

At length he said to him, "Assuredly I saw some strolling vagrant women on this walk, my dear friend: I wish we could find them, for there is little doubt that they are concealed here in your woods."

"I wish we *could* find them," answered Wringhim; "we would have fine sport maltreating and abusing them."

"That we should, that we should! Now tell me, Robert, if you found a malevolent woman, the latent enemy of your prosperity, lurking in these woods to betray you, what would you inflict on her?"

"I would tear her to pieces with my dogs, and feed them with her flesh. O, my dear friend, there is an old strumpet who lived with my unnatural father, whom I hold in such utter detestation, that I stand constantly in dread of her, and would sacrifice the half of my estate to shed her blood!"

"What will you give me if I will put her in your power, and give you a fair and genuine excuse for making away with her; one for which you shall answer at any bar, here or hereafter?"

"I should like to see the vile hag put down. She is in possession of the family plate, that is mine by right, as well as a thousand valuable relics, and great riches besides, all of which the old profligate gifted shamefully away. And it is said, besides all these, that she has sworn my destruction."

"She has, she has. But I see not how she can accomplish that, seeing the deed was done so suddenly, and in the silence of the night?"

"It was said there were some on-lookers.—But where shall we find that disgraceful Miss Logan?"

"I will show you her by and by. But will you then consent to the other meritorious deed? Come, be a man, and throw away scruples."

"If you can convince me that the promise is binding, I will."

"Then step this way, till I give you a piece of information."

They walked a little way out of hearing, but went not out of sight; therefore, though the women were in a terrible quandary, they durst not stir, for they had some hopes that this extraordinary person was on a mission of the same sort with themselves, knew of them, and was going to make use of their testimony. Mrs. Logan was several times on the point of falling into a swoon, so much did the appearance of the young man impress her, until her associate covered her face that she might listen without embarrassment. But this latter dialogue aroused different feelings within them; namely, those arising from imminent personal danger. They saw his waggish associate point out the place of their concealment to Wringhim, who came toward them, out of curiosity to see what his friend meant by what he believed to be a joke, manifestly without crediting it in the least degree. When he came running away, the other called after him, "If she is too hard for you, call to me." As he said this, he hasted out of sight, in the contrary direction, apparently much delighted with the joke.

Wringhim came rushing through the thicket impetuously, to the very spot where Mrs. Logan lay squatted. She held the wrapping close about her head, but he tore it off and discovered her. "The curse of God be on thee!" said he: "What fiend has brought thee here, and for what purpose art thou come? But, whatever has brought thee, *I have thee!*" and with that he seized her by the throat. The two women, when they heard what jeopardy they were in from such a wretch, had squatted among the underwood at a small distance from each other, so that he had never observed Mrs. Calvert; but no sooner had he seized her benefactor, than, like a wild cat, she sprung out of the thicket, and had both her hands fixed at his throat, one of them twisted in his stock, in a twinkling. She brought him back-over among the brushwood, and the two, fixing on him like two harpies, mastered him with ease. Then indeed was he wofully beset. He deemed for a while that his friend was at his back, and turning his bloodshot eyes toward the path, he attempted to call; but there was no friend there, and the women cut short his cries by another twist of his stock. "Now, gallant and rightful Laird of Dalcastle," said Mrs. Logan, "what hast thou to say for thyself? Lay thy account to dree the weird thou hast so well earned. Now shalt thou suffer due penance for murdering thy brave and only brother."

"Thou liest, thou hag of the pit! I touched not my brother's life."

"I saw thee do it with these eyes that now look thee in the face; ay, when his back was to thee too, and while he was hotly engaged with thy friend," said Mrs. Calvert.

"I heard thee confess it again and again this same hour," said Mrs. Logan.

"Ay, and so did I," said her companion.—"Murder will out, though the Almighty should lend hearing to the ears of the willow, and speech to the seven tongues of the woodriff."

"You are liars, and witches!" said he, foaming with rage, "and creatures fitted from the beginning for eternal destruction. I'll have your bones and your blood sacrificed on your cursed altars!

O, Gil-Martin! Gil-Martin! where art thou now? Here, here is the proper food for blessed vengeance!—Hilloa!"

There was no friend, no Gil-Martin there to hear or assist him: he was in the two women's mercy, but they used it with moderation. They mocked, they tormented, and they threatened him; but, finally, after putting him in great terror, they bound his hands behind his back, and his feet fast with long straps of garters which they chanced to have in their baskets, to prevent him from pursuing them till they were out of his reach. As they left him, which they did in the middle of the path, Mrs. Calvert said, "We could easily put an end to thy sinful life, but our hands shall be free of thy blood. Nevertheless thou art still in our power, and the vengeance of thy country shall overtake thee, thou mean and cowardly murderer, ay, and that more suddenly than thou art aware!"

The women posted to Edinburgh; and as they put themselves under the protection of an English merchant, who was journeying thither with twenty horses loaden, and armed servants, so they had scarcely any conversation on the road. When they arrived at Mrs. Logan's house, then they spoke of what they had seen and heard, and agreed that they had sufficient proof to condemn young Wringhim, who they thought richly deserved the severest doom of the law.

"I never in my life saw any human being," said Mrs. Calvert, "whom I thought so like a fiend. If a demon could inherit flesh and blood, that youth is precisely such a being as I could conceive that demon to be. The depth and the malignity of his eye is hideous. His breath is like the airs from a charnel house, and his flesh seems fading from his bones, as if the worm that never dies were gnawing it away already."

"He was always repulsive, and every way repulsive," said the other; "but he is now indeed altered greatly to the worse. While we were handfasting him, I felt his body to be feeble and emaciated; but yet I know him to be so puffed up with spiritual pride, that I believe he weens every one of his actions justified before God, and instead of having stings of conscience for these, he takes great merit to himself in having effected them. Still my thoughts are less about him than the extraordinary being who accompanies him. He does every thing with so much ease and indifference, so much velocity and effect, that all bespeak him an adept in wickedness. The likeness to my late hapless young master is so striking, that I can hardly believe it to be a chance model; and I think he imitates him in every thing, for some purpose, or some effect on his sinful associate. Do you know that he is so like in every lineament, look, and gesture, that, against the clearest light of reason, I cannot in my mind separate the one from the other, and have a certain indefinable impression on my mind, that they are one and the same being, or that the one was a prototype of the other."

still fighting to keep faith in her reason

"If there is an earthly crime," said Mrs. Calvert, for the due punishment of which the Almighty may be supposed to subvert the order of nature, it is fratricide. But tell me, dear friend, did you remark to what the subtile and hellish villain was endeavouring to prompt the assassin?"

"No, I could not comprehend it. My senses were altogether so bewildered, that I thought they had combined to deceive me, and I gave them no credit."

"Then hear me: I am almost certain he was using every persuasion to induce him to make away with his mother; and I likewise conceive that I heard the incendiary give his consent!"

"This is dreadful. Let us speak and think no more about it, till we see the issue. In the meantime, let us do that which is our bounden duty,—go and divulge all that we know relating to this foul murder."

Accordingly the two women went to Sir Thomas Wallace of Craigie, the Lord Justice Clerk, (who was, I think, either uncle or grandfather to young Drummond, who was outlawed, and obliged to fly his country on account of Colwan's death,) and to that gentleman they related every circumstance of what they had seen and heard. He examined Calvert very minutely, and seemed deeply interested in her evidence—said he knew she was relating the truth, and in testimony of it, brought a letter of young Drummond's from his desk, wherein that young gentleman, after protesting his innocence in the most forcible terms, confessed having been with such a woman in such a house, after leaving the company of his friends; and that on going home, Sir Thomas's servant had let him in, in the dark, and from these circumstances he found it impossible to prove an *alibi*. He begged of his relative, if ever an opportunity offered, to do his endeavour to clear up that mystery, and remove the horrid stigma from his name in his country, and among his kin, of having stabbed a friend behind his back.

Lord Craigie, therefore, directed the two women to the proper authorities, and after hearing their evidence there, it was judged proper to apprehend the present Laird of Dalcastle, and bring him to his trial. But before that, they sent the prisoner in the tolbooth, he who had seen the whole transaction along with Mrs. Calvert, to take a view of Wringhim privately; and his discrimination being so well known as to be proverbial all over the land, they determined secretly to be ruled by this report. They accordingly sent him on a pretended mission of legality to Dalcastle, with orders to see and speak with the proprietor, without giving him a hint what was wanted. On his return, they examined him, and he told them that he found all things at the place in utter confusion and dismay; that the lady of the place was missing, and could not be found, dead or alive. On being asked if he had ever seen the proprietor before, he looked astounded, and unwilling to answer. But it came out that he had; and that he had once seen him kill a man on such a spot at such an hour.

Officers were then despatched, without delay, to apprehend the monster, and bring him to justice. On these going to the mansion, and inquiring for him, they were told he was at home; on which they stationed guards, and searched all the premises, but he was not to be found. It was in vain that they overturned beds, raised floors, and broke open closets: Robert Wringhim Colwan was lost once and for ever. His mother also was lost; and strong suspicions attached to some of the farmers and house servants, to whom she was obnoxious, relating to her disappearance. The Honourable Thomas Drummond became a distinguished officer in the Austrian service, and died in the memorable year for Scotland, 1715;[1] and this is all with which history, justiciary records, and tradition, furnish me relating to these matters.

I have now the pleasure of presenting my readers with an original document of a most singular nature, and preserved for their perusal in a still more singular manner. I offer no remarks on it, and make as few additions to it, leaving every one to judge for himself. We have heard much of the rage of fanaticism in former days, but nothing to this.

---

1   The year of the first of two Jacobite Rebellions, in which supporters of James Edward Stuart, the "Old Pretender" to the crown, headed south with the intention of invading England. They met with the pro-Hanovarian forces at the Battle of Sheriffmuir, near Stirling. Afterwards, both sides claimed victory.

MY life has been a life of trouble and turmoil; of change and vicissitude; of anger and exultation; of sorrow and of vengeance. My sorrows have all been for a slighted gospel, and my vengeance has been wreaked on its adversaries. Therefore, in the might of heaven I will sit down and write: I will let the wicked of this world know what I have done in the faith of the promises, and justification by grace, that they may read and tremble, and bless their gods of silver and of gold, that the minister of heaven was removed from their sphere before their blood was mingled with their sacrifices.

I was born an outcast in the world, in which I was destined to act so conspicuous a part. My mother was a burning and a shining light, in the community of Scottish worthies, and in the days of her virginity had suffered much in the persecution of the saints. But it so pleased Heaven, that, as a trial of her faith, she was married to one of the wicked; a man all over spotted with the leprosy of sin. As well might they have conjoined fire and water together, in hopes that they would consort and amalgamate, as purity and corruption: She fled from his embraces the first night after their marriage, and from that time forth, his iniquities so galled her upright heart, that she quitted his society altogether, keeping her own apartments in the same house with him.

I was the second son of this unhappy marriage, and, long ere ever I was born, my father according to the flesh disclaimed all relation or connection with me, and all interest in me, save what the law compelled him to take, which was to grant me a scanty maintenance; and had it not been for a faithful minister of the gospel, my mother's early instructor, I should have remained an outcast from the church visible. He took pity on me, admitting me not only into that, but into the bosom of his own household and ministry also, and to him am I indebted, under Heaven, for the high conceptions and glorious discernment between good and evil, right and wrong, which I attained even at an early age. It was he who directed my studies aright, both in the learning of the ancient fathers, and the doctrines of the reformed church, and designed me for his assistant and successor in the holy office. I missed no opportunity of perfecting myself particularly in all the minute points of theology in which my reverend father and mother took great delight; but at length I acquired so much skill, that I astonished my teachers, and made them gaze at one another. I remember that it was the custom, in my patron's house, to ask the questions of the Single Catechism round every Sabbath night. He asked the first, my mother the second, and so on, every one saying the question asked, and then asking the next. It fell to my mother to ask Effectual Calling at me. I said the answer with propriety and emphasis. "Now, madam," added I, "my question to you is, What is *In*effectual Calling?"

"Ineffectual Calling? There is no such thing, Robert," said she. "But there is, madam," said I; "and that answer proves how much you say these fundamental precepts by rote, and without any consideration. Ineffectual Calling is, *the outward call of the gospel* without any effect on the hearts of unregenerated and impenitent sinners. Have not all these the same calls, warnings, doctrines, and reproofs, that we have? and is not this Ineffectual Calling? Has not Ardinferry the same? Has not Patrick M'Lure the same? Has not the Laird of Dalcastle and his reprobate heir the same? And will any tell me, that *this is not In*effectual Calling?"

"What a wonderful boy he is!" said my mother.

"I'm feared he turn out to be a conceited gowk," said old Barnet, the minister's man.

"No," said my pastor, and *father*, (as I shall henceforth denominate him,) "No, Barnet, he *is* a wonderful boy; and no marvel, for I have prayed for these talents to be bestowed on him from his infancy: and do you think that Heaven would refuse a prayer so disinterested? No, it is impossible. But my dread is, madam," continued he, turning to my mother, "that he is yet in the bond of iniquity."

"God forbid!" said my mother.

"I have struggled with the Almighty long and hard," continued he; "but have as yet had no certain token of acceptance in his behalf. I have indeed fought a hard fight, but have been repulsed by him who hath seldom refused my request; although I cited his own words against him, and endeavoured to hold him at his promise, he hath so many turnings in the supremacy of his power, that I have been rejected. How dreadful is it to think of our darling being still without the pale of the covenant! But I have vowed a vow, and in that there is hope."

My heart quaked with terror, when I thought of being still living in a state of reprobation, subjected to the awful issues of death, judgment, and eternal misery, by the slightest accident or casualty, and I set about the duty of prayer myself with the utmost earnestness. I prayed three times every day, and seven times on the Sabbath; but the more frequently and fervently that I prayed, I sinned still the more. About this time, and for a long period afterwards, amounting to several years, I lived in a hopeless and deplorable state of mind; for I said to myself, "If my name is not written in the book of life from all eternity, it is in vain for me to presume that either vows or prayers of mine, or those of all mankind combined, can ever procure its insertion now." I had come under many vows, most solemnly taken, every one of which I had broken; and I saw with the intensity of juvenile grief, that there was no hope for me. I went on sinning every hour, and all the while most strenuously warring against sin, and repenting of every one transgression, as soon after the commission of it as I got leisure to think. But O what a wretched state this unregenerated state is, in which every effort after righteousness only aggravates our offences! I found it vanity to contend; for after communing with my heart, the conclusion was as follows: "If I could repent me of all my sins, and shed tears of blood for them, still have I not a load of original transgression pressing on me, that is enough to crush me to the lowest hell. I may be angry with my first parents for having sinned, but how I shall repent me of their sin, is beyond what I am able to comprehend."

Still, in those days of depravity and corruption, I had some of those principles implanted in my mind, which were afterward to spring up with such amazing fertility among the heroes of the faith and the promises. In particular, I felt great indignation against all the wicked of this world and often wished for the means of ridding it of such a noxious burden. I liked John Barnet, my reverend father's serving-man, extremely ill; but, from a supposition that he might be one of the justified, I refrained from doing him any injury. He gave always his word against me, and when we were by ourselves, in the barn or the fields, he rated me with such severity for my faults, that my heart could brook it no longer. He discovered some notorious lies that I had framed, and taxed me with them in such a manner that I could in nowise get off. My cheek burnt with offence, rather than shame; and he, thinking he had got the mastery of me, exulted over me most unmercifully, telling me I was a selfish and conceited blackguard, who made great pretences towards religious devotion to cloak a disposition tainted with deceit, and that it would not much astonish him if I brought myself to the gallows.

I gathered some courage from his over severity, and answered him as follows: "Who made thee a judge of the actions or dispositions of the Almighty's creatures—thou who art a worm, and no man in his sight? How it befits thee to deal out judgments and anathemas! Hath he not made one vessel to honour, and another to dishonour, as in the case with myself and thee? Hath he not builded his stories in the heavens, and laid the foundations thereof in the earth, and how can a being like thee judge between good and evil, that are both subjected to the workings of his hand; or of the opposing principles in the soul of man, correcting, modifying, and refining one another?"

I said this with that strong display of fervor for which I was remarkable at my years, and expected old Barnet to be utterly confounded; but he only shook his head, and, with the most provoking grin, said, "There he goes! sickan sublime and ridiculous sophistry I never heard come out of another mouth but ane. There needs nae aiths to be sworn afore the session wha is your father, young goodman. I ne'er, for my part, saw a son sae like a dad, sin' my een first opened." With that he went away, saying, with an ill-natured wince, "You made to honour and me to dishonour! Dirty bowkail thing that thou be'st!"

"I will have the old rascal on the hip for this, if I live," thought I. So I went and asked my mother if John was a righteous man? She could not tell, but supposed he was, and therefore I got no encouragement from her. I went next to my reverend father, and inquired his opinion, expecting as little from that quarter. He knew the elect as it were by instinct, and could have told you of all those in his own, and some neighbouring parishes, who were born within the boundaries of the covenant of promise, and who were not.

"I keep a good deal in company with your servant, old Barnet, father," said I.

"You do, boy; you do, I see," said he.

"I wish I may not keep too much in his company," said I, "not knowing what kind of society I am in;—is John a good man, father?"

"Why, boy, he is but so, so. A morally good man John is, but very little of the leaven of true righteousness, which is faith, within. I am afraid old Barnet, with all his stock of morality, will be a cast-away."

My heart was greatly cheered by this remark; and I sighed very deeply, and hung my head to one side. The worthy father observed me, and inquired the cause? when I answered as follows: "How dreadful the thought, that I have been going daily in company and fellowship with one, whose name is written on the red-letter side of the book of life; whose body and soul have been, from all eternity, consigned over to everlasting destruction, and to whom the blood of the atonement can never, never reach! Father, this is an awful thing, and beyond my comprehension."

"While we are in the world, we must mix with the inhabitants thereof," said he; "and the stains which adhere to us by reason of this admixture, which is unavoidable, shall all be washed away. It is our duty, however, to shun the society of wicked men as much as possible, lest we partake of their sins, and become sharers with them in punishment. John, however, is a morally good man, and may yet get a cast of grace."

"I always thought him a good man till to day," said I, "when he threw out some reflections on your character, so horrible that I quake to think of the wickedness and malevolence of his heart. He was rating me very impertinently for some supposed fault, which had no being save in his own jealous brain, when I attempted to reason him out of his belief in the spirit of calm Christian argument. But how do you think he answered me? He did so, sir, by twisting his mouth at me, and remarking that such sublime and ridiculous sophistry never came out of another mouth but one, (meaning yours,) and that no oath before a kirk session was necessary to prove who was my dad, for that he had never seen a son so like a father as I was like mine."

"He durst not for his soul's salvation, and for his daily bread, which he values much more, say such a word, boy; therefore take care what you assert," said my reverend father.

"He said these very words, and will not deny them, sir," said I.

My reverend father turned about in great wrath and indignation, and went away in search of John; but I kept out of the way, and listened at a back window; for John was dressing the plot of ground behind the house; and I hope it was no sin in me that I did rejoice in the dialogue which took place, it being the victory of righteousness over error.

"Well, John, this is a fine day for your delving work."

"Ey, it's a tolerable day, sir."

"Are you thankful in your heart, John, for such temporal mercies as these?"

"Aw doubt we're a' ower little thankfu', sir, baith for temporal an' speeritual mercies; but it isna aye the maist thankfu' heart that maks the greatest fraze wi' the tongue."

"I hope there is nothing personal under that remark, John?"

"Gin the bannet fits ony body's head, they're unco welcome to it, sir, for me."

"John, I do not approve of these innuendoes. You have an arch malicious manner of vending your aphorisms, which the men of the world are too apt to read the wrong way, for your dark hints are sure to have *one* very bad meaning."

"Hout na, sir, it's only bad folks that think sae. They find ma bits o' gibes come hame to their hearts wi' a kind o' yerk, an' that gars them wince."

"That saying is ten times worse than the other, John; it is a manifest insult: it is just telling me to my face, that you think me a bad man."

"A body canna help his thoughts, sir."

"No, but a man's thoughts are generally formed from observation. Now I should like to know, even from the mouth of a misbeliever, what part of my conduct warrants such a conclusion?"

"Nae particular pairt, sir; I draw a' my conclusions frae the haill o' a man's character, an' I'm no that aften far wrang."

"Well, John, and what sort of general character do you suppose mine to be?"

"Yours is a Scripture character, sir, an' I'll prove it."

"I hope so, John. Well, which of the Scripture characters do you think approximates nearest to my own?"

"Guess, sir, guess; I wish to lead a proof."

"Why, if it be an Old Testament character, I hope it is Melchizedek,[1] for at all events you cannot deny there is one point of resemblance: I, like him, am a preacher of righteousness. If it be a New Testament character, I suppose you mean the Apostle of the Gentiles[2], of whom I am an unworthy representative."

"Na, na, sir, better nor that still, an' fer closer is the resemblance. When ye bring me to the point, I maun speak. Ye are the just Pharisee, sir, that gaed up wi' the poor publican to pray in the Temple;[3]

---

1 Old Testament king of Salem, referred to in Genesis as "the priest of the most high God" (14:18). In Hebrews, Christ is described as a "high priest after the order of Melchisedec" (5:10).

2 i.e. St Paul

3 The Pharisees were a Jewish order strict in their observance of tradition and textual edict. Barnet's reference is to Luke 18:10–14: "Two men went

an' ye're acting the very same pairt at this time, an' saying i' your heart, 'God, I thank thee that I am not as other men are, an' in nae way like this poor misbelieving unregenerate sinner, John Barnet.'"

"I hope I may say so indeed."

"There now! I tauld you how it was! But, d'ye hear, maister: Here stands the poor sinner, John Barnet, your beadle an' servant-man, wha wadna change chances wi' you in the neist world, nor consciences in this, for ten times a' that you possess,—your justification by faith an' awthegither."

"You are extremely audacious and impertinent, John; but the language of reprobation cannot affect me: I came only to ask you one question, which I desire you to answer candidly. Did you ever say to any one that I was the boy Robert's natural father?"

Rev. totally claus off truth of statement

"Hout na, sir! Ha—ha—ha! Aih, fie na, sir! I durstna say that for my life. I doubt the black stool, an' the sack gown, or maybe the juggs wad hae been my portion had I said sic a thing as that. Hout, hout! Fie, fie! Unco-like doings thae for a Melchizedek or a Saint Paul!"

"John, you are a profane old man, and I desire that you will not presume to break your jests on me. Tell me, dare you say, or dare you think, that I am the natural father of that boy?"

"Ye canna hinder me to think whatever I like, sir, nor can I hinder mysel."

"But did you ever *say* to any one, that he resembled me, and fathered himself well enough?"

"I hae said mony a time, that he resembled you, sir. Naebody can mistake that."

"But, John, there are many natural reasons for such likenesses, besides that of consanguinity. They depend much on the thoughts and affections of the mother; and, it is probable, that the mother of this boy, being deserted by her worthless husband, having turned

---

up into the temple to pray; the one a Pharisee, and the other a publican. The Pharisee stood and prayed thus with himself, God I thank thee, that I am not as other men *are*, extortioners, unjust, adulterers, or even as this publican. I fast twice in the week, I give tithes of all that I possess. And the publican, standing afar off, would not lift up so much as *his* eyes unto heaven, but smote upon his breast, saying, God be merciful to me a sinner. I tell you, this man went down to his house justified *rather* than the other: for every one that exalteth himself shall be abased; and he that humbleth himself shall be exalted."

her thoughts on me, as likely to be her protector, may have caused this striking resemblance."

"Ay, it may be, sir. I coudna say."

"I have known a lady, John, who was delivered of a blackamoor child, merely from the circumstance of having got a start by the sudden entrance of her negro servant, and not being able to forget him for several hours."

"It may be, sir; but I ken this;—an I had been the laird, I wadna hae ta'en that story in."

"So, then, John, you positively think, from a casual likeness, that this boy is my son?"

"Man's thoughts are vanity, sir; they come unasked, an' gang away without a dismissal, an' he canna help them. I'm neither gaun to say that I *think* he's your son, nor that I think he's *no* your son: sae ye needna pose me nae mair about it."

"Hear then my determination, John: If you do not promise to me, in faith and honour, that you never will say, or insinuate such a thing again in your life, as that that boy is my natural son, I will take the keys of the church from you, and dismiss you my service."

John pulled out the keys, and dashed them on the gravel at the reverend minister's feet. "There are the keys o' your kirk, sir! I hae never had muckle mense o' them sin' ye entered the door o't. I hae carried them this three an thretty year, but they hae aye been like to burn a hole i' my pouch sin' ever they were turned for your admittance. Tak them again, an' gie them to wha you will, and muckle gude may he get o' them. Auld John may dee a beggar in a hay barn, or at the back of a dike, but he sall aye be master o' his ain thoughts, an' gie them vent or no, as he likes."

He left the manse that day, and I rejoiced in the riddance; for I disdained to be kept so much under, by one who was in the bond of iniquity, and of whom there seemed no hope, as he rejoiced in his frowardness, and refused to submit to that faithful teacher, his master.

It was about this time that my reverend father preached a sermon, one sentence of which affected me most disagreeably: It was to the purport, that every unrepented sin was productive of a new sin with each breath that a man drew; and every one of these new sins added to the catalogue in the same manner. I was utterly confounded at the multitude of my transgressions; for I was sensible that there were great numbers of sins of which I had never been able thoroughly to repent, and these momentary ones, by a moderate calculation, had, I saw, long ago, amounted to a hundred and fifty thousand in the minute, and I saw no end to the series of repentances to which I had subjected myself. A life-time was nothing to enable me to accomplish the sum, and then being, for any thing I was certain of, in my state of nature, and the grace of repentance withheld from me,—what was I to do, or what was to become of me? In the meantime, I went on sinning without measure; but I was still more troubled about the multitude than the magnitude of my transgressions, and the small minute ones puzzled me more than those that were more heinous, as the latter had generally some good effects in the way of punishing wicked men, froward boys, and deceitful women; and I rejoiced, even then in my early youth, at being used as a scourge in the hand of the Lord; another Jehu, a Cyrus, or a Nebuchadnezzar.[1]

On the whole, I remember that I got into great confusion relating to my sins and repentances, and knew neither where to begin nor how to proceed, and often had great fears that I was wholly without Christ, and that I would find God a consuming fire to me. I could not help running into new sins continually; but then I was mercifully dealt with, for I was often made to repent of them most heartily, by reason of bodily chastisements received on these delinquencies being discovered. I was particularly prone to lying, and I cannot but admire the mercy that has freely forgiven me all these juvenile sins. Now that I know them all to be blotted out, and that I am an accepted person, I may the more freely confess them: the truth is, that one lie always paved the way for another, from hour to hour, from day to day, and from year to year; so that I found myself constantly involved in a labyrinth of deceit, from which it was impossible to extricate myself. If I knew a person to be a godly one, I could almost have kissed his feet; but against the carnal portion of mankind, I set my face continually. I esteemed the true ministers of the gospel; but the prelatic party, and the preachers up of good works I abhorred, and to this hour I account them the worst and most heinous of all transgressors.

There was only one boy at Mr. Wilson's class who kept always the upper hand of me in every part of education. I strove against

---

1 Jehu (c.842–815BC) was king of Israel. Cyrus (c.580–529BC), King of Persia in 6th century BC, freed Jews from Babylonia. Nebuchadnezzar (c.630–562BC) was king of Babylonia (605–561BC) and responsible for the destruction of Jerusalem and the exile of the Jews.

him from year to year, but it was all in vain; for he was a very wicked boy, and I was convinced he had dealings with the devil. Indeed it was believed all over the country that his mother was a witch; and I was at length convinced that it was no human ingenuity that beat me with so much ease in the Latin, after I had often sat up a whole night with my reverend father, studying my lesson in all its bearings. I often read as well and sometimes better than he; but the moment Mr. Wilson began to examine us, my opponent popped up above me. I determined, (as I knew him for a wicked person, and one of the devil's hand-fasted children,) to be revenged on him, and to humble him by some means or other. Accordingly I lost no opportunity of setting the Master against him, and succeeded several times in getting him severely beaten for faults of which he was innocent. I can hardly describe the joy that it gave to my heart to see a wicked creature suffering, for though he deserved it not for one thing, he richly deserved it for others. This may be by some people accounted a great sin in me; but I deny it, for I did it as a duty, and what a man or boy does for the right, will never be put into the sum of his transgressions.

jealousy

This boy, whose name was M'Gill, was, at all his leisure hours, engaged in drawing profane pictures of beasts, men, women, houses, and trees, and, in short, of all things that his eye encountered. These profane things the Master often smiled at, and admired; therefore I began privately to try my hand likewise. I had scarcely tried above once to draw the figure of a man, ere I conceived that I had hit the very features of Mr. Wilson. They were so particular, that they could not be easily mistaken, and I was so tickled and pleased with the droll likeness that I had drawn, that I laughed immoderately at it. I tried no other figure but this; and I tried it in every situation in which a man and a schoolmaster could be placed. I often wrought for hours together at this likeness, nor was it long before I made myself so much master of the outline, that I could have drawn it in any situation whatever, almost off hand. I then took M'Gill's account book of algebra home with me, and at my leisure put down a number of gross caricatures of Mr. Wilson here and there, several of them in situations notoriously ludicrous. I waited the discovery of this treasure with great impatience; but the book, chancing to be one that M'Gill was not using, I saw it might be long enough before I enjoyed the consummation of my grand scheme: therefore, with all the ingenuity I was master of, I brought it before our dominie's eye. But never shall I forget the rage that gleamed in the tyrant's phiz![1] I was actually terrified to look at him, and trembled at his voice. M'Gill was called upon, and examined relating to the obnoxious figures. He denied flatly that any of them were of his doing. But the Master inquiring at him whose they were, he could not tell, but affirmed it to be some trick. Mr. Wilson at one time, began, as I thought, to hesitate; but the evidence was so strong against M'Gill, that at length his solemn asseverations of innocence only proved an aggravation of his crime. There was not one in the school who had ever been known to draw a figure but himself, and on him fell the whole weight of the tyrant's vengeance. It was dreadful; and I was once in hopes that he would not leave life in the culprit. He, however, left the school for several months, refusing to return to be subjected to punishment for the faults of others, and I stood king of the class.

Matters were at last made up between M'Gill's parents and the schoolmaster, but by that time I had got the start of him, and never in my life did I exert myself so much as to keep the mastery. It was in vain; the powers of enchantment prevailed, and I was again turned down with the tear in my eye. I could think of no amends but one, and being driven to desperation, I put it in practice. I told a lie of him. I came boldly up to the master, and told him that M'Gill had in my hearing cursed him in a most shocking manner, and called him vile names. He called M'Gill, and charged him with the crime, and the proud young coxcomb was so stunned at the atrocity of the charge, that his face grew as red as crimson, and the words stuck in his throat as he feebly denied it. His guilt was manifest, and he was again flogged most nobly, and dismissed the school for ever in disgrace, as a most incorrigible vagabond.

This was a great victory gained, and I rejoiced and exulted exceedingly in it. It had, however, very nigh cost me my life; for not long thereafter, I encountered M'Gill in the fields, on which he came up and challenged me for a liar, daring me to fight him. I refused, and said that I looked on him as quite below my notice; but he would not quit me, and finally told me that he should either *lick me*, or I should *lick* him, as he had no other means of being revenged on such a scoundrel. I tried to intimidate him, but it would not do; and I believe I would have given all that I had in the world to be quit of him. He at length went so far as first to

---

1 Abbreviation of "physiognomy."

kick me, and then strike me on the face; and, being both older and stronger than he, I thought it scarcely became me to take such insults patiently. I was, nevertheless, well aware that the devilish powers of his mother would finally prevail; and either the dread of this, or the inward consciousness of having wronged him, certainly unnerved my arm, for I fought wretchedly, and was soon wholly overcome. I was so sore defeated, that I kneeled, and was going to beg his pardon; but another thought struck me momentarily, and I threw myself on my face, and inwardly begged aid from heaven; at the same time I felt as if assured that my prayer was heard, and would be answered. While I was in this humble attitude, the villain kicked me with his foot and cursed me; and I being newly encouraged, arose and encountered him once more. We had not fought long at this second turn, before I saw a man hastening toward us; on which I uttered a shout of joy, and laid on valiantly; but my very next look assured me, that the man was old John Barnet, whom I had likewise wronged all that was in my power, and between these two wicked persons I expected any thing but justice. My arm was again enfeebled, and that of my adversary prevailed. I was knocked down and mauled most grievously, and while the ruffian was kicking and cuffing me at his will and pleasure, up came old John Barnet, breathless with running, and at one blow with his open hand, levelled my opponent with the earth. "Tak ye that, maister!" says John, "to learn ye better breeding. Hout awa, man! anye will fight, fight fair. Gude sauf us, ir ye a gentleman's brood, that ye will kick an' cuff a lad when he's down?"

When I heard this kind and unexpected interference, I began once more to value myself on my courage, and springing up, I made at my adversary; but John, without saying a word, bit his lip, and seizing me by the neck, threw me down. M'Gill begged of him to stand and see fair play, and suffer us to finish the battle; for, added he, "he is a liar, and a scoundrel, and deserves ten times more than I can give him."

"I ken he's a' that ye say, an' mair, my man," quoth John: "But am I sure that ye're no as bad, an' waur? It says nae muckle for ony o' ye to be tearing like tikes at ane anither here."

John cocked his cudgel and stood between us, threatening to knock the one dead, who first offered to lift his hand against the other; but, perceiving no disposition in any of us to separate, he drove me home before him like a bullock, keeping close guard behind me, lest M'Gill had followed. I felt greatly indebted to John, yet I complained of his interference to my mother, and the old cannot honestly express emotion officious sinner got no thanks for his pains.

As I am writing only from recollection, so I remember of nothing farther in these early days, in the least worthy of being recorded. That I was a great, a transcendent sinner, I confess. But still I had hopes of forgiveness, because I never sinned from principle, but accident; and then I always *tried* to repent of these sins by the slump, for individually it was impossible; and though not always successful in my endeavours, I could not help that; the grace of repentance being withheld from me, I regarded myself as in no degree accountable for the failure. Moreover, there were many of the most deadly sins into which I never fell, for I dreaded those mentioned in the Revelations as excluding sins, so that I guarded against them continually. In particular, I brought myself to despise, if not to abhor, the beauty of women, looking on it as the greatest snare to which mankind are subjected, and though young men and maidens, and even old women, (my mother among the rest,) taxed me with being an unnatural wretch, I gloried in my acquisition; and to this day, am thankful for having escaped the most dangerous of all snares.

I kept myself also free of the sins of idolatry, and misbelief, both of a deadly nature; and, upon the whole, I think I had not then broken, that is, absolutely broken, above four out of the ten commandments; but for all that, I had more sense than to regard either my good works, or my evil deeds, as in the smallest degree influencing the eternal decrees of God concerning me, either with regard to my acceptance or reprobation. I depended entirely on the bounty of free grace, holding all the righteousness of man as filthy rags, and believing in the momentous and magnificent truth, that the more heavily loaden with transgressions, the more welcome was the believer at the throne of grace. And I have reason to believe that it was this dependence and this belief that at last ensured my acceptance there.

I come now to the most important period of my existence,—the period that has modelled my character, and influenced every action of my life,—without which, this detail of my actions would have been as a tale that hath been told—a monotonous *farrago*[1]—an uninteresting harangue—in short, a thing of nothing. Whereas,

---

1   A confused medley or mixture.

lo! it must now be a relation of great and terrible actions, done in the night, and by the commission of heaven. *Amen.*

Like the sinful king of Israel,[1] I had been walking softly before the Lord for a season. I had been humbled for my transgressions, and, as far as I recollect, sorry on account of their numbers and heinousness. My reverend father had been, moreover, examining me every day regarding the state of my soul, and my answers sometimes appeared to give him satisfaction, and sometimes not. As for my mother, she would harp on the subject of my faith for ever; yet, though I knew her to be a Christian, I confess that I always despised her motley instructions, nor had I any great regard for her person. If this was a crime in me, I never could help it. I confess it freely, and believe it was a judgment from heaven inflicted on her for some sin of former days, and that I had no power to have acted otherwise toward her than I did.   *refuses to accept responsibility*

In this frame of mind was I, when my reverend father one morning arose from his seat, and, meeting me as I entered the room, he embraced me, and welcomed me into the community of the just upon earth. I was struck speechless, and could make no answer save by looks of surprise. My mother also came to me, kissed, and wept over me; and after showering unnumbered blessings on my head, she also welcomed me into the society of *the just made perfect.* Then each of them took me by a hand, and my reverend father explained to me how he had wrestled with God, as the patriarch of old had done, not for a night, but for days and years, and that in bitterness and anguish of spirit, on my account; but that *he* had at last prevailed, and had now gained the long and earnestly desired assurance of my acceptance with the Almighty, in and through the merits and sufferings of his Son: That I was now a justified person, adopted among the number of God's children—my name written in the Lamb's book of life, and that no bypast transgression, nor any future act of my own, or of other men, could be instrumental in altering the decree. "All the powers of darkness," added he, "shall never be able to pluck you again out of your Redeemer's hand. And now, my son,

[marginal notes: this revelation external—not internal]

[contra-diction: according to Calvinism, your actions don't influence God's decisions]

---

1   Ahab (c.874–853BC), seventh King of Israel. In the Old Testament he is rebuked by Elijah: "And it came to pass when Ahab heard those words that he rent his clothes, and put sackcloth upon his flesh, and fasted, and lay in sackcloth, and went softly" (*1 Kings* 21:27).

be strong and stedfast in the truth. Set your face against sin, and sinful men, and resist even to blood, as many of the faithful of this land have done, and your reward shall be double. I am assured of your acceptance by the word and spirit of him who cannot err, and your sanctification and repentance unto life will follow in due course. Rejoice and be thankful, for you are plucked as a brand out of the burning, and now your redemption is sealed and sure."

I wept for joy to be thus assured of my freedom from all sin, and of the impossibility of my ever again falling away from my new state. I bounded away into the fields and the woods, to pour out my spirit in prayer before the Almighty for his kindness to me: my whole frame seemed to be renewed; every nerve was buoyant with new life; I felt as if I could have flown in the air, or leaped over the tops of the trees. An exaltation of spirit lifted me, as it were, far above the earth, and the sinful creatures crawling on its surface; and I deemed myself as an eagle among the children of men, soaring on high, and looking down with pity and contempt on the grovelling creatures below.

As I thus wended my way, I beheld a young man of a mysterious appearance coming towards me. I tried to shun him, being bent on my own contemplations; but he cast himself in my way, so that I could not well avoid him; and more than that, I felt a sort of invisible power that drew me towards him, something like the force of enchantment, which I could not resist. As we approached each other, our eyes met, and I can never describe the strange sensations that thrilled through my whole frame at that impressive moment; a moment to me fraught with the most tremendous consequences; the beginning of a series of adventures which has puzzled myself, and will puzzle the world when I am no more in it. That time will now soon arrive, sooner than any one can devise who knows not the tumult of my thoughts, and the labour of my spirit; and when it hath come and passed over,—when my flesh and my bones are decayed, and my soul has passed to its everlasting home, then shall the sons of men ponder on the events of my life; wonder and tremble, and tremble and wonder how such things should be.

That stranger youth and I approached each other in silence, and slowly, with our eyes fixed on each other's eyes. We approached till not more than a yard intervened between us, and then stood still and gazed, measuring each other from head to foot. What was my astonishment, on perceiving that he was the same being as myself!

The clothes were the same to the smallest item. The form was the same; the apparent age; the colour of the hair; the eyes; and, as far as recollection could serve me from viewing my own features in a glass, the features too were the very same. I conceived at first, that I saw a vision, and that my guardian angel had appeared to me at this important era of my life; but this singular being read my thoughts in my looks, anticipating the very words that I was going to utter.

"You think I am your brother," said he; "or that I am your second self. I am indeed your brother, not according to the flesh, but in my belief of the same truths, and my assurance in the same mode of redemption, than which, I hold nothing so great or so glorious on earth."

"Then you are an associate well adapted to my present state," said I. "For this time is a time of great rejoicing in spirit to me. I am on my way to return thanks to the Most High for my redemption from the bonds of sin and misery. If you will join with me heart and hand in youthful thanksgiving, then shall we two go and worship together; but if not, go your way, and I shall go mine."

"Ah, you little know with how much pleasure I will accompany you, and join with you in your elevated devotions," said he fervently. "Your state is a state to be envied indeed; but I have been advised of it, and am come to be a humble disciple of yours; to be initiated into the true way of salvation by conversing with you, and perhaps by being assisted by your prayers."

My spiritual pride being greatly elevated by this address, I began to assume the preceptor, and questioned this extraordinary youth with regard to his religious principles, telling him plainly, if he was one who expected acceptance with God at all, on account of good works, that I would hold no communion with him. He renounced these at once, with the greatest vehemence, and declared his acquiescence in my faith. I asked if he believed in the eternal and irrevocable decrees of God, regarding the salvation and condemnation of all mankind? He answered that he did so: aye, what would signify all things else that he believed, if he did not believe in that? We then went on to commune about all our points of belief; and in every thing that I suggested, he acquiesced, and, as I thought that day, often carried them to extremes, so that I had a secret dread he was advancing blasphemies. Yet he had such a way with him, and paid such a deference to all my opinions, that I was quite captivated, and, at the same time, I stood in a sort of awe of him, which I could not account for, and several times was seized with an involuntary inclination to escape from his presence, by making a sudden retreat. But he seemed constantly to anticipate my thoughts, and was sure to divert my purpose by some turn in the conversation that particularly interested me. He took care to dwell much on the theme of the impossibility of those ever falling away, who were once accepted and received into covenant with God, for he seemed to know, that in that confidence, and that trust, my whole hopes were centred.

We moved about from one place to another, until the day was wholly spent. My mind had all the while been kept in a state of agitation resembling the motion of a whirlpool, and when we came to separate, I then discovered that the purpose for which I had sought the fields had been neglected, and that I had been diverted from the worship of God, by attending to the quibbles and dogmas of this singular and unaccountable being, who seemed to have more knowledge and information than all the persons I had ever known put together.

We parted with expressions of mutual regret, and when I left him I felt a deliverance, but at the same time a certain consciousness that I was not thus to get free of him, but that he was like to be an acquaintance that was to stick to me for good or for evil. I was astonished at his acuteness and knowledge about every thing; but as for his likeness to me, that was quite unaccountable. He was the same person in every respect, but yet he was not always so; for I observed several times, when we were speaking of certain divines and their tenets, that his face assumed something of the appearance of theirs; and it struck me, that by setting his features to the mould of other people's, he entered at once into their conceptions and feelings. I had been greatly flattered, and greatly interested by his conversation; whether I had been the better for it or the worse, I could not tell. I had been diverted from returning thanks to my gracious Maker for his great kindness to me, and came home as I went away, but not with the same buoyancy and lightness of heart. Well may I remember that day in which I was first received into the number, and made an heir to all the privileges of the children of God, and on which I first met this mysterious associate, who from that day forth contrived to wind himself into all my affairs, both spiritual and temporal, to this day on which I am writing the account of it. It was on the 25th day of March 1704, when I had just entered the eighteenth year of my age. Whether it behoves me to bless God for the events of that day,

[handwritten marginal note:] v. much like what Robert did to George

or to deplore them, has been hid from my discernment, though I have inquired into it with fear and trembling; and I have now lost all hopes of ever discovering the true import of these events until that day when my accounts are to make up and reckon for in another world.

When I came home, I went straight into the parlour, where my mother was sitting by herself. She started to her feet, and uttered a smothered scream. "What ails you, Robert?" cried she. "My dear son, what is the matter with you?"

"Do you see any thing the matter with me?" said I. "It appears that the ailment is with yourself, and either in your crazed head or your dim eyes, for there is nothing the matter with me."

"Ah, Robert, you are ill!" cried she; "you are very ill, my dear boy; you are quite changed; your very voice and manner are changed. Ah, Jane, haste you up to the study, and tell Mr. Wringhim to come here on the instant and speak to Robert."

"I beseech you, woman, to restrain yourself," said I. "If you suffer your frenzy to run away with your judgment in this manner, I will leave the house. What do you mean? I tell you, there is nothing ails me: I never was better."

She screamed, and ran between me and the door, to bar my retreat: in the meantime my reverend father entered, and I have not forgot how he gazed, through his glasses, first at my mother, and then at me. I imagined that his eyes burnt like candles, and was afraid of him, which I suppose made my looks more unstable than they would otherwise have been.

"What is all this for?" said he. "Mistress! Robert! What is the matter here?"

"Oh, sir, our boy!" cried my mother; "our dear boy, Mr. Wringhim! Look at him, and speak to him: he is either dying or translated, sir!"

He looked at me with a countenance of great alarm; mumbling some sentences to himself, and then taking me by the arm, as if to feel my pulse, he said, with a faltering voice, "Something has indeed befallen you, either in body or mind, boy, for you are transformed, since the morning, that I could not have known you for the same person. Have you met with any accident?"

"No."

"Have you seen any thing out of the ordinary course of nature?"

"No."

"Then, Satan, I fear, has been busy with you, tempting you in no ordinary degree at this momentous crisis of your life?"

My mind turned on my associate for the day, and the idea that he might be an agent of the devil, had such an effect on me, that I could make no answer.

"I see how it is," said he; "you are troubled in spirit, and I have no doubt that the enemy of our salvation has been busy with you. Tell me this, has he overcome you, or has he not?"

"He has not, my dear father," said I. "In the strength of the Lord, I hope I have withstood him. But indeed, if he has been busy with me, I knew it not. I have been conversant this day with one stranger only, whom I took rather for an angel of light."

"It is one of the devil's most profound wiles to appear like one," said my mother.

"Woman, hold thy peace!" said my reverend father: "thou pretendest to teach what thou knowest not. Tell me this, boy: Did this stranger, with whom you met, adhere to the religious principles in which I have educated you?"

"Yes, to every one of them, in their fullest latitude," said I.

"Then he was no agent of the wicked one with whom you held converse," said he; "for that is the doctrine that was made to overturn the principalities and powers, the might and dominion of the kingdom of darkness.—Let us pray."

After spending about a quarter of an hour in solemn and sublime thanksgiving, this saintly man and minister of Christ Jesus, gave out that the day following should be kept by the family as a day of solemn thanksgiving, and spent in prayer and praise, on account of the calling and election of one of its members; or rather for the election of that individual being revealed on earth, as well as confirmed in heaven.

The next day was with me a day of holy exultation. It was begun by my reverend father laying his hands upon my head and blessing me, and then dedicating me to the Lord in the most awful and impressive manner. It was in no common way that he exercised this profound rite, for it was done with all the zeal and enthusiasm of a devotee to the true cause, and a champion on the side he had espoused. He used these remarkable words, which I have still treasured up in my heart:—"I give him unto Thee only, to Thee wholly, and to Thee for ever. I dedicate him unto Thee, soul, body, and spirit. Not as the wicked of this world, or the hirelings of a church profanely called by Thy name, do I dedicate this Thy servant to Thee: Not in words and form, learned by rote, and dictated by the limbs of Antichrist, but, Lord, I give him into Thy hand, as a captain putteth a sword into the hand of his sovereign, wherewith to lay waste his enemies. May he be a two-edged weapon in Thy hand, and a spear coming out of Thy mouth, to destroy, and overcome, and pass over; and may the enemies of Thy church fall down before him, and be as dung to fat the land!"

From that moment, I conceived it decreed, not that I should be a minister of the gospel, but a champion of it, to cut off the enemies of the Lord from the face of the earth; and I rejoiced in the commission, finding it more congenial to my nature to be cutting sinners off with the sword, than to be haranguing them from the pulpit, striving to produce an effect, which God, by his act of absolute predestination, had for ever rendered impracticable. The more I pondered on these things, the more I saw of the folly and inconsistency of ministers, in spending their lives, striving and remonstrating with sinners, in order to induce them to do that which they had it not in their power to do. Seeing that God had from all eternity decided the fate of every individual that was to be born of woman, how vain was it in man to endeavour to save those whom their Maker had, by an unchangeable decree, doomed to destruction. I could not disbelieve the doctrine which the best of men had taught me, and toward which he made the whole of the Scriptures to bear, and yet it made the economy of the Christian world appear to me as an absolute contradiction. How much more wise would it be, thought I, to begin and cut sinners off with the sword! for till that is effected, the saints can never inherit the earth in peace. Should I be honoured as an instrument to begin this great work of purification, I should rejoice in it. But then, where had I the means, or under what direction was I to begin? There was one thing clear, I was now the Lord's, and it behoved me to bestir myself in his service. O that I had an host at my command, then would I be as a devouring fire among the workers of iniquity!

Full of these great ideas, I hurried through the city, and sought again the private path through the field and wood of Finnieston,[1] in which my reverend preceptor had the privilege of walking for study, and to which he had a key that was always at my command. Near one of the stiles, I perceived a young man sitting in a devout posture, reading on a Bible. He rose, lifted his hat, and made an obeisance to me, which I returned and walked on. I had not well

---

1   A district in the city of Glasgow.

crossed the stile, till it struck me I knew the face of the youth, and that he was some intimate acquaintance, to whom I ought to have spoken. I walked on, and returned, and walked on again, trying to recollect who he was; but for my life I could not. There was, however, a fascination in his look and manner, that drew me back toward him in spite of myself, and I resolved to go to him, if it were merely to speak and see who he was.

I came up to him and addressed him, but he was so intent on his book, that, though I spoke, he lifted not his eyes. I looked on the book also, and still it seemed a Bible, having columns, chapters, and verses; but it was in a language of which I was wholly ignorant, and all intersected with red lines, and verses. A sensation resembling a stroke of electricity came over me, on first casting my eyes on that mysterious book, and I stood motionless. He looked up, smiled, closed his book, and put it in his bosom. "You seem strangely affected, dear sir, by looking on my book," said he mildly.

"In the name of God, what book is that?" said I: "Is it a Bible?"

"It is *my* Bible, sir," said he; "but I will cease reading it, for I am glad to see you. Pray, is not this a day of holy festivity with you?"

I stared in his face, but made no answer, for my senses were bewildered.

"Do you not know me?" said he. "You appear to be somehow at a loss. Had not you and I some sweet communion and fellowship yesterday?"

"I beg your pardon, sir," said I. "But surely if you are the young gentleman with whom I spent the hours yesterday, you have the cameleon art of changing your appearance; I never could have recognized you."

"My countenance changes with my studies and sensations," said he. "It is a natural peculiarity in me, over which I have not full control. If I contemplate a man's features seriously, mine own gradually assume the very same appearance and character. And what is more, by contemplating a face minutely, I not only attain the same likeness, but, with the likeness, I attain the very same ideas as well as the same mode of arranging them, so that, you see, by looking at a person attentively, I by degrees assume his likeness, and by assuming his likeness I attain to the possession of his most secret thoughts. This, I say, is a peculiarity in my nature, a gift of the God that made me; but whether or not given me for a blessing, he knows himself, and so do I. At all events, I have this privilege, I can never be mistaken of a character in whom I am interested."

"It is a rare qualification," replied I, "and I would give worlds to possess it. Then, it appears, that it is needless to dissemble with you, since you can at any time extract our most secret thoughts from our bosoms. You already know my natural character?"

"Yes," said he, "and it is that which attaches me to you. By assuming your likeness yesterday, I became acquainted with your character, and was no less astonished at the profundity and range of your thoughts, than at the heroic magnanimity with which these were combined. And now, in addition to these, you are dedicated to the great work of the Lord; for which reasons I have resolved to attach myself as closely to you as possible, and to render you all the service of which my poor abilities are capable."

I confess that I was greatly flattered by these compliments paid to my abilities by a youth of such superior qualifications; by one who, with a modesty and affability rare at his age, combined a height of genius and knowledge almost above human comprehension. Nevertheless, I began to assume a certain superiority of demeanour toward him, as judging it incumbent on me to do so, in order to keep up his idea of my exalted character. We conversed again till the day was near a close; and the things that he strove most to inculcate on my mind, were the infallibility of the elect, and the pre-ordination of all things that come to pass. I pretended to controvert the first of these, for the purpose of showing him the extent of my argumentative powers, and said, that "indubitably there were degrees of sinning which would induce the Almighty to throw off the very elect." But behold my hitherto humble and modest companion took up the argument with such warmth, that he put me not only to silence, but to absolute shame.

"Why, sir," said he, "by vending such an insinuation, you put discredit on the great atonement, in which you trust. Is there not enough of merit in the blood of Jesus to save thousands of worlds, if it was for these worlds that he died? Now, when you know, as you do, (and as every one of the elect may know of himself,) that this Saviour died for you, namely and particularly, dare you say that there is not enough of merit in his great atonement to annihilate all your sins, let them be as heinous and atrocious as they may? And, moreover, do you not acknowledge that God hath pre-ordained and decreed whatsoever comes to pass? Then, how is it that you should deem it in your power to eschew one action of your life, whether good or evil? Depend on it, the advice of the great preacher is genuine: 'What thine hand findeth to do, do it with all thy might, for none of us knows what a day may bring

forth?' That is, none of us knows what is pre-ordained, but whatever is pre-ordained we *must* do, and none of these things will be
laid to our charge."

I could hardly believe that these sayings were genuine or ortho-
dox; but I soon felt, that, instead of being a humble disciple of
mine, this new acquaintance was to be my guide and director, and
all under the humble guise of one stooping at my feet to learn the
right. He said that he saw I was ordained to perform some great
action for the cause of Jesus and his church, and he earnestly cov-
eted being a partaker with me; but he besought of me never to
think it possible for me to fall from the truth, or the favour of him
who had chosen me, else that misbelief would baulk every good
work to which I set my face.

There was something so flattering in all this, that I could not *temptation*
resist it. Still, when he took leave of me, I felt it as a great relief;
and yet, before the morrow, I wearied and was impatient to see
him again. We carried on our fellowship from day to day, and all
the while I knew not who he was, and still my mother and reverend father kept insisting that I was an altered youth, changed in
my appearance, my manners, and my whole conduct; yet something always prevented me from telling them more about my new
acquaintance than I had done on the first day we met. I rejoiced
in him, was proud of him, and soon could not live without him;
yet, though resolved every day to disclose the whole history of my
connection with him, I had it not in my power: Something always
prevented me, till at length I thought no more of it, but resolved
to enjoy his fascinating company in private, and by all means to
keep my own with him. The resolution was vain: I set a bold face
to it, but my powers were inadequate to the task; my adherent,
with all the suavity imaginable, was sure to carry his point. I sometimes fumed, and sometimes shed tears at being obliged to yield to
proposals against which I had at first felt every reasoning power of
my soul rise in opposition; but, for all that, he never failed in carrying conviction along with him in effect, for he either forced me
to acquiesce in his measures, and assent to the truth of his posi-
tions, or he put me so completely down, that I had not a word left
to advance against them.

After weeks, and I may say months of intimacy, I observed, somewhat to my amazement, that we had never once prayed together;
and more than that, that he had constantly led my attentions away
from that duty, causing me to neglect it wholly. I thought this a bad
mark of a man seemingly so much set on inculcating certain impor-

tant points of religion, and resolved next day to put him to the test, and request of him to perform that sacred duty in name of us both. He objected boldly; saying there were very few people indeed, with whom he could join in prayer, and he made a point of never doing it, as he was sure they were to ask many things of which he disapproved, and that if he were to officiate himself, he was as certain to allude to many things that came not within the range of their faith. He disapproved of prayer altogether, in the manner it was generally gone about, he said. Man made it merely a selfish concern, and was constantly employed asking, asking, for every thing. Whereas it became all God's creatures to be content with their lot, and only to kneel before him in order to thank him for such benefits as he saw meet to bestow. In short, he argued with such energy, that before we parted I acquiesced, as usual, in his position, and never mentioned prayer to him any more.

Having been so frequently seen in his company, several people happened to mention the circumstance to my mother and reverend father; but at the same time had all described him differently. At length, they began to examine me with respect to the company I kept, as I absented myself from home day after day. I told them I kept company only with one young gentleman, whose whole manner of thinking on religious subjects, I found so congenial with my own, that I could not live out of his society. My mother began to lay down some of her old hackneyed rules of faith, but I turned from hearing her with disgust; for, after the energy of my new friend's reasoning, hers appeared so tame I could not endure it. And I confess with shame, that my reverend preceptor's religious dissertations began, about this time, to lose their relish very much, and by degrees became exceedingly tiresome to my ear. They were so inferior, in strength and sublimity, to the most common observations of my young friend, that in drawing a comparison the former appeared as nothing. He, however, examined me about many things relating to my companion, in all of which I satisfied him, save in one: I could neither tell him who my friend was, what was his name, nor of whom he was descended; and I wondered at myself how I had never once adverted to such a thing, for all the time we had been intimate.

I inquired the next day what his name was; as I said I was often at a loss for it, when talking with him. He replied, that there was no occasion for any one friend ever naming another, when their society was held in private, as ours was; for his part he had never once named me since we first met, and never intended to do so,

if hers is tame, his must be beyond control

unless by my own request. "But if you cannot converse without naming me, you may call me Gil for the present," added he; "and if I think proper to take another name at any future period, it shall be with your approbation."

"Gil!" said I; "Have you no name but Gil? Or which of your names is it? Your Christian or surname?"

"O, you must have a surname too, must you!" replied he, "Very well, you may call me Gil-Martin. It is not my *Christian* name; but it *is* a name which may serve your turn." *his turn is not a Christian one*

"This is very strange!" said I. "Are you ashamed of your parents, that you refuse to give your real name?"

"I have no parents save one, whom I do not acknowledge," said he proudly; "therefore, pray drop that subject, for it is a disagreeable one. I am a being of a very peculiar temper, for though I have servants and subjects more than I can number, yet, to gratify a certain whim, I have left them, and retired to this city, and for all the society it contains, you see I have attached myself only to you. This is a secret, and I tell it you only in friendship, therefore pray let it remain one, and say not another word about the matter."

I assented, and said no more concerning it; for it instantly struck me that this was no other than the Czar Peter of Russia,[1] I having heard that he had been travelling through Europe in disguise, and I cannot say that I had not thenceforward great and mighty hopes of high preferment, as a defender and avenger of the oppressed Christian Church, under the influence of this great potentate. He had hinted as much already, as that it was more honourable, and of more avail to put down the wicked with the sword, than try to reform them, and I thought myself quite justified in supposing that he intended me for some great employment, that he had thus selected me for his companion out of all the rest in Scotland, and even pretended to learn the great truths of religion from my mouth. From that time I felt disposed to yield to such a great prince's suggestions without hesitation.

Nothing ever astonished me so much, as the uncommon powers with which he seemed invested. In our walk one day, we met with a Mr. Blanchard, who was reckoned a worthy, pious

---

1   Peter the Great (1672-1725) visited Britain in 1698 as part of a long fact-finding European excursion during which he studied, among other things, shipbuilding technologies.

divine, but quite of the moral cast, who joined us; and we three walked on, and rested together in the fields. My companion did not seem to like him, but, nevertheless, regarded him frequently with deep attention, and there were several times, while he seemed contemplating him, and trying to find out his thoughts, that his face became so like Mr. Blanchard's, that it was impossible to have distinguished the one from the other. The antipathy between the two was mutual, and discovered itself quite palpably in a short time. When my companion the prince was gone, Mr. Blanchard asked me anent him, and I told him that he was a stranger in the city, but a very uncommon and great personage. Mr. Blanchard's answer to me was as follows: "I never saw any body I disliked so much in my life, Mr. Robert; and if it be true that he is a stranger here, which I doubt, believe me he is come for no good."

"Do you not perceive what mighty powers of mind he is possessed of?" said I, "and also how clear and unhesitating he is on some of the most interesting points of divinity?"

"It is for his great mental faculties that I dread him," said he. "It is incalculable what evil such a person as he may do, if so disposed. There is a sublimity in his ideas, with which there is to me a mixture of terror; and when he talks of religion, he does it as one that rather dreads its truths than reverences them. He, indeed, pretends great strictness of orthodoxy regarding some of the points of doctrine embraced by the reformed church; but you do not seem to perceive, that both you and he are carrying these points to a dangerous extremity. Religion is a sublime and glorious thing, the bond of society on earth, and the connector of humanity with the Divine nature; but there is nothing so dangerous to man as the wresting of any of its principles, or forcing them beyond their due bounds: this is of all others the readiest way to destruction. Neither is there any thing so easily done. There is not an error into which a man can fall, which he may not press Scripture into his service as proof of the probity of, and though your boasted theologian shunned the full discussion of the subject before me, while you pressed it, I can easily see that both you and he are carrying your ideas of absolute predestination, and its concomitant appendages, to an extent that overthrows all religion and revelation together; or, at least, jumbles them into a chaos, out of which human capacity can never select what is good, Believe me, Mr. Robert, the less you associate with that illustrious stranger the better, for it appears to me that your creed and his carries damnation on the very front of it."

I was rather stunned at this; but I pretended to smile with disdain, and said, it did not become youth to control age; and, as I knew our principles differed fundamentally, it behoved us to drop the subject. He, however, would not drop it, but took both my principles and me fearfully to task, for Blanchard was an eloquent and powerful-minded old man; and, before we parted, I believe I promised to drop my new acquaintance, and was *all but* resolved to do it.

As well might I have laid my account with shunning the light of day. He was constant to me as my shadow, and by degrees he acquired such an ascendency over me, that I never was happy out of his company, nor greatly so in it. When I repeated to him all that Mr. Blanchard had said, his countenance kindled with indignation and rage; and then by degrees his eyes sunk inward, his brow lowered, so that I was awed, and withdrew my eyes from looking at him. A while afterward, as I was addressing him, I chanced to look him again in the face, and the sight of him made me start violently. He had made himself so like Mr. Blanchard, that I actually believed I had been addressing that gentleman, and that I had done so in some absence of mind that I could not account for. Instead of being amused at the quandary I was in, he seemed offended: indeed, he never was truly amused with any thing. And he then asked me sullenly, if I conceived such personages as he to have no other endowments than common mortals?

I said I never conceived that princes or potentates had any greater share of endowments than other men, and frequently not so much. He shook his head, and bade me think over the subject again; and there was an end of it. I certainly felt every day the more disposed to acknowledge such a superiority in him, and from all that I could gather, I had now no doubt that he was Peter of Russia. Every thing combined to warrant the supposition, and, of course, I resolved to act in conformity with the discovery I had made.

For several days the subject of Mr. Blanchard's doubts and doctrines formed the theme of our discourse. My friend deprecated them most devoutly; and then again he would deplore them, and lament the great evil that such a man might do among the human race. I joined with him in allowing the evil in its fullest latitude; and, at length, after he thought he had fully prepared my nature for such a trial of its powers and abilities, he proposed calmly that we two should make away with Mr. Blanchard. I was so shocked, that my bosom became as it were a void, and the beatings of my heart sounded loud and hollow in it; my breath cut, and my tongue and palate became dry and speechless. He mocked at my cowardice, and began a-reasoning on the matter with such powerful eloquence, that before we parted, I felt fully convinced that it was my bounden duty to slay Mr. Blanchard; but my will was far, very far from consenting to the deed.

Robert weak

I spent the following night without sleep, or nearly so; and the next morning, by the time the sun arose, I was again abroad, and in the company of my illustrious friend. The same subject was resumed, and again he reasoned to the following purport: That supposing me placed at the head of an army of Christian soldiers, all bent on putting down the enemies of the church, would I have any hesitation in destroying and rooting out these enemies?— None surely.—Well then, when I saw and was convinced, that here was an individual who was doing more detriment to the church of Christ on earth, than tens of thousands of such warriors were capable of doing, was it not my duty to cut him off, and save the elect? "He, who would be a champion in the cause of Christ and his Church, my brave young friend," added he, "must begin early, and no man can calculate to what an illustrious eminence small beginnings may lead. If the man Blanchard is worthy, he is only changing his situation for a better one; and if unworthy, it is better that one fall, than that a thousand souls perish. Let us be up and doing in our vocations. For me, my resolution is taken; I have but one great aim in this world, and I never for a moment lose sight of it."

I was obliged to admit the force of his reasoning; for though I cannot from memory repeat his words, his eloquence was of that overpowering nature, that the subtility of other men sunk before it; and there is also little doubt that the assurance I had that these words were spoken by a great potentate, who could raise me to the highest eminence, (provided that I entered into his extensive and decisive measures,) assisted mightily in dispelling my youthful scruples and qualms of conscience; and I thought moreover, that having such a powerful back friend to support me, I hardly needed to be afraid of the consequences. I consented! But begged a little time to think of it. He said the less one thought of a duty the better; and we parted.

But the most singular instance of this wonderful man's power over my mind was, that he had as complete influence over me by night as by day. All my dreams corresponded exactly with his suggestions; and when he was absent from me, still his arguments sunk deeper in my heart than even when he was present. I dreamed that night of a great triumph obtained, and though the whole scene was but dimly and confusedly defined in my vision, yet the overthrow and death of Mr. Blanchard was the first step by which I attained the eminent station I occupied. Thus, by dreaming of the event by night, and discoursing of it by day, it soon became so familiar to my mind, that I almost conceived it as done. It was resolved on: which was the first and greatest victory gained; for there was no difficulty in finding opportunities enow of cutting off a man, who, every good day, was to be found walking by himself in private grounds. I went and heard him preach for two days, and in fact I held his tenets scarcely short of blasphemy; they were such as I had never heard before, and his congregation, which was numerous, were turning up their ears and drinking in his doctrines with the utmost delight; for O, they suited their carnal natures and self-sufficiency to a hair! He was actually holding it forth, as a fact, that "it was every man's own blame if he was not saved!" What horrible misconstruction! And then he was alleging, and trying to prove from nature and reason, that no man ever was guilty of a sinful action, who might not have declined it had he so chosen! "Wretched controvertist!" thought I to myself an hundred times, "shall not the sword of the Lord be moved from its place of peace for such presumptuous and absurd testimonies as these!"

When I began to tell the prince about these false doctrines, to my astonishment I found that he had been in the church himself, and had every argument that the old divine had used *verbatim*; and he remarked on them with great concern, that these were not the tenets that corresponded with his views in society, and that he had agents in every city, and every land, exerting their powers to put them down. I asked, with great simplicity, "Are all your subjects Christians, prince?"

"All my European subjects are, or deem themselves so," returned he; "and they are the most faithful and true subjects I have."

Who could doubt, after this, that he was the Czar of Russia? I have nevertheless had reasons to doubt of his identity since that period, and which of my conjectures is right, I believe the God of heaven only knows, for I do not. I shall go on to write such things as I remember, and if any one shall ever take the trouble to read over these confessions, such a one will judge for himself. It will be observed, that since ever I fell in with this extraordinary person, I have written about him only, and I must continue to do so to the end of this memoir, as I have performed no great or interesting action in which he had not a principal share.

He came to me one day and said, "We must not linger thus in executing what we have resolved on. We have much before our hands to perform for the benefit of mankind, both civil as well as religious. Let us do what we have to do here, and then we must wend our way to other cities, and perhaps to other countries. Mr. Blanchard is to hold forth in the high church of Paisley[1] on Sunday next, on some particularly great occasion: this must be defeated; he must not go there. As he will be busy arranging his discourses, we may expect him to be walking by himself in Finnieston Dell the greater part of Friday and Saturday. Let us go and cut him off. What is the life of a man more than the life of a lamb, or any guiltless animal? It is not half so much, especially when we consider the immensity of the mischief this old fellow is working among our fellow-creatures. Can there be any doubt that it is the duty of one consecrated to God, to cut off such a mildew?"

"I fear me, great sovereign," said I, "that your ideas of retribution are too sanguine, and too arbitrary for the laws of this country. I dispute not that your motives are great and high; but have you debated the consequences, and settled the result?"

"I have," returned he, "and hold myself amenable for the action, to the laws of God and of equity; as to the enactments of men I despise them. Fain would I see the weapon of the Lord of Hosts, begin the work of vengeance that awaits it to do!"

I could not help thinking, that I perceived a little derision of countenance on his face as he said this, nevertheless I sunk dumb before such a man, and aroused myself to the task, seeing he would not have it deferred. I approved of it in theory, but my spirit stood aloof from the practice. I saw and was convinced that the elect of God would be happier, and purer, were the wicked and unbelievers all cut off from troubling and misleading them, but if it had not been the instigations of this illustrious stranger, I should never have presumed to begin so great a work myself. Yet, though he often aroused my zeal to the highest pitch, still my heart at times shrunk from the shedding of life-blood, and it was only at the earnest and unceasing instigations of my enlightened and voluntary patron, that I at length put my hand to the conclusive work. After I said all that I could say, and all had been overborne, (I remember my actions

---

1   A town near Glasgow.

and words as well as it had been yesterday,) I turned round hesitatingly, and looked up to Heaven for direction; but there was a dimness came over my eyes that I could not see. The appearance was as if there had been a veil drawn over me, so nigh that I put up my hand to feel it; and then Gil-Martin (as this great sovereign was pleased to have himself called,) frowned, and asked me what I was grasping at? I knew not what to say, but answered, with fear and shame, "I have no weapons, not one; nor know I where any are to be found."

"The God whom thou servest will provide these," said he; "if thou provest worthy of the trust committed to thee."

I looked again up into the cloudy veil that covered us, and thought I beheld golden weapons of every description let down in it, but all with their points towards me. I kneeled, and was going to stretch out my hand to take one, when my patron seized me, as I thought, by the clothes, and dragged me away with as much ease as I had been a lamb, saying, with a joyful and elevated voice,— "Come, my friend, let us depart: thou art dreaming—thou art dreaming. Rouse up all the energies of thy exalted mind, for thou art an highly-favoured one; and doubt thou not, that he whom *thou* servest, will be ever at thy right and left hand, to direct and assist thee."

These words, but particularly the vision I had seen, of the golden weapons descending out of Heaven, inflamed my zeal to that height that I was as one beside himself; which my parents perceived that night, and made some motions toward confining me to my room. I joined in the family prayers, and then I afterwards sung a psalm and prayed by myself; and I had good reasons for believing that that small oblation of praise and prayer was not turned to sin. But there are strange things, and unaccountable agencies in nature: He only who dwells between the Cherubim can unriddle them, and to him the honour must redound for ever. *Amen.*

I felt greatly strengthened and encouraged that night, and the next morning I ran to meet my companion, out of whose eye I had now no life. He rejoiced at seeing me so forward in the great work of reformation by blood, and said many things to raise my hopes of future fame and glory; and then, producing two pistols of pure beaten gold, he held them out and proffered me the choice of one, saying, "See what thy master hath provided thee!" I took one of them eagerly, for I perceived at once that they were two of the very weapons that were let down from Heaven in the cloudy veil, the dim tapestry of the firmament; and I said to myself, "Surely this is the will of the Lord."

The little splendid and enchanting piece was so perfect, so complete, and so ready for executing the will of the donor, that I now longed to use it in his service. I loaded it with my own hand, as Gil-Martin did the other, and we took our stations behind a bush of hawthorn and bramble on the verge of the wood, and almost close to the walk. My patron was so acute in all his calculations that he never mistook an event. We had not taken our stand above a minute and a half, till old Mr. Blanchard appeared, coming slowly on the path. When we saw this, we cowered down, and leaned each of us a knee upon the ground, pointing the pistols through the bush, with an aim so steady, that it was impossible to miss our victim.

He came deliberately on, pausing at times so long, that we dreaded he was going to turn. Gil-Martin dreaded it, and I said I did, but wished in my heart that he might. He, however, came onward, and I will never forget the manner in which he came! No—I don't believe I ever can forget it, either in the narrow bounds of time or the ages of eternity! He was a boardly ill-shaped man, of a rude exterior, and a little bent with age; his hands were clasped behind his back, and below his coat, and he walked with a slow swinging air that was very peculiar. When he paused and looked abroad on nature, the act was highly impressive: he seemed conscious of being all alone, and conversant only with God and the elements of his creation. Never was there such a picture of human inadvertency! a man approaching step by step to the one that was to hurl him out of one existence into another, with as much ease and indifference as the ox goeth to the stall. Hideous vision, wilt thou not be gone from my mental sight! If not, let me bear with thee as I can!

When he came straight opposite to the muzzles of our pieces, Gil-Martin called out "Eh!" with a short quick sound. The old man, without starting, turned his face and breast toward us, and looked into the wood, but looked over our heads. "Now!" whispered my companion, and fired. But my hand refused the office, for I was not at that moment sure about becoming an assassin in the cause of Christ and his Church. I thought I heard a sweet voice behind me, whispering me to beware, and I was going to look round, when my companion exclaimed, "Coward, we are ruined!"

I had no time for an alternative: Gil-Martin's ball had not taken effect, which was altogether wonderful, as the old man's breast was within a few yards of him. "Hilloa!" cried Blanchard; "what is that for, you dog!" and with that he came forward to look over the bush. I hesitated, as I said, and attempted to look behind me; but there was no time: the next step discovered two assassins lying in covert, waiting for blood. "Coward, we are ruined!" cried my indignant friend; and that moment my piece was discharged. The effect was as might have been expected: the old man first stumbled to one side, and then fell on his back. We kept our places, and I perceived my companion's eyes gleaming with an unnatural joy. The wounded man raised himself from the bank to a sitting posture, and I beheld his eyes swimming; he, however, appeared sensible, for we heard him saying in a low and rattling voice, "Alas, alas! whom have I offended, that they should have been driven to an act like this! Come forth and shew yourselves, that I may either forgive you before I die, or curse you in the name of the Lord." He then fell a-groping with both hands on the ground, as if feeling for something he had lost, manifestly in the agonies of death; and, with a solemn and interrupted prayer for forgiveness, he breathed his last.

I had become rigid as a statue, whereas my associate appeared to be elevated above measure. "Arise, thou faint-hearted one, and let us be going," said he. "Thou hast done well for once; but wherefore hesitate in such a cause? This is but a small beginning of so great a work as that of purging the Christian world. But the first victim is a worthy one, and more of such lights must be extinguished immediately." *light of God?*

We touched not our victim, nor any thing pertaining to him, for fear of staining our hands with his blood; and the firing having brought three men within view, who were hasting towards the spot, my undaunted companion took both the pistols, and went forward as with intent to meet them, bidding me shift for myself. I ran off in a contrary direction, till I came to the foot of the Pearman Sike, and then, running up the hollow of that, I appeared on the top of the bank as if I had been another man brought in view by hearing the shots in such a place. I had a full view of a part of what passed, though not of all. I saw my companion going straight to meet the men, apparently with a pistol in every hand, waving in a careless manner. They seemed not quite clear of meeting with him, and so he went straight on, and passed between them. They looked after him, and came onward; but when they came to the old man lying stretched in his blood, then they turned and pursued my companion, though not so quickly as they might have done; and I understood that from the first they saw no more of him.

Great was the confusion that day in Glasgow. The most popular of all their preachers of morality was (what they called) murdered in cold blood, and a strict and extensive search was made for the assassin. Neither of the accomplices was found, however, that is certain, nor was either of them so much as suspected; but another man was apprehended under circumstances that warranted suspicion.— This was one of the things that I witnessed in my life, which I never understood, and it surely was one of my patron's most dexterous tricks, for I must still say, what I have thought from the beginning, that like him there never was a man created. The young man who was taken up was a preacher; and it was proved that he had purchased fire arms in town, and gone out with them that morning. But the far greatest mystery of the whole was, that two of the men, out of the three who met my companion, swore, that that unfortunate preacher was the man whom they met with a pistol in each hand, fresh from the death of the old divine. The poor fellow made a confused speech himself, which there is not the least doubt was quite true; but it was laughed to scorn, and an expression of horror ran through both the hearers and jury. I heard the whole trial, and so did Gil-Martin; but we left the journeyman preacher to his fate, and from that time forth I have had no faith in the justice of criminal trials. If once a man is prejudiced on one side, he will swear any thing in support of such prejudice. I tried to expostulate with my mysterious friend on the horrid injustice of suffering this young man to die for our act, but the prince exulted in it more than the other, and said the latter was the most dangerous man of the two.

The alarm in and about Glasgow was prodigious. The country being divided into two political parties, the court and the country party, the former held meetings, issued proclamations, and offered rewards, ascribing all to the violence of party spirit, and deprecating the infernal measures of their opponents. I did not understand their political differences; but it was easy to see that the true Gospel preachers joined all on one side, and the upholders of pure morality and a blameless life on the other, so that this division proved a test to us, and it was forthwith resolved, that we two should pick out some of the leading men of this unsaintly and heterodox cabal, and cut them off one by one, as occasion should suit.

Now, the ice being broke, I felt considerable zeal in our great work, but pretended much more; and we might soon have kidnapped them all through the ingenuity of my patron, had not our next attempt miscarried, by some awkwardness or mistake of mine. The consequence was, that he was discovered fairly, and very nigh seized. I also was seen, and suspected so far, that my reverend father, my mother, and myself were examined privately. I denied all knowledge of the matter; and they held it in such a ridiculous light, and their conviction of the complete groundlessness of the suspicion was so perfect, that their testimony prevailed, and the affair was hushed. I was obliged, however, to walk circumspectly, and saw my companion the prince very seldom, who was prowling about every day, quite unconcerned about his safety. He was every day a new man, however, and needed not to be alarmed at any danger; for such a facility had he in disguising himself, that if it had not been for a pass-word which we had between us, for the purposes of recognition, I never could have known him myself.

It so happened that my reverend father was called to Edinburgh about this time, to assist with his council in settling the national affairs. At my earnest request I was permitted to accompany him, at which both my associate and I rejoiced, as we were now about to move in a new and extensive field. All this time I never knew where my illustrious friend resided. He never once invited me to call on him at his lodgings, nor did he ever come to our house, which made me sometimes to suspect, that if any of our great efforts in the cause of true religion were discovered, he intended leaving me in the lurch. Consequently, when we met in Edinburgh (for we travelled not in company) I proposed to go with him to look for lodgings, telling him at the same time what a blessed religious family my reverend instructor and I were settled in. He said he rejoiced at it, but he made a rule of never lodging in any particular house, but took these daily, or hourly, as he found it convenient, and that he never was at a loss in any circumstance.

"What a mighty trouble you put yourself to, great sovereign!" said I, "and all, it would appear, for the purpose of seeing and knowing more and more of the human race."

"I never go but where I have some great purpose to serve," returned he, "either in the advancement of my own power and dominion, or in thwarting my enemies."

"With all due deference to your great comprehension, my illustrious friend," said I, "it strikes me that you can accomplish very little either the one way or the other here, in the humble and private capacity you are pleased to occupy."

"It is your own innate modesty that prompts such a remark," said he. "Do you think the gaining of *you* to my service, is not an attainment worthy of being envied by the greatest potentate in Christendom? Before I had missed such a prize as the attainment of your services, I would have travelled over one half of the habitable globe."—I bowed with great humility, but at the same time how could I but feel proud and highly flattered? He continued. "Believe me, my dear friend, for such a prize I account no effort too high. For a man who is not only dedicated to the King of Heaven, in the most solemn manner, soul, body, and spirit, but also chosen of him from the beginning, justified, sanctified, and received into a communion that never shall be broken, and from which no act of his shall ever remove him,—the possession of such a man, I tell you, is worth kingdoms; because every deed that he performs, he does it with perfect safety to himself and honour to me."—I bowed again, lifting my hat, and he went on.—"I am now going to put his courage in the cause he has espoused, to a severe test—to a trial at which common nature would revolt, but he who is dedicated to be the sword of the Lord, must raise himself above common humanity. You have a father and a brother according to the flesh, what do you know of them?"

"I am sorry to say I know nothing good," said I. "They are reprobates, cast-aways, beings devoted to the wicked one, and, like him, workers of every species of iniquity with greediness."

"They must both fall!" said he, with a sigh and melancholy look: "It is decreed in the councils above, that they must both fall by your hand."

"The God of heaven forbid it!" said I. "They are enemies to Christ and his church, that I know and believe; but they shall live and die in their iniquity for me, and reap their guerdon[1] when their time cometh. There my hand shall not strike."

"The feeling is natural, and amiable," said he; "but you *must* think again. Whether are the bonds of carnal nature, or the bond, and vows of the Lord, strongest?"

"I will not reason with you on this head, mighty potentate," said I, "for whenever I do so it is but to be put down. I shall only express my determination, not to take vengeance out of the Lord's hand in this instance. It availeth not. These are men that have the

---

1 Reward

mark of the beast in their foreheads and right hands; they are lost beings themselves, but have no influence over others. Let them perish in their sins; for they shall not be meddled with by me."

"How preposterously you talk, my dear friend!" said he. "These people are your greatest enemies; they would rejoice to see you annihilated. And now that you have taken up the Lord's cause of being avenged on *his* enemies, wherefore spare those that are your own as well as his? Besides, you ought to consider what great advantages would be derived to the cause of righteousness and truth, were the estate and riches of that opulent house in your possession, rather than in that of such as oppose the truth and all manner of holiness."

This was a portion of the consequence of following my illustrious adviser's summary mode of procedure, that had never entered into my calculation—I disclaimed all idea of being influenced by it; however, I cannot but say that the desire of being enabled to do so much good, by the possession of these bad men's riches, made some impression on my heart, and I said I would consider of the matter. I did consider it, and that right seriously as well as frequently; and there was scarcely an hour in the day on which my resolves were not animated by my great friend, till at length I began to have a longing desire to kill my brother, in particular. Should any man ever read this scroll, he will wonder at this confession, and deem it savage and unnatural. So it appeared to me at first, but a constant thinking of an event changes every one of its features. I have done all for the best, and as I was prompted, by one who knew right and wrong much better that I did. I *had* a desire to slay him, it is true, and such a desire too as a thirsty man has to drink; but at the same time, this longing desire was mingled with a certain terror, as if I had dreaded that the drink for which I longed was mixed with deadly poison. My mind was so much weakened, or rather softened about this time, that my faith began a little to give way, and I doubted most presumptuously of the least tangible of all Christian tenets, namely, of *the infallibility of the elect*. I hardly comprehended the great work I had begun, and doubted of *my own* infallibility, or that of any created being. But I was brought over again by the unwearied diligence of my friend to repent of my backsliding, and view once more the superiority of the Almighty's counsels in its fullest latitude. *Amen.*

I prayed very much in secret about this time, and that with great fervor of spirit, as well as humility; and my satisfaction at finding all my requests granted is not to be expressed.

My illustrious friend still continuing to sound in my ears the imperious duty to which I was called, of making away with my sinful relations, and quoting many parallel actions out of the Scriptures, and the writings of the holy Fathers, of the pleasure the Lord took in such as executed his vengeance on the wicked, I was obliged to acquiesce in his measures, though with certain limitations. It was not easy to answer his arguments, and yet I was afraid that he soon perceived a leaning to his will on my part. "If the acts of Jehu, in rooting out the whole house of his master, were ordered and approved of by the Lord," said he, "would it not have been more praiseworthy if one of Ahab's[1] own sons had stood up for the cause of the God of Israel, and rooted out the sinners and their idols out of the land?"

"It would certainly," said I. "To our duty to God all other duties must yield."

"Go thou then and do likewise," said he. "Thou art called to a high vocation; to cleanse the sanctuary of thy God in this thy native land by the shedding of blood; go thou forth then like a ruling energy, a master spirit of desolation in the dwellings of the wicked, and high shall be your reward both here and hereafter."

My heart now panted with eagerness to look my brother in the face: On which my companion, who was never out of the way, conducted me to a small square in the suburbs of the city, where there were a number of young noblemen and gentlemen playing at a vain, idle, and sinful game, at which there was much of the language of the accursed going on; and among these blasphemers he instantly pointed out my brother to me. I was fired with indignation at seeing him in such company, and so employed; and I placed myself close beside him to watch all his motions, listen to his words, and draw inferences from what I saw and heard. In what a sink of sin was he wallowing! I resolved to take him to task, and if he refused to be admonished, to inflict on him some condign punishment; and knowing that my illustrious friend and director was looking on, I resolved to show some spirit. Accordingly, I waited until I heard him profane his Maker's name three times, and then, my spiritual indignation being roused above all restraint, I went up and kicked him. Yes, I went boldly up and struck him with my foot, and meant to have given him a more severe blow than it was my fortune to inflict.

---

1   King of Israel, 874–853 BC.

It had, however, the effect of rousing up his corrupt nature to quarrelling and strife, instead of taking the chastisement of the Lord in humility and meekness. He ran furiously against me in the choler that is always inspired by the wicked one; but I overthrew him, by reason of impeding the natural and rapid progress of his unholy feet, running to destruction. I also fell slightly; but his fall proving a severe one, he arose in wrath, and struck me with the mall which he held in his hand, until my blood flowed copiously; and from that moment I vowed his destruction in my heart. But I chanced to have no weapon at that time, nor any means of inflicting due punishment on the caitiff, which would not have been returned double on my head, by him and his graceless associates. I mixed among them at the suggestion of my friend, and following them to their den of voluptuousness and sin, I strove to be admitted among them, in hopes of finding some means of accomplishing my great purpose, while I found myself moved by the spirit within me so to do. But I was not only debarred, but, by the machinations of my wicked brother and his associates, cast into prison.

I was not sorry at being thus honoured to suffer in the cause of righteousness, and at the hands of sinful men; and as soon as I was alone, I betook myself to prayer, deprecating the long-suffering of God toward such horrid sinners. My jailer came to me, and insulted me. He was a rude unprincipled fellow, partaking much of the loose and carnal manners of the age; but I remembered of having read, in the Cloud of Witnesses,[1] of such men formerly, having been converted by the imprisoned saints; so I set myself, with all my heart, to bring about this man's repentance and reformation.

"Fat the deil are ye yoolling an' praying that gate for, man?" said he, coming angrily in. "I thought the days o' praying prisoners had been a' ower. We had rowth o' them aince; an' they were the poorest an' the blackest bargains that ever poor jailers saw. Gie up your crooning, or I'll pit you to an in-by place, where ye sall get plenty o't."

"Friend," said I, "I am making my appeal at that bar where all human actions are seen and judged, and where you shall not be forgot, sinful as you are. Go in peace, and let me be."

---

1   This book, collecting the last speeches and testaments of executed Covenanters, was in fact published anonymously in 1714, two years after the end of the Robert's confession. See Appendix A3.

"Hae ye naebody nearer-hand hame to mak your appeal to, man?" said he; "because an ye haena, I dread you an' me may be unco weel acquaintit by an' by?"

I then opened up the mysteries of religion to him in a clear and perspicuous manner, but particularly the great doctrine of the election of grace; and then I added, "Now, friend, you must tell me if you pertain to this chosen number. It is in every man's power to ascertain this, and it is every man's duty to do it."

"An' fat the better wad you be for the kenning o' this, man?" said he.

"Because, if you are one of my brethren, I will take you into sweet communion and fellowship," returned I; "but if you belong to the unregenerate, I have a commission to slay you."

"The deil you hae, callant!" said he, gaping and laughing. "An' pray now, fa was it that gae you siccan a braw commission?"

"My commission is sealed by the signet above," said I, "and that I will let you and all sinners know. I am dedicated to it by the most solemn vows and engagements. I am the sword of the Lord, and Famine and Pestilence are my sisters. Wo then to the wicked of this land, for they must fall down dead together, that the church may be purified!"

"Oo, foo, foo! I see how it is," said he; "yours is a very braw commission, but you will have the small opportunity of carrying it through here. Take my advising, and write a bit of a letter to your friends, and I will send it, for this is no place for such a great man. If you cannot steady your hand to write, as I see you have been at your great work, a word of a mouth may do; for I do assure you this is not the place at all, of any in the world, for your operations."

The man apparently thought I was deranged in my intellect. He could not swallow such great truths at the first morsel. So I took his advice, and sent a line to my reverend father, who was not long in coming, and great was the jailer's wonderment when he saw all the great Christian noblemen of the land sign my bond of freedom.

My reverend father took this matter greatly to heart, and bestirred himself in the good cause till the transgressors were ashamed to shew their faces. My illustrious companion was not idle: I wondered that he came not to me in prison, nor at my release; but he was better employed, in stirring up the just to the execution of God's decrees; and he succeeded so well, that my brother and all his associates had nearly fallen victims to their wrath: But many were wounded, bruised, and imprisoned, and much commotion prevailed in the city. For my part, I was greatly strengthened in my resolution by the anathemas of my reverend father, who, privately, (that is in a family capacity,) in his prayers, gave up my father and brother, according to the flesh, to Satan, making it plain to all my senses of perception, that they were beings given up of God, to be devoured by fiends or men, at their will and pleasure, and that *whosoever* should slay them, would do God good service.

The next morning my illustrious friend met me at an early hour, and he was greatly overjoyed at hearing my sentiments now chime so much in unison with his own. I said, "I longed for the day and the hour that I might look my brother in the face at Gil gal,[1] and visit on him the iniquity of his father and himself, for that I was now strengthened and prepared for the deed."

"I have been watching the steps and movements of the profligate one," said he; "and lo, I will take you straight to his presence. Let your heart be as the heart of the lion, and your arms strong as the shekels of brass, and swift to avenge as the bolt that descendeth from Heaven, for the blood of the just and the good hath long flowed in Scotland. But already is the day of their avengement begun; the hero is at length arisen, who shall send all such as bear enmity to the true church, or trust in works of their own, to Tophet!"[2]

Thus encouraged, I followed my friend, who led me directly to the same court in which I had chastised the miscreant on the foregoing day; and behold, there was the same group again assembled. They eyed me with terror in their looks, as I walked among them and eyed them with looks of disapprobation and rebuke; and I saw that the very eye of a chosen one lifted on these children of Belial, was sufficient to dismay and put them to flight. I walked aside to my friend, who stood at a distance looking on, and he said to me, "What thinkest thou now?" and I answered in the words of the venal prophet, "Lo now, if I had a sword into mine hand, I would even kill him."[3]

"Wherefore lackest thou it?" said he. "Dost thou not see that they tremble at thy presence, knowing that the avenger of blood is among them."

---

1 Joshua's camp, lying to the east of Jericho.
2 A place near Jerusalem where humans were ritually sacrificed.
3 The venal prophet is Balaam who says these words in Numbers 22:29 to an ass through which God has just spoken.

My heart was lifted up on hearing this, and again I strode into the midst of them, and eyeing them with threatening looks, they were so much confounded, that they abandoned their sinful pastime, and fled every one to his house!

This was a palpable victory gained over the wicked, and I thereby knew that the hand of the Lord was with me. My companion also exulted, and said, "Did not I tell thee? Behold thou dost not know one half of thy might, or of the great things thou art destined to do. Come with me and I will show thee more than this, for these young men cannot subsist without the exercises of sin. I listened to their councils, and I know where they will meet again."

Accordingly he led me a little farther to the south, and we walked aside till by degrees we saw some people begin to assemble; and in a short time we perceived the same group stripping off their clothes to make them more expert in the practice of madness and folly. Their game was begun before we approached, and so also were the oaths and cursing. I put my hands in my pockets, and walked with dignity and energy into the midst of them. It was enough: Terror and astonishment seized them. A few of them cried out against me, but their voices were soon hushed amid the murmurs of fear. One of them, in the name of the rest, then came and besought of me to grant them liberty to amuse themselves; but I refused peremptorily, dared the whole multitude so much as to touch me with one of their fingers, and dismissed them in the name of the Lord.

Again they all fled and dispersed at my eye, and I went home in triumph, escorted by my friend, and some well-meaning young Christians, who, however, had not learned to deport themselves with soberness and humility. But my ascendency over my enemies was great indeed; for wherever I appeared I was hailed with approbation, and wherever my guilty brother made his appearance, he was hooted and held in derision, till he was forced to hide his disgraceful head, and appear no more in public.

Immediately after this I was seized with a strange distemper, which neither my friends nor physicians could comprehend, and it confined me to my chamber for many days; but I knew, myself, that I was bewitched, and suspected my father's reputed concubine of the deed. I told my fears to my reverend protector, who hesitated concerning them, but I knew by his words and looks that he was conscious I was right. I generally conceived myself to be two people. When I lay in bed, I deemed there were two of us in it; when

I sat up, I always beheld another person, and always in the same position from the place where I sat or stood, which was about three paces off me towards my left side. It mattered not how many or how few were present: this my second self was sure to be present in his place; and this occasioned a confusion in all my words and ideas that utterly astounded my friends, who all declared, that instead of being deranged in my intellect, they had never heard my conversation manifest so much energy or sublimity of conception; but for all that, over the singular delusion that I was two persons, my reasoning faculties had no power. The most perverse part of it was, that I rarely conceived *myself* to be any of the two persons. I thought for the most part that my companion was one of them, and my brother the other; and I found, that to be obliged to speak and answer in the character of another man, was a most awkward business at the long run.

Who can doubt, from this statement, that I was bewitched, and that my relatives were at the ground of it? The constant and unnatural persuasion that I was my brother, proved it to my own satisfaction, and must, I think, do so to every unprejudiced person. This victory of the wicked one over me kept me confined in my chamber, at Mr. Millar's house, for nearly a month, until the prayers of the faithful prevailed, and I was restored. I knew it was a chastisement for my pride, because my heart was lifted up at my superiority over the enemies of the church; nevertheless, I determined to make short work with the aggressor, that the righteous might not be subjected to the effect of his diabolical arts again.

I say I was confined a month. I beg he that readeth to take note of this, that he may estimate how much the word, or even the oath, of a wicked man, is to depend on. For a month I saw no one but such as came into my room, and for all that, it will be seen, that there were plenty of the same set to attest upon oath that I saw my brother every day during that period; that I persecuted him with my presence day and night, while all the time I never saw his face, save in a delusive dream. I cannot comprehend what manoeuvres my illustrious friend was playing off with them about this time; for he, having the art of personating whom he chose, had peradventure deceived them, else so many of them had never all attested the same thing. I never saw any man so steady in his friendships and attentions as he; but as he made a rule of never calling at private houses, for fear of some discovery being made of his person, so I never saw him while my malady lasted; but as soon as I grew better, I knew I had nothing ado but to attend at some of our places of meeting, to see him again. He was punctual, as usual, and I had not to wait.

My reception was precisely as I apprehended. There was no flaring, no flummery, nor bombastical pretensions, but a dignified return to my obeisance, and an immediate recurrence, in converse, to the important duties incumbent on us, in our stations, as reformers and purifiers of the Church.

"I have marked out a number of most dangerous characters in this city," said he, "all of whom must be cut off from cumbering the true vineyard before we leave this land. And if you bestir not yourself in the work to which you are called, I must raise up others who shall have the honour of it."

"I am, most illustrious prince, wholly at your service," aid I. "Show but what ought to be done, and here is the heart to dare, and the hand to execute. You pointed out my relations, according to the flesh, as brands fitted to be thrown into the burning. I approve peremptorily of the award; nay, I thirst to accomplish it; for I myself have suffered severely from their diabolical arts. When once that trial of my devotion to the faith is accomplished, then be your future operations disclosed."

"You are free of your words and promises," said he.

"So will I be of my deeds in the service of my master, and that shalt thou see," said I. "I lack not the spirit, nor the will, but I lack experience wofully; and because of that shortcoming, must bow to your suggestions."

"Meet me here to-morrow betimes," said he, "and perhaps you may hear of some opportunity of displaying your zeal in the cause of righteousness."

I met him as he desired me; and he addressed me with a hurried and joyful expression, telling me that my brother was astir, and that a few minutes ago he had seen him pass on his way to the mountain. "The hill is wrapped in a cloud," added he, "and never was there such an opportunity of executing divine justice on a guilty sinner. You may trace him in the dew, and shall infallibly find him on the top of some precipice; for it is only in secret that he dares show his debased head to the sun."

"I have no arms, else assuredly I would pursue him and discomfit him," said I.

"Here is a small dagger," said he; "I have nothing of weapon-kind about me save that, but it is a potent one; and should you require it, there is nothing more ready or sure."

"Will not you accompany me?" said I: "Sure you will?"

"I will be with you, or near you," said he. "Go you on before."

I hurried away as he directed me, and imprudently asked some of Queensberry's guards if such and such a young man passed by them going out from the city. I was answered in the affirmative, and till then had doubted of my friend's intelligence, it was so inconsistent with a profligate's life to be so early astir. When I got the certain intelligence that my brother was before me, I fell a-running, scarcely knowing what I did; and looking several times behind me, I perceived nothing of my zealous and arbitrary friend. The consequence of this was, that by the time I reached St. Antho-ny's well,[1] my resolution began to give way. It was not my courage, for now that I had once shed blood in the cause of the true faith, I was exceedingly bold and ardent; but whenever I was left to myself, I was subject to sinful doubtings. These always hankered on one point: I doubted if the elect were infallible, and if the Scripture promises to them were binding in all situations and relations. I confess this, and that it was a sinful and shameful weakness in me, but my nature was subject to it, and I could not eschew it. I never doubted that I was one of the elect myself; for, besides the strong inward and spiritual conviction that I possessed, I had my kind father's assurance; and these had been revealed to him in that way and measure that they could not be doubted.

In this desponding state, I sat myself down on a stone, and bethought me of the rashness of my understanding. I tried to ascertain, to my own satisfaction, whether or not I really had been commissioned of God to perpetrate these crimes in his behalf, for in the eyes, and by the laws of men, they were great and crying transgressions. While I sat pondering on these things, I was involved in a veil of white misty vapour, and looking up to heav-en, I was just about to ask direction from above, when I heard as it were a still small voice[2] close by me, which uttered some words of

---

1 The ruins of a 15th century chapel and well on a crag above Holyrood Park.

2 Douglas Mack suggests that Hogg lifted this phrase from 1 Kings 19:12, where God speaks to the prophet Elijah in "a still small voice." He goes on to argue that "Hogg's contemporaries would have immediately recognised the Bibical reference, and would have understood it as an indication that the vision of the lady robed in white is of Heavenly origin" ("The Rage of Fanaticism in Former Days" 47).

derision and chiding. I looked intensely in the direction whence it seemed to come, and perceived a lady, robed in white, who hasted toward me. She regarded me with a severity of look and gesture that appalled me so much, I could not address her; but she waited not for that, but coming close to my side, said, without stopping, "Preposterous wretch! how dare you lift your eyes to heaven with such purposes in your heart? Escape homeward, and save your soul, or farewell for ever!"

These were all the words that she uttered, as far as I could ever recollect, but my spirits were kept in such a tumult that morning, that something might have escaped me. I followed her eagerly with my eyes, but in a moment she glided over the rocks above the holy well, and vanished. I persuaded myself that I had seen a vision, and that the radiant being that had addressed me was one of the good angels, or guardian spirits, commissioned by the Almighty to watch over the steps of the just. My first impulse was to follow her advice, and make my escape home; for I thought to myself, "How is this interested and mysterious foreigner, a proper judge of the actions of a free Christian?"

The thought was hardly framed, nor had I moved in a retrograde direction six steps, when I saw my illustrious friend and great adviser descending the ridge towards me with hasty and impassioned strides. My heart fainted within me; and when he came up and addressed me, I looked as one caught in a trespass. "What hath detained thee, thou desponding trifler?" said he. "Verily now shall the golden opportunity be lost which may never be recalled. I have traced the reprobate to his sanctuary in the cloud, and lo he is perched on the pinnacle of a precipice an hundred fathoms high. One ketch with thy foot, or toss with thy finger, shall throw him from thy sight into the foldings of the cloud, and he shall be no more seen, till found at the bottom of the cliff dashed to pieces. Make haste therefore, thou loiterer, if thou wouldst ever prosper and rise to eminence in the work of thy Lord and master."

"I go no farther on this work," said I, "for I have seen a vision that has reprimanded the deed."

"A vision?" said he: "Was it that wench who descended from the hill?"

"The being that spake to me, and warned me of my danger, was indeed in the form of a lady," said I.

"She also approached me and said a few words," returned he; "and I thought there was something mysterious in her manner.

Pray, what did she say? for the words of such a singular message, and from such a messenger, ought to be attended to. If I understood her aright, she was chiding us for our misbelief and preposterous delay."

I recited her words, but he answered that I had been in a state of sinful doubting at the time, and it was to these doubtings she had adverted. In short, this wonderful and clear-sighted stranger soon banished all my doubts and despondency, making me utterly ashamed of them, and again I set out with him in the pursuit of my brother. He showed me the traces of his footsteps in the dew, and pointed out the spot where I should find him. "You have nothing more to do than go softly down behind him," said he; "which you can do to within an ell of him, without being seen; then rush upon him, and throw him from his seat, where there is neither footing nor hold. I will go, meanwhile, and amuse his sight by some exhibition in the contrary direction, and he shall neither know nor perceive who has done him this *kind office*: for, exclusive of more weighty concerns, be assured of this, that the sooner he falls, the fewer crimes will he have to answer for, and his estate in, the other world will be proportionally more tolerable, than if he spent a long unregenerate life steeped in iniquity to the loathing of the soul."

"Nothing can be more plain or more pertinent," said I: "therefore I fly to perform that which is both a duty toward God and toward man!"

"You shall yet rise to great honour and preferment," said he.

"I value it not, provided I do honour and justice to the cause of my master here," said I.

"You shall be lord of your father's riches and demesnes," added he.

"I disclaim and deride every selfish motive thereto relating," said I, "farther than as it enables me to do good."

"Ay, but that is a great and a heavenly consideration, *that longing for ability to do good*," said he;—and as he said so, I could not help remarking a certain derisive exultation of expression which I could not comprehend; and indeed I have noted this very often in my illustrious friend, and sometimes mentioned it civilly to him, but he has never failed to disclaim it. On this occasion I said nothing, but concealing his poniard in my clothes, I hasted up the mountain, determined to execute my purpose before any misgivings should again visit me; and I never had more ado, than in keeping firm my resolution. I could not help my thoughts, and there are

certain trains and classes of thoughts that have great power in ener-
vating the mind. I thought of the awful thing of plunging a fellow
creature from the top of a cliff into the dark and misty void
below—of his being dashed to pieces on the protruding rocks, and
of hearing his shrieks as he descended the cloud, and beheld the
shagged points on which he was to alight. Then I thought of
plunging a soul so abruptly into hell, or, at the best, sending it to
hover on the confines of that burning abyss—of its appearance at
the bar of the Almighty to receive its sentence. And then I thought,
"Will there not be a sentence pronounced against me there, by a
jury of the just made perfect, and written down in the registers of
heaven?"

These thoughts, I say, came upon me unasked, and instead of
being able to dispel them, they mustered, upon the summit of my
imagination, in thicker and stronger array: and there was another
that impressed me in a very particular manner, though, I have reason to believe, not so strongly as those above written. It was this:
"What if I should fail in my first effort? Will the consequence not
be that I am tumbled from the top of the rock myself?" and then
all the feelings anticipated, with regard to both body and soul, must
happen to me! This was a spine-breaking reflection; and yet,
though the probability was rather on that side, my zeal in the cause
of godliness was such that it carried me on, maugre all danger and
dismay.

I soon came close upon my brother, sitting on the dizzy pinnacle, with his eyes fixed stedfastly in the direction opposite to me. I
descended the little green ravine behind him with my feet foremost, and every now and then raised my head, and watched his
motions. His posture continued the same, until at last I came so
near him I could have heard him breathe, if his face had been
towards me. I laid my cap aside, and made me ready to spring upon
him, and push him over. I could not for my life accomplish it! I do
not think it was that I durst not, for I have always felt my courage
equal to any thing in a good cause. But I had not the heart, or
something that I ought to have had. In short, it was not done in
time, as it easily might have been. These THOUGHTS are hard
enemies wherewith to combat! And I was so grieved that I could
not effect my righteous purpose, that I laid me down on my face
and shed tears. Then, again, I thought of what my great enlightened
friend and patron would say to me, and again my resolution rose
indignant, and indissoluble save by blood. I arose on my right knee
and left foot, and had just begun to advance the latter forward: the

next step my great purpose had been accomplished, and the culprit had suffered the punishment due to his crimes. But what moved him I knew not: in the critical moment he sprung to his feet, and dashing himself furiously against me, he overthrew me, at the imminent peril of my life. I disencumbered myself by main force, and fled, but he overhied me, knocked me down, and threatened, with dreadful oaths, to throw me from the cliff. After I was a little recovered from the stunning blow, I aroused myself to the combat; and though I do not recollect the circumstances of that deadly scuffle very minutely, I know that I vanquished him so far as to force him to ask my pardon, and crave a reconciliation. I spurned at both, and left him to the chastisements of his own wicked and corrupt heart.

My friend met me again on the hill, and derided me, in a haughty and stern manner, for my imbecility and want of decision. I told him how nearly I had effected my purpose, and excused myself as well as I was able. On this, seeing me bleeding, he advised me to swear the peace against my brother, and have him punished in the mean time, he being the first aggressor. I promised compliance, and we parted, for I was somewhat ashamed of my failure, and was glad to be quit for the present of one of whom I stood so much in awe.

When my reverend father beheld me bleeding a second time by the hand of a brother, he was moved to the highest point of displeasure; and, relying on his high interest and the justice of his cause, he brought the matter at once before the courts. My brother and I were first examined face to face. His declaration was a mere romance: mine was not the truth; but as it was by the advice of my reverend father, and that of my illustrious friend, both of whom I knew to be sincere Christians and true believers, that I gave it, I conceived myself completely justified on that score. I said, I had gone up into the mountain early on the morning to pray, and had withdrawn myself, for entire privacy, into a little sequestered dell—had laid aside my cap, and was in the act of kneeling, when I was rudely attacked by my brother, knocked over, and nearly slain. They asked my brother if this was true. He acknowledged that it was; that I was bare-headed, and in the act of kneeling when he ran foul of me without any intent of doing so. But the judge took him to task on the improbability of this, and put the profligate sore out of countenance. The rest of his tale told still worse, insomuch that he was laughed at by all present, for the judge remarked to him, that granting it was true that he had at first run against me on an open mountain, and overthrown me by accident, how was it, that after I had extricated myself and fled, that he had pursued, overtaken, and knocked me down a second time? Would he pretend that all that was likewise by chance? The culprit had nothing to say for himself on this head, and I shall not forget my exultation and that of my reverend father, when the sentence of the judge was delivered. It was, that my wicked brother should be thrown into prison, and tried on a criminal charge of assault and battery, with the intent of committing murder. This was a just and righteous judge, and saw things in their proper bearings, that is, he could discern between a righteous and a wicked man, and then there could be no doubt as to which of the two were acting right, and which wrong.

Had I not been sensible that a justified person could do nothing wrong, I should not have been at my ease concerning the statement I had been induced to give on this occasion. I could easily perceive, that by rooting out the weeds from the garden of the Church, I heightened the growth of righteousness; but as to the tardy way of giving false evidence on matters of such doubtful issue, I confess I saw no great propriety in it from the beginning. But I now only moved by the will and mandate of my illustrious friend: I had no peace or comfort when out of his sight, nor have I ever been able to boast of much in his presence; so true is it that a Christian's life is one of suffering.

My time was now much occupied, along with my reverend preceptor, in making ready for the approaching trial, as the prosecutors. Our counsel assured us of a complete victory, and that banishment would be the mildest award of the law on the offender. Mark how different was the result! From the shifts and ambiguities of a wicked Bench, who had a fellow-feeling of iniquity with the defenders,—my suit was cast, the graceless libertine was absolved, and I was incarcerated, and bound over to keep the peace, with heavy penalties, before I was set at liberty.

I was exceedingly disgusted at this issue, and blamed the counsel of my friend to his face. He expressed great grief, and expatiated on the wickedness of our judicatories, adding, "I see I cannot depend on you for quick and summary measures, but for your sake I shall be revenged on that wicked judge, and that you shall see in a few days." The Lord Justice Clerk died that same week! But he died in his own house and his own bed, and by what means my friend effected it, I do not know. He would not tell me a single word of the matter, but the judge's sudden death made a great noise, and I made so many curious inquiries regarding the particulars of it, that some suspicions were like to attach to our family, of some unfair means used. For my part I know nothing, and rather think he died by the visitation of Heaven, and that my friend had foreseen it, by symptoms, and soothed me by promises of complete revenge.

completely out of touch w/ reality

It was some days before he mentioned my brother's meditated death to me again, and certainly he then found me exasperated against him personally to the highest degree. But I told him that I could not now think any more of it, owing to the late judgment of the court, by which, if my brother were missing or found dead, I would not only forfeit my life, but my friends would be ruined by the penalties.

"I suppose you know and believe in the perfect safety of your soul," said he, "and that that is a matter settled from the beginning of time, and now sealed and ratified both in heaven and earth?"

"I believe in it thoroughly and perfectly," said I; "and whenever I entertain doubts of it, I am sensible of sin and weakness."

"Very well, so then am I," said he. "I think I can now divine, with all manner of certainty, what will be the high and merited guerdon of your immortal part. Hear me then farther: I give you my solemn assurance, and bond of blood, that no human hand shall ever henceforth be able to injure your life, or shed one drop of your precious blood, but it is on the condition that you walk always by my directions."

"I will do so with cheerfulness," said I; "for without your enlightened counsel, I feel that I can do nothing. But as to your power of protecting my life, you must excuse me for doubting of it. Nay, were we in your own proper dominions, you could not ensure that."

"In whatever dominion or land I am, my power accompanies me," said he; "and it is only against human might and human weapon that I ensure your life; on that will I keep an eye, and on that you may depend. I have never broken word or promise with you. Do you credit me?"

"Yes, I do," said I; "for I see you are in earnest. I believe, though I do not comprehend you."

"Then why do you not at once challenge your brother to the field of honour? Seeing you now act without danger, cannot you also act without fear?"

"It is not fear," returned I; "believe me, I hardly know what fear is. It is a doubt, that on all these emergencies constantly haunts my mind, that in performing such and such actions I may fall from my upright state. This makes fratricide a fearful task."

"This is imbecility itself," said he. "We have settled, and agreed on that point an hundred times. I would therefore advise that you challenge your brother to single combat. I shall ensure your safety, and he cannot refuse giving you satisfaction."

"But then the penalties?" said I.

"We will try to evade these," said he; "and supposing you should be caught, if once you are Laird of Dalcastle and Balgrennan, what are the penalties to you?"

"Might we not rather pop him off in private and quietness, as we did the deistical divine?" said I.

"The deed would be alike meritorious, either way," said he. "But may we not wait for years before we find an opportunity? My advice is to challenge him, as privately as you will, and there cut him off."

"So be it then," said I. "When the moon is at the full, I will send for him forth to speak with one, and there will I smite him and slay him, and he shall trouble the righteous no more."

"Then this is the very night," said he. "The moon is nigh to the full, and this night your brother and his sinful mates hold carousal; for there is an intended journey to-morrow. The exulting profligate leaves town, where we must remain till the time of my departure hence; and then is he safe, and must live to dishonour God, and not only destroy his own soul, but those of many others. Alack, and wo is me! The sins that he and his friends will commit this very night, will cry to heaven against us for our shameful delay! When shall our great work of cleansing the sanctuary be finished, if we proceed at this puny rate?"

"I see the deed *must* be done, then," said I; "and since it is so, it shall be done. I will arm myself forthwith, and from the midst of his wine and debauchery you shall call him forth to me, and there will I smite him with the edge of the sword, that our great work be not retarded."

"If thy execution were equal to thy intent, how great a man you soon might be!" said he. "We shall make the attempt once more; and if it fail again, why, I must use other means to bring about my high purposes relating to mankind.—Home and make ready. I will go and procure what information I can regarding their motions, and will meet you in disguise twenty minutes hence, at the first turn of Hewie's lane beyond the loch."

"I have nothing to make ready," said I; "for I do not choose to go home. Bring me a sword, that we may consecrate it with prayer and vows, and if I use it not to the bringing down of the wicked and profane, then may the Lord do so to me, and more also!"

We parted, and there was I left again to the multiplicity of my own thoughts for the space of twenty minutes, a thing my friend never failed in subjecting me to, and these were worse to contend with than hosts of sinful men. I prayed inwardly, that these deeds of mine might never be brought to the knowledge of men who were incapable of appreciating the high motives that led to them; and then I sung part of the 10th Psalm,[1] likewise in spirit; but for all these efforts, my sinful doubts returned, so that when my illustrious friend joined me, and proffered me the choice of two gilded rapiers, I declined accepting any of them, and began, in a very bold and energetic manner, to express my doubts regarding the justification of all the deeds of perfect men. He chided me severely, and branded me with cowardice, a thing that my nature never was subject to; and then he branded me with falsehood, and breach of the most solemn engagements both to God and man.

I was compelled to take the rapier, much against my inclination; but for all the arguments, threats, and promises that he could use, I would not consent to send a challenge to my brother by his mouth. There was one argument only that he made use of which had some weight with me, but yet it would not preponderate. He told me my brother was gone to a notorious and scandalous habitation of women, and that if I left him to himself for ever so short a space longer, it might embitter his state through ages to come. This was a trying concern to me; but I resisted it, and reverted to my doubts. On this he said that he had meant to do me honour, but since I put it out of his power, he would do the deed, and take the responsibility on himself. "I have with sore travail procured a guardship of your life," added he. "For my own, I have not; but, be that as it will, I shall not be baffled in my attempts to benefit my friends without a trial. You will at all events accompany me, and see that I get justice?"

"Certes, I will do thus much," said I; "and wo be to him if his arm prevail against my friend and patron!"

His lip curled with a smile of contempt, which I could hardly brook; and I began to be afraid that the eminence to which I had been destined by him was already fading from my view. And I

---

1 The Psalmist prays that God's wrath might fall on the "wicked man" and "heathen people" who beset the humble, righteous believer.

thought what I should then do to ingratiate myself again with him, for without his countenance I had no life. "I will be a man in act," thought I, "but in sentiment I will not yield, and for this he must surely admire me the more."

As we emerged from the shadowy lane into the fair moonshine, I started so that my whole frame underwent the most chilling vibrations of surprise. I again thought I had been taken at unawares, and was conversing with another person. My friend was equipped in the Highland garb, and so completely translated into another being, that, save by his speech, all the senses of mankind could not have recognized him. I blessed myself, and asked whom it was his pleasure to personify to-night? He answered me carelessly, that it was a spark whom he meant should bear the blame of whatever might fall out to-night; and that was all that passed on the subject.

We proceeded by some stone steps at the foot of the North Loch, in hot argument all the way. I was afraid that our conversation might be overheard, for the night was calm and almost as light as day, and we saw sundry people crossing us as we advanced. But the zeal of my friend was so high, that he disregarded all danger, and continued to argue fiercely and loudly on my delinquency, as he was pleased to call it. I stood on one argument alone, which was, "that I did not think the Scripture promises to the elect, taken in their utmost latitude, warranted the assurance that they could do no wrong; and that, therefore, it behoved every man to look well to his steps."

There was no religious scruple that irritated my enlightened friend and master so much as this. He could not endure it. And the sentiments of our great covenanted reformers being on his side, there is not a doubt that I was wrong. He lost all patience on hearing what I advanced on this matter, and taking hold of me, he led me into a darksome booth in a confined entry; and, after a friendly but cutting reproach, he bade me remain there in secret and watch the event; "and if I fall," said he, "you will not fail to avenge my death?"

I was so entirely overcome with vexation that I could make no answer, on which he left me abruptly, a prey to despair; and I saw or heard no more, till he came down to the moonlight green followed by my brother. They had quarrelled before they came within my hearing, for the first words I heard were those of my brother, who was in a state of intoxication, and he was urging a reconciliation, as was his wont on such occasions. My friend spurned at the suggestion, and dared him to the combat; and after a good deal of boastful altercation, which the turmoil of my spirits prevented me from remembering, my brother was compelled to draw his sword and stand on the defensive. It was a desperate and terrible engagement. I at first thought that the royal stranger and great champion of the faith would overcome his opponent with ease, for I considered heaven as on his side, and nothing but the arm of sinful flesh against him. But I was deceived: The sinner stood firm as a rock, while the assailant flitted about like a shadow, or rather like a spirit. I smiled inwardly, conceiving that these lightsome manoeuvres were all a sham to show off his art and mastership in the exercise, and that whenever they came to close fairly, that instant my brother would be overcome. Still I was deceived: My brother's arm seemed invincible, so that the closer they fought the more palpably did it prevail. They fought round the green to the very edge of the water, and so round, till they came close up to the covert where I stood. There being no more room to shift ground, my brother then forced him to come to close quarters, on which, the former still having the decided advantage, my friend quitted his sword, and called out. I could resist no longer; so, springing from my concealment, I rushed between them with my sword drawn, and parted them as if they had been two schoolboys: then turning to my brother, I addressed him as follows:—"Wretch! miscreant! knowest thou what thou art attempting? Wouldst thou lay thine hand on the Lord's anointed, or shed his precious blood? Turn thee to me, that I may chastise thee for all thy wickedness, and not for the many injuries thou hast done to me!" To it we went, with full thirst of vengeance on every side. The duel was fierce; but the might of heaven prevailed, and not my might. The ungodly and reprobate young man fell, covered with wounds, and with curses and blasphemy in his mouth, while I escaped uninjured. Thereto his power extended not.

I will not deny, that my own immediate impressions of this affair in some degree differed from this statement. But this is precisely as my illustrious friend described it to me afterwards, and I can rely implicitly on his information, as he was at that time a looker-on, and my senses all in a state of agitation, and he could have no motive for saying what was not the positive truth.

Never till my brother was down did we perceive that there had been witnesses to the whole business. Our ears were then astounded by rude challenges of unfair play, which were quite appalling to me; but my friend laughed at them, and conducted me off in perfect safety. As to the unfairness of the transaction, I can say thus much, that my royal friend's sword was down ere ever mine was presented. But if it still be accounted unfair to take up a conqueror, and punish him in his own way, I answer: That if a man is sent on a positive mission by his master, and hath laid himself under vows to do his work, he ought not to be too nice in the means of accomplishing it; and farther, I appeal to holy writ, wherein many instances are recorded of the pleasure the Lord takes in the final extinction of the wicked and profane; and this position I take to be unanswerable.

I was greatly disturbed in my mind for many days, knowing that the transaction had been witnessed, and sensible also of the perilous situation I occupied, owing to the late judgment of the court against me. But, on the contrary, I never saw my enlightened friend in such high spirits. He assured me there was no danger; and again repeated, that he warranted my life against the power of man. I thought proper, however, to remain in hiding for a week; but, as he said, to my utter amazement, the blame fell on another, who was not only accused, but pronounced guilty by the general voice, and outlawed for non-appearance! how could I doubt, after this, that the hand of heaven was aiding and abetting me? The matter was beyond my comprehension; and as for my friend, he never explained any thing that was past, but his activity and art were without a parallel.

He enjoyed our success mightily; and for his sake I enjoyed it somewhat, but it was on account of his comfort only, for I could not for my life perceive in what degree the church was better or purer than before these deeds were done. He continued to flatter me with great things, as to honours, fame, and emolument; and, above all, with the blessing and protection of him to whom my body and soul were dedicated. But after these high promises, I got no longer peace; for he began to urge the death of my father with such an unremitting earnestness, that I found I had nothing for it but to comply. I did so; and cannot express his enthusiasm of approbation. So much did he hurry and press me in this, that I was forced to devise some of the most openly violent measures, having no alternative. Heaven spared me the deed, taking, in that instance, the vengeance in its own hand; for before my arm could effect the sanguine but meritorious act, the old man followed his son to the grave. My illustrious and zealous friend seemed to regret this somewhat; but he comforted himself with the reflection, that still I had the merit of it, having not only consented to it, but in fact effected it, for by doing the one action I had brought about both.

No sooner were the obsequies of the funeral over, than my friend and I went to Dalcastle, and took undisputed possession of the houses, lands, and effects that had been my father's; but his plate, and vast treasures of ready money, he had bestowed on a voluptuous and unworthy creature, who had lived long with him as a mistress. Fain would I have sent her after her lover, and gave my friend some hints on the occasion; but he only shook his head, and said that we must lay all selfish and interested motives out of the question.

For a long time, when I awaked in the morning, I could not believe my senses, that I was indeed the undisputed and sole proprietor of so much wealth and grandeur; and I felt so much gratified, that I immediately set about doing all the good I was able, hoping to meet with all approbation and encouragement from my friend. I was mistaken: He checked the very first impulses towards such a procedure, questioned my motives, and uniformly made them out to be wrong. There was one morning that a servant said to me, there was a lady in the back chamber who wanted to speak with me, but he could not tell me who it was, for all the old servants had left the mansion, every one on hearing of the death of the late laird, and those who had come knew none of the people in the neighbourhood. From several circumstances, I had suspicions of private confabulations[1] with women, and refused to go to her, but bid the servant inquire what she wanted. She would not tell; she could only state the circumstances to me; so I, being sensible that a little dignity of manner became me in my elevated situation, returned for answer, that if it was business that could not be transacted by my steward, it must remain untransacted. The answer which the servant brought back was of a threatening nature. She stated that she *must* see me, and if I refused her satisfaction there, she would compel it where I should not evite her.

My friend and director appeared pleased with my dilemma, and rather advised that I should hear what the woman had to say; on which I consented, provided she would deliver her mission in his presence. She came in with manifest signs of anger and indignation, and began with a bold and direct charge against me of a shameful assault on one of her daughters; of having used the basest of means in order to lead her aside from the paths of rectitude; and

---

1   Conversations.

on the failure of these, of having resorted to the most unqualified measures.

I denied the charge in all its bearings, assuring the dame that I had never so much as seen either of her daughters to my knowledge, far less wronged them; on which she got into great wrath, and abused me to my face as an accomplished vagabond, hypocrite, and sensualist; and she went so far as to tell me roundly, that if I did not *marry* her daughter, she would bring me to the gallows, and that in a very short time.

"Marry your daughter, honest woman!" said I, "on the faith of a Christian, I never saw your daughter; and you may rest assured in this, that I will neither marry you nor her. Do you consider how short a time I have been in this place? How much that time has been occupied? And how there was even a *possibility* that I could have accomplished such villainies?"

"And how long does your Christian reverence suppose you have remained in this place since the late laird's death?" said she.

"That is too well known to need recapitulation," said I: "only a very few days, though I cannot at present specify the exact number; perhaps from thirty to forty, or so. But in all that time, certes, I have never seen either you or any of your two daughters that you talk of. You must be quite sensible of that."

My friend shook his head three times during this short sentence, while the woman held up her hands in amazement and disgust, exclaiming, "There goes the self-righteous one! There goes the consecrated youth, who cannot err! You, sir, know, and the world shall know of the faith that is in this most just, devout, and religious miscreant! Can you deny that you have already been in this place four months and seven days? Or that in that time you have been forbid my house twenty times? Or that you have persevered in your endeavours to effect the basest and most ungenerous of purposes? Or that you have attained them? hypocrite and deceiver as you are! Yes, sir; I say, dare you deny that you *have* attained your vile, selfish, and degrading purposes towards a young, innocent, and unsuspecting creature, and thereby ruined a poor widow's only hope in this world? No, you cannot look in my face, and deny aught of this."

"The woman is raving mad!" said I. "You, illustrious sir, know, that in the first instance, I have not yet been in this place *one* month." My friend shook his head again, and answered me, "You are wrong, my dear friend; you are wrong. It is indeed the space of time that the lady hath stated, to a day, since you came here, and I came with you; and I am sorry that I know for certain that you have been frequently haunting her house, and have often had private correspondence with one of the young ladies too. Of the nature of it I presume not to know."

"You are mocking me," said I. "But as well may you try to reason me out of my existence, as to convince me that I have been here even one month, or that any of those things you allege against me has the shadow of truth or evidence to support it. I will swear to you, by the great God that made me; and by——"

"Hold, thou most abandoned profligate!" cried she violently, "and do not add perjury to your other detestable crimes. Do not, for mercy's sake, any more profane that name whose attributes you have wrested and disgraced. But tell me what reparation you propose offering to my injured child?"

"I again declare, before heaven, woman, that to the best of my knowledge and recollection, I never saw your daughter. I now think I have some faint recollection of having seen your face, but where, or in what place, puzzles me quite."

"And, why?" said she. "Because for months and days you have been in such a state of extreme inebriety, that your time has gone over like a dream that has been forgotten. I believe, that from the day you came first to my house, you have been in a state of utter delirium, and that principally from the fumes of wine and ardent spirits."

"It is a manifest falsehood!" said I; "I have never, since I entered on the possession of Dalcastle, tasted wine or spirits, saving once, a few evenings ago; and, I confess to my shame, that I was led too far; but I have craved forgiveness and obtained it. I take my noble and distinguished friend there for a witness to the truth of what I assert; a man who has done more, and sacrificed more for the sake of genuine Christianity, than any this world contains. Him you will believe."

"I hope you have attained forgiveness," said he, seriously. "Indeed it would be next to blasphemy to doubt it. But, of late, you have been very much addicted to intemperance. I doubt if, from the first night you tasted the delights of drunkenness, that you have ever again been in your right mind until Monday last. Doubtless you have been for a good while most diligent in your addresses to this lady's daughter."

"This is unaccountable," said I. "It is impossible that I can have been doing a thing, and not doing it at the same time. But indeed, honest woman, there have several incidents occurred to me in the course of my life which persuade me I have a second self; or that there is some other being who appears in my likeness."

Here my friend interrupted me with a sneer, and a hint that I was talking insanely; and then he added, turning to the lady, "I know my friend Mr. Colwan will do what is just and right. Go and bring the young lady to him, that he may see her, and he will then recollect all his former amours with her."

"I humbly beg your pardon, sir," said I. "But the mention of such a thing as *amours* with any woman existing, to me, is really so absurd, so far from my principles, so far from the purity of nature and frame to which I was born and consecrated, that I hold it as an insult, and regard it with contempt."

I would have said more in reprobation of such an idea, had not my servant entered, and said, that a gentleman wanted to see me on business. Being glad of an opportunity of getting quit of my lady visitor, I ordered the servant to show him in; and forthwith a little lean gentleman, with a long acquiline nose, and a bald head, daubed all over with powder and pomatum, entered. I thought I recollected having seen him too, but could not remember his name, though he spoke to me with the greatest familiarity; at least, that sort of familiarity that an official person generally assumes. He bustled about and about, speaking to every one, but declined listening for a single moment to any. The lady offered to withdraw, but he stopped her.

"No, no, Mrs. Keeler, you need not go; you need not go; you *must* not go, madam. The business I came about, concerns you— yes, that it does—Bad business yon of Walker's? Eh? Could not help it—did all I could, Mr. Wringhim. Done your business. Have it all cut and dry here, sir—No, this is not it—Have it among them, though—I'm at a little loss for your name, sir, (addressing my friend,)—seen you very often, though exceedingly often—quite well acquainted with you."

"No, sir, you are not," said my friend, sternly.—The intruder never regarded him; never so much as lifted his eyes from his bundle of law papers, among which he was bustling with great hurry and importance, but went on—

"*Im*possible! Have seen a face very like it, then—what did you say your name was, sir?—very like it indeed. Is it not the young laird who was murdered whom you resemble so much?"

Here Mrs. Keeler uttered a scream, which so much startled me, that it seems I grew pale. And on looking at my friend's face, there was something struck me so forcibly in the likeness between him and my late brother, that I had very nearly fainted. The woman exclaimed, that it was my brother's spirit that stood beside me.

"Im*poss*ible!" exclaimed the attorney; "at least I hope not, else his signature is not worth a pin. There is some balance due on yon business, madam. Do you wish your account? because I have it here, ready discharged, and it does not suit letting such things lie over. This business of Mr. Colwan's will be a severe one on you, madam, *rat*her a severe one."

"What business of mine, if it be your will, sir," said I. "For my part I never engaged you in business of any sort, less or more." He never regarded me, but went on. "You may appeal, though: Yes, yes, there are such things as appeals for the refractory. Here it is, gentlemen,—here they are all together—Here is, in the first place, sir, your power of attorney, regularly warranted, sealed, and signed with your own hand."

"I declare solemnly that I never signed that document," said I.

"Ay, ay, the system of denial is not a bad one in general," said my attorney; "but at present there is no occasion for it. You do not deny your own hand?"

"I deny every thing connected with the business," cried I; "I disclaim it *in toto*, and declare that I know no more about it than the child unborn."

"That is exceedingly good!" exclaimed he; "I like your pertinacity vastly! I have three of your letters, and three of your signatures; that part is all settled, and I hope so is the whole affair; for here is the original grant to your father, which he has never thought proper to put in requisition. Simple gentleman! But here have I, Lawyer Linkam, in one hundredth part of the time that any other notary, writer, attorney, or writer to the signet in Britain, would have done it, procured the signature of his Majesty's commissioner, and thereby confirmed the charter to you and your house, sir, for ever and ever,—Begging your pardon, madam." The lady, as well as myself, tried several times to interrupt the loquacity of Linkum, but in vain: he only raised his hand with a quick flourish, and went on:—

"Here it is:—'JAMES, by the grace of God, King of Great Britain, France, and Ireland, to his right trust cousin, sendeth greeting: And whereas his right leal and trust-worthy cousin, George Colwan, of Dalcastle and Balgrennan, hath suffered great losses, and undergone much hardship, on behalf of his Majesty's rights and titles; he therefore, for himself, and as prince and steward of Scotland, and by the consent of his right trusty cousins and councillors, hereby grants to the said George Colwan, his heirs and assignees whatsomever, heritably and irrevocably, all and haill the lands and others underwritten: *To wit,* All and haill, the five merk land of Kipplerig; the five pound land of Easter Knockward, with all the towers, fortalices, manor-places, houses, biggings, yards, orchards, tofts, crofts, mills, woods, fishings, mosses, muirs, meadows, commonties, pasturages, coals, coal-heughs, tenants, tenantries, services of free tenants, annexes, connexes, dependencies, parts, pendicles, and pertinents of the same whatsomever; to be peaceably brooked, joysed, set, used, and disposed of by him and his aboves, as specified, heritably and irrevocably, in all time coming: And, in testimony thereof, His Majesty, for himself, and as prince and steward of Scotland, with the advice and consent of his foresaids, knowledge, proper motive, and kingly power, makes, erects, creates, unites, annexes, and incorporates, the whole lands above mentioned in an haill and free barony, by all the rights, miethes, and marches thereof, old and divided, as the same lies, in length and breadth, in houses, biggings, mills, multures, hawking, hunting, fishing; with court, plaint, herezeld, fock, fork, sack, sock, thole, thame, vert, wraik, waith, wair, venison, outfang thief, infang thief, pit and gallows, and all and sundry other commodities. Given at our Court of Whitehall, &c. &c. God save the King.

'*Compositio* 5 *lib.* 13. 8.

'Registrate 26th September, 1687.'

"See, madam, here are ten signatures of privy councillors of that year, and here are other ten of the present year, with his Grace the Duke of Queensberry at the head. All right—See here it is, sir,—all right—done your work. So you see, madam, this gentleman is the true and sole heritor of all the land that your father possesses, with all the rents thereof for the last twenty years, and upwards—Fine job for my employers!—sorry on your account, madam—can't help it."

I was again going to disclaim all interest or connection in the matter, but my friend stopped me; and the plaints and lamentations of the dame became so overpowering, that they put an end to all farther colloquy; but Lawyer Linkum followed me, and stated his great outlay, and the important services he had rendered me, until I was obliged to subscribe an order to him for £100 on my banker.

I was now glad to retire with my friend, and ask seriously for some explanation of all this. It was in the highest degree unsatisfactory. He confirmed all that had been stated to me; assuring me, that I had not only been assiduous in my endeavours to seduce a young lady of great beauty, which it seemed I had effected, but that I had taken counsel, and got this supposed, old, false, and forged grant, raked up and new signed, to ruin the young lady's family quite, so as to throw her entirely on myself for protection, and be wholly at my will.

This was to me wholly incomprehensible. I could have freely made oath to the contrary of every particular. Yet the evidences were against me, and of a nature not to be denied. Here I must confess, that, highly as I disapproved of the love of women, and all intimacies and connections with the sex, I felt a sort of indefinite pleasure, an ungracious delight in having a beautiful woman solely at my disposal. But I thought of her spiritual good in the meantime. My friend spoke of my backslidings with concern; requesting me to make sure of my forgiveness, and to forsake them; and then he added some words of sweet comfort. But from this time forth I began to be sick at times of my existence. I had heart-burnings, longings, and yearnings, that would not be satisfied; and I seemed hardly to be an accountable creature; being thus in the habit of executing transactions of the utmost moment, without being sensible that I did them. I was a being incomprehensible to myself. Either I had a second self, who transacted business in my likeness, or else my body was at times possessed by a spirit over which it had no controul, and of whose actions my own soul was wholly unconscious. This was an anomaly not to be accounted for by any philosophy of mine, and I was many times, in contemplating it, excited to terrors and mental torments hardly describable. To be in a state of consciousness and unconsciousness, at the same time, in the same body and same spirit, was impossible. I was under the greatest anxiety, dreading some change would take place momently in my nature; for of dates I could make nothing: one-half, or two-thirds of my time, seemed to me to be totally lost. I often, about this time, prayed with great fervour, and lamented my hopeless condition, especially in being liable to the commission of crimes, which I was not sensible of, and could not eschew. And I confess, notwithstanding the promises on which I had been taught to rely, I began to have secret terrors, that the great enemy of man's salvation was exercising powers over me, that might eventually lead to my ruin. These were but temporary and sinful fears, but they added greatly to my unhappiness.

The worst thing of all was, what hitherto I had never felt, and, as yet, durst not confess to myself, that the presence of my illustrious and devoted friend was becoming irksome to me. When I was by myself, I breathed freer, and my step was lighter; but, when he approached, a pang went to my heart, and, in his company, I moved and acted as if under a load that I could hardly endure. What a state to be in! And yet to shake him off was impossible—we were incorporated together—identified with one another, as it were, and the power was not in me to separate myself from him. I still knew nothing who he was, farther than that he was a potentate of some foreign land, bent on establishing some pure and genuine doctrines of Christianity, hitherto only half understood, and less than half exercised. Of this I could have no doubts, after all that he had said, done, and suffered in the cause. But, alongst with this, I was also certain, that he was possessed of some supernatural power, of the source of which I was wholly ignorant. That a man could be a Christian, and at the same time a powerful necromancer, appeared inconsistent, and adverse to every principle taught in our church; and from this I was led to believe, that he inherited his powers from on high, for I could not doubt either of the soundness of his principles, or that he accomplished things impossible to account for.

Thus was I sojourning in the midst of a chaos of confusion. I looked back on my bypast life with pain, as one looks back on a perilous journey, in which he has attained his end, without gaining any advantage either to himself, or others; and I looked forward, as on a darksome waste, full of repulsive and terrific shapes, pitfalls, and precipices, to which there was no definite bourne, and from which I turned with disgust. With my riches, my unhappiness was increased tenfold; and here, with another great acquisition of property, for which I had pleaded, and which I had gained in a dream, my miseries and difficulties were increasing. My principal feeling, about this time, was an insatiable longing for something that I cannot describe or denominate properly, unless I say it was for *utter oblivion* that I longed. I desired to sleep; but it was for a deeper and longer sleep, than that in which the senses were nightly steeped. I longed to be at rest and quiet, and close my eyes on the past and the future alike, as far as this frail life was concerned. But what had been formerly and finally settled in the counsels above, I presumed not to call in question.

In this state of irritation and misery, was I dragging on an existence, disgusted with all around me, and in particular with my mother, who, with all her love and anxiety, had such an insufferable mode of manifesting them, that she had by this time rendered herself exceedingly obnoxious to me. The very sound of her voice at a distance, went to my heart like an arrow, and made all my nerves to shrink; and as for the beautiful young lady of whom they told me I had been so much enamoured, I shunned all intercourse with her or hers, as I would have done with the devil. I read some of their letters and burnt them, but refused to see either the young lady or her mother, on any account.

About this time it was, that my worthy and reverend parent came with one of his elders to see my mother and myself. His presence always brought joy with it into our family, for my mother was uplifted, and I had so few who cared for me, or for whom I cared, that I felt rather gratified at seeing him. My illustrious friend was also much more attached to him, than any other person, (except myself,) for their religious principles tallied in every point, and their conversation was interesting, serious, and sublime. Being anxious to entertain well and highly the man to whom I had been so much indebted, and knowing that with all his integrity and righteousness, he disdained not the good things of this life, I brought from the late laird's well-stored cellars, various fragrant and salubrious wines, and we drank and became merry, and I found that my miseries and overpowering calamities, passed away over my head like a shower that is driven by the wind. I became elevated and happy, and welcomed my guests an hundred times; and then I joined them in religious conversation, with a zeal and enthusiasm which I had not often experienced, and which made all their hearts rejoice, so that I said to myself, "Surely every gift of God is a blessing, and ought to be used with liberality and thankfulness."

The next day I waked from a profound and feverish sleep, and called for something to drink. There was a servant answered whom I had never seen before, and he was clad in my servant's clothes and livery. I asked for Andrew Handyside, the servant who had waited at table the night before; but the man answered with a stare and a smile.

"What do you mean, sirrah," said I. "Pray what do you here? or what are you pleased to laugh at? I desire you to go about your business, and send me up Handyside. I want him to bring me something to drink."

"Ye sanna want a drink, maister," said the fellow: "Tak a hearty ane, and see if it will wauken ye up something, sae that ye dinna ca' for ghaists through your sleep. Surely ye haena forgotten that Andrew Handyside has been in his grave these six months?"

This was a stunning blow to me. I could not answer farther, but sunk back on my pillow as if I had been a lump of lead, refusing to take a drink or any thing else at the fellow's hand, who seemed thus mocking me with so grave a face. The man seemed sorry, and grieved at my being offended, but I ordered him away, and continued sullen and thoughtful. Could I have again been for a season in utter oblivion to myself, and transacting business which I neither approved of, nor had any connection with! I tried to recollect something in which I might have been engaged, but nothing was pourtrayed on my mind subsequent to the parting with my friends at a late hour the evening before. The evening before it certainly was: but if so, how came it, that Andrew Handyside, who served at table that evening, should have been in his grave six months! This was a circumstance somewhat equivocal; therefore, being afraid to arise lest accusations of I knew not what might come against me, I was obliged to call once more in order to come at what intelligence I could. The same fellow appeared to receive my orders as before, and I set about examining him with regard to particulars. He told me his name was Scrape; that I hired him myself; of whom I hired him; and at whose recommendation. I smiled, and nodded so as to let the knave see I understood he was telling me a chain of falsehoods, but did not choose to begin with any violent asseverations to the contrary.

"And where is my noble friend and companion?" said I. "How has he been engaged in the interim?"

"I dinna ken him, sir," said Scrape; "but have heard it said, that the strange mysterious person that attended you, him that the maist part of folks countit uncanny, had gane awa wi' a Mr. Ringan o' Glasko last year, and had never returned."

I thanked the Lord in my heart for this intelligence, hoping that the illustrious stranger had returned to his own land and people, and that I should thenceforth be rid of his controlling and appalling presence. "And where is my mother?" said I.—The man's breath cut short, and he looked at me without returning any answer.—"I ask you where my mother is?" said I.

"God only knows, and not I, where she is," returned he. "He knows where her soul is, and as for her body, if you dinna ken something o' it, I suppose nae man alive does."

"What do you mean, you knave?" said I. "What dark hints are these you are throwing out? Tell me precisely and distinctly what you know of my mother?"

"It is unco queer o' ye to forget, or pretend to forget every thing that gate, the day, sir," said he. "I'm sure you heard enough about it yestreen; an' I can tell you, there are some gayan ill-faurd stories gaun about that business. But as the thing is to be tried afore the circuit lords, it wad be far wrang to say either this or that to influence the public mind; it is best just to let justice tak its swee. I hae naething to say, sir. Ye hae been a good enough maister to me, and paid my wages regularly, but ye hae muckle need to be innocent, for there are some heavy accusations rising against you."

"I fear no accusations of man," said I, "as long as I can justify my cause in the sight of Heaven; and that I can do this I am well aware. Go you and bring me some wine and water, and some other clothes than these gaudy and glaring ones."

I took a cup of wine and water; put on my black clothes, and walked out. For all the perplexity that surrounded me, I felt my spirits considerably buoyant. It appeared that I was rid of the two greatest bars to my happiness, by what agency I knew not. My mother, it seemed, was gone, who had become a grievous thorn in my side of late, and my great companion and counsellor, who tyrannized over every spontaneous movement of my heart, had likewise taken himself off. This last was an unspeakable relief; for I found that for a long season I had only been able to act by the motions of his mysterious mind and spirit. I therefore thanked God for my deliverance, and strode through my woods with a daring and heroic step; with independence in my eye, and freedom swinging in my right hand.

At the extremity of the Colwan wood, I perceived a figure approaching me with slow and dignified motion. The moment that I beheld it, my whole frame received a shock as if the ground on which I walked had sunk suddenly below me. Yet, at that moment, I knew not who it was; it was the air and motion of some one that I dreaded, and from whom I would gladly have escaped; but this I even had not power to attempt. It came slowly onward, and I advanced as slowly to meet it; yet when we came within speech, I still knew not who it was. It bore the figure, air, and features of my late brother, I thought, exactly; yet in all these there were traits so forbidding, so mixed with an appearance of misery, chagrin, and despair, that I still shrunk from the view, not knowing on whose face I looked. But when the being spoke, both my mental and bodily frame received another shock more terrible than the first, for it was the voice of the great personage I had so long denominated my friend, of whom I had deemed myself for ever freed, and whose presence and counsels I now dreaded more than hell. It was his voice, but so altered—I shall never forget it till my dying day.

opposite of music & of proof of God's power)

Nay, I can scarce conceive it possible that any earthly sounds could be so discordant, so repulsive to every feeling of a human soul, as the tones of the voice that grated on my ear at that moment. They were the sounds of the pit, wheezed through a grated cranny, or seemed so to my distempered imagination.

"So! Thou shudderest at my approach now, dost thou?" said he. "Is this all the gratitude that you deign for an attachment of which the annals of the world furnish no parallel? An attachment which has caused me to forego power and dominion, might, homage, conquest and adulation, all that I might gain one highly valued and sanctified spirit, to my great and true principles of reformation among mankind. Wherein have I offended? What have I done for evil, or what have I not done for your good, that you would thus shun my presence?"

"Great and magnificent prince," said I humbly, "let me request of you to abandon a poor worthless wight to his own wayward fortune, and return to the dominion of your people. I am unworthy of the sacrifices you have made for my sake; and after all your efforts, I do not feel that you have rendered me either more virtuous or more happy. For the sake of that which is estimable in human nature, depart from me to your own home, before you render me a being either altogether above, or below the rest of my fellow creatures. Let me plod on towards heaven and happiness in my own way, like those that have gone before me, and I promise to stick fast by the great principles which you have so strenuously inculcated, on condition that you depart and leave me for ever."

"Sooner shall you make the mother abandon the child of her bosom; nay, sooner cause the shadow to relinquish the substance, than separate me from your side. Our beings are amalgamated, as it were, and consociated in one, and never shall I depart from this country until I can carry you in triumph with me."

I can in nowise describe the effect this appalling speech had on me. It was like the announcement of death to one who had of late deemed himself free, if not of something worse than death, and of longer continuance. There was I doomed to remain in misery, subjugated, soul and body, to one whose presence was become more intolerable to me than ought on earth could compensate: And at that moment, when he beheld the anguish of my soul, he could not conceal that he enjoyed it. I was troubled for an answer, for which he was waiting: it became incumbent on me to say something after such a protestation of attachment; and, in some degree to shake the validity of it, I asked, with great simplicity, where he had been all this while?

"Your crimes and your extravagancies forced me from your side for a season," said he; "but now that I hope the day of grace is returned, I am again drawn towards you by an affection that has neither bounds nor interest; an affection for which I receive not even the poor return of gratitude, and which seems to have its radical sources in fascination. I have been far, far abroad, and have seen much, and transacted much, since I last spoke with you. During that space, I grievously suspect that you have been guilty of great crimes and misdemeanours, crimes that would have sunk an unregenerated person to perdition; but as I knew it to be only a temporary falling off, a specimen of that liberty by which the chosen and elected ones are made free, I closed my eyes on the wilful debasement of our principles, knowing that the transgressions could never be accounted to your charge, and that in good time you would come to your senses, and throw the whole weight of your crimes on the shoulders that had voluntarily stooped to receive the load."

"Certainly I will," said I, "as I and all the justified have a good right to do. But what crimes? What misdemeanours and transgressions do you talk about? For my part, I am conscious of none, and am utterly amazed at insinuations which I do not comprehend."

"You have certainly been left to yourself for a season," returned he, "having gone on rather like a person in a delirium, than a Christian in his sober senses. You are accused of having made away with your mother privately; as also of the death of a beautiful young lady, whose affections you had seduced."

"It is an intolerable and monstrous falsehood!" cried I, interrupting him; "I never laid a hand on a woman to take away her life, and have even shunned their society from my childhood: I know nothing of my mother's exit, nor of that young lady's whom you mention—Nothing whatever."

"I hope it is so," said he. "But it seems there are some strong presumptuous proofs against you, and I came to warn you this day that a precognition is in progress, and that unless you are perfectly convinced, not only of your innocence, but of your ability to prove it, it will be the safest course for you to abscond, and let the trial go on without you."

"Never shall it be said that I shrunk from such a trial as this," said I. "It would give grounds for suspicions of guilt that never had existence, even in thought. I will go and show myself in every public place, that no slanderous tongue may wag against me. I have shed the blood of sinners, but of these deaths I am guiltless; therefore, I will face every tribunal, and put all my accusers down."

"Asseveration will avail you but little," answered he, composedly: "It is, however, justifiable in its place, although to me it signifies nothing, who know too well that you *did* commit both crimes, in your own person, and with your own hands. Far be it from me to betray you; indeed, I would rather endeavour to palliate the offences; for though adverse to nature, I can prove them not to be so to the cause of pure Christianity, by the mode of which we have approved of it, and which we wish to promulgate."

"If this that you tell me be true," said I, "then is it as true that I have two souls, which take possession of my bodily frame by turns, the one being all unconscious of what the other performs; for as sure as I have at this moment a spirit within me, fashioned and destined to eternal felicity, as sure am I utterly ignorant of the crimes you now lay to my charge."

"Your supposition may be true in effect," said he. "We are all subjected to two distinct natures in the same person. I myself have suffered grievously in that way. The spirit that now directs my energies is not that with which I was endowed at my creation. It is changed within me, and so is my whole nature. My former days were those of grandeur and felicity. But, would you believe it? *I was not then a Christian.* Now I am. I have been converted to its truths by passing through the fire, and since my final conversion, my misery has been extreme. You complain that I have not been able to render you more happy than you were. Alas! do you expect it in the difficult and exterminating career which you have begun. I, however, promise you this—a portion of the only happiness which I enjoy, sublime in its motions, and splendid in its attainments—I will place you on the right hand of my throne, and show you the grandeur of my domains, and the felicity of my millions of true professors."

I was once more humbled before this mighty potentate, and promised to be ruled wholly by his directions, although at that moment my nature shrunk from the concessions, and my soul longed rather to be inclosed in the deeps of the sea, or involved once more in utter oblivion. I was like Daniel in the den of lions,[1]

---

1 In the Old Testament, Daniel is cast into the den of lions but is saved by God. (*Daniel* 6: 4-27).

without his faith in divine support, and wholly at their mercy. I felt as one round whose body a deadly snake is twisted, which continues to hold him in its fangs, without injuring him, farther than in moving its scaly infernal folds with exulting delight, to let its victim feel to whose power he has subjected himself; and thus did I for a space drag an existence from day to day, in utter weariness and helplessness; at one time worshipping with great fervour of spirit, and at other times so wholly left to myself, as to work all manner of vices and follies with greediness. In these my enlightened friend never accompanied me, but I always observed that he was the first to lead me to every one of them, and then leave me in the lurch. The next day, after these my fallings off, he never failed to reprove me gently, blaming me for my venial transgressions; but then he had the art of reconciling all, by reverting to my justified and infallible state, which I found to prove a delightful healing salve for every sore.

But, of all my troubles, this was the chief: I was every day and every hour assailed with accusations of deeds of which I was wholly ignorant; of acts of cruelty, injustice, defamation, and deceit; of pieces of business which I could not be made to comprehend; with law-suits, details, arrestments of judgment, and a thousand interminable quibbles from the mouth of my loquacious and conceited attorney. So miserable was my life rendered by these continued attacks, that I was often obliged to lock myself up for days together, never seeing any person save my man Samuel Scrape, who was a very honest blunt fellow, a staunch Cameronian,[1] but withal very little conversant in religious matters. He said he came from a place called Penpunt,[2] which I thought a name so ludicrous, that I called him by the name of his native village, an appellation of which he was very proud, and answered every thing with more civility and perspicuity when I denominated him Penpunt, than Samuel, his own Christian name. Of this peasant was I obliged to make a companion on sundry occasions, and strange indeed were the details

---

1 Followers of Richard Cameron (1648–80), the Cameronians were unyielding in their adherence to the Scottish covenants of 1638 and 1643. Many of their number were executed and their last testimonies recorded in *A Cloud of Witnesses*, the book which Robert mentions having read above (155).
2 A village in Dumfries and Galloway, in the south of Scotland.

which he gave me concerning myself, and the ideas of the country people concerning me. I took down a few of these in writing, to put off the time, and here leave them on record to show how the best and greatest actions are misconstrued among sinful and ignorant men.

"You say, Samuel, that I hired you myself—that I have been a good enough master to you, and have paid you your weekly wages punctually. Now, how is it that you say this, knowing, as you do, that I never hired you, and never paid you a sixpence of wages in the whole course of my life, excepting this last month?"

"Ye may as weel say, master, that water's no water, or that stanes are no stanes. But that's just your gate, an' it is a great pity aye to do a thing an' profess the clean contrair. Weel then, since you havena paid me ony wages, an' I can prove day and date when I was hired, an' came hame to your service, will you be sae kind as to pay me now? That's the best way o' curing a man o' the mortal disease o' leasing-making that I ken o'."

"I should think that Penpunt and Cameronian principles, would not admit of a man taking twice payment for the same article."

"In sic a case as this, sir, it disna hinge upon principles, but a piece o' good manners; an' I can tell you that at sic a crisis, a Cameronian is a gayan weel-bred man. He's driven to this, that he maun either make a breach in his friend's good name, or in his purse; an' O, sir, whilk o' thae, think you, is the most precious? For instance, an a Galloway drover had comed to the town o' Penpunt, an' said to a Cameronian, (the folk's a' Cameronians there,) 'Sir, I want to buy your cow.' 'Vera weel,' says the Cameronian, 'I just want to sell the cow, see gie me twanty punds Scots, an' take her w'ye.' It's a bargain. The drover takes away the cow, an' gies the Cameronian his twanty pund Scots. But after that, he meets him again on the white sands, amang a' the drovers an' dealers o' the land, an' the Galloway-man, he says to the Cameronian, afore a' thae witnesses, 'Come, Master Whiggam, I hae never paid you for yon bit useless cow, that I bought, I'll pay her the day, but you maun mind the luck-penny; there's muckle need for't,'—or something to that purpose. The Cameronian then turns out to be a civil man, an' canna bide to make the man baith a feele an' liar at the same time, afore a' his associates; an' therefore he pits his principles aff at the side, to be a kind o' sleepin partner, as it war, an' brings up his good breeding to stand at the counter: he pockets the money, gies the Galloway drover time o' day, an' comes his way. An' wha's to blame? *Man mind yoursel* is the first commandment. A Cameronian's principles never came atween him an' his purse, nor sanna in the present case; for as I canna bide to make you out a leear, I'll thank you for my wages."

"Well, you shall have them, Samuel, if you declare to me that I hired you myself in this same person, and bargained with you with this same tongue, and voice, with which I speak to you just now."

"That I do declare, unless ye hae twa persons o' the same appearance, and twa tongues to the same voice. But, od saif us, sir, do you ken what the auld wives o' the clachan say about you?"

"How should I, when no one repeats it to me?"

"Oo, I trow it's a' stuff;—folk shouldna heed what's said by auld crazy kimmers. But there are some o' them weel kend for witches too; an' they say,—lord have a care o' us!—they say the deil's often seen gaun sidie for sidie w'ye, whiles in ae shape, an' whiles in another. An' they say that he whiles takes your ain shape, or else enters into you, and then your turn a deil yoursel."

I was so astounded at this terrible idea that had gone abroad, regarding my fellowship with the prince of darkness, that I could make no answer to the fellow's information, but sat like one in a stupor; and if it had not been for my well-founded faith, and conviction that I was a chosen and elected one before the world was made, I should at that moment have given into the popular belief, and fallen into the sin of despondency; but I was preserved from such a fatal error by an inward and unseen supporter. Still the insinuation was so like what I felt myself, that I was greatly awed and confounded.

The poor fellow observed this, and tried to do away the impression by some farther sage remarks of his own.

"Hout, dear sir, it is balderdash, there's nae doubt o't. It is the crownhead o' absurdity to tak in the havers o' auld wives for gospel. I told them that my master was a peeous man, an' a sensible man; an' for praying, that he could ding auld Macmillan[1] himsel. 'Sae could the deil,' they said, 'when he liket, either at preaching or praying, if these war to answer his ain ends.' 'Na, na,' says I, 'but he's a strick believer in a' the truths o' Christianity, my master.' They said, sae was Satan, for that he was the firmest believer in a' the truths of Christianity that was out o' heaven; an' that, sin' the Revolution that the gospel had turned see rife, he had been often

---

1 John Macmillan (1670–1753), Cameronian minister and founder of the Reformed Presbyterian Church.

driven to the shift o' preaching it himsel, for the purpose o' getting some wrang tenets introduced into it, and thereby turning it into blasphemy and ridicule."

I confess, to my shame, that I was so overcome by this jumble of nonsense, that a chillness came over me, and in spite of all my efforts to shake off the impression it had made, I fell into a faint. Samuel soon brought me to myself, and after a deep draught of wine and water, I was greatly revived, and felt my spirit rise above the sphere of vulgar conceptions, and the restrained views of unregenerate men. The shrewd but loquacious fellow, perceiving this, tried to make some amends for the pain he had occasioned to me, by the following story, which I noted down, and which was brought on by a conversation to the following purport:—

"Now, Penpunt, you may tell me all that passed between you and the wives of the clachan. I am better of that stomach qualm, with which I am sometimes seized, and shall be much amused by hearing the sentiments of noted witches regarding myself and my connections."

"Weel, you see, sir, I says to them, 'It will be lang afore the deil intermeddle wi' as serious a professor, and as fervent a prayer as my master, for gin he gets the upper hand o' sickan men, wha's to be safe?' An', what think ye they said, sir? There was ane Lucky Shaw set up her lang lantern chafts, an' answered me, an' a' the rest shanned and noddit in assent an' approbation: 'Ye silly, sauchless, Cameronian cuif!' quo she, 'is that a' that ye ken about the wiles and doings o' the prince o' the air, that rules an' works in the bairns of disobedience? Gin ever he observes a proud professor, wha has mae than ordinary pretensions to a divine calling, and that reards and prays till the very howlets learn his preambles, that's the man Auld Simmie fixes on to mak a dishclout o'. He canna get rest in hell, if he sees a man, or a set of men o' this stamp, an' when he sets fairly to wark, it is seldom that he disna bring them round till his ain measures by hook or by crook. Then, O it is a grand prize for him, an' a proud deil he is, when he gangs hame to his ain ha', wi' a batch o' the souls o' sic strenuous professors on his back. Ay, I trow, auld Ingleby, the Liverpool packman, never came up Glasco street wi' prouder pomp, when he had ten horse-laids afore him o' Flanders lace, an' Hollin lawn,[1] an' silks an' satins frae the eastern Indians, than Satan wad strodge into

---

1 A fine linen.

hell with a pack-laid o' the souls o' proud professors on his braid shoulders. Ha, ha, ha! I think I see how the auld thief wad be gaun through his gizened dominions, crying his wares, in derision, 'Wha will buy a fresh, cauler divine, a bouzy bishop, a fasting zealot, or a piping priest? For a' their prayers an' their praises, their aumuses, an' their penances, their whinings, their howlings, their rantings, an' their ravings, here they come at last! Behold the end! Here go the rare and precious wares! A fat professor for a bodle, an' a lean ane for half a merk!' I declare, I trembled at the auld hag's ravings, but the lave o' the kimmers applauded the sayings as sacred truths. An' then Lucky went on: 'There are many wolves in sheep's claithing, among us, my man; mony deils aneath the masks o' zealous professors, roaming about in kirks and meeting-houses o' the land. It was but the year afore the last, that the people o' the town o' Auchtermuchty[1] grew so rigidly righteous, that the meanest hind among them became a shining light in ither towns an' parishes. There was nought to be heard, neither night nor day, but preaching, praying, argumentation, an' catechising in a' the famous town o' Auchtermuchty. The young men wooed their sweethearts out o' the Song o' Solomon,[2] an' the girls returned answers in strings o' verses out o' the Psalms. At the lint-swinglings, they said questions round; an read chapters, and sang hymns at bridals; auld an young prayed in their dreams, an' prophesied in their sleep, till the deils in the farrest nooks o' hell were alarmed, and moved to commotion. Gin it had hadna been an auld carl, Robin Ruthven, Auchtermuchty wad at that time hae been ruined and lost for ever. But Robin was a cunning man, an' had rather mae wits than his ain, for he had been in the hands o' the fairies when he was young, an' a' kinds o' spirits were visible to his een, an' their language as familiar to him as his ain mother tongue. Robin was sitting on the side o' the West Lowmond, ae still gloomy night in September, when he saw a bridal o' corbie craws coming east the lift, just on the edge o' the gloaming. The moment that Robin saw them, he kenned, by their movements, that they were craws o' some ither warld than this; so he signed himself, and crap into the middle o' his bourock. The corbie craws came a' an' sat down round about him, an' they poukit their black sooty wings, an' spread them out to the breeze to cool; and Robin heard ae corbie

[margin note: takes a Secularist to see the devil]

---

1   A village in Fife, in eastern Scotland.
2   A book in the Old Testament, notable for its erotic allusions.

speaking, an' another answering him; and the tane said to the tither: 'Where will the ravens find a prey the night?'—'On the lean crazy souls o' Auchtermuchty,' quo the tither.—'I fear they will be o'er weel wrappit up in the warm flannens o' faith, an' clouted wi' the dirty duds o' repentance, for us to mak a meal o',' quo the first.— 'Whaten vile sounds are these that I hear coming bumming up the hill?' 'O these are the hymns and praises o' the auld wives and creeshy louns o' Auchtermuchty, wha are gaun crooning their way to heaven; an' gin it warna for the shame o' being beat, we might let our great enemy tak them. For sic a prize as he will hae! Heaven, forsooth! What shall we think o' heaven, if it is to be filled wi' vermin like thae, amang whom there is mair poverty and pollution, than I can name.' 'No matter for that,' said the first, 'we cannot have our power set at defiance; though we should put them in the thief's hole, we must catch them, and catch them with their own bait too. Come all to church to-morrow, and I'll let you hear how I'll gull the saints of Auchtermuchty. In the mean time, there is a feast on the Sidlaw hills tonight, below the hill of Macbeth,—Mount, Diabolus, and fly.' Then, with loud croaking and crowing, the bridal of corbies again scaled the dusky air, and left Robin Ruthven in the middle of his cairn.

"'The next day the congregation met in the kirk of Auchtermuchty, but the minister made not his appearance. The elders ran out and in, making inquiries; but they could learn nothing, save that the minister was missing. They ordered the clerk to sing a part of the 119th Psalm, until they saw if the minister would cast up. The clerk did as he was ordered, and by the time he reached the 77th verse,[1] a strange divine entered the church, by the *western door*, and advanced solemnly up to the pulpit. The eyes of all the congregation were riveted on the sublime stranger, who was clothed in a robe of black sackcloth, that flowed all around him, and trailed far behind, and they weened him an angel, come to exhort them, in disguise. He read out his text from the Prophecies of Ezekiel,[2] which consisted of these singular words: 'I will overturn, overturn, overturn it; and it shall be no more, until he come, whose right it is, and I will give it him.'

---

1 "And let thy tender mercies come to me, that I may live; Because thy holy laws to me sweet delectation give." *Psalm* 119, verse 77.

2 *Ezekiel* 21:27, prophesying the destruction of the temple at Jerusalem.

"'From these words he preached such a sermon as never was heard by human ears, at least never by ears of Auchtermuchty. It was a true, sterling, gospel sermon—it was striking, sublime, and awful in the extreme. He finally made out the IT, mentioned in the text, to mean, properly and positively, the notable town of Auchtermuchty. He proved all the people in it, to their perfect satisfaction, to be in the gall of bitterness and bond of iniquity, and he assured them, that God would overturn them, their principles, and professions; and that they should be no more, until the devil, the town's greatest enemy, came, and then it should be given unto him for a prey, for it was his right, and to him it belonged, if there was not forthwith a radical change made in all their opinions and modes of worship.

"'The inhabitants of Auchtermuchty were electrified—they were charmed; they were actually raving mad about the grand and sublime truths delivered to them, by this eloquent and impressive preacher of Christianity. 'He is a prophet of the Lord,' said one, 'sent to warn us, as Jonah was sent to the Ninevites.' 'O, he is an angel sent from heaven, to instruct this great city,' said another, 'for no man ever uttered truths so sublime before.' The good people of Auchtermuchty were in perfect raptures with the preacher, who had thus sent them to hell by the slump, tag, rag, and bobtail! Nothing in the world delights a truly religious people so much, as consigning them to eternal damnation. They wondered after the preacher—they crowded together, and spoke of his sermon with admiration, and still as they conversed, the wonder and the admiration increased; so that honest Robin Ruthven's words would not be listened to. It was in vain that he told them he heard a raven speaking, and another raven answering him: the people laughed him to scorn, and kicked him out of their assemblies, as a one who spoke evil of dignities; and they called him a warlock, an' a daft body, to think to mak language out o' the crouping o' craws.

"'The sublime preacher could not be heard of, although all the country was sought for him, even to the minutest corner of St. Johnston and Dundee; but as he had announced another sermon on the same text, on a certain day, all the inhabitants of that populous country, far and near, flocked to Auchtermuchty.[1] Cupar,

---

1 St. Johnston, Dundee, Cupar, Newburgh and Strathmiglo are all places in Fife, in eastern Scotland. Perth is a city further to the west, on the banks of the river Tay, while the Grampian Hills lie to the north. A "nook" or "neuk" is a piece of land projecting into the sea, in this case the North Sea.

Newburgh, and Strathmiglo, turned out men, women, and children. Perth and Dundee gave their thousands; and from the East Nook of Fife to the foot of the Grampian hills, there was nothing but running and riding that morning to Auchtermuchty. The kirk would not hold the thousandth part of them. A splendid tent was erected on the brae north of the town, and round that the countless congregation assembled. When they were all waiting anxiously for the great preacher, behold, Robin Ruthven set up his head in the tent, and warned his countrymen to beware of the doctrines they were about to hear, for he could prove, to their satisfaction, that they were all false, and tended to their destruction!

" 'The whole multitude raised a cry of indignation against Robin, and dragged him from the tent, the elders rebuking him, and the multitude threatening to resort to stronger measures; and though he told them a plain and unsophisticated tale of the black corbies, he was only derided. The great preacher appeared once more, and went through his two discourses with increased energy and approbation. All who heard him were amazed, and many of them went into fits, writhing and foaming in a state of the most horrid agitation. Robin Ruthven sat on the outskirts of the great assembly, listening with the rest, and perceived what they, in the height of their enthusiasm, perceived not,—the ruinous tendency of the tenets so sublimely inculcated. Robin kenned the voice of his friend the corby-craw again, and was sure he would not be wrang: sae when public worship was finished, a' the elders an' a' the gentry flocked about the great preacher, as he stood on the green brae in the sight of the hale congregation, an' a' war alike anxious to pay him some mark o' respect. Robin Ruthven came in amang the thrang, to try to effect what he had promised; and, with the greatest readiness and simplicity, just took haud o' the side an' wide gown, an' in sight of a' present, held it aside as high as the preacher's knee, and behold, there was a pair o' cloven feet! The auld thief was fairly catched in the very height o' his proud conquest, an' put down by an auld carl. He could feign nae mair, but gnashing on Robin wi' his teeth, he dartit into the air like a fiery dragon, an' keust a reid rainbow our the taps o' the Lowmonds.

" 'A' the auld wives an' weavers o' Auchtermuchty fell down flat wi' affright, an' betook them to their prayers aince again, for they saw the dreadfu' danger they had escapit, an' frae that day to this it is a hard matter to gar an Auchtermuchty man listen to a sermon at a', an' a harder ane still to gar him applaud ane, for he thinks aye that he sees the cloven foot peeping out frae aneath ilka sentence.

"'Now, this is a true story, my man,' quo the auld wife; 'an' whenever you are doubtfu' of a man, take auld Robin Ruthven's plan, an' look for the cloven foot, for it's a thing that winna weel hide; an' it appears whiles where ane wadna think o't. It will keek outfrae aneath the parson's gown, the lawyer's wig, and the Cameronian's blue bannet; but still there is a gouden rule whereby to detect it, an' that never, never fails.'—The auld witch didna gie me the rule, an' though I hae heard tell o't often an' often, shame fa' me an I ken what it is! But ye will ken it well, an' it wad be nae the waur of a trial on some o' your friends, maybe; for they say there's a certain gentleman seen walking wi' you whiles, that, wherever he sets his foot, the grass withers as gin it war scoudered wi' a het ern. His presence be about us! What's the matter wi' you, master? Are ye gaun to take the calm o' the stamock again?"

The truth is, that the clown's absurd story, with the still more ridiculous application, made me sick at heart a second time. It was not because I thought my illustrious friend was the devil, or that I took a fool's idle tale as a counterbalance to divine revelation, that had assured me of my justification in the sight of God before the existence of time. But, in short, it gave me a view of my own state, at which I shuddered, as indeed I now always did, when the image of my devoted friend and ruler presented itself to my mind. I often communed with my heart on this, and wondered how a connection, that had the well-being of mankind solely in view, could be productive of fruits so bitter, I then went to try my works by the Saviour's golden rule,[1] as my servant had put it into my head to do; and, behold, not one of them would stand the test. I had shed blood on a ground on which I could not admit that any man had a right to shed mine; and I began to doubt the motives of my adviser once more, not that they were intentionally bad, but that his was some great mind led astray by enthusiasm, or some overpowering passion.

He seemed to comprehend every one of these motions of my heart, for his manner towards me altered every day. It first became any thing but agreeable, then supercilious, and finally, intolerable; so that I resolved to shake him off, cost what it would, even though I should be reduced to beg my bread in a foreign land. To do it at

---

1 "Therefore all things whatsoever ye would that men should do to you, do ye even so to them" (Matthew 7:12)

home was impossible, as he held my life in his hands, to sell it whenever he had a mind; and besides, his ascendancy over me was as complete as that of a huntsman over his dogs. I was even so weak, as, the next time I met with him, to look stedfastly at his foot, to see if it was not cloven into two hoofs. It was the foot of a gentleman, in every respect, so far as appearances went, but the form of his counsels was somewhat equivocal, and if not double, they were amazingly crooked.

But, if I had taken my measures to abscond and fly from my native place, in order to free myself of this tormenting, intolerant, and bloody reformer, he had likewise taken his to expel me, or throw me into the hands of justice. It seems, that about this time, I was haunted by some spies connected with my late father and brother, of whom the mistress of the former was one. My brother's death had been witnessed by two individuals; indeed, I always had an impression that it was witnessed by more than one, having some faint recollection of hearing voices and challenges close beside me; and this woman had searched about until she found these people; but, as I shrewdly suspected, not without the assistance of the only person in my secret,—my own warm and devoted friend. I say this, because I found that he had them concealed in the neighbour-hood, and then took me again and again where I was fully exposed to their view, without being aware. One time in particular, on pre-tence of gratifying my revenge on that base woman, he knew so well where she lay concealed, that he led me to her, and left me to the mercy of two viragos, who had very nigh taken my life. My time of residence at Dalcastle was wearing to a crisis. I could no longer live with my tyrant, who haunted me like my shadow; and besides, it seems there were proofs of murder leading against me from all quarters. Of part of these I deemed myself quite free, but the world deemed otherwise; and how the matter would have gone, God only knows, for, the case never having undergone a judicial trial, I do not. It perhaps, however, behoves me here to relate all that I know of it, and it is simply this:

On the first of June 1712, (well may I remember the day,) I was sitting locked in my secret chamber, in a state of the utmost despondency, revolving in my mind what I ought to do to be free of my persecutors, and wishing myself a worm, or a moth, that I might be crushed and at rest, when behold Samuel entered, with eyes like to start out of his head, exclaiming, "For God's sake, mas-ter, fly and hide yourself, for your mother's found, an' as sure as you're a living soul, the blame is gaun to fa' on you!"

"My mother found!" said I. "And, pray, where has she been all this while?" In the mean time, I was terribly discomposed at the thoughts of her return.

"Been, sir! Been? Why, she has been where ye pat her, it seems,—lying buried in the sands o' the linn. I can tell you, ye will see her a frightsome figure, sic as I never wish to see again. An' the young lady is found too, sir: an' it is said the devil—I beg pardon sir, *your friend*, I mean,—it is said your *friend* has made the discovery, an' the folk are away to raise officers, an' they will be here in an hour or two at the farthest, sir; an' sae you hae not a minute to lose, for there's proof, sir, strong proof, an' sworn proof, that ye were last seen wi' them baith; sae, unless ye can gie a' the better an account o' baith yoursel an' them, either hide, or flee for your bare life."

"I will neither hide nor fly," said I; "for I am as guiltless of the blood of these women as the child unborn."

"The country disna think sae, master; an' I can assure you, that should evidence fail, you run a risk o' being torn limb frae limb. They are bringing the corpse here, to gar ye touch them baith afore witnesses, an' plenty o' witnesses there will be!"

"They shall not bring them here," cried I, shocked beyond measure at the experiment about to be made: "Go, instantly, and debar them from entering my gate with their bloated and mangled carcases."

"The body of your own mother, sir!" said the fellow emphatically. I was in terrible agitation; and, being driven to my wit's end, I got up and strode furiously round an' round the room. Samuel wist not what to do, but I saw by his staring he deemed me doubly guilty. A tap came to the chamber door: we both started like guilty creatures; and as for Samuel, his hairs stood all on end with alarm, so that when I motioned to him, he could scarcely advance to open the door. He did so at length, and who should enter but my illustrious friend, manifestly in the utmost state of alarm. The moment that Samuel admitted him, the former made his escape by the prince's side as he entered, seemingly in a state of distraction. I was little better, when I saw this dreaded personage enter my chamber, which he had never before attempted; and being unable to ask his errand, I suppose I stood and gazed on him like a statue.

"I come with sad and tormenting tidings to you, my beloved and ungrateful friend," said he; "but having only a minute left to save your life, I have come to attempt it. There is a mob coming towards you with two dead bodies, which will place you in circumstances disagreeable enough: but that is not the worst, for of that you may be able to clear yourself. At this moment there is a party of officers, with a Justiciary warrant from Edinburgh, surrounding the house, and about to begin the search of it, for you. If you fall into their hands, you are inevitably lost; for I have been making earnest inquiries, and find that every thing is in train for your ruin."

"Ay, and who has been the cause of all this?" said I, with great bitterness. But he stopped me short, adding, "There is no time for such reflections at present: I gave you my word of honour that your life should be safe from the hand of man. So it shall, if the power remain with me to save it. I am come to redeem my pledge, and to save your life by the sacrifice of my own. Here,—Not one word of expostulation, change habits with me, and you may then pass by the officers, and guards, and even through the approaching mob, with the most perfect temerity. There is a virtue in this garb, and instead of offering to detain you, they shall pay you obeisance. Make haste, and leave this place for the present, flying where you best may, and if I escape from these dangers that surround me, I will endeavour to find you out, and bring you what intelligence I am able."

I put on his green frock coat, buff belt, and a sort of a turban that he always wore on his head, somewhat resembling a bishop's mitre: he drew his hand thrice across my face, and I withdrew as he continued to urge me. My hall door and postern gate were both strongly guarded, and there were sundry armed people within, searching the closets; but all of them made way for me, and lifted their caps as I passed by them. Only one superior officer accosted me, asking if I had seen the culprit? I knew not what answer to make, but chanced to say, with great truth and propriety, "He is safe enough." The man beckoned with a smile, as much as to say, "Thank you, sir, that is quite sufficient;" and I walked deliberately away.

I had not well left the gate, till, hearing a great noise coming from the deep glen toward the east, I turned that way, deeming myself quite secure in this my new disguise, to see what it was, and if matters were as had been described to me. There I met a great mob, sure enough, coming with two dead bodies stretched on boards, and decently covered with white sheets. I would fain have examined their appearance, had I not perceived the apparent fury in the looks of the men, and judged from that how much more safe it was for me not to intermeddle in the affray. I cannot tell how it was, but I felt a strange and unwonted delight in viewing this scene, and a certain pride of heart in being supposed the perpetrator of the unnatural crimes laid to my charge. This was a feeling quite new to me; and if there were virtues in the robes of the illustrious foreigner, who had without all dispute preserved my life at this time; I say, if there was any inherent virtue in these robes of his, as he had suggested, this was one of their effects, that they turned my heart towards that which was evil, horrible, and disgustful.

I mixed with the mob to hear what they were saying. Every tongue was engaged in loading me with the most opprobrious epithets! One called me a monster of nature; another an incarnate devil; and another a creature made to be cursed in time and eternity. I retired from them, and winded my way southward, comforting myself with the assurance, that so mankind had used and persecuted the greatest fathers and apostles of the Christian church, and that their vile opprobrium could not alter the counsels of heaven concerning me.

On going over that rising ground called Dorington Moor, I could not help turning round and taking a look of Dalcastle. I had little doubt that it would be my last look, and nearly as little ambition that it should not. I thought how high my hopes of happiness and advancement had been on entering that mansion, and taking possession of its rich and extensive domains, and how miserably I had been disappointed. On the contrary, I had experienced nothing but chagrin, disgust, and terror; and I now consoled myself with the hope that I should henceforth shake myself free of the chains of my great tormentor, and for that privilege was I willing to encounter any earthly distress. I could not help perceiving, that I was now on a path which was likely to lead me into a species of distress hitherto unknown, and hardly dreamed of by me, and that was total destitution. For all the riches I had been possessed of a few hours previous to this, I found that here I was turned out of my lordly possessions without a single merk, or the power of lifting and commanding the smallest sum, without being thereby discovered and seized. Had it been possible for me to have escaped in my own clothes, I had a considerable sum secreted in these, but, by the sudden change, I was left without a coin for present necessity. But I had hope in heaven, knowing that the just man would not be left destitute; and that though many troubles surrounded him, he would at last be set free from them all. I was possessed of strong and brilliant parts, and a liberal education; and though I had some-how unaccountably suffered my theological qualifications to fall into desuetude, since my acquaintance with the ablest and most rigid of all theologians, I had nevertheless hopes that, by preaching up redemption by grace, pre-ordination, and eternal purpose, I should yet be enabled to benefit mankind in some country, and rise to high distinction.

These were some of the thoughts by which I consoled myself as I posted on my way southward, avoiding the towns and villages, and falling into the cross ways that led from each of the great roads passing east and west, to another. I lodged the first night in the house of a country weaver, into which I stepped at a late hour, quite overcome with hunger and fatigue, having travelled not less than thirty miles from my late home. The man received me ungra-ciously, telling me of a gentleman's house at no great distance, and of an inn a little farther away; but I said I delighted more in the society of a man like him, than that of any gentleman of the land, for my concerns were with the poor of this world, it being easier for a camel to go through the eye of a needle, than for a rich man to enter into the kingdom of heaven. The weaver's wife, who sat with a child on her knee, and had not hitherto opened her mouth, hearing me speak in that serious and religious style, stirred up the fire, with her one hand; then drawing a chair near it, she said, "Come awa, honest lad, in by here; sin' it be sae that you belang to Him wha gies us a' that we hae, it is but right that you should share a part. You are a stranger, it is true, but *them* that winna entertain a stranger will never entertain an angel unawares."

I never was apt to be taken with the simplicity of nature; in gen-eral I despised it; but, owing to my circumstances at the time, I was deeply affected by the manner of this poor woman's welcome. The weaver continued in a churlish mood throughout the evening, apparently dissatisfied with what his wife had done in entertaining me, and spoke to her in a manner so crusty that I thought proper to rebuke him, for the woman was comely in her person, and vir-tuous in her conversation; but the weaver her husband was large of make, ill-favoured, and pestilent; therefore did I take him severely to task for the tenor of his conduct; but the man was froward, and answered me rudely, with sneering and derision, and, in the height of his caprice, he said to his wife, "Whan focks are sae keen of a chance o' entertaining angels, gudewife, it wad maybe be worth their while to tak tent what kind o' angels they are. It wadna won-der me vera muckle an ye had entertained your friend the deil the night, for aw thought aw fand a saur o' reek an' brimstane about him. *He's nane o' the best o' angels, an' focks winna hae muckle credit by entertaining him.*"

Certainly, in the assured state I was in, I had as little reason to be alarmed at mention being made of the devil as any person on earth: of late, however, I felt that the reverse was the case, and that any allusion to my great enemy, moved me exceedingly. The weaver's speech had such an effect on me, that both he and his wife were alarmed at my looks. The latter thought I was angry, and chided her husband gently for his rudeness; but the weaver himself rather seemed to be confirmed in his opinion that I was the devil, for he looked round like a startled roe-buck, and immediately betook him to the family Bible.

I know not whether it was on purpose to prove my identity or not, but I think he was going to desire me either to read a certain portion of Scripture that he had sought out, or to make family worship, had not the conversation at that instant taken another turn; for the weaver, not knowing how to address me, abruptly asked my name, as he was about to put the Bible into my hands. Never having considered myself in the light of a malefactor, but rather as a champion in the cause of truth, and finding myself perfectly safe under my disguise, I had never once thought of the utility of changing my name, and when the man asked me, I hesitated; but being compelled to say something, I said my name was Cowan. The man stared at me, and then at his wife, with a look that spoke a knowledge of something alarming or mysterious.

"Ha! Cowan?" said he. "That's most extrordinar! Not Colwan, I hope?"

"No: Cowan is my sirname," said I. "But why not Colwan, there being so little difference in the sound?"

"I was feared ye might be that waratch that the deil has taen the possession oi, an' eggit him on to kill baith his father an' his mother, his only brother, an' his sweetheart," said he; "an' to say the truth, I'm no that sure about you yet, for I see you're gaun wi' arms on ye."

"Not I, honest man," said I; "I carry no arms; a man conscious of his innocence and uprightness of heart, needs not to carry arms in his defence now."

"Ay, ay, maister," said he; "an' pray what div ye ca' this bit windlestrae that's appearing here?" With that he pointed to something on the inside of the breast of my frock-coat. I looked at it, and there certainly was the gilded haft of a poniard, the same weapon I had seen and handled before, and which I knew my illustrious companion always carried about with him; but till that moment I knew not that I was in possession of it. I drew it out: a more dangerous or insidious looking weapon could not be conceived. The weaver and his wife were both frightened, the latter in particular; and she being my friend, and I dependant on their hospitality, for that night, I said, "I declare I knew not that I carried this small rapier, which has been in my coat by chance, and not by any design of mine. But lest you should think that I meditate any mischief to any under this roof, I give it into your hands, requesting of you to lock it by till to-morrow, or when I shall next want it."

The woman seemed rather glad to get hold of it; and, taking it from me, she went into a kind of pantry out of my sight, and locked the weapon up; and then the discourse went on.

"There cannot be such a thing in reality," said I, "as the story you were mentioning just now, of a man whose name resembles mine."

"It's likely that you ken a wee better about the story than I do, maister," said he, "suppose you do leave the *L* out of your name. An' yet I think sic a waratch, an' a murderer, wad hae taen a name wi' some gritter difference in the sound. But the story is just that true, that there were twa o' the Queen's officers here nae mair than an hour ago, in pursuit o' the vagabond, for they gat some intelligence that he had fled this gate; yet they said he had been last seen wi' black claes on, an' they supposed he was clad in black. His ain servant is wi' them, for the purpose o' kennin the scoundrel, an' they're galloping through the country like madmen. I hope in God they'll get him, an' rack his neck for him!"

I could not say *Amen* to the weaver's prayer, and therefore tried to compose myself as well as I could, and made some religious comment on the causes of the nation's depravity. But suspecting that my potent friend had betrayed my flight and disguise, to save his life, I was very uneasy, and gave myself up for lost. I said prayers in the family, with the tenor of which the wife was delighted, but the weaver still dissatisfied; and, after a supper of the most homely fare, he tried to start an argument with me, proving, that every thing for which I had interceded in my prayer, was irrelevant to man's present state. But I, being weary and distressed in mind, shunned the contest, and requested a couch whereon to repose.

I was conducted into the other end of the house, among looms, treadles, pirns, and confusion without end; and there, in a sort of box, was I shut up for my night's repose, for the weaver, as he left me, cautiously turned the key of my apartment, and left me to shift for myself among the looms, determined that I should escape from the house with nothing. After he and his wife and children were crowded into their den, I heard the two mates contending furiously about me in suppressed voices, the one maintaining the probability that I was the murderer, and the other proving the impossibility of it. The husband, however, said as much as let me understand, that he had locked me up on purpose to bring the military, or officers of justice, to seize me. I was in the utmost perplexity, yet, for all that, and the imminent danger I was in, I fell asleep, and a more troubled and tormenting sleep never enchained a mortal frame. I had such dreams that they will not bear repetition, and early in the morning I awaked, feverish, and parched with thirst.

I went to call mine host, that he might let me out to the open air, but before doing so, I thought it necessary to put on some clothes. In attempting to do this, a circumstance arrested my attention, (for which I could in nowise account, which to this day I cannot unriddle, nor shall I ever be able to comprehend it while I live,) the frock and turban, which had furnished my disguise on the preceding day, were both removed, and my own black coat and cocked hat laid down in their place. At first I thought I was in a dream, and felt the weaver's beam, web, and treadle-strings with my hands, to convince myself that I was awake. I was certainly awake; and there was the door locked firm and fast as it was the evening before. I carried my own black coat to the small window, and examined it. It was my own in verity; and the sums of money, that I had concealed in case of any emergency, remained untouched. I trembled with astonishment; and on my return from the small window, went doiting in amongst the weaver's looms, till I entangled myself, and could not get out again without working great deray amongst the coarse linen threads that stood in warp from one end of the apartment unto the other. I had no knife whereby to cut the cords of this wicked man, and therefore was obliged to call out lustily for assistance. The weaver came half naked, unlocked the door, and, setting in his head and long neck, accosted me thus:

"What now, Mr. Satan? What for are ye roaring that gate? Are you fawn inna little hell, instead o' the big muckil ane? Deil be in your reistit trams! What for have ye abscondit yoursel into ma leddy's wab for?"

"Friend, I beg your pardon," said I; "I wanted to be at the light, and have somehow unfortunately involved myself in the intricacies of your web, from which I cannot get clear without doing you a great injury. Pray do, lend your experienced hand to extricate me."

"May a the pearls o' damnation light on your silly snout, an I dinna estricat ye weel enough! Ye ditit, donnart, deil's burd that ye be! what made ye gang howkin in there to be a poor man's ruin? Come out, ye vile rag-of-a-muffin, or I gar ye come out wi' mair shame and disgrace, an' fewer haill banes in your body."

My feet had slipped down through the double warpings of a web, and not being able to reach the ground with them, (there being a small pit below,) I rode upon a number of yielding threads, and there being nothing else that I could reach, to extricate myself was impossible. I was utterly powerless; and besides, the yarn and cords hurt me very much. For all that, the destructive weaver seized a loomspoke, and began a-beating me most unmercifully, while, entangled as I was, I could do nothing but shout aloud for mercy, or assistance, whichever chanced to be within hearing. The latter, at length, made its appearance, in the form of the weaver's wife, in the same state of dishabille with himself, who instantly interfered, and that most strenuously, on my behalf. Before her arrival, however, I had made a desperate effort to throw myself out of the entanglement I was in; for the weaver continued repeating his blows and cursing me so, that I determined to get out of his meshes at any risk. This effort made my case worse; for my feet being wrapt among the nether threads, as I threw myself from my saddle on the upper ones, my feet brought the others up through these, and I hung with my head down, and my feet as firm as they had been in a vice. The predicament of the web being thereby increased, the weaver's wrath was doubled in proportion, and he laid on without mercy.

At this critical juncture the wife arrived, and without hesitation rushed before her offended lord, withholding his hand from injuring me farther, although then it was uplifted along with the loom-spoke in overbearing ire.

"Dear Johnny! I think ye be gaen dementit this morning. Be quiet, my dear, an' dinna begin a Boddel Brigg[1] business in your ain house. What for ir ye persecutin' a servant o' the Lord's that gate, an' pitting the life out o' him wi' his head down an' his heels up?"

---

1 Bothwell Bridge, where the Royalists under Monmouth defeated the Covenanters, June 22, 1679.

"Had ye said a servant o' the deil's, Nans, ye wad hae been nearer the nail, for gin he binna the auld ane himsel, he's gayan sib till him. There, didna I lock him in on purpose to bring the military on him; an' in place o' that, hasna he keepit me in a sleep a' this while as deep as death? An' here do I find him abscondit like a speeder i' the mids o' my leddy's wab, an' me dreamin' a' the night that I had the deil i' my house, an' that he was clapper-clawin me ayont the loom. Have at you, ye brunstane thief!" and, in spite of the good woman's struggles, he lent me another severe blow.

"Now, Johnny Dods, my man! O Johnny Dods, think if that be like a Christian, and ane o' the heroes o' Boddel Brigg, to enter-tain a stranger, an' then bind him in a web wi' his head down, an' mell him to death! O Johnny Dods, think what you are about! Slack a pin, an' let the good honest religious lad out."

The weaver was rather overcome, but still stood to his point that I was the deil, though in better temper; and as he slackened the web to release me, he remarked, half laughing, "Wha wad hae thought that John Dods should hae escapit a' the snares an' dangers that circumfauldit him, an' at last should hae weaved a net to catch the deil."

The wife released me soon, and carefully whispered me, at the same time, that it would be as well for me to dress and be going. I was not long in obeying, and dressed myself in my black clothes, hardly knowing what I did, what to think, or whither to betake myself. I was sore hurt by the blows of the desperate ruffian; and, what was worse, my ankle was so much strained, that I could hard-ly set my foot to the ground. I was obliged to apply to the weaver once more, to see if I could learn any thing about my clothes, or how the change was effected. "Sir," said I, "how comes it that you have robbed me of my clothes, and put these down in their place over night?"

"Ha! thae claes? Me pit down thae claes!" said he, gaping with astonishment, and touching the clothes with the point of his fore-finger; "I never saw them afore, as I have death to meet wi': So help me God!"

He strode into the work-house where I slept, to satisfy himself that my clothes were not there, and returned perfectly aghast with consternation. "The doors were baith fast lockit," said he. "I could hae defied a rat either to hae gotten out or in. My dream has been true! My dream has been true! The Lord judge between thee and me; but, in his name, I charge you to depart out o' this house; an', gin it be your will, dinna tak the braidside o't w'ye, but gang quietly out at the door wi' your face foremost. Wife, let nought o' this enchanter's remain i' the house, to be a curse, an' a snare to us; gang an' bring him his gildit weapon, an' may the Lord protect a' his ain against its hellish an' deadly point!"

The wife went to seek my poniard, trembling so excessively that she could hardly walk, and shortly after, we heard a feeble scream from the pantry. The weapon had disappeared with the clothes, though under double lock and key; and the terror of the good people having now reached a disgusting extremity, I thought proper to make a sudden retreat, followed by the weaver's anathemas.

My state both of body and mind was now truly deplorable. I was hungry, wounded, and lame; an outcast and a vagabond in society; my life sought after with avidity, and all for doing that to which I was predestined by him who fore-ordains whatever comes to pass. I knew not whither to betake me. I had purposed going into England, and there making some use of the classical education I had received, but my lameness rendered this impracticable for the present. I was therefore obliged to turn my face towards Edinburgh, where I was little known—where concealment was more practicable than by skulking in the country, and where I might turn my mind to something that was great and good. I had a little money, both Scots and English, now in my possession, but not one friend in the whole world on whom I could rely. One devoted friend, it is true, I had, but he was become my greatest terror. To escape from him, I now felt that I would willingly travel to the farthest corners of the world, and be subjected to every deprivation; but after the certainty of what had taken place last night, after I had travelled thirty miles by secret and bye-ways, I saw not how escape from him was possible.

Miserable, forlorn, and dreading every person that I saw, either behind or before me, I hasted on towards Edinburgh, taking all the bye and unfrequented paths; and the third night after I left the weaver's house, I reached the West Port, without meeting with any thing remarkable. Being exceedingly fatigued and lame, I took lodgings in the first house I entered, and for these I was to pay two groats a-week, and to board and sleep with a young man who wanted a companion to make his rent easier. I liked this; having found from experience, that the great personage who had attached himself to me, and was now become my greatest terror among many surrounding evils, generally haunted me when I was alone, keeping aloof from all other society.

My fellow lodger came home in the evening, and was glad at my coming. His name was Linton, and I changed mine to Elliot. He was a flippant unstable being, one to whom nothing appeared a difficulty, in his own estimation, but who could effect very little, after all. He was what is called by some a compositor, in the Queen's printing house, then conducted by a Mr. James Watson.[1] In the course of our conversation that night, I told him that I was a first-rate classical scholar, and would gladly turn my attention to some business wherein my education might avail me something; and that there was nothing would delight me so much as an engagement in the Queen's printing office. Linton made no difficulty in bringing about that arrangement. His answer was, "Oo, gud sir, you are the very man we want. Gud bless your breast and your buttons, sir! Ay, that's neither here nor there—That's all very well—Ha-ha-ha—A byeword in the house, sir. But, as I was saying, you are the very *man* we want—You will get any money you like to ask, sir—*Any* money you like, sir. God bless your buttons!— That's settled—All done—Settled, settled—I'll do it, I'll do it—No more about it; no more about it. Settled, settled."

The next day I went with him to the office, and he presented me to Mr. Watson as the most wonderful genius and scholar ever known. His recommendation had little sway with Mr. Watson, who only smiled at Linton's extravagancies, as one does at the prattle of an infant. I sauntered about the printing office for the space of two or three hours, during which time Watson bustled about with green spectacles on his nose, and took no heed of me. But seeing that I still lingered, he addressed me at length, in a civil gentlemanly way, and inquired concerning my views. I satisfied him with all my answers, in particular those to his questions about the Latin and Greek languages; but when he came to ask testimonials of my character and acquirements, and found that I could produce none, he viewed me with a jealous eye, and said he dreaded I was some ne'er-do-weel, run from my parents or guardians, and he did not chuse to employ any such. I said my parents were both dead; and that being thereby deprived of the means of following out my education, it behoved me to apply to some business in which my education might be of some use to

---

1   Edinburgh-based printer and publisher; he became Queen's printer in Scotland in 1711.

me. He said he would take me into the office, and pay me according to the business I performed, and the manner in which I deported myself; but he could take no man into her Majesty's printing office upon a regular engagement, who could not produce the most respectable references with regard to morals. I could not but despise the man in my heart who laid such a stress upon morals, leaving grace out of the question; and viewed it as a deplorable instance of human depravity and self conceit; but for all that, I was obliged to accept of his terms, for I had an inward thirst and longing to distinguish myself in the great cause of religion, and I thought if once I could print my own works, how I would astonish mankind, and confound their self wisdom and their esteemed morality—blow up the idea of any dependence on good works, and *morality*, forsooth! And I weened that I might thus get me a name even higher than if I had been made a general of the Czar Peter's troops against the infidels.

I attended the office some hours every day, but got not much encouragement, though I was eager to learn every thing, and could soon have set types considerably well. It was here that I first conceived the idea of writing this journal, and having it printed, and applied to Mr. Watson to print it for me, telling him it was a religious parable such as the Pilgrim's Progress.[1] He advised me to print it close, and make it a pamphlet, and then if it did not sell, it would not cost me much; but that religious pamphlets, especially if they had a shade of allegory in them, were the very rage of the day. I put my work to the press, and wrote early and late; and encouraging my companion to work at odd hours, and on Sundays, before the press-work of the second sheet was begun, we had the work all in types, corrected, and a clean copy thrown off for farther revisal. The first sheet was wrought off; and I never shall forget how my heart exulted when at the printing house this day, I saw what numbers of my works were to go abroad among mankind, and I determined with myself that I would not put the Border name of Elliot, which I had assumed, to the work.

THUS far have my History and Confessions been carried.

---

1   *The Pilgrim's Progress* (1678), a religious allegory by John Bunyan.

I must now furnish my Christian readers with a key to the process, management, and winding up of the whole matter; which I propose, by the assistance of God, to limit to a very few pages.

Chesters, July 27, 1712.—My hopes and prospects are a wreck. My precious journal is lost! consigned to the flames! My enemy hath found me out, and there is no hope of peace or rest for me on this side the grave.

In the beginning of the last week, my fellow lodger came home, running in a great panic, and told me a story of the devil having appeared twice in the printing house, assisting the workmen at the printing of my book, and that some of them had been frightened out of their wits. That the story was told to Mr. Watson, who till that time had never paid any attention to the treatise, but who, out of curiosity, began and read a part of it, and thereupon flew into a great rage, called my work a medley of lies and blasphemy, and ordered the whole to be consigned to the flames, blaming his foreman, and all connected with the press, for letting a work go so far, that was enough to bring down the vengeance of heaven on the concern.

If ever I shed tears through perfect bitterness of spirit it was at that time, but I hope it was more for the ignorance and folly of my countrymen than the overthrow of my own hopes. But my attention was suddenly aroused to other matters, by Linton mentioning that it was said by some in the office the devil had inquired for me.

"Surely you are not such a fool," said I, "as to believe that the devil really was in the printing office?"

"Oo, gud bless you sir! saw him myself, gave him a nod, and good-day. Rather a gentlemanly personage—Green Circassian[1] hunting coat and turban—Like a foreigner—Has the power of vanishing in one moment though—Rather a suspicious circumstance that. Otherwise, his appearance not much against him."

If the former intelligence thrilled me with grief, this did so with terror. I perceived who the personage was that had visited the printing house in order to further the progress of my work; and at the approach of every person to our lodgings, I from that instant trembled every bone, lest it should be my elevated and

---

1   A type worn by inhabitants of Moslem Circassia, a region in the Northern Caucasus between the Black and Caspian Seas.

dreaded friend. I could not say I had ever received an office at his hand that was not friendly, yet these offices had been of a strange tendency; and the horror with which I now regarded him was unaccountable to myself. It was beyond description, conception, or the soul of man to bear. I took my printed sheets, the only copy of my unfinished work existing; and, on pretence of going straight to Mr. Watson's office, decamped from my lodgings at Portsburgh a little before the fall of evening, and took the road towards England.

As soon as I got clear of the city, I ran with a velocity I knew not before I had been capable of. I flew out the way towards Dalkeith[1] so swiftly, that I often lost sight of the ground, and I said to myself, "O that I had the wings of a dove, that I might fly to the farthest corners of the earth, to hide me from those against whom I have no power to stand!"

I travelled all that night and the next morning, exerting myself beyond my power; and about noon the following day I went into a yeoman's house, the name of which was Ellanshaws, and request-ed of the people a couch of any sort to lie down on, for I was ill, and could not proceed on my journey. They showed me to a sta-ble-loft where there were two beds, on one of which I laid me down; and, falling into a sound sleep, I did not awake till the evening, that other three men came from the fields to sleep in the same place, one of whom lay down beside me, at which I was exceedingly glad. They fell all sound asleep, and I was terribly alarmed at a conversation I overheard somewhere outside the sta-ble. I could not make out a sentence, but trembled to think I knew one of the voices at least, and rather than not be mistaken, I would that any man had run me through with a sword. I fell into a cold sweat, and once thought of instantly putting hand to my own life, as my only means of relief, (May the rash and sinful thought be in mercy forgiven!) when I heard as it were two persons at the door, contending, as I thought, about their right and interest in me. That the one was forcibly preventing the admission of the other, I could hear distinctly, and their language was mixed with something dreadful and mysterious. In an agony of terror, I awakened my snoring companion with great difficulty, and asked him, in a low whisper, who these were at the door? The man lay silent, and lis-

---

1   A town south east of Edinburgh.

tening, till fairly awake, and then asked if I had heard any thing? I said I had heard strange voices contending at the door.

"Then I can tell you, lad, it has been something neither good nor canny," said he: "It's no for naething that our horses are snorking that gate."

For the first time, I remarked that the animals were snorting and rearing as if they wished to break through the house. The man called to them by their names, and ordered them to be quiet; but they raged still the more furiously. He then roused his drowsy companions, who were alike alarmed at the panic of the horses, all of them declaring that they had never seen either Mause or Jolly start in their lives before. My bed-fellow and another then ventured down the ladder, and I heard one of them then saying, "Lord be wi' us! What can be i' the house? The sweat's rinning off the poor beasts like water."

They agreed to sally out together, and if possible to reach the kitchen and bring a light. I was glad at this, but not so much so when I heard the one man saying to the other, in a whisper, "I wish that stranger man may be canny enough."

"God kens!" said the other: "It doesnae look unco weel."

The lad in the other bed, hearing this, set up his head in manifest affright as the other two departed for the kitchen; and, I believe, he would have been glad to have been in their company. This lad was next the ladder, at which I was extremely glad, for had he not been there, the world should not have induced me to wait the return of these two men. They were not well gone, before I heard another distinctly enter the stable, and come towards the ladder. The lad who was sitting up in his bed, intent on the watch, called out, "Wha's that there? Walker, is that you? Purdie, I say, is it you?"

The darkling intruder paused for a few moments, and then came towards the foot of the ladder. The horses broke loose, and snorting and neighing for terror, raged through the house. In all my life I never heard so frightful a commotion. The being that occasioned it all, now began to mount the ladder toward our loft, on which the lad in the bed next the ladder sprung from his couch, crying out, "the L—d A——y preserve us! what can it be?" With that he sped across the loft, and by my bed, praying lustily all the way; and, throwing himself from the other end of the loft into a manger, he darted, naked as he was, through among the furious horses, and making the door, that stood open, in a moment he vanished and left me in the lurch. Powerless with terror, and calling out fearfully, I tried to follow his example; but not knowing the situation of the places with regard to one another, I missed the manger, and fell on the pavement in one of the stalls. I was both stunned and lamed on the knee; but terror prevailing, I got up and tried to escape. It was out of my power; for there were divisions and cross divisions in the house, and mad horses smashing every thing before them, so that I knew not so much as on what side of the house the door was. Two or three times was I knocked down by the animals, but all the while I never stinted crying out with all my power. At length, I was seized by the throat and hair of the head, and dragged away, I wist not whither. My voice was now laid, and all my powers, both mental and bodily, totally overcome; and I remember no more till I found myself lying naked on the kitchen table of the farm house, and something like a horse's rug thrown over me. The only hint that I got from the people of the house on coming to myself was, that my absence would be good company; and that they had got me in a woful state, one which they did not chuse to describe, or hear described.

As soon as day-light appeared, I was packed about my business, with the hisses and execrations of the yeoman's family, who viewed me as a being to be shunned, ascribing to me the visitations of that unholy night. Again was I on my way southward, as lonely, hopeless, and degraded a being as was to be found on life's weary round. As I limped out the way, I wept, thinking of what I might have been, and what I really had become: of my high and flourishing hopes, when I set out as the avenger of God on the sinful children of men; of all that I had dared for the exaltation and progress of the truth; and it was with great difficulty that my faith remained unshaken, yet was I preserved from that sin, and comforted myself with the certainty, that the believer's progress through life is one of warfare and suffering.

My case was indeed a pitiable one. I was lame, hungry, fatigued, and my resources on the very eve of being exhausted. Yet these were but secondary miseries, and hardly worthy of a thought, compared with those I suffered inwardly. I not only looked around me with terror at every one that approached, but I was become a terror to myself; or rather, my body and soul were become terrors to each other; and, had it been possible, I felt as if they would have gone to war. I dared not look at my face in a glass, for I shuddered at my own image and likeness. I dreaded the dawning, and trembled at the approach of night, nor was there one thing in nature that afforded me the least delight.

In this deplorable state of body and mind, was I jogging on towards the Tweed, by the side of the small river called Ellan,[1] when, just at the narrowest part of the glen, whom should I meet full in the face, but the very being in all the universe of God I would the most gladly have shunned. I had no power to fly from him, neither durst I, for the spirit within me, accuse him of falsehood; and renounce his fellowship. I stood before him like a condemned criminal, staring him in the face, ready to be winded, twisted, and tormented as he pleased. He regarded me with a sad and solemn look. How changed was now that majestic countenance, to one of haggard despair—changed in all save the extraordinary likeness to my late brother, a resemblance which misfortune and despair tended only to heighten. There were no kind greetings passed between us at meeting, like those which pass between the men of the world; he looked on me with eyes that froze the currents of my blood, but spoke not, till I assumed as much courage as to articulate "You here! I hope you have brought me tidings of comfort?"

"Tidings of despair!" said he. "But such tidings as the timid and the ungrateful deserve, and have reason to expect. You are an outlaw, and a vagabond in your country, and a high reward is offered for your apprehension. The enraged populace have burnt your house, and all that is within it; and the farmers on the land bless themselves at being rid of you. So fare it with every one who puts his hand to the great work of man's restoration to freedom, and draweth back, contemning the light that is within him! Your enormities caused me to leave you to yourself for a season, and you see what the issue has been. You have given some evil ones power over you, who long to devour you, both soul and body, and it has required all my power and influence to save you. Had it not been for my hand, you had been torn in pieces last night; but for once I prevailed. We must leave this land forthwith, for here there is neither peace, safety, nor comfort for us. Do you now, and here, pledge yourself to one who has so often saved your life, and has put his own at stake to do so? Do you pledge yourself that you will henceforth be guided by my counsel, and follow me whithersoever I chuse to lead?"

"I have always been swayed by your counsel," said I, "and for your sake, principally, am I sorry, that all our measures have proved

---

1   The Tweed and Ellan are rivers in south east Scotland.

abortive. But I hope still to be useful in my native isle, therefore let me plead that your highness will abandon a poor despised and outcast wretch to his fate, and betake you to your realms, where your presence cannot but be greatly wanted."

"Would that I could do so!" said he wofully. "But to talk of that is to talk of an impossibility. I am wedded to you so closely, that I feel as if I were the same person. Our essences are one, our bodies and spirits being united, so, that I am drawn towards you as by magnetism, and wherever you are, there must my presence be with you."

Perceiving how this assurance affected me, he began to chide me most bitterly for my ingratitude; and then he assumed such looks, that it was impossible for me longer to bear them; therefore I staggered out the way, begging and beseeching of him to give me up to my fate, and hardly knowing what I said; for it struck me, that, with all his assumed appearance of misery and wretchedness, there were traits of exultation in his hideous countenance, manifesting a secret and inward joy at my utter despair.

It was long before I durst look over my shoulder, but when I did so, I perceived this ruined and debased potentate coming slowly on the same path, and I prayed that the Lord would hide me in the bowels of the earth, or depths of the sea. When I crossed the Tweed, I perceived him still a little behind me; and my despair being then at its height, I cursed the time I first met with such a tormentor; though, on a little recollection it occurred, that it was at that blessed time when I was solemnly dedicated to the Lord, and assured of my final election, and confirmation, by an eternal decree never to be annulled. This being my sole and only comfort, I recalled my curse upon the time, and repented me of my rashness.

After crossing the Tweed, I saw no more of my persecutor that day, and had hopes that he had left me for a season; but, alas, what hope was there of my relief after the declaration I had so lately heard! I took up my lodgings that night in a small miserable inn in the village of Ancrum,[1] of which the people seemed alike poor and ignorant. Before going to bed, I asked if it was customary with them to have family worship of evenings? The man answered, that they were so hard set with the world, they often could not get

---

1 A village near the southern border of Scotland.

time, but if I would be so kind as officiate they would be much obliged to me. I accepted the invitation, being afraid to go to rest lest the commotions of the foregoing night might be renewed, and continued the worship as long as in decency I could. The poor people thanked me, hoped my prayers would be heard both on their account and my own, seemed much taken with my abilities, and wondered how a man of my powerful eloquence chanced to be wandering about in a condition so forlorn. I said I was a poor student of theology, on my way to Oxford. They stared at one another with expressions of wonder, disappointment, and fear. I afterwards came to learn, that the term *theology* was by them quite misunderstood, and that they had some crude conceptions that nothing was taught at Oxford but the *black arts*, which ridiculous idea prevailed over all the south of Scotland. For the present I could not understand what the people meant, and less so, when the man asked me, with deep concern, "If I was serious in my intentions of going to Oxford? He hoped not, and that I would be better guided."

I said my education wanted finishing;—but he remarked, that the Oxford arts were a bad finish for a religious man's education.—Finally, I requested him to sleep with me, or in my room all the night, as I wanted some serious and religious conversation with him, and likewise to convince him that the study of the fine arts, though not absolutely necessary, were not incompatible with the character of a Christian divine. He shook his head, and wondered how I could call them *Fine arts*—hoped I did not mean to convince him by any ocular demonstration, and at length reluctantly condescended to sleep with me, and let the lass and wife sleep together for one night. I believe he would have declined it, had it not been some hints from his wife, stating, that it was a good arrangement, by which I understood there were only two beds in the house, and that when I was preferred to the lass's bed, she had one to shift for.

The landlord and I accordingly retired to our homely bed, and conversed for some time about indifferent matters, till he fell sound asleep. Not so with me: I had that within which would not suffer me to close my eyes; and about the dead of night, I again heard the same noises and contention begin outside the house, as I had heard the night before; and again I heard it was about a sovereign and peculiar right in me. At one time the noise was on the top of the house, straight above our bed, as if the one party were breaking through the roof, and the other forcibly preventing it; at another time it was at the door, and at a third time at the window; but still mine host lay sound by my side, and did not waken. I was seized with terrors indefinable, and prayed fervently, but did not attempt rousing my sleeping companion until I saw if no better could be done. The women, however, were alarmed, and, rushing into our apartment, exclaimed that all the devils in hell were besieging the house. Then, indeed, the landlord awoke, and it was time for him, for the tumult had increased to such a degree, that it shook the house to its foundations, being louder and more furious than I could have conceived the heat of battle to be when the volleys of artillery are mixed with groans, shouts, and blasphemous cursing. It thundered and lightened; and there were screams, groans, laughter, and execrations, all intermingled.

I lay trembling and bathed in a cold perspiration, but was soon obliged to bestir myself, the inmates attacking me one after the other.

"O, Tam Douglas! Tam Douglas! haste ye an' rise out fra-yont that incarnal devil!" cried the wife: "Ye are in ayont the auld ane himsel, for our lass Tibbie saw his cloven cloots last night."

"Lord forbid!" roared Tam Douglas, and darted over the bed like a flying fish. Then, hearing the unearthly tumult with which he was surrounded, he returned to the side of the bed, and addressed me thus, with long and fearful intervals:

"If ye be the deil, rise up, an' depart in peace out o' this house—afore the bedstrae take kindling about ye, an' than it'll maybe be the waur for ye—Get up—an' gang awa out amang your cronies, like a good—lad—There's nae body here wishes you ony ill—D'ye hear me?"

"Friend," said I, "no Christian would turn out a fellow creature on such a night as this, and in the midst of such a commotion of the villagers."

"Na, if ye be a mortal man," said he, "which I rather think, from the use you made of the holy book—Nane o' your practical jokes on strangers an' honest foks. These are some o' your Oxford tricks, an' I'll thank you to be ower wi' them.—Gracious heaven, they are brikkin through the house at a' the four corners at the same time!"

The lass Tibby, seeing the innkeeper was not going to prevail with me to rise, flew toward the bed in desperation, and seizing me by the waist, soon landed me on the floor, saying: "Be ye deil, be ye chiel, ye's no lie there till baith the house an' us be swallowed up!"

Her master and mistress applauding the deed, I was obliged to attempt dressing myself, a task to which my powers were quite inadequate in the state I was in, but I was readily assisted by every one of the three; and as soon as they got my clothes thrust on in a loose way, they shut their eyes lest they should see what might drive them distracted, and thrust me out to the street, cursing me, and calling on the fiends to take their prey and begone.

The scene that ensued is neither to be described, nor believed, if it were. I was momently surrounded by a number of hideous fiends, who gnashed on me with their teeth, and clenched their crimson paws in my face; and at the same instant I was seized by the collar of my coat behind, by my dreaded and devoted friend, who pushed me on, and, with his gilded rapier waving and brandishing around me, defended me against all their united attacks. Horrible as my assailants were in appearance, (and they had all monstrous shapes,) I felt that I would rather have fallen into their hands, than be thus led away captive by my defender at his will and pleasure, without having the right or power to say my life, or any part of my will, was my own. I could not even thank him for his potent guardianship, but hung down my head, and moved on I knew not whither, like a criminal led to execution, and still the infernal combat continued, till about the dawning, at which time I looked up, and all the fiends were expelled but one, who kept at a distance; and still my persecutor and defender pushed me by the neck before him.

At length he desired me to sit down and take some rest, with which I complied, for I had great need of it, and wanted the power to withstand what he desired. There, for a whole morning did he detain me, tormenting me with reflections on the past, and pointing out the horrors of the future, until a thousand times I wished myself non-existent. "I have attached myself to your wayward fortune," said he; "and it has been my ruin as well as thine. Ungrateful as you are, I cannot give you up to be devoured; but this is a life that it is impossible to brook longer. Since our hopes are blasted in this world, and all our schemes of grandeur overthrown; and since our everlasting destiny is settled by a decree which no act of ours can invalidate, let us fall by our own hands, or by the hands of each other; die like heroes; and, throwing off this frame of dross and corruption, mingle with the pure ethereal essence of existence, from which we derived our being."

I shuddered at a view of the dreadful alternative, yet was obliged to confess that in my present circumstances existence was not to be borne. It was in vain that I reasoned on the sinfulness of the deed, and on its damning nature; he made me condemn myself out of my own mouth, by allowing the absolute nature of justifying grace, and the impossibility of the elect ever falling from the faith, or the glorious end to which they were called; and then he said, this granted, self-destruction was the act of a hero, and none but a coward would shrink from it, to suffer a hundred times more every day and night that passed over his head.

I said I was still contented to be that coward; and all that I begged of him was, to leave me to my fortune for a season, and to the just judgment of my creator; but he said his word and honour were engaged on my behoof, and these, in such a case, were not to be violated. "If you will not pity yourself, have pity on me," added he: "turn your eyes on me, and behold to what I am reduced."

Involuntarily did I turn round at the request, and caught a half glance of his features. May no eye destined to reflect the beauties of the New Jerusalem inward upon the beatific soul, behold such a sight as mine then beheld! My immortal spirit, blood, and bones, were all withered at the blasting sight; and I arose and withdrew, with groanings which the pangs of death shall never wring from me.

Not daring to look behind me, I crept on my way, and that night reached this hamlet on the Scottish border; and being grown reckless of danger, and hardened to scenes of horror, I took up my lodging with a poor hind, who is a widower, and who could only accommodate me with a bed of rushes at his fire-side. At midnight I heard some strange sounds, too much resembling those to which I had of late been inured; but they kept at a distance, and I was soon persuaded that there was a power protected that house superior to those that contended for, or had the mastery over me. Overjoyed at finding such an asylum, I remained in the humble cot. This is the third day I have lived under the roof, freed of my hellish assailants, spending my time in prayer, and writing out this my journal, which I have fashioned to stick in with my printed work, and to which I intend to add portions while I remain in this pilgrimage state, which, I find too well, cannot be long.

August 3, 1712.—This morning the hind has brought me word from Redesdale,[1] whither he had been for coals, that a stranger gentleman had been traversing that country, making the most earnest inquiries after me, or one of the same appearance; and from

---

1 A village in the south of Scotland.

the description that he brought of this stranger, I could easily perceive who it was. Rejoicing that my tormentor has lost traces of me for once, I am making haste to leave my asylum, on pretence of following this stranger, but in reality to conceal myself still more completely from his search. Perhaps this may be the last sentence ever I am destined to write. If so, farewell Christian reader! May God grant to thee a happier destiny than has been allotted to me here on earth, and the same assurance of acceptance above! *Amen.*

Ault-Righ, August 24, 1712.—Here am I, set down on the open moor to add one sentence more to my woful journal; and then, farewell all beneath the sun!

On leaving the hind's cottage on the Border, I hasted to the north-west, because in that quarter I perceived the highest and wildest hills before me. As I crossed the mountains above Hawick,[1] I exchanged clothes with a poor homely shepherd, whom I found lying on a hill side, singing to himself some woful love ditty. He was glad of the change, and proud of his saintly apparel; and I was no less delighted with mine, by which I now supposed myself completely disguised; and I found moreover that in this garb of a common shepherd I was made welcome in every house. I slept the first night in a farm-house nigh to the church of Roberton,[2] without hearing or seeing aught extraordinary; yet I observed next morning that all the servants kept aloof from me, and regarded me with looks of aversion. The next night I came to this house, where the farmer engaged me as a shepherd; and finding him a kind, worthy, and religious man, I accepted of his terms with great gladness. I had not, however, gone many times to the sheep, before all the rest of the shepherds told my master, that I knew nothing about herding, and begged of him to dismiss me. He perceived too well the truth of their intelligence; but being much taken with my learning, and religious conversation, he would not put me away, but set me to herd his cattle.

It was lucky for me, that before I came here, a report had prevailed, perhaps for an age, that this farm-house was haunted at certain seasons by a ghost. I say it was lucky for me, for I had not been in it many days before the same appalling noises began to prevail around me about midnight, often continuing till near the dawn-

---

1 A town in the south of Scotland.
2 A village near Hawick.

ing. Still they kept aloof, and without doors; for this gentleman's house, like the cottage I was in formerly, seemed to be a sanctuary from all demoniacal power. He appears to be a good man and a just, and mocks at the idea of supernatural agency, and he either does not hear these persecuting spirits, or will not acknowledge it, though of late he appears much perturbed.

The consternation of the menials has been extreme. They ascribe all to the ghost, and tell frightful stories of murders having been committed there long ago. Of late, however, they are beginning to suspect that it is I that am haunted; and as I have never given them any satisfactory account of myself, they are whispering that I am a murderer, and haunted by the spirits of those I have slain.

August 30.—This day I have been informed, that I am to be banished the dwelling-house by night, and to sleep in an out-house by myself, to try if the family can get any rest when freed of my presence. I have peremptorily refused acquiescence, on which my master's brother struck me, and kicked me with his foot. My body being quite exhausted by suffering, I am grown weak and feeble both in mind and bodily frame, and actually unable to resent any insult or injury. I am the child of earthly misery and despair, if ever there was one existent. My master is still my friend; but there are so many masters here, and every one of them alike harsh to me, that I wish myself in my grave every hour of the day. If I am driven from the family sanctuary by night, I know I shall be torn in pieces before morning; and then who will deign or dare to gather up my mangled limbs, and give them honoured burial.

My last hour is arrived: I see my tormentor once more approaching me in this wild. Oh, that the earth would swallow me up, or the hill fall and cover me! Farewell for ever!

September 7, 1712.—My devoted, princely, but sanguine friend, has been with me again and again. My time is expired, and I find a relief beyond measure, for he has fully convinced me that no act of mine can mar the eternal counsel, or in the smallest degree alter or extenuate one event which was decreed before the foundations of the world were laid. He said he had watched over me with the greatest anxiety, but perceiving my rooted aversion towards him, he had forborn troubling me with his presence. But now, seeing that I was certainly to be driven from my sanctuary that night, and that there would be a number of infernals watching to make a prey of my body, he came to caution me not to despair, for that he would protect me at all risks, if the power remained with him. He then repeated an ejaculatory prayer, which I was to pronounce, if in great extremity. I objected to the words as equivocal, and susceptible of being rendered in a meaning perfectly dreadful; but he reasoned against this, and all reasoning with him is to no purpose. He said he did not ask me to repeat the words, unless greatly straitened; and that I saw his strength and power giving way, and when perhaps nothing else could save me.

The dreaded hour of night arrived; and, as he said, I was expelled from the family residence, and ordered to a byre, or cow-house, that stood parallel with the dwelling-house behind, where, on a divot loft, my humble bedstead stood, and the cattle grunted and puffed below me. How unlike the splendid halls of Dalcastle! And to what I am now reduced, let the reflecting reader judge. Lord, thou knowest all that I have done for thy cause on earth! Why then art thou laying thy hands so sore upon me? Why hast thou set me as a butt of thy malice? But thy will must be done! Thou wilt repay me in a better world. *Amen.*

September 8.—My first night of trial in this place is overpast! Would that it were the last that I should ever see in this detested world! If the horrors of hell are equal to those I have suffered, eternity will be of short duration there, for no created energy can support them for one single month, or week. I have been buffeted as never living creature was. My vitals have all been torn, and every faculty and feeling of my soul racked, and tormented into callous insensibility. I was even hung by the locks over a yawning chasm, to which I could perceive no bottom, and then—not till then, did I repeat the tremendous prayer!—I was instantly at liberty; and what I now am, the Almighty knows! *Amen.*

September 18, 1712.—Still am I living, though liker to a vision than a human being; but this is my last day of mortal existence. Unable to resist any longer, I pledged myself to my devoted friend, that on this day we should die together, and trust to the charity of the children of men for a grave. I am solemnly pledged; and though I dared to repent, I am aware he will not be gainsaid, for he is raging with despair at his fallen and decayed majesty, and there is some miserable comfort in the idea that my tormentor shall fall with me. Farewell, world, with all thy miseries; for comforts or enjoyments hast thou none! Farewell, woman, whom I have despised and shunned; and man, whom I have hated; whom, nevertheless, I desire to leave in charity! And thou, sun, bright emblem of a far brighter effulgence, I bid farewell to thee also! I do not now take my last look of thee, for to thy glorious orb shall a poor suicide's last earthly look be raised. But, ah! who is yon that

I see approaching furiously—his stern face blackened with horrid despair! My hour is at hand.—Almighty God, what is this that I am about to do! The hour of repentance is past, and now my fate is inevitable.—*Amen, for ever!* I will now seal up my little book, and conceal it; and cursed be he who trieth to alter or amend!

END OF THE MEMOIR

WHAT can this work be? Sure, you will say, it must be an allegory; or (as the writer calls it) a religious PARABLE, showing the dreadful danger of self-righteousness? I cannot tell. Attend to the sequel: which is a thing so extraordinary, so unprecedented, and so far out of the common course of human events, that if there were ~~not true~~ not hundreds of living witnesses to attest the truth of it, I would not bid any rational being believe it.

In the first place, take the following extract from an authentic letter, published in *Blackwood's Magazine for August*, 1823.[1]

"On the top of a wild height called Cowanscroft, where the lands of three proprietors meet all at one point, there has been for long and many years the grave of a suicide marked out by a stone standing at the head, and another at the feet. Often have I stood musing over it myself, when a shepherd on one of the farms, of which it formed the extreme boundary, and thinking what could induce a young man, who had scarcely reached the prime of life, to brave his Maker, and rush into his presence by an act of his own erring hand, and one so unnatural and preposterous. But it never once occurred to me, as an object of curiosity, to dig up the mouldering bones of the culprit, which I considered as the most revolting of all objects. The thing was, however, done last month, and a discovery made of one of the greatest natural phenomena that I have heard of in this country.

"The little traditionary history that remains of this unfortunate youth, is altogether a singular one. He was not a native of the place, nor would he ever tell from what place he came; but he was

---

1   This letter, signed "James Hogg," appeared under the title "A Scots Mummy: To Sir Christopher North" in *Blackwood's Edinburgh Magazine* 14 (1823): 188-90.

remarkable for a deep, thoughtful, and sullen disposition. There was nothing against his character that any body knew of here, and he had been a considerable time in the place. The last service he was in was with a Mr. Anderson of Eltrive, (Ault-Righ, *the King's burn,*) who died about 100 years ago, and who had hired him during the summer to herd a stock of young cattle in Eltrive Hope. It happened one day in the month of September, that James Anderson, his master's son, went with this young man to the Hope to divert himself. The herd had his dinner along with him, and about one o'clock, when the boy proposed going home, the former pressed him very hard to stay and take share of his dinner; but the boy refused, for fear his parents might be alarmed about him, and said he *would* go home: on which the herd said to him, 'Then, if ye winna stay with me, James, ye may depend on't I'll cut my throat afore ye come back again.'

"I have heard it likewise reported, but only by one person, that there had been some things stolen out of his master's house a good while before, and that the boy had discovered a silver knife and fork, that was a part of the stolen property, in the herd's possession that day, and that it was this discovery that drove him to despair.

"The boy did not return to the Hope that afternoon; and, before evening, a man coming in at the pass called *The Hart Loup*, with a drove of lambs, on the way for Edinburgh, perceived something like a man standing in a strange frightful position at the side of one of Eldinhope hay-ricks. The driver's attention was riveted on this strange uncouth figure, and as the drove-road passed at no great distance from the spot, he first called, but receiving no answer, he went up to the spot, and behold it was the above-mentioned young man, who had hung himself in the hay rope that was tying down the rick.

"This was accounted a great wonder; and every one said, if the devil had not assisted him it was impossible the thing could have been done; for, in general, these ropes are so brittle, being made of green hay, that they will scarcely bear to be bound over the rick. And the more to horrify the good people of this neighbourhood, the driver said, when he first came in view, *he could almost give his oath* that he saw two people busily engaged at the hay-rick, going round it and round it, and he thought they were dressing it.

"If this asseveration approximated at all to truth, it makes this evident at least, that the unfortunate young man had hanged himself after the man with the lambs came in view. He was, however, quite dead when he cut him down. He had fastened two of the old hay-ropes at the bottom of the rick on one side, (indeed they are all fastened so when first laid on,) so that he had nothing to do but to loosen two of the ends on the other side. These he had tied in a knot round his neck, and then slackening his knees, and letting himself down gradually, till the hay-rope bore all his weight, he had contrived to put an end to his existence in that way. Now the fact is, that if you try all the ropes that are thrown over all the outfield hay-ricks in Scotland, there is not one among a thousand of them will hang a colley dog; so that the manner of this wretch's death was rather a singular circumstance.

"Early next morning, Mr. Anderson's servants went reluctantly away, and, taking an old blanket with them for a winding sheet, they rolled up the body of the deceased, first in his own plaid, letting the hay-rope still remain about his neck, and then rolling the old blanket over all, they bore the loathed remains away to the distance of three miles or so, on spokes, to the top of Cowan's-Croft, at the very point where the Duke of Buccleuch's land, the Laird of Drummelzier's, and Lord Napier's, meet, and there they buried him, with all that he had on and about him, silver knife and fork and altogether. Thus far went tradition, and no one ever disputed one jot of the disgusting oral tale.

"A nephew of that Mr. Anderson's who was with the hapless youth that day he died, says, that, as far as he can gather from the relations of friends that he remembers, and of that same uncle in particular, it is one hundred and five years next month, (that is September, 1823), since that event happened; and I think it likely that this gentleman's information is correct. But sundry other people, much older than he, whom I have consulted, pretend that it is six or seven years more. They say they have heard that Mr. James Anderson was then a boy ten years of age; that he lived to an old age, upwards of fourscore, and it is two and forty years since he died. Whichever way it may be, it was about that period some way, of that there is no doubt.

"It so happened, that two young men, William Shiel and W. Sword, were out, on an adjoining height, this summer, casting peats, and it came into their heads to open this grave in the wilderness, and see if there were any of the bones of the suicide of former ages and centuries remaining. They did so, but opened only one half of the grave, beginning at the head and about the middle at the same time. It was not long till they came upon the old blanket—I think they said not much more than a foot from the surface. They tore that open, and there was the hay rope lying stretched down alongst his breast, so fresh that they saw at first sight that it was made of *risp*, a sort of long sword-grass that grows about marshes and the sides of lakes. One of the young men seized the rope and pulled by it, but the old enchantment of the devil remained,—it would not break; and so he pulled and pulled at it, till behold the body came up into a sitting posture, with a broad blue bonnet on its head, and its plaid around it, all as fresh as that day it was laid in! I never heard of a preservation so wonderful, if it be true as was related to me, for still I have not had the curiosity to go and view the body myself. The features were all so plain, that an acquaintance might easily have known him. One of the lads gripped the face of the corpse with his finger and thumb, and the cheeks felt quite soft and fleshy, but the dimples remained and did not spring out again. He had fine yellow hair, about nine inches long; but not a hair of it could they pull out till they cut part of it off with a knife. They also cut off some portions of his clothes, which were all quite fresh, and distributed them among their acquaintances, sending a portion to me, among the rest, to keep as natural curiosities. Several gentlemen have in a manner forced me to give them fragments of these enchanted garments: I have, however, retained a small portion for you, which I send along with this, being a piece of his plaid, and another of his waistcoat breast, which you will see are still as fresh as that day they were laid in the grave.

"His broad blue bonnet was sent to Edinburgh several weeks ago, to the great regret of some gentlemen connected with the land, who wished to have it for a keep-sake. For my part, fond as I am of blue bonnets, and broad ones in particular, I declare I durst not have worn that one. There was nothing of the silver knife and fork discovered, that I heard of, nor was it very likely it should: but it would appear he had been very near run of cash, which I dare-say had been the cause of his utter despair; for, on searching his pockets, nothing was found but three old Scots halfpennies. These young men meeting with another shepherd afterwards, his curiosity was so much excited that they went and digged up the curious remains a second time, which was a pity, as it is likely that by these exposures to the air, and from the impossibility of burying it up again as closely as it was before, the flesh will now fall to dust."

★ ★ ★ ★ ★ ★

The letter from which the above is an extract, is signed JAMES HOGG, and dated from Altrive Lake, *August 1st*, 1823. It bears the

[Margin note: ? v. unlikely the boy would do this]

[Margin note: v. anticlimactic that's what happens when you dig up past]

Hogg creates unauthentic lines in his article ↓

stamp of authenticity in every line; yet, so often had I been hoaxed by the ingenious fancies displayed in that Magazine, that when this relation met my eye, I did not believe it; but from the moment that I perused it, I half formed the resolution of investigating these wonderful remains personally, if any such existed; for, in the immediate vicinity of the scene, as I supposed, I knew of more attractive metal than the dilapidated remains of mouldering suicides.

Accordingly, having some business in Edinburgh in September last, and being obliged to wait a few days for the arrival of a friend from London, I took that opportunity to pay a visit to my townsman and fellow collegian, Mr. L——t of C——d, advocate.[1] I mentioned to him Hogg's letter, asking him if the statement was founded at all on truth. His answer was, "I suppose so. For my part I never doubted the thing, having been told that there has been a deal of *Hogg makes fun of himself* talking about it up in the Forest for some time past. But, God knows! Hogg has imposed as ingenious lies on the public ere now."

I said, if it was within reach, I should like exceedingly to visit both the Shepherd and the Scots mummy he had described. Mr. L——t assented at the first proposal, saying he had no objections to take a ride that length with me, and make the fellow produce his credentials: That we would have a delightful jaunt through a romantic and now classical country, and some good sport into the bargain, provided he could procure a horse for me, from his father-in-law, next day. He sent up to a Mr. L——w[2] to inquire, who returned for answer, that there was an excellent pony at my service, and that he himself would accompany us, being obliged to attend a great sheep fair at Thirlestane; and that he was certain the Shepherd would be there likewise.

Mr. L——t said that was the very man we wanted to make our party complete; and at an early hour next morning we started for the ewe fair of Thirlestane, taking Blackwood's Magazine for August along with us. We rode through the ancient royal burgh of Selkirk,—halted and corned our horses at a romantic village, nigh to some deep linns on the Ettrick, and reached the market ground at Thirlestane-green a little before midday. We soon found Hogg,

---

1 John Lockhart of Chiefswood (1794-1854). Lockhart was Walter Scott's son-in-law and biographer, a frequent contributor to *Blackwood's*, and friend to that magazine's editor, John Wilson.

2 William Laidlaw (1780-1845), a steward to Scott.

standing near the *foot* of the market, as he called it, beside a great drove of *paulies*, a species of stock that I never heard of before. They were small sheep, striped on the backs with red chalk. Mr. L——t introduced me to him as a great wool-stapler, come to raise the price of that article; but he eyed me with distrust, and turning his back on us, answered, "I hae sell'd mine."

I followed, and shewing him the above-quoted letter, said I was exceedingly curious to have a look of these singular remains he had so ingeniously described; but he only answered me with the remark, that "It was a queer fancy for a woo-stapler to tak."

His two friends then requested him to accompany us to the spot, and to take some of his shepherds with us to assist in raising the body; but he spurned at the idea, saying, "Od bless ye, lad! I hae ither matters to mind. I hae a' thae paulies to sell, an' a' yon Highland stotts down on the green every ane; an' then I hae ten scores o' yowes to buy after, an' if I canna first sell my ain stock, I canna buy nae ither body's. I hae mair ado than I can manage the day, foreby ganging to houk up hunder-year-auld banes."

Finding that we could make nothing of him, we left him with his *paulies*, Highland stotts, grey jacket, and broad blue bonnet, to go in search of some other guide. L——w soon found one, for he seemed acquainted with every person in the fair. We got a fine old shepherd, named W——m B——e,[1] a great original, and a very obliging and civil man, who asked no conditions but that we should not speak of it, because he did not wish it to come to his master's ears, that he had been engaged in *sic a profane thing*. We promised strict secrecy; and accompanied by another farmer, Mr. S——t, and old B——e, we proceeded to the grave, which B——e described as about a mile and a half distant from the market ground.

We went into a shepherd's cot to get a drink of milk, when I read to our guide Mr. Hogg's description, asking him if he thought it correct? He said there was hardly a bit o't correct, for the grave was not on the hill of Cowan's-Croft, nor yet on the point where three lairds' lands met, but on the top of a hill called the Faw-Law, where there was no land that was not the Duke of Buccleuch's within a quarter of a mile. He added that it was a wonder how the

---

1 Possibly William Beattie. David Groves suggests the artist and poet William Blake (*Scottish Literary Journal* 18 [1991] 27-45).

poet could be mistaken there, who once herded the very ground where the grave is, and saw both hills from his own window. Mr. L——w testified great surprise at such a singular blunder, as also how the body came *not* to be buried at the meeting of three or four lairds' lands, which had always been customary in the south of Scotland. Our guide said he had always heard it reported, that the Eltrive men, with Mr. David Anderson at their head, had risen before day on the Monday morning, it having been on the Sabbath day that the man *put down* himself; and that they set out with the intention of burying him on Cowan's-Croft, where three marches met at a point. But it having been an invariable rule to bury such *lost sinners* before the rising of the sun, these five men were over-taken by day-light, as they passed the house of Berry-Knowe; and by the time they reached the top of the Faw-Law, the sun was beginning to skair the east. On this they laid down the body, and digged a deep grave with all expedition; but when they had done, it was too short, and the body being stiff, it would not go down, on which Mr. David Anderson looking to the east, and perceiving that the sun would be up on them in a few minutes, set his foot on the suicide's brow, and tramped down his head into the grave with his iron-heeled shoe, until his nose and skull crashed again, and at the same time uttered a terrible curse on the wretch who had dis-graced the family, and given them all this trouble. This anecdote, our guide said, he had heard when a boy, from the mouth of Robert Laidlaw, one of the five men who buried the body.

We soon reached the spot, and I confess I felt a singular sensa-tion, when I saw the grey stone standing at the head, and another at the feet, and the one half of the grave manifestly new digged, and closed up again as had been described. I could still scarcely deem the thing to be a reality, for the ground did not appear to be wet, but a kind of dry rotten moss. On looking around, we found some fragments of clothes, some teeth, and part of a pocket-book, which had not been returned into the grave, when the body had been last raised, for it had been twice raised before this, but only from the loins upward.

To work we fell with two spades, and soon cleared away the whole of the covering. The part of the grave that had been opened before, was filled with mossy mortar, which impeded us exceed-ingly, and entirely prevented a proper investigation of the fore parts of the body. I will describe every thing as I saw it before four respectable witnesses, whose names I shall publish at large if per-mitted. A number of the bones came up separately; for with the

constant flow of liquid stuff into the deep grave, we could not see
to preserve them in their places. At length great loads of coarse
clothes, blanketing, plaiding, &c. appeared; we tried to lift these
regularly up, and on doing so, part of a skeleton came up, but no
flesh, save a little that was hanging in dark flitters about the spine,
but which had no consistence; it was merely the appearance of
flesh without the substance. The head was wanting; and I being
very anxious to possess the skull, the search was renewed among
the mortar and rags. We first found a part of the scalp, with the long
hair firm on it; which, on being cleaned, is neither black nor fair,
but of a darkish dusk, the most common of any other colour. Soon
afterwards we found the skull, but it was not complete. A spade had
damaged it, and one of the temple quarters was wanting. I am no
phrenologist, not knowing one organ from another, but I thought
the skull of that wretched man no study. If it was particular for any
thing, it was for a smooth, almost perfect rotundity, with only a little protuberance above the vent of the ear.

When we came to the part of the grave that had never been
opened before, the appearance of every thing was quite different.
There the remains lay under a close vault of moss, and within a
vacant space; and I suppose, by the digging in the former part of
the grave, that part had been deepened, and drawn the moisture
away from this part, for here all was perfect. The breeches still suited the thigh, the stocking the leg, and the garters were wrapt as
neatly and as firm below the knee as if they had been newly tied.
The shoes were all opened in the seams, the hemp having decayed,
but the soles, upper leathers, and wooden heels, which were made
of birch, were all as fresh as any of those we wore. There was one
thing I could not help remarking, that in the inside of one of the
shoes there was a layer of cow's dung, about one eighth of an inch
thick, and in the hollow of the sole fully one fourth of an inch. It
was firm, green, and fresh; and proved that he had been working
in a byre. His clothes were all of a singular ancient cut, and no less
singular in their texture. Their durability certainly would have
been prodigious; for in thickness, coarseness, and strength, I never
saw any cloth in the smallest degree to equal them. His coat was a
frock coat, of a yellowish drab colour, with wide sleeves. It is
tweeled, milled, and thicker than a carpet. I cut off two of the skirts
and brought them with me. His vest was of striped serge, such as I
have often seen worn by country people. It was lined and backed
with white stuff. The breeches were a sort of striped plaiding,
which I never saw worn, but which our guide assured us was very

common in the country once, though, from the old clothes which he had seen remaining of it, he judged that it could not be less than 200 years since it was in fashion. His garters were of worsted, and striped with black or blue; his stockings gray, and wanting the feet. I brought samples of all along with me. I have likewise now got possession of the bonnet, which puzzles me most of all. It is not conformable with the rest of the dress. It is neither a broad bonnet, nor a Border bonnet; for there is an open behind, for tying, which no genuine Border bonnet, I am told, ever had. It seems to have been a Highland bonnet, worn in a flat way like a scone on the crown, such as is sometimes still seen in the west of Scotland. All the limbs, from the loins to the toes, seemed perfect and entire, but they could not bear handling. Before we got them returned again into the grave, they were all shaken to pieces, except the thighs, which continued to retain a kind of flabby form.

All his clothes that were sewed with linen yarn were lying in separate portions, the thread having rotten; but such as were sewed with worsted remained perfectly firm and sound. Among such a confusion, we had hard work to find out all his pockets, and our guide supposed, that, after all, we did not find above the half of them. In his vest pocket was a long clasp knife, very sharp; the haft was thin, and the scales shone as if there had been silver inside. Mr. Sc—t took it with him, and presented it to his neighbour, Mr. R——n of W—n L—e[1] who still has it in his possession. We found a comb, a gimblet, a vial, a small neat square board, a pair of plated knee-buckles, and several samples of cloth of different kinds, rolled neatly up within one another. At length, while we were busy on the search, Mr. L——t picked up a leathern case, which seemed to have been wrapped round and round by some ribbon, or cord, that had been rotten from it, for the swaddling marks still remained. Both L——w and B——e called out that "it was the tabacco spleuchan, and a well-filled ane too;" but on opening it out, we found, to our great astonishment, that it contained *a printed pamphlet*. We were all curious to see what sort of a pamphlet such a person would read; what it could contain that he seemed to have had such a care about? for the slough in which it was rolled, was fine chamois leather; what colour it had been, could not be known. But

---

1 It is unclear whose names these are. John Carey, in his 1969 Oxford edition, speculates that the initial "R" in the second name is a misread "A," in which case a "Mr Anderson of Wilton Lodge" would fit.

the pamphlet was wrapped so close together, and so damp, rotten, and yellow, that it seemed one solid piece. We all concluded, from some words that we could make out, that it was a religious tract, but that it would be impossible to make any thing of it. Mr. L——w remarked that it was a great pity if a few sentences could not be made out, for that it was a question what might be contained in that little book; and then he requested Mr. L——t to give it to me, as he had so many things of literature and law to attend to, that he would never think more of it. He replied, that either of us were heartily welcome to it, for that he had thought of returning it into the grave, if he could have made out but a line or two, to have seen what was its tendency.

"Grave, man!" exclaimed L——w, who speaks excellent strong broad Scots: "My truly, but ye grave weel! I wad esteem the contents o' that spleuchan as the most precious treasure. I'll tell you what it is, sir: I hae often wondered how it was that this man's corpse has been miraculously preserved frae decay, a hunder times langer than ony other body's, or than even a tanner's. But now I could wager a guinea, it has been for the preservation o' that little book. And Lord kens what may be in't! It will maybe reveal some mystery that mankind disna ken naething about yet."

"If there be any mysteries in it," returned the other, "it is not for your handling, my dear friend, who are too much taken up about mysteries already." And with these words he presented the mysterious pamphlet to me. With very little trouble, save that of a thorough drying, I unrolled it all with ease, and found the very tract which I have here ventured to lay before the public, part of it in small bad print, and the remainder in manuscript. The title page is written, and is as follows:

THE PRIVATE MEMOIRS
AND CONFESSIONS
OF A JUSTIFIED SINNER:
WRITTEN BY HIMSELF.
FIDEI CERTA MERCES.[1]

And, alongst the head, it is the same as given in the present edition of the work. I altered the title to *A Self-justified Sinner*, but my

---

1 "To the faithful, reward is certain."

booksellers did not approve of it; and there being a curse pronounced by the writer on him that should dare to alter or amend, I have let it stand as it is. Should it be thought to attach discredit to any received principle of our church, I am blameless. The printed part ends at page 340,[1] and the rest is in a fine old hand, extremely small and close. I have ordered the printer to procure a fac-simile of it, to be bound in with the volume.

With regard to the work itself, I dare not venture a judgment, for I do not understand it. I believe no person, man or woman, will ever peruse it with the same attention that I have done, and yet I confess that I do not comprehend the writer's drift. It is certainly impossible that these scenes could ever have occurred, that he describes as having himself transacted. I think it *may be* possible that he had some hand in the death of his brother, and yet I am disposed greatly to doubt it; and the numerous distorted traditions, &c. which remain of that event, may be attributable to the work having been printed and burnt, and of course the story known to all the printers, with their families and gossips. That the young Laird of Dalcastle came by a violent death, there remains no doubt; but that this wretch slew him, there is to me a good deal. However, allowing this to have been the case, I account all the rest either dreaming or madness; or, as he says to Mr. Watson, a religious parable, on purpose to illustrate something scarcely tangible, but to which he seems to have attached great weight. Were the relation at all consistent with reason, it corresponds so minutely with traditionary facts, that it could scarcely have missed to have been received as authentic; but in this day, and with the present generation, it will not go down, that a man should be daily tempted by the devil, in the semblance of a fellow-creature; and at length lured to self-destruction, in the hopes that this same fiend and tormentor was to suffer and fall along with him. It was a bold theme for an allegory, and would have suited that age well had it been taken up by one fully qualified for the task, which this writer was not. In short, we must either conceive him not only the greatest fool, but the greatest wretch, on whom was ever stamped the form of humanity; or, that he was a religious maniac, who wrote and wrote about a deluded creature, till he arrived at that height of madness, that he believed himself the very object whom he had been all

---

1 In the present edition the printed memoir ends at page 208.

along describing. And in order to escape from an ideal tormentor, committed that act for which, according to the tenets he embraced, there was no remission, and which consigned his memory and his name to everlasting detestation.

FINIS

Appendix A: Contexts of Reference

[The following documents relate to the religious contexts of the novel: election and predestination, Calvinism and Antinomianism (see also Introduction).]

1. The Epistle of Paul the Apostle to the Romans (King James Version).

i. *Romans* Chapter 3
19 Now we know that what things soever the law saith, it saith to them who are under the law: that every mouth may be stopped, and all the world may become guilty before God.
20 Therefore by the deeds of the law there shall no flesh be justified in his sight: for by the law *is* the knowledge of sin.
21 But now the righteousness of God without the law is manifested, being witnessed by the law and the prophets;
22 Even the righteousness of God *which is* by faith of Jesus Christ unto all and upon all them that believe: for there is no difference:
23 For all have sinned, and come short of the glory of God;
24 Being justified freely by his grace through the redemption that is in Christ Jesus:
25 Whom God hath set forth *to be* a propitiation through faith in his blood, to declare his righteousness for the remission of sins that are past, through the forbearance of God;
26 To declare, *I say*, at this time his righteousness: that he might be just, and the justifier of him which believeth in Jesus.
27 Where *is* boasting then? It is excluded. By what law? of works? Nay: but by the law of faith.
28 Therefore we conclude that a man is justified by faith without the deeds of the law.
29 *Is he* the God of the Jews only? *is he* not also of the Gentiles? Yes, of the Gentiles also:
30 Seeing *it is* one God, which shall justify the circumcision by faith, and uncircumcision through faith.
31 Do we then make void the law through faith? God forbid: yea, we establish the law.

ii. *Romans* Chapter 4
1 What shall we say then that Abraham our father, as pertaining to the flesh, hath found?

2 For if Abraham were justified by works, he hath *whereof* to glory; but not before God.

3 For what saith the scripture? Abraham believed God, and it was counted unto him for righteousness.

4 Now to him that worketh is the reward not reckoned of grace, but of debt.

5 But to him that worketh not, but believeth on him that justifieth the ungodly, his faith is counted for righteousness.

6 Even as David also describeth the blessedness of the man, unto whom God imputeth righteousness without works,

7 *Saying,* Blessed *are* they whose iniquities are forgiven, and whose sins are covered.

8 Blessed *is* the man to whom the Lord will not impute sin.

9 *Cometh* this blessedness then upon the circumcision *only,* or upon the uncircumcision also? for we say that faith was reckoned to Abraham for righteousness.

10 How was it then reckoned? when he was in circumcision, or in uncircumcision? Not in circumcision, but in uncircumcision.

11 And he received the sign of circumcision, a seal of the righteousness of the faith which *he had yet* being uncircumcised: that he might be the father of all them that believe, though they be not circumcised; that righteousness might be imputed unto them also:

12 And the father of circumcision to them who are not of the circumcision only, but who also walk in the steps of that faith of our father Abraham, which *he had* being *yet* uncircumcised.

13 For the promise, that he should be the heir of the world, *was* not to Abraham, or to his seed, through the law, but through the righteousness of faith.

14 For if they which are of the law *be* heirs, faith is made void, and the promise made of none effect:

15 Because the law worketh wrath: for where no law is, *there is* no transgression.

16 Therefore *it is* of faith, that *it might be* by grace; to the end the promise might be sure to all the seed; not to that only which is of the law, but to that also which is of the faith of Abraham; who is the father of us all.

iii. *Romans* Chapter 6

14 For sin shall not have dominion over you: for ye are not under the law, but under grace.

15 What then? shall we sin, because we are not under the law, but under grace? God forbid.

16 Know ye not, that to whom ye yield yourselves servants to obey, his servants ye are to whom ye obey; whether of sin unto death, or of obedience unto righteousness?

17 But God be thanked, that ye were the servants of sin, but ye have obeyed from the heart that form of doctrine which was delivered you.

18 Being then made free from sin, ye became the servants of righteousness.

19 I speak after the manner of men because of the infirmity of your flesh: for as ye have yielded your members servants to uncleanness and to iniquity unto iniquity; even so now yield your members servants to righteousness unto holiness.

20 For when ye were the servants of sin, ye were free from righteousness.

21 What fruit had ye then in those things whereof ye are now ashamed? for the end of those things *is* death.

22 But now being made free from sin, and become servants to God, ye have your fruit unto holiness, and the end everlasting life.

23 For the wages of sin *is* death; but the gift of God *is* eternal life through Jesus Christ our Lord.

iv. *Romans* Chapter 7

1 Know ye not, brethren, (for I speak to them that know the law,) how that the law hath dominion over a man as long as he liveth?

2 For the woman which hath an husband is bound by the law to *her* husband so long as he liveth; but if the husband be dead, she is loosed from the law of *her* husband.

3 So then if, while *her* husband liveth, she be married to another man, she shall be called an adulteress: but if her husband be dead, she is free from that law; so that she is no adulteress, though she be married to another man.

4 Wherefore, my brethren, ye also are become dead to the law by the body of Christ; that ye should be married to another, *even* to him who is raised from the dead, that we should bring forth fruit unto God.

5 For when we were in the flesh, the motions of sins, which were by the law, did work in our members to bring forth fruit unto death.

6 But now we are delivered from the law, that being dead wherein we were held; that we should serve in newness of spirit, and not *in* the oldness of the letter.

v. *Romans* Chapter 8

28 And we know that all things work together for good to them that love God, to them who are the called according to *his* purpose.

29 For whom he did foreknow, he also did predestinate *to be* conformed to the image of his Son, that he might be the firstborn among many brethren.

30 Moreover whom he did predestinate, them he also called: and whom he called, them he also justified: and whom he justified, them he also glorified.

31 What shall we then say to these things? If God *be* for us, who *can be* against us?

32 He that spared not his own Son, but delivered him up for us all, how shall he not with him also freely give us all things?

33 Who shall lay any thing to the charge of God's elect? *It is* God that justifieth.

34 Who *is* he that condemneth? *It is* Christ that died, yea rather, that is risen again, who is even at the right hand of God, who also maketh intercession for us.

35 Who shall separate us from the love of Christ? *shall* tribulation, or distress, or persecution, or famine, or nakedness, or peril, or sword?

36 As it is written, For thy sake we are killed all the day long; we are accounted as sheep for the slaughter.

37 Nay, in all these things we are more than conquerors through him that loved us.

38 For I am persuaded, that neither death, nor life, nor angels, nor principalities, nor powers, nor things present, nor things to come,

39 Nor height, nor depth, nor any other creature, shall be able to separate us from the love of God, which is in Christ Jesus our Lord.

vi. *Romans* Chapter 10

1 Brethren, my heart's desire and prayer to God for Israel is, that they might be saved.

2 For I bear them record that they have a zeal of God, but not according to knowledge.

3 For they being ignorant of God's righteousness, and going about to establish their own righteousness, have not submitted themselves unto the righteousness of God.

4 For Christ *is* the end of the law for righteousness to every one that believeth.

5 For Moses describeth the righteousness which is of the law, That the man which doeth those things shall live by them.

6 But the righteousness which is of faith speaketh on this wise, Say not in thine heart, Who shall ascend into heaven? (that is, to bring Christ down *from above*:)

7 Or, Who shall descend into the deep? (that is, to bring up Christ again from the dead.)

8 But what saith it? The word is nigh thee, *even* in thy mouth, and in thy heart: that is, the word of faith, which we preach;

9 That if thou shalt confess with thy mouth the Lord Jesus, and shalt believe in thine heart that God hath raised him from the dead, thou shalt be saved.

10 For with the heart man believeth unto righteousness; and with the mouth confession is made unto salvation.

11 For the scripture saith, Whosoever believeth on him shall not be ashamed.

vii. *Romans* Chapter 11

1 I say then, Hath God cast away his people? God forbid. For I also am an Israelite, of the seed of Abraham, *of* the tribe of Benjamin.

2 God hath not cast away his people which he foreknew. Wot ye not what the scripture saith of Elias? how he maketh intercession to God against Israel, saying,

3 Lord, they have killed thy prophets, and digged down thine altars; and I am left alone, and they seek my life.

4 But what saith the answer of God unto him? I have reserved to myself seven thousand men, who have not bowed the knee to *the image of* Baal.

5 Even so then at this present time also there is a remnant according to the election of grace.

6 And if by grace, then *is it* no more of works: otherwise grace is no more grace. But if *it be* of works, then is it no more grace: otherwise work is no more work.

2. Jean Calvin

i. *Institutes of the Christian Religion* III. xi. 2[1]
"Justification by Faith"
[L]et us first explain the meaning of these expressions, *To be justified in the sight of God, To be justified by faith or by works*. He is said

---

1   Book and chapter headings correspond to those in John Allen's 1813 translation (London: J. Walker et al).

to be *justified in the sight of God*, who in the Divine judgment is reputed righteous, and accepted on account of his righteousness: for as iniquity is abominable to God, so no sinner can find favour in his sight, as a sinner, or so long as he is considered as such. Wherever sin is, therefore, it is accompanied with the wrath and vengeance of God. He is justified who is considered not as a sinner, but as a righteous person, and on that account stands in safety before the tribunal of God, where all sinners are confounded and ruined... [H]e is justified before God, who, not being numbered among sinners, has God for a witness and assertor of his righteousness. Thus he must be said, therefore, to be *justified by faith*, whose life discovers such purity and holiness, as to deserve the character of righteousness before the throne of God; or who, by the integrity of his works, can answer and satisfy the Divine judgment. On the other hand, he will be *justified by faith*, who, being excluded from the righteousness of works, apprehends by faith the righteousness of Christ, invested in which, he appears, in the sight of God, not as a sinner, but as a righteous man. Thus we simply explain justification to be an acceptance, by which God receives us into his favour and esteems us as righteous persons: and we say that it consists in the remission of sins and the imputation of the righteousness of Christ...

ii. *Institutes* III xi.13

But as many persons imagine righteousness to be composed of faith and works, let us also prove, before we proceed, that the righteousness of faith is so exceedingly different from that of works, that if one be established, the other must necessarily be subverted... If, by establishing our own righteousness, we reject the righteousness of God; then, in order to obtain the latter, the former must doubtless be entirely renounced... [A]s long as there remains the least particle of righteousness in our works, we retain some cause for boasting. But if faith excludes all boasting, the righteousness of works can by no means be associated with the righteousness of faith... [R]ighteousness is attributed to faith through grace. Therefore it is not from the merit of works. Adieu, therefore, to the fanciful notion of those who imagine a righteousness compounded of faith and works...

iii. *Institutes* III. xi. 21

We are informed, that sin makes a division between man and God, and turns the Divine countenance away from the sinner. Nor can it be otherwise; because it is incompatible with his righteousness to have any commerce with sin. Hence the apostle teaches, that man is an enemy to God, till he be reconciled to him by Christ. Whom therefore the Lord receives into fellowship with him, him he is said to justify; because he cannot receive any one into favour or into fellowship with himself, without making him from a sinner to be a righteous person. This, we add, is accomplished by the remission of sins. For if they, whom the Lord hath reconciled to himself, be judged according to their works, they will still be found actually sinners; who, notwithstanding, must be absolved and free from sin. It appears then, that those whom God receives, are made righteous no otherwise, than as they are purified by being cleansed from all their defilements by the remission of their sins: so that such a righteousness may, in one word, be denominated, a remission of sins...

iv. *Institutes* III. xi. 23
Hence it is also evident, that we obtain justification before God, solely by the intervention of the righteousness of Christ. Which is equivalent to saying, that a man is righteous, not in himself, but because the righteousness of Christ is communicated to him by imputation; and this is a point which deserves an attentive consideration. For it supersedes that idle notion, that a man is justified by faith, because faith receives the Spirit of God by whom he is made righteous; which is too repugnant to the foregoing doctrine, ever to be reconcilable to it. For he must certainly be destitute of all righteousness of his own, who is taught to seek a righteousness out of himself... We see that our righteousness is not in ourselves, but in Christ; and that all our title to it, rests solely on our being partakers of Christ; for in possessing him, we possess all his riches with him...

v. *Institutes* III. xix. 2
"Justification and Christian Liberty"
Christian liberty, according to my judgment, consists of three parts. The first part is, that the consciences of the faithful, when seeking an assurance of their justification before God, should raise themselves above the law, and forget all the righteousness of the law... The whole life of Christians ought to be an exercise of piety, since they are called to sanctification. It is the office of the law to remind them of their duty, and thereby to excite them to the pursuit of holiness and integrity. But when their consciences are solicitous

how God may be propitiated, what answer they shall make, and on what they shall rest their confidence, if called to his tribunal; there must then be no consideration of the requisitions of the law, but Christ alone must be proposed for righteousness, who exceeds all the perfection of the law...

vi. *Institutes* III. xix. 4
The second part of Christian liberty, which is dependent on the first, is, that their consciences do not observe the law, as being under any legal obligation; but that, being liberated from the yoke of the law, they yield a voluntary obedience to the will of God. For being possessed with perpetual terrors, as long as they remain under the dominion of the law, they will never engage with alacrity and promptitude in the service of God, unless they have previously received this liberty...

vii. *Institutes* III. xix. 5
In short, they who are bound by the yoke of the law, are like slaves who have certain daily tasks appointed by their masters. They think they have done nothing, and presume not to enter into the presence of their masters without having finished the work prescribed to them. But children, who are treated by their parents in a more liberal manner, hesitate not to present to them their imperfect, and in some respects faulty works, in confidence that their obedience and promptitude of mind will be accepted by them, though they have not performed all that they wished. Such children ought we to be, feeling a certain confidence that our services, however small, rude, and imperfect, will be approved by our most indulgent father...

viii. *Institutes* III. xix. 7
The third part of Christian liberty teaches us, that we are bound by no obligation before God respecting external things, which in themselves are indifferent; but that we may indifferently sometimes use, and at other times omit them. And the knowledge of this liberty also is very necessary for us; for without it we shall have no tranquillity of conscience, nor will there be any end of superstitions...

ix. *Institutes* III.xxi. 1
"Predestination and the Doctrine of Election"
If it be evidently the result of the Divine will, that salvation is freely offered to some, and others are prevented from attaining it; this

immediately gives rise to important and difficult questions, which are incapable of any other explication, than by the establishment of pious minds in what ought to be received concerning election and predestination:—a question, in the opinion of many, full of perplexity; for they consider nothing more unreasonable, than that of the common mass of mankind some should be predestined to salvation, and others to destruction... We shall never be clearly convinced as we ought to be, that our salvation flows from the fountain of God's free mercy, till we are acquainted with his eternal election, which illustrates the grace of God by this comparison, that he adopts not all promiscuously to the hope of salvation, but gives to some what he refuses to others...

x. *Institutes* III. xxi. 5

Predestination we call the eternal decree of God, by which he hath determined in himself, what he would have to become of every individual of mankind. For they are not all created with a similar destiny; but eternal life is fore-ordained for some, and eternal damnation for others, Every man therefore, being created for one or the other of these ends, we say, he is predestined either to life or to death...

xi. *Institutes* III. xxi. 7

In conformity, therefore, to the clear doctrine of the Scripture, we assert, that by an eternal and immutable counsel, God hath once for all determined, both whom he would admit to salvation, and whom he would condemn to destruction. We affirm that this counsel, as far as concerns the elect, is founded on his gratuitous mercy, totally irrespective of human merit: but that to those whom he devotes to condemnation, the gate of life is closed by a just and irreprehensible, but incomprehensible, judgment. In the elect, we consider calling as an evidence of election, and justification as another token of its manifestation, till they arrive in glory, which constitutes its completion. As God seals his elect by vocation and justification, so by excluding the reprobate from the knowledge of his name and the sanctification of his Spirit, he affords an indication of the judgment that awaits them...

xii. *Institutes* III. xxii. 10

It is objected by some, that God will be inconsistent with himself, if he invites all men universally to come to him, and receives only a few elect... What they assume, I deny, as being false in two respects. For he who threatens drought to one city while it rains upon another, and who denounces to another place a famine of doctrine, lays himself under no positive obligation to call all men alike. And he who, forbidding Paul to preach the word in Asia, and suffering him not to go into Bithynia, calls him into Macedonia, demonstrates his right to distribute this treasure to whom he pleases. In Isaiah, he still more fully declares his destination of the promises of salvation exclusively for the elect: for of them only, and not indiscriminately of all mankind, he declares that they shall be his disciples. Whence it appears, that when the doctrine of salvation is offered to all for their effectual benefit, it is a corrupt prostitution of that which is declared to be reserved particularly for the children of the Church. At present let this suffice, that though the voice of the gospel addresses all men generally, yet the gift of faith is bestowed on few...

xiii: *Institutes* III. xxiv. 10
Now the elect are not gathered into the fold of Christ by calling, immediately from their birth, nor all at the same time, but according as God is pleased to dispense his grace to them. Before they are gathered to that chief Shepherd, they go astray, scattered in the common wilderness, and differing in no respect for others, except in being protected by the special mercy of God from rushing down the precipice of eternal death. If you observe them therefore, you will see the posterity of Adam, partaking of the common corruption of the whole species. That they go not to the most desperate extreme of impiety, is not owing to any innate goodness of theirs, but because the eye of God watches over them, and his hand is extended for their preservation...

3. *A Cloud of Witnesses, for the Royal Prerogatives of Jesus Christ; or, The Last Speeches and Testimonies of those who have suffered for the Truth, in Scotland, since the Year 1680* (n.p., 1714).

i. *A Cloud of Witnesses* i–iii
The Glorious Frame and Contrivance of Religion, Revealed by the Ever-blessed JEHOVAH, in the *Face* or Person of JESUS CHRIST, for the Recovery of lost Mankind into a State of Favour and Reconcilement with Himself, is so excellently ordered in the Counsels of Infinite Wisdom, and exactly adjusted to the Real Delight, Contentment and Happiness of the Rational World; that it might justly be wondered, why so many Men in all Ages, other-

wise of good Intellectuals, have not only had a secret Disgust thereat themselves, but laboured to rob others of the Comfort and Benefit of it, and make the World a Chaos of Confusion by Persecutions raised against it; Had not the Holy Spirit in the Scriptures laid open the hidden Springs of this Malice and Enmity, which exerts its self in so many of the Children of Men. We are told in these Divinely inspired Writings, that the first Source of this Opposition that the true Religion meets within the World, flows originally from Satan, that inveterate Enemy of GOD's Glory and Man's Happiness; Who having himself *left his Original State* of Obedience to, and Enjoyment of GOD his Creator, hath no other *Levamen* of his inevitable Miseries, but to draw the Race of Mankind into the like Ruin, which is the only Satisfaction, that malicious Spirit is capable of. This restless Adversary perceiving, That through the Grace and Love of GOD manifested in CHRIST, a great Number of these, whom he thought he had secured to his Slavery, are redeemed, and called by the Gospel out of that intolerable Servitude, into a *Glorious Liberty*, and secured by Faith to Salvation; Labours by two great Engines of *Open Force* and *Secret Fraud*, to keep them in or regain them to his Obedience; Hence the sacred Scriptures describe him, both as a *Dragon* for *Cruelty*, and a *Serpent* for *Subtilty*: But because he either cannot, or thinks not fit to do this visibly in Person; therefore he does it more invisibly, and so more successfully by his Agents, in whom he works, who, because of their Unreasonable Unbelief, are called *Children of Impersuasion*: These he Acts and Animates, as it were so many Machines, to endeavour by *Crafty Seduction*, or *Violent Persecution*, to draw, or drive the *Followers of the Lamb* from their Subjection, Obedience and Loyalty to the *Captain of their Salvation*, that he may *drown them in Perdition and Destruction*. This is the latent Origin of all Persecution, the Mint where all the other more visible Causes of the bloody Violence, the People of GOD meet withal, are struck and framed. This is the Grand Design to which they tend, to root out the *Obedience of Faith* out of the World, and deprive the Son of GOD of his rightful Dominion over his Subjects, whom he has chosen, redeemed and sanctified for himself.

As this holds true of all the Persecutions, raised against the Church and Truths of GOD, whether in the Persons of *Jews* or *Christians*, by whatever hands, *Pagan* or *Antichristian*, so 'tis eminently verified of the Persecutions of the Church of *Scotland*, prosecuted by a profane wicked Generation of *Malignant Prelatics*, during the Reigns of the late King *Charles 2*, *James 7...*

JESUS CHRIST the only Begotten of the Father having received the Church of *Scotland*, as one of the *utmost Isles of the Earth for His Possession* by Solemn grant from JEHOVAH, was pleased, as to call her from the Deplorable State of *Pagan*, and Reform her from the Ruinous Condition of *Antichristian* darkness; so to dignify her in a peculiar manner, to contend and Suffer for that Truth, THAT HE IS A KING AND LAW-GIVER TO HIS CHURCH, having power to institute her Form of Government, to give her Laws, Officers, and Censures whereby she should be Governed, and hath not left it Ambulatory and uncertain what Government he will have in force for the ordering of His House, but hath expressly determined in His Word every necessary part thereof, and hath not put any Power into the hands of any Mortal, whether Pope, Prelate, Prince, or Potentate, as a vicarious Head in His Personal absence, whereby they may alter the Form of Government at their pleasure and make what kind of Officers, Canons and Censures they please; but all the Power that this king hath left in his Church, concerning her Government, is purely and properly Ministerial under the Direction and Regulation of His Sovereign Pleasure, Revealed in His written Word.

This, this is the most radiant Pearl in the Church of *Scotland's* Garland; that she hath been honoured valiantly to stand up for the *Headship* and *Royal Prerogative* of Her King and Husband, Jesus Christ, in all the Periods of her Reformation. For no sooner had She thrown off the Yoke of the *Popes* pretended Jurisdiction and Authority, but presently, while She was labouring by means of these Censures, which Christ had Institute, to Root out the Damnable Heresies which that Enemy had sown, all on a sudden King *James* VI. naturally Ambitious, and instigated by Interested and Projecting Counsellors, attempts a Rape upon Her Chastity and Loyalty to Her Husband and Lord... Upon the same bottom of a pretended Royal Jurisdiction over the Church, He attempted, and in a great measure effected, the Establishment of *Popish Hierarchy* and *Romish Ceremonies*, by setting up Prelates, and bringing in the *Perth* Articles,[1] flattering some, and overawing others of the Ministry into a compliance therewith... And in like manner *Charles* I. following his Father's Example and Instructions, endeavoured upon pretence of

---

1 Liturgical innovations imposed by James at the meeting of the General Assembly of the Church of Scotland in Perth, 1618, in an effort to bring the Kirk into line with Anglican practice.

the same Prerogative to improve upon what his Father had begun and complete the Church's slavery by obtruding upon her a Liturgy and Canons framed *à la mode d'Angleterre*...

ii. *A Cloud of Witnesses* vii.
[It is certain the Royalists] had nothing else before them, but to bring People to a tame Submission and slavish Compliance with the whole Course of their Christ-dethroning, and Land-enslaving Constitutions and Administrations; for they intended the same thing by urging People to say, *God Save the King,* as by the *Oath of Allegiance,* Declaration, or Test, namely an acknowledgement of their Authority, wherewith they had vested him in the forementioned Articles and others of like Nature. Less than this could never serve their Design, which was still the same, whatever alteration might appear to be in their way of prosecuting it...

iii. *A Cloud of Witnesses* x
Their finest Topic wherein they [the interrogators of the Covenanters] insulted and Gloried most, was the Death of *James Sharp* Arch-Bishop of *St. Andrews,*[1] which they reckoned a cruel Murder, and therefore hoped, that if the Sufferers should approve of the same, they would have a Colour to destroy 'em as being Men of assassinating and Bloody Principles, deserving to be exterminate out of any well Governed Common Wealth: And therefore it was still one of their Questions, *Was the Bishop's Death Murder?* To which Question some answered directly that it was a Just and Lawful Execution of GOD's Law upon him, for his Perjurious Treachery, and bloody Cruelty...

iv. *A Cloud of Witnesses* 24
"The Testimony of David Hackstoun"
(I) *Whether or not had you any hand, in the Murdering of the late Bishop of* St. Andrews? Answered, He was not obliged to answer that Question, nor be his own Accuser. (II) *What he would declare as to the King's Authority?* Answered, That Authority that disowns the Interest of GOD, and States itself in Opposition to Jesus Christ is no more to be owned; but so it is, the King's Authority is now such; therefore, it ought not to be owned. (III) *Whether the killing*

---

1 Sharp was assassinated by a group of Covenanters (including David Hackstoun, whose last testimony is quoted from here) on 3 May 1678.

of the *Arch Bishop of* St. Andrews *was Murder, yea or not?* Answered, That he thought it no sin to dispatch a bloody Monster. (IV) *If he owned the New Covenant, taken at the* Queensferry, *from Mr.* Cargil *one of their preachers?* Answered, That he did own it in every particular thereof, and would fain see the Man that in Conscience or Reason would Debate the contrary. (V) *If he were at Liberty, and had the Power to kill any of the King's Counsel, and Murder them as he did the Bishop of* St. Andrews, *whether he would do it, yea, or not?* Answered, that he had no spare Time to answer such frivolous and Childish Questions.

v. *A Cloud of Witnesses* 52
"James Skeen: Letter to Brother"
He asked, did I own the King's Authority? I said in so far as it was against the Covenant and Interest of Christ, I disowned it. He asked me, thought I it not a sinful Murder, the Killing of the *Arch Prelate?* I said, I thought it was their duty to kill him, when God gave them Opportunity; for he had been the Author of much Bloodshed. They asked me, why I carried Arms, I told them, I was for self Defence, and the Defence of the Gospel. They asked me, why I poisoned my Ball? I told them, I wished none of them to recover whom I Shot. They asked, would I Kill the Soldiers, being the King's? I said it was my duty if I could, when they persecuted GOD's People. They asked, if I would Kill any of them? I said they were all stated Enemies to our Lord Jesus Christ, and by the Declaration at *Sanquhair*,[1] I counted them my Enemies. They asked, if I would think it duty to Kill the King. I said he had stated himself an Enemy to God's interest, and there was War declared against him: I said the Covenant made with God was the Glory of *Scotland*; tho they unthankfully counted it their shame... The *Chancellor* asked, if I knew *His Royal Highness?* I said I never saw such a Person. *York* looks out by, for he sat in the shadow of Bishop *Burnet*; and said why did I wish the King so ill? I told, I wish no ill to any; but as they were in opposition to GOD, I wished them brought down. And he spoke no more. The *Chancellor* said; would I not adhere to the *Acts of Parliament* of this Kingdom? I said I would not own any of them which were in opposition to GOD

---

1 Made on 22 June 1680 at the cross of Sanquhar (in Dumfriesshire, southern Scotland) the declaration made war on the king and his co-religionists "as enemies to our Lord Jesus Christ, and his cause and covenants."

and his Covenant. Mr. *M kenzie* said, if the King were Riding by in Coach, would ye think it no Sin to Kill him? I said by the *Sanquhair Declaration* there was War declared against him, and so he needed not put that in Question.

vi. *A Cloud of Witnesses* 151–5
"The last Testimony of Robert Gray"
I having got my Sentence of Death from Men, who are unjustly taking away my Life, merely for adhering to my Principles, and have no *Matter of Fact* to prove against me; but only adhering to the Truths of JESUS CHRIST, and testifying against their sinful Laws and Actions, which my *Indictment* will testify. They take away my Life for declining their Authority, and calling *Charles Stuart* a Tyrant, and speaking against their *Test*, that they have made to turn over the whole Work of *Reformation*, in calling it the *Black Test*... And let such as will Condemn me, mind that Scripture, *It is GOD that justifieth, who is he that condemneth?* I bless the Lord, that ever I was Honoured to Testify against the wrongs done to my Lord and Master Jesus Christ, either by word or write. O! wonder what am I, that ever he should have chosen the like of me, who have been one of the vilest of sinners! if the World had seen me, as he saw me, they would not have chosen me, no not to have kept Company with: But O wonder that His condescending Love has not only taken me to be Servant, but to be one of the Children of the family... It is a Year bygone, being the first Week of *May* 1681, since I personally Subscribed my Name to be the Lords; for before that I played many times fast and loose with GOD, for which I take shame and Confusion of Face to my self (which is my due) but since I have been kept free of what formerly I was guilty of, tho' the assaults of Satan have not been wanting. I durst not look back, nor yet take my Word again: But desired to act and contend for my LORD and Master, Jesus Christ's Rights, and not to quit them to any, which he helped and owned me in...

For our LORD is now taking a narrow Look of *Scotland*, and seeing who did put the Hand to the Plough to carry on the Work of Reformation, to banish *Popery*, and this *Popish Duke*, that has gotten his Foot in *Scotland*, which will be the blackest Sight that every poor *Scotland* saw: But who ever of the Nobles or Gentry of the Land is guilty, yet I will assure you, as sure as the LORD is in Heaven, Ministers, yea, *Presbyterian* Ministers are not free of *Popery's* coming into the Land; because they have not testified against it, who should *have set the Trumpet to their Mouth*, and have *given faithful Warning*, and so they would have delivered their Souls and the Souls of others, whereas now poor things are insnared; but their Blood will be required at Ministers Hands; and ye that are old wily Professors, that have taken the *Lee side of the Brae*,[1] and are advising others to do so, ye are not free of the innocent Blood shed in *Scotland*, and the Loss of poor Souls, because of your Practice of seeming Piety and Holiness, so ye blind their Eyes, and what ye do, that is a godly Man, in the Town or Country Parishes, in going to hear the Curates that have taken that black *Test*, or any other thing, because ye do it to save your Gear, they follow your Practice; but assure your selves the Loss of their Souls will be required at your Hands, who are Ring leaders in an evil Course, be who ye will, in Prison or out of Prison; our LORD is now near his coming, and is begun to tread upon *Scotland's* Sea, and will within a little tread upon the Necks of his Enemies, and come and deliver his Church, which *I* die in the Faith of: But it will be a costly delivery...

Now my Time here is but short; and I think it needless to write any more, the Testimonies of the *Worthies* being so little Valued by this Generation, that nothing will do at it but Wrath and Judgments that tho' an Angel should come down from Heaven it will avail nothing; for nothing I can see, but wrath, wrath, wrath, Judgments, Judgments, said Judgments coming to this Land very suddenly; but my Eyes shall be closed, and I shall not see it, and well is me for this; therefore I am content, and, heartily content, seeing I get my Soul for a Prey...

4. Edward Fisher

i. *The Marrow of Modern Divinity* (Edinburgh: John Mosman, 1718) 118-9.

[The] *Covenant* that Believers are to have regard unto for Life and Salvation, is the free and gracious *Covenant* that is betwixt Christ, or God in Christ and them, and in this *Covenant* there is not any Condition or Law to be performed on Man's Part by himself; no, there is no more for him to do, but only to know and believe that Christ hath done all for him; wherefore my dear Neighbour *Neophytus*, to turn my Speech particularly to you; because I see you are in Heaviness, I beseech you be persuaded, that here you are to work nothing, here you are to do nothing, here you are to render

---

1   i.e. the sheltered side of the hill.

nothing unto God, but only to receive the Treasure, which is Jesus Christ, and apprehend him in your Heart by Faith, although you be never so great a Sinner, and so shall you obtain Forgiveness for Sins, Righteousness, and eternal Happiness, not as an Agent, but as a Patient; not by doing, but by receiving, nothing here cometh betwixt but Faith only, apprehending Christ in the Promise; this then is perfect Righteousness, to hear nothing, to know nothing, to do nothing of the *Law of Works*, but only to know and believe that Jesus Christ is now gone to the Father, and sitteth at his right Hand, not as a Judge, *But is made unto you of God, Wisdom, Righteousness, Sanctification and Redemption*, wherefore as *Paul* and *Silas* said to the Jailor, so say I unto you, *Believe on the Lord Jesus Christ, and thou shalt be saved*; that is, be verily persuaded in your Heart, that Jesus Christ is yours, and that you shall have Life and Salvation by him, that whatsoever Christ did for the Redemption of Mankind, he did it for you...

ii. *Marrow* 121-2

I beseech you to consider, that although some Men be ordained to Condemnation, yet so long as the Lord hath concealed their Names and not set a Mark of Reprobation upon any Man in particular, but offers the pardon generally to all, without having any Respect either to Election, or Reprobation, surely it is great Folly in any Man to say, it may be I am not elected, and therefore shall not have Benefit by it...Wherefore I beseech you, do not you say, it may be I am not elected, and therefore I will not believe in Christ, but rather say, I do believe in Christ, and therefore, I am sure I am elected, and check your own heart...

iii. *Marrow* 150-4

Truly, as it is the *Covenant of Works*, you are wholly and altogether delivered and set free from, you are dead to it, and it is dead to you, and if it be dead to you, then it can do you neither Good nor Hurt; and if you be dead to it, you can expect neither Good nor Hurt from it: Consider Man, I pray you, that as I said before, you are now under another *Covenant*, to wit, the *Covenant of Grace*, and you cannot be under *two Covenants* at once, neither wholly nor partly; and therefore as before you believed you were wholly under the *Covenant of Works*, as *Adam* left both you, and all his Posterity after his Fall, so now since you have believed you are wholly under the *Covenant of Grace*; assure your self then, that no Minister or Preacher of *God's Word* hath any Warrant to say unto you hereafter,

Either do this and this Duty contained in the Law, and avoid this and this Sin forbidden in the Law, and God will justify thee, and save thy soul; or do it not, and he will condemn thee, and damn thee: No, no, you are now set free, both from the commanding and the condemning Power of the *Covenant of Works*... God cannot by Virtue of the *Covenant of Works*, either require of you any Obedience, or punish you for any Disobedience: No, he cannot by Virtue of that *Covenant* so much as threaten you, or give you an angry Word, or shew you an angry Look; for indeed he can see no Sin in you as a Transgression of that *Covenant*, *For*, saith the *Apostle*, *Where there is no Law, there is no Transgression*, Rom. iv. 15. And therefore though hereafter you do through Frailty transgress any of all the *Ten Commandments*, yet do you not thereby transgress the *Covenant of Works*, there is no such *Covenant* now betwixt *God* and you...

Nay the Truth is, *God* never speaks to a Believer out of Christ; and in Christ he speaks not a Word in the Terms of the *Covenant of Works*; and if the Law of it self should presume to come into your *Conscience*, and say, Herein, and herein thou hast transgressed and broken me, and therefore thou owest so much, and so much to *divine Justice* which must be satisfied, or else I will take hold on thee: Then answer you and say, O *Law*, be it known unto thee that I am now married unto Christ, and so I am under Covert, and therefore if thou charge me with any *Debt*, thou must enter thine action against my Husband Christ, for the Wife is not sueable at the *Law*, but the Husband; but the Truth is, I through him am dead to thee, O *Law*, and thou are dead to me, and therefore Justice hath nothing to do with me, for it judgeth according to the *Law*. And if it yet reply and say, I, but *good Works* must be done, and the *Commandments* must be kept if thou wilt obtain Salvation; then answer you and say, I am already saved before thou camest, therefore I have no Need of thy Presence, for in Christ I have all Things at once, neither need I any Thing more that is necessary to Salvation, he is my Righteousness, my Treasure, and my Work: I confess, O Law, that I am neither godly nor righteous, but yet this I am sure of, that he is godly and righteous for me, and to tell thee the Truth, O *Law*, I am now with him in the Bride-Chamber, where it maketh no Matter what I am, or what I have done, but what Christ my sweet Husband is, hath done, and doth for me, and therefore leave off Law to dispute with me; for by Faith I apprehend him who hath apprehended me, and put me into his Bosom; wherefore I will be bold to bid *Moses* with his Tables, and all Lawyers with their Books, and all Men with their works, hold their Peace and give Place; so that I say unto thee, O Law, be gone; and if it will not be gone, then thrust it by Force, saith Luther.[1] ...

5. James Hadow

i. *The Antinomianism of the Marrow of Modern Divinity Detected* (Edinburgh: John Mosman, 1721), Preface i-iii
The following Treatise, written on Occasion of some Pamphlets, published in favours of the *Marrow of Modern Divinity*, was communicated only to a few in Private: But after that a *Representation*, in Defence of the *Marrow*, signed by twelve Brethren, had been given in to the late General Assembly, craving, That the Fifth Act of the General Assembly 1720, wherein it was censured as erroneous, might be repealed;[2] Some who had seen this Treatise in Manuscript, thought the publishing of it might be of Use to prevent the spreading of the *Antinomian* Gangreen of that Book; The Infection appearing the more Dangerous, in that twelve Ministers had undertaken to maintain its Reputation against the Censure of the supreme Judicatory of this Church; And advised, that the sooner some Remedy were applied, it might prove the more seasonable. These Considerations prevailed with me, to let this Essay go abroad such as it is.

The *Antinomian* Scheme was always formerly set forth under the specious Shew of a peculiar Zeal for free Grace: and the same Pretext is still the most plausible for the promoting of it. The Brethren in their Representation go on in the same Way. In their Zeal for the Reputation of the *Marrow*, they charge the General Assembly with injuring the Doctrine of free Grace; as if it could not be preserved in its Purity, without admitting the censured Errors of that Book. But the Charge, as themselves may and ought to know, is unjust. This Church doth steadfastly maintain the Sovereignty, Freedom and Efficacy of Grace; but according to the Gospel Revelation, without extending it to all and every one...

ii. *Antinomianism*, Preface to the Recommenders ix-x
I find my self very far disappointed: For in stead of obeying the

---

1 Martin Luther (1483-1546), German Protestant reformer.
2 On 20 May 1720 the General Assembly of the Church of Scotland proscribed Fisher's book. In May of the following year a petition in support of *The Marrow* was lodged by twelve ministers, among them James Hog of Carnock and Thomas Boston of Ettrick.

Authority of our General Assembly, I see the Undertakings and Resolutions to support the Credit of that Book, still rising higher and higher, notwithstanding of the Act of the penult Assembly past against it, without a contradictory Voice, except three or four, which one would have thought might have been sufficient to extinguish the Flame; but in stead thereof, the Act is contemned, and new Measures taken to enervate its Force: Pains are used, with too great Success, to raise Prejudices against the Church, in the Minds of serious Christians, to maintain the Reputation of the *Marrow*, not only in private, but from Pulpits: Pamphlets and Libels are handed about, containing bitter and reproachful Reflections, having no other Tendency than to harden the profane, and foment Divisions among weak Christians, and raise in them a Dislike at pure Gospel Ordinances, administered by some worthy Pastors, at whom these Libels directly point. 'Tis very well known that Effects of this Nature are too too visible in the City of *Edinburgh* especially: For tho' the Ordinances of the Gospel are dispensed there in as much Purity and Plenty, by faithful Ambassadors of JESUS CHRIST...as in any Place of the Earth; are not Gospel Administrations in their Hands, falling under Contempt with some Professors: And tho' none in *Scotland* have such frequent and easy Access to the Sacrament of the Lord's Supper, as People in that Place, by Reason of its Frequency there, and in other neighbouring Congregations; are not these blessed Occasions slighted by some who used to attend them, who seem to place too much Religion in communicating with such Ministers as support new Schemes; there are not a few who turn their Backs upon Communions in *Edinburgh*, or the Suburbs thereof, and choose at the very same precise Time, to attend them, perhaps at the Distance of a Day's Journey; as if the Efficacy or Ordinances were to proceed from Ministers, who distinguish themselves, by some singular Opinions: And does not daily Experience testify, that many Professors cannot hear these new Schemes, or the *Marrow* in the least condemned, and the Care of the Church to maintain our Purity against them commended, but they lose that meek and calm Temper of Spirit, that's necessary to Christian Love and Unity...

iii. *Antinomianism* 16
Will the Reverend Recommender of the *Marrow* aver, that its Author doth here refute the *Antinomian* Error, *That the Believer ought not to mourn for his Sins?* Though the Believer be not under

the Law, as it requires perfect personal Obedience for his Righteousness; and as it binds over unto the Curse for every Transgression, without giving Hope of Relief: Yet is he not still under the Law, as the Commanding Will of his Creator and Sovereign Lord? Will the Reverend Recommender justify the *Marrow* in these horrid Tenets? Will he maintain that Murder, Adultery, Theft, Lying, are in a Believer no Sins, no Transgressions of the Law of his Creator, which is indispensably binding upon all *Adam*'s Posterity? Will he say that Lying, disingenuous Tricking, &c. are, in a Believer no Sins? or that they have no Guilt annexed to them, and do not deserve eternal Wrath, which would be actually inflicted, had not the Death and Satisfaction of our blessed Redeemer interposed? ...

iv. *Antinomianism* 20-1
I observe, That the Author of the *Marrow* overturneth the Necessity of seeking after an Assurance, by Marks of saving Faith; seeing he placeth Assurance in the Nature and Essence of that Faith, which the Gospel requireth of all its Hearers. He describes believing on Christ to be a Man's persuading himself in his Heart that Jesus Christ is his, and that he shall have Life and Salvation by him; and that whatsoever Christ did for the Redemption of Mankind, he did it for him in particular. He teacheth, That a Sinner is to make sure his Election by believing it...and that by Christ he is freely and fully justified and acquitted from all his Sins...

v. *Antinomianism* 143-5
The truth is, the more sober *Antinomians*, with whom I rank the Author of the *Marrow*, do exclaim against the lewd and licentious Practices of more Gross *Libertines*, and are not for Believers giving up themselves to unbridled Lusts and vile Affections, but teach that true Faith leads to Holiness of Life; yet they entertain several unfounded Notions, which tend to weaken a Believer's Obligation unto Obedience, and slacken his Diligence in the Practice of Holiness. They are not for Believers being bound to do Good and eschew Evil, by the commanding Power of a Law, and Divine Authority of the Law-giver; lest the moral Coaction of the Law should hinder their Freedom in doing Good of their own Accord. But they would have Believers to be only under the Physical Operation and Impulse of the Spirit, whereby they are excited and carried on to the Good Things commanded, which are the Matter of the Law. And so they set the holy and binding Rule of the Law, in Opposition unto the gracious Operation of

the Sanctifying Spirit, as if these were inconsistent in a Believer's Obedience...

Hence they do not allow inherent Holiness, and the Practice of Good Works to be necessary unto Salvation, by the Command of God, or even as a Means appointed of God, and necessary to fit the Believer for the Possession of Glory.

When we assert the Necessity of Holiness and Good Works, we do not mean that they are the Matter and Ground of our Justification, or that they are meritorious of Salvation, or the procuring Cause of the Right and Title to Eternal Life... But in Believers that are continued sometime in this Life, we say that they are necessary by the Commandment of God, and as Means to make them meet for the Inheritance of the Saints in Light. *Antinomians* oppose this Doctrine, and the *Marrow* agrees with them therein...

vi. *Antinomianism* 150

The *Marrow*...does plainly deny the necessity of Good Works, in order to Salvation, and that upon the *Antinomian* Principle, That a Believer is already saved, and needs nothing more that is necessary to Salvation: And therefore Holiness and Good Works, in his Opinion, are not necessary to Salvation...

vii. *Antinomianism* 169-72

Many Instances might have been given of other Errors in *the Marrow of Modern Divinity*; these already treated of, may suffice for a Proof of the *Antinomianism* of its Author: I have shewed that he agrees with *Antinomians*, in teaching that a Believer is not obliged to mourn for Sin; and that Faith is not to be tried by distinguishing Marks, seeing he makes Assurance to be of the Nature and Essence of Faith. That he maintains the *Antinomian* universal Attonement, and makes Pardon of Sin to be prior to Believing, seeing he'll have the Sinner called directly to believe, that his Sins are pardoned; and so makes Justification by Faith, to be but declarative. That he denies, that true Repentance goes before Justification, and that Ministers of the Gospel ought to call Sinners to repent or forsake their Sins, in Order to the Pardon of them; and holds that Gospel-Repentance flows from a Man's Assurance of the Love of God to him, in pardoning his Sins; and that when a Man becomes a Believer, the Command to repent of his Sins, doth not appertain to him. That by his Account of his Threefold Law, *of Works, of Faith, and of Christ*, Faith and Repentance are excluded from the Commands of God. That he will have the Moral Law of Creation deprived of all Penal Sanction, before the Form of a Covenant of Works was put upon it. That under the Law of Works, from which he will have a Believer set free, he comprehends not only the Form of the Covenant of Works, requiring perfect, personal Obedience, as the Condition of Eternal Life; but also the Moral Law, as enacted and established by the Authority of God the Creator, and as delivered to the Church by the Angel of the Covenant from Mount *Sinai*: Yea, he comprehends all Divine Laws, which have any Authoritative Compulsion or Binding Force to influence Obedience, and which have Promises of Eternal Life, or Threatenings of Wrath, and Eternal Death annexed to them. And hence maintains, That a Believer is not under the Law, but is altogether delivered from it; That a Believer doth not commit Sin; That the Lord can see no Sin in a Believer; That the Lord is not angry with a Believer for his Sins; And that a Believer hath no Cause, either to confess his Sins, or to crave Pardon at the Hand of God for them, either yet to fast, or mourn, or humble himself before the Lord for them. That the Law of Christ, in his Account of it, is a mere passive Rule, and the Matter of the Law, without a commanding, binding Power, to enforced Obedience from the Authority of the Divine Law-Giver, and without a Promise of Eternal Life, or Threatening of Wrath annexed to it. A Law, which commandeth no Moral Duty to be done, either for eschewing of Punishment, or upon Promise of Reward Temporal or Eternal. A Law which is delivered only to such as are in Christ, and doth not reach unto the Unbelieving Hearers of the Gospel. And a Law, which neither justifies nor condemns. That he agrees with *Antinomians* in denying Personal Holiness and Good Works, to be necessary to Salvation; and maintains this *Antinomian* Tenet upon *Antinomian* Principles, in that he confounds Justification with Sanctification, which he makes Imputative, asserting, that Christ is Godly for the Believer freed from the Commanding Power of the Law, so as Holiness may not be necessary by the command of God, nor Sin in a Believer be either hurtful to him, or displeasing to God.

In detecting those Errors of the *Marrow*, I have suggested some Things to contribute unto the Vindication of the Fifth Act of the General Assembly 1720, and to shew that they had good Ground and Reason to pass their Censure against that Book, when they found it so highly recommended, and industriously dispersed among People in several Parts of this national Church...

6. Robert Burns

Holy Willie's Prayer[1]

O Thou, wha in the heavens dost dwell,
Wha, as it pleases best thysel',
Sends ane to heaven and ten to hell,
A' for thy glory,
And no for ony guid or ill
They've done afore thee!

I bless and praise thy matchless might,
Whan thousands thou hast left in night,
That I am here afore thy sight,
For gifts an' grace
A burnin' an' a shinin' light,
To a' this place.

What was I, or my generation,
That I should get sic exaltation?
I, wha deserve most just damnation,
For broken laws,
Sax thousand years 'fore my creation,
Thro' Adam's cause.

When frae my mither's womb I fell,
Thou might hae plungéd me in hell,
To gnash my gums, to weep and wail,
In burnin lakes,
Where damnéd devils roar and yell,
Chained to their stakes;

Yet I am here a chosen sample,
To show thy grace is great and ample;
I'm here a pillar in thy temple,
Strong as a rock,
A guide, a buckler, an example
To a' thy flock.

---

1 The Willie of the title was a censorious church elder at Mauchline, one William
Fisher, who was charged with drunkenness and the theft of church funds.

O Lord, thou kens what zeal I bear,
When drinkers drink, and swearers swear.
And singin' there and dancin' here,
Wi' great an' sma':
For I am keepit by thy fear
Free frae them a'.

But yet, O Lord! confess I must
At times I'm fashed wi' fleshy lust;
An' sometimes too, wi' warldly trust,
Vile self gets in;
But thou remembers we are dust,
Defiled in sin.

O Lord! yestreen, thou kens, wi' Meg—
Thy pardon I sincerely beg;
O! may't ne'er be a livin' plague
To my dishonour,
An' I'll ne'er lift a lawless leg
Again upon her.

Besides I farther maun allow,
Wi' Lizzie's lass, three times I trow—
But, Lord, that Friday I was fou,
When I cam near her,
Or else thou kens thy servant true
Wad never steer her.

May be thou lets this fleshly thorn
Beset thy servant e'en and morn
Lest he owre high and proud should turn,
That he's sae gifted;
If sae, thy hand maun e'en be borne,
Until thou lift it.

Lord, bless thy chosen in this place,
For here thou hast a chosen race;
But God confound their stubborn face,
And blast their name,
Wha bring thy elders to disgrace
An' public shame.

Lord, mind Gavin Hamilton's[1] deserts,
He drinks, an swears, an plays at cartes,
Yet has sae mony takin arts
Wi' great an' sma',
Frae God's ain priest the people's hearts
He steals awa'.

An' when we chastened him therefor,
Thou kens how he bred sic a splore
As set the warld in a roar
O laughin' at us;
Curse thou his basket and his store,
Kail and potatoes.

Lord, hear my earnest cry an' pray'r,
Against that presbytery o' Ayr;
Thy strong right hand, Lord, make it bare
Upo' their heads;
Lord, weigh it down, and dinna spare,
For their misdeeds.

O Lord my God, that glib-tongued Aiken,[2]
My very heart and soul are quakin',
To think how we stood sweatin, shakin,
An' pissed wi' dread,
While he, wi' hangin lips and snakin,
Held up his head.

Lord in the day of vengeance try him;
Lord, visit them wha did employ him,
And pass not in thy mercy by them,
Nor hear their pray'r:
But, for thy people's sake, destroy them,
An dinna spare.

---

1   Gavin Hamilton, lawyer and friend of Burns's, accused of Sabbath-breaking by the
    Mauchline elders.
2   Robert Aiken, lawyer who helped clear Hamilton of the charges against him.

But, Lord, remember me and mine
Wi' mercies temp'ral and divine,
That I for gear and grace may shine
Excelled by nane,
And a' the glory shall be thine,
Amen, Amen!

Appendix B: Contexts of Production

[The following extracts are from literary and psychoanalytical sources contemporaneous with the *Confessions* (see Introduction).]

1. E.T.A. Hoffmann

i. *The Devil's Elixir* (Edinburgh: *Blackwood's*, 1824) I, iv.
[*Lately rejected by the young woman of his affections, the sixteen-year-old narrator, Medardus, has entered a Capuchin monastery, determined to take the vows of the order.*]

My vocation to the monastic life was thus, according to my own opinion, rendered clear and unalterable. On that very day after the fatal music party [at which he had been rejected by Therese], I hastened, as soon as I could escape from my usual studies at the school, to the Capuchin Prior, and informed him that it was my fixed intention directly to begin my noviciate, and that I had already, by letters, announced my design to my mother, and to the Abbess. Leonardus seemed surprised at my sudden zeal, and without being impolitely urgent, he yet endeavoured, by one means or another, to find out what could have led me all at once to this resolve, to which he rightly concluded that some extraordinary event must have given rise.

A painful emotion of shame, which I could not overcome, prevented me from telling the truth. On the other hand, I dwelt, with all the fervour of excitement, on the visions, warnings, and strange adventures of my youth, which all seemed decidedly to point to a monastic retirement. Without in the least disputing the authenticity of the events which I had described, he suggested that I might, nevertheless, have drawn from them false conclusions, as there was no certainty that I had interpreted correctly the warnings, whatever they might be, which I had received.

Indeed, the Prior did not at any time speak willingly of supernatural agency—not even of those instances recorded by inspired writers, so that there were moments in which I had almost set him down for an infidel and a sceptic. Once I emboldened myself so far, as to force from him some decided expressions as to the adversaries of our Catholic faith, who stigmatize all belief of that which cannot be interpreted according to the laws of our corporeal senses, with the name of Superstition. "My son," said Leonardus, "infidelity itself is indeed the worst species of that mental weakness, which, under the name of Superstition, such people ascribe to believers." Thereafter he directly changed the subject to lighter and more ordinary topics of discourse.

Not till long afterwards was I able to enter into his admirable views of the mysteries of our religion, which involves the supernatural communing of our spirits with beings of a celestial order, and was then obliged to confess, that Leonardus, with great propriety, reserved these ideas for students who were sufficiently advanced in years and experience...

The reciprocal confidence and friendship of the brethren with regard to each other—the internal arrangements of the convent—and, in short, the whole mode of life among the Capuchins, appeared to me for a long time exactly as it had done at first. That composure of spirit, which was universally apparent, failed not by sympathy to pour the balm of peace into my soul; and I was visited often by delightful inspirations, especially by faery dreams, derived from the period of my earliest years in the Convent of the Holy Lime-Tree.

I must not omit to mention, that, during the solemn act of my investiture, I beheld the choirmaster's sister [Therese]. She looked quite sunk in melancholy, and her eyes evidently shone in tears. But the time of temptation was now past and gone; and, perhaps, out of a sinful pride over a triumph too easily won, I could not help smiling, which did not fail to be remarked by a certain monk, named Cyrillus, who at that moment stood near me. "What makes you so merry, brother?" said he.

—"When I am renouncing this contemptible world," said I. "and its vanities, ought I not to rejoice?"

It was not to be denied, however, that, at the moment when I pronounced these words, an involuntary feeling of regret vibrated through my inmost heart, and was at direct variance with what I had said. Yet this was the last attack of earthly passion, after which composure of spirit gradually gained complete ascendancy. Oh, had it never departed! But who may trust to the strength of his armour? Who may rely on his own courage, if the supernatural and unseen powers of darkness are combined against him, and for ever on the watch?

ii. *The Devil's Elixir* (I v)
[*After five years in the convent, Medardus is charged with care of the reliquary chamber. Brother Cyrillus tells him the story of the most mysterious and important of the relics.*]

At last, Brother Cyrillus had recourse to an old and strangely carved wooden press, which he carefully unlocked, and out of which he took a small square box. "Herein, Brother Medardus," said he, "is contained the most wonderful and mysterious relic of which our convent is possessed. As long as I have been resident here, no one but the Prior and myself has had this box in his hands. Even the other brethren (not to speak of strangers) are unaware of its existence. For my own part, I cannot even touch this casket without an inward shuddering; for it seems to me as if there were some malignant spell, or rather, some living demon, locked up within it, which, were the bonds broken by which this evil principle is now confined, would bring destruction on all who came within its accursed range.

"That which is therein contained is known to have been derived immediately from the Arch-Fiend, at the time when he was still allowed *visibly*, and in personal shape, to contend against the weal of mankind."

I looked at Brother Cyrillus with the greatest astonishment; but without leaving me time to answer, he went on.

"I shall abstain, Brother Medardus, from offering you any opinion of my own on this mysterious affair, but merely relate to you faithfully what our documents say upon the subject. You will find the papers in that press, and can read them afterwards at your leisure.

"The life of St Anthony is already well known to you. You are aware, that in order to be completely withdrawn from the distractions of the world, he went out into the desert, and there devoted himself to the severest penitential exercises. The Devil, of course, followed him, and came often in his way, in order to disturb him in his pious contemplations.

"One evening it happened accordingly, that St Anthony was returning home, and had arrived near his cell, when he perceived a dark figure approaching him rapidly along the heath. As his visitant came nearer, he observed with surprise, through the holes in a torn mantle worn by the stranger, the long necks of oddly-shaped bottles, which of course produced an effect the most extraordinary and grotesque. It was the Devil, who, in this absurd masquerade, smiled on him ironically, and inquired if he would not choose to taste of the Elixir which he carried in these bottles? At this insolence, St Anthony was not even incensed, but remained perfectly calm; for the Enemy, having now become powerless and contemptible, was no longer in a condition to venture a real combat, but must confine himself to scornful words.

"The Saint, however, inquired for what reason he carried about so many bottles in that unheard-of manner.

"'For this very reason,' said the Devil, 'that people may be induced to ask me the question; for as soon as any mortal meets with me, he looks on me with astonishment, makes the same inquiry that you have done, and, the next place, cannot forbear desiring to taste, and try what sort of elixirs I am possessed of. Among so many bottles, if he finds one which suits his taste, and *drinks it out*, and becomes drunk, he is irrecoverably mine, and belongs to me and my kingdom for ever.'

"So far the story is the same in all legends, though some of them add, that, according to the Devil's confession, if two individuals should drink out of the same flask, they would henceforth become addicted to the same crimes, possessing a wonderful reciprocity of thoughts and feelings, yet mutually and unconsciously acting for the destruction of each other. By our own manuscripts, it is narrated farther, that when the Devil went from thence, he left some of his flasks on the ground, which St Anthony directly took with him into his cave, fearing that they might fall into the way of accidental travellers, or even deceive some of his own pupils, who came to visit him in that retirement. By chance, so we are also told, St Anthony once opened one of these bottles, out of which there arose directly a strange and stupefying vapour, whereupon all sorts of hideous apparitions and spectral phantoms from hell had environed the Saint, in order to terrify and delude him. Above all, too, there were forms of women, who sought to entice him into shameless indecencies. These altogether tormented him, until, by constant prayer, and severe penitential exercises, he had driven them again out of the field.

"In this very box there is now deposited a bottle of that kind, saved from the relics of St Anthony; and the documents thereto relating, are so precise and complete, that the fact of its having been derived from the Saint is hardly to be doubted. Besides, I can assure you, Brother Medardus, that so often as I have chanced to touch this bottle, or even the box in which it is contained, I have been stuck with a mysterious horror. It seems to me also, as if I smelt a peculiar, odoriferous vapour, which stuns the senses, and the effects of which do not stop there, but utterly rob me of composure of spirit afterwards, and distract my attention from devotional exercises.

"Whether I do or not believe in this immediate intercourse with the devil in visible shape, yet, that such distraction proceeds from the direct influence of some hostile power, there can be no doubt. However, I overcame this gradually by zealous and unceasing prayer. As for you, Brother Medardus, whose fervent imagination will colour all things with a strength beyond that of reality, and who, in consequence of youth, also will be apt to trust too much to your own power of resistance, I would earnestly impress on you this advice,— 'Never, or at least, for many years, to open this box; and in order that it may not tempt and entice you, to put it as much as possible out of your reach and sight.'"

Hereupon Brother Cyrillus shut up the mysterious Box in the press from which it had come, and consigned over to me a large bunch of keys, among which that of the formidable press had its place. The whole story had made on me a deep impression, and the more that I felt an inward longing to contemplate the wonderful relic, the more I was resolved to render this to myself difficult, or even impossible...

iii. *The Devil's Elixir* (I vi)
[*Now an impassioned and celebrated preacher, Medardus becomes convinced of his divinely inspired ability to spread 'a kind of religious delirium' among his hearers. During his St Anthony's Day sermon he sees for the first time the vision of the mysterious painter who, like a good angel, will continue to appear at critical moments in Medardus's life.*]

Thus vanity gradually, by imperceptible, but sure approaches, took possession of my heart. Almost unconsciously, I began to look upon myself as the *one elect*,—the pre-eminently *chosen* of Heaven. Then the miraculous circumstances attending my birth at the Lime-Tree; my father's forgiveness of a mortal crime; the visionary adventures of my childhood;—all seemed to indicate that my lofty spirit, in immediate commerce with supernatural beings, belonged not properly to earth, but to Heaven, and was but suffered, for a space, to wander here, for the benefit and consolation of mortals! It became, according to my own judgment, quite certain, that the venerable old Pilgrim, together with the wonderful boy that he had brought with him, had been *supernatural* visitants,—that they had descended on earth, for the express purpose of greeting me as the chosen saint, who was destined for the instruction of mankind, to sojourn transiently among them.

But the more vividly all these ideas come before me, the more did my present situation become oppressive and disagreeable. That unaffected cheerfulness and inward serenity which had formerly brightened my existence, was completely banished form my soul. Even all the good-hearted expressions of the Prior, and friendly behaviour of the monks, awoke within me only discontent and resentment. By their mode of conduct, my vanity was bitterly mortified. In me they ought clearly to have recognised the chosen saint who was above them so highly elevated. Nay, they should even have prostrated themselves in the dust, and implored my intercession before the throne of Heaven!

I considered them, therefore, as beings influenced by the most deplorable obduracy and refractoriness of spirit. Even in my discourses I contrived to interweave certain mysterious allusions. I ventured to assert, that now a wholly new and mighty revolution had begun, as with the roseate light of morning, to dawn upon the earth, announcing to pious believers, that one of the specially elect of Heaven had been sent for a space to wander in sublunary regions. My supposed mission I continued to clothe in mysterious and obscure imagery, which, indeed, the less it was understood, seemed the more to work like a charm among the people.

Leonardus now became visibly colder in his manner, avoiding to speak with me, unless before witnesses. At last, one day, when we were left alone in the great *alee* of the convent garden, he broke out— "Brother Medardus, I can no longer conceal from you, that for some time past your whole behaviour has been such as to excite in me the greatest displeasure. There has arisen in your mind some adverse and hostile principle, by which you have become wholly alienated from a life of pious simplicity. In your discourses, there prevails a dangerous obscurity; and from this darkness many things appear ready, if you dared utter them, to start forward, which if plainly spoken, would effectually separate you and me for ever. To be candid—at this moment you bear about with you, and betray that unalterable curse of our sinful origin, by which every powerful struggle of our spiritual energies is rendered a means of opening to us the realms of destruction, whereinto we thoughtless mortals are, alas! too apt to go astray!" ...

His words had indeed penetrated my heart; but, alas! the impressions that they had left were only those of anger, distrust, and resentment. He had spoken of the approbation, nay, the admiration and respect, which I had obtained by my wonderful talents; and it became but too obvious that only pitiful envy had been the real source of that displeasure, which he so candidly expressed towards me.

Silent, and wrapt up within myself, I remained at the next meeting of the brethren, a prey to devouring indignation. Still buoyed up and excited by the wild inspirations which had risen up within me, I continued through whole days and long sleepless nights my laborious contrivances how I might best commit to paper (without a too candid avowal of my self-idolatry) the glorious ideas that crowded on my mind.

Meanwhile, the more that I became estranged from Leonardus and the monks, the better I succeeded in attracting the homage of the people; and my discourses never failed to rivet their attention.

On St Anthony's day this year, it happened that the church was more than ever thronged—in such manner, that the vestry-men were obliged to keep the doors open, in order that those who could not get in might at least hear me from without. Never had I spoken more ardently, more impressively,—in a word, with more *onction*. I had related, as usual, many wonderful anecdotes from the lives of the saints, and had demonstrated in what degree their examples, though not imitable in their fullest extent, might yet be advantageously applied in real life. I spoke, too, of the manifold arts of the Devil, to whom the fall of our first parents had given the power of seducing mankind; and involuntarily, before I was aware, the stream of eloquence led me away into the legend of the Elixir, which I wished to represent as an ingenious allegory.

Then suddenly, my looks, in wandering through the church, fell upon a tall haggard figure, who had mounted upon a bench, and stood in a direction nearly opposite to me, leaning against a pillar. He was in a strange foreign garb, with a dark violet-coloured mantle, of which the folds were twined round his crossed arms. His countenance was deadly pale; but there was an unearthly glare in his large black staring eyes, which struck into my very heart. I trembled involuntarily—a mysterious horror pervaded my whole frame. I turned away my looks, however, and, summoning up my utmost courage, forced myself to continue my discourse. But, as if constrained by some inexplicable spell of an enchanter—as if fascinated by the basilisk's eyes—I was always obliged to look back again, where the man stood as before, changeless and motionless, with his large spectral eyes glaring upon me.

On his high wrinkled forehead, and in the lineaments of his down-drawn mouth, there was an expression of bitter scorn, of disdain mixed almost with hatred. His whole figure presented something indescribably and supernaturally horrid, such as belonged not to this life. The whole truth now came on my remembrance. It was, it could be no other, than the unknown miraculous painter from the Lime-Tree, whose form, beheld in infancy, had never wholly vanished from my mind, and who now haunted me like the visible impersonification of that hereditary guilt by which my life was overshadowed.

I felt as if seized on and grappled with by ice-cold talons: My periods faltered;—my whole discourse became always more and more confused. There arose a whispering and murmuring in the church;—but the stranger remained utterly unmoved; and the fixed regard of his eyes never for a moment relented. At last, in the full paroxysm—the climax of terror and despair—I screamed aloud— "Thou revenant!—Thou accursed sorcerer!—Away with thee from hence!—Begone! for I myself am he!—I am the blessed St Anthony!"

iv. *The Devil's Elixir* (I x)
[*Newly empowered by having drunk of the Elixir, Medardus quits the monastery and heads for Rome by way of solitary mountain paths.*]

The dark pine-tree woods became always more and more dense, and the ground more steep and uneven. Suddenly I heard near me a rustling in the thickets, and then a horse neighed aloud, which was there bound to a tree. I advanced some steps farther, as the path guided me onwards, till, almost petrified with terror, I suddenly found myself on the verge of a tremendous precipice, beyond which the river, which I have already mentioned, was thundering and foaming at an immeasurable distance below.

With astonishment, too, I beheld, on a projecting point of rock which jutted over the chasm, what appeared to me the figure of a man. At first, I suspected some new delusion; but, recovering in some degree from my fear, I ventured nearer, and perceived a young man in uniform, on the very outermost point of the rocky cliff. His sabre, his hat, with a high plume of feathers, and a porte-feuille, lay beside him;—with half his body hanging over the abyss, he seemed to be asleep, and always to sink down lower and lower! His fall was inevitable!

I ventured nearer. Seizing him with one hand, and endeavouring to pull him back, I shouted aloud, "For God's sake, sir, awake! For Heaven's sake, beware!"—I said no more; for, at that moment, starting from his sleep, and at the same moment losing his equilibrium, he fell down into the cataract!

His mangled form must have dashed from point to point of the rocks in his descent. I heard one piercing yell of agony, which echoed through the immeasurable abyss, from which at last only a hollow moaning arose, which soon also died away.

Struck with unutterable horror, I stood silent and motionless. At last, by a momentary impulse, I seized the hat, the sword, the portefeuille, and wished to withdraw myself as quickly as possible from the fatal spot.

Now, however, I observed a young man dressed as a *chasseur* emerge from the wood, and coming to meet me. At first, he looked at me earnestly and scrutinizingly—then, all at once, broke out into immoderate laughter; whereat an ice-cold shuddering vibrated through all my frame.

"*Sapperment!* my Lord Count," said the youth, "your masquerade is indeed admirable and complete; and if the Lady Baroness were not apprized before hand, I question if even she would recognize you in this disguise.—But what have you done with the uniform, my lord?"

"As for that," replied I, "I threw it down the rocks into the water."—Yet these words were *not mine!* I only gave utterance, involuntarily and almost unconsciously, to expressions, which, by means of some supernatural influence, rose up within me...

When I had recovered myself in some measure from my confusion, and reflected on the adventure, I was obliged to confess, that I had become wholly the victim of chance or destiny, which had at once thrown me into the most extraordinary circumstances. It was quite obvious, that an exact resemblance of my face and figure with those of the unfortunate Count, had deceived the chasseur; and that his master must have chosen the dress of a capuchin, in order to carry on some adventure in the castle, of which the completion had now devolved upon me! Death had overtaken him, and at the same moment a wonderful fatality had *forced* me into his place. An inward irresistible impulse to act the part of the deceased Count, overpowered every doubt, and stunned the warning voice of conscience, which accused me of murder *now*, and of shameless intended crimes *yet to come!*

v. *The Devil's Elixir* (I. xv)

[*Medardus does not know that the man in fact survived the fall; nor is he made aware until much later that the man is his identical half-brother, Victorin. All the subsequent action arises from the complications surrounding the identity of the two men and the apparent interchangeability of their personalities. Medardus, mistaken for Victorin, becomes engrossed in his brother's schemes at the manor of the Baron F., where he ends up murdering both the Baron's young wife, Euphemia, and his son, Hermogen.*]

When Hermogen fell, I ran in wild frenzy down stairs. Then I heard shrilling voices through the castle, that cried aloud, "Murder! murder!"

Lights hovered about here and there, and I heard hasty steps sounding along the corridor and passages. Terror now utterly overpowered me, so that, from exhaustion, I fell down on a remote private staircase. The noise always became louder, and there was more and more light in the castle. I heard too that the outcries came nearer and nearer— "Murder! murder!" At last I distinguished the voices of the Baron and Reinhold, who spoke violently with their servants. Whither now could I possibly fly? Where conceal myself? Only a few moments before, when I had spoken, for the last time, with the detestable Euphemia, it had seemed to me, as if, with the deadly weapon in my hand, I could have boldly stepped forth, and that no one would have dared to withstand me.

Now, however, I contended in vain with my unconquerable fear. At last, I found myself on the great staircase. The tumult had withdrawn itself to the chambers of the Baroness, and there was an interval, therefore, of comparative tranquillity. I roused myself accordingly; and, with three vehement bounds, clinging by the staircase rail, I was arrived at the ground-floor, and within a few steps of the outward gate.

Then, suddenly, I heard a frightful piercing shriek, which reverberated through the vaulted passages, and resembled that which I had observed on the preceding night. "She is dead," said I to myself, in a hollow voice; "she has worked her own destruction, by means of the poison that she had prepared for me!"

But now, once more, I heard new and fearful shrieks from the apartments of the Baroness. It was the voice of Aurelia [the Baron's daughter, whom Medardus desires], screaming in terror, for help; and, by this, my whole feelings were once more changed. Again the reiterated cry of "Murder! murder!" sounded through the castle. The footsteps approached nearer through a staircase leading downwards. They were bearing, as I conceived, the dead body of Hermogen.

"Haste, haste, after him!—seize the murderer!" These words were uttered in the voice of Reinhold.

Hereupon I broke out into a vehement and horrid laughter, so that my voice echoed through the vaulted corridors, and I cried aloud, "Poor insane wretches! would you strive to interfere with and arrest that destiny, which inflicts only just and righteous punishment on the guilty?"

They stopped suddenly. They remained as if rooted to one spot on the staircase. I wished no longer to fly. I thought rather of advancing decidedly and boldly to meet them, and announcing the vengeance of God in words of thunder on the wicked.

But, oh horrible sight! at that moment arose, and stood bodily before me, the hideous blood-stained and distorted figure of Victorin! Methought it was not *I*, but *he*, that had spoken the words in which I thought to triumph! At the first glance of this apparition, (whether real or imaginary,) my hair stood on end with horror.

I thought no longer of resistance, but of flight. I rushed through the gates of the castle, and fled in delirious terror away through the well-known walks of the park.

vi. *The Devil's Elixir* (I. xxi)
[*From this point on Medardus is pursued by his mysterious "double."*]

In another part of the building , which was of considerable extent, the old man shewed me a small and neatly-fitted-up appartment, in which was a bed, and where I found my luggage already deposited. There he left me, with the assurance that the early disturbance in the house would not break my sleep, as I was quite separated from the other inhabitants of the castle, and might rest as long as I chose. My breakfast would not be carried in until I rung the bell, or came down stairs to order it. He added, that I should not see him again till we met at the dinner-table, as he should set out early with his lads to the forest, and would not return before mid-day.

I gave myself no farther trouble therefore, but being much fatigued, undressed hastily, and threw myself into bed, where I soon fell into a deep sleep. After this, however, I was persecuted by a horrible dream. In a manner the most extraordinary, it began with the consciousness of slumber. I said to myself, "Now this is fortunate, that I have fallen asleep so readily; I shall by this means quite recover from my fatigue, and, for fear of awaking, must only take special care to keep my eyes shut."

Notwithstanding this resolution, it seemed to me as if I must, of necessity, open my eyes, and yet continued at the same time to sleep. Then the door of my room opened, and a dark form entered, in whom, to my extreme horror and amazement, I recognised *myself* in the capuchin habit, with the beard and tonsure!

The monk came nearer and nearer to the bed, till he stood leaning over me, and grinned scornfully. "Now, then," said he, in a hollow sepulchral voice, and yet with a strange cadence of exultation—"now, then, thou shalt come along with me; we shalt mount on the *altan* [balcony] on the roof of the house beside the weather-cock, who will sing us a merry bridal-song, because the owl tonight holds his wedding-feast—there shall we contend together, and whoever beats the other from the roof of the house is king, and may drink blood!"

I felt now that the figure seized upon me, and tried to lift me from the bed. Then despair gave me courage, and I exclaimed, "Thou art not Medardus!—thou art the devil!" and as if with the claws of a demon, I grappled at the throat and visage of this detestable spectre.

But when I did so, it seemed as if my fingers forced their way into empty skeleton sockets, or held only dry withered joints, and the spectre laughed aloud in shrilling tones of scorn and mockery.

At that moment, as if forcibly roused by some one violently wrenching me about, I awoke!

The laughter still continued in the room. I raised myself up. The morning had broken in bright gleams through the window, and I actually beheld at the table, with his back turned towards me, a figure dressed in the capuchin habit!

I was petrified with horror. The abominable dream had started into real life! The capuchin tossed and tumbled among the things which lay upon the table, till by accident he turned round, and thereupon I recovered all my courage, for his visage, thank Heaven, was *not mine!* Certain features, indeed, bore the closest resemblance, but I was in health and vigour; he was, on the contrary, worn and emaciated, disguised too by an overgrown head of hair, and grizzly black beard. Moreover his eyes rolled and glared with the workings of a thoughtless and vacant delirium.

vii. *The Devil's Elixir* (II ix)
[*The mad monk gives the story of his own life in terms strikingly similar to Medardus's own: having once been a great preacher, he drank of the Devil's Elixir, then embarked on a career of shameful crime. Medardus is arrested for the murders of Euphemia and Hermogen but he convinces his accusers that he is in fact a Polish gentleman named Krczynski. The mad monk, who is in fact Victorin, confesses to the murders. The day Medardus (still under disguise as the Polish gentleman) is set to marry Aurelia coincides with the day of the insane monk's execution.*]

At that moment a hollow rumbling noise, and a tumult of voices on the street, attracted our attention. At Aurelia's request I hastened to the window. There, just before the palace, was a *leiter-wagen*, which, on account of some obstacle, had stopped in the street. The car was surrounded by the executioners of justice; and within it, I perceived the horrible monk, who sat looking backwards, while before him was a capuchin, earnestly engaged in prayer. His countenance was deadly pale, and again disfigured by a grizzly beard, but the features of my detestable *double* were to me but too easily recognizable.

When the carriage, that had been for a short space interrupted by the crowd. began to roll on, he seemed awoke from his reverie, and turning up his staring spectral eyes towards me, instantly became animated. He laughed and howled aloud— *"Brüd-er-lein— Brüd-er-lein!"* cried he.— "Bride-groom!—Bride-groom!—Come quickly—come quickly.—Up—up to the roof of the house. There the owl holds his wedding-feast; the weather-cock sings aloud! There shall we contend together, and whoever casts the other down, is king, and may drink blood!"

The howling voice in which he uttered these words, the glare of his eyes, and the horrible writhings of his visage, that was like that of an animated corse, were more than, weakened as I was by previous agitation, I was able to withstand. From that moment I lost all self-possession; I became also utterly insane, and unconscious what I did! At first I tried to speak calmly. "Horrible wretch!" said I; "what mean'st thou? What would'st thou from me?"

Then I grinned, jabbered, and howled back to the madman; and Aurelia, in an agony of terror, broke from her attendants, and ran up to me. With all her strength, she seized my arms, and endeavoured to draw me from the window. "For God's sake," cried she, "leave that horrible spectacle; they are dragging Medardus, the murderer of my brother, to the scaffold. Leonard!—Leonard!"

Then all the demons of hell seemed awoke within me, and manifested, in its utmost extent, that power which they are allowed to exercise over an obdurate and unrepentant sinner. With reckless cruelty I repulsed Aurelia, who trembled, as if shook by convulsions, in every limb.— "Ha—ha—ha!" I almost shrieked aloud— "foolish, insane girl! I myself, thy lover, thy chosen bridegroom, am the murderer of thy brother! Would'st thou by thy complaints bring down destruction from heaven on thy sworn husband?— Ho—ho—ho! I am king—I am king—and will drink blood!"

I drew out the stiletto—I struck at Aurelia—blood streamed over my arm and hand, and she fell lifeless at my feet. I rushed down stairs,—forced my way through the crowd to the carriage—seized the monk by the collar, and with supernatural strength tore him from the car. Then I was arrested by the executioner; but with the stiletto in my hand, I defended myself so furiously, that I broke loose, and rushed into the thick of the mob, where, in a few moments, I found myself wounded by a stab in the side; but the people were struck with such terror, that I made my way through them as far as to the neighbouring wall of the park, which, by frightful effort, I leapt over.

"Murder—murder!—Stop—stop the murderer!" I had fallen down, almost fainting, on the other side of the wall, but these outcries instantly gave me new strength. Some were knocking with great violence, in vain endeavours to break open one of the park gates, which, not being the regular entrance, was always kept closed. Others were striving to clamber over the wall, which I had cleared by an incredible leap. I rose, and exerting my utmost speed, ran forward. I came, ere long, to a broad *frosse*, by which the park was separated from the adjoining forest. By another tremendous effort, I jumped over, and continued to run on through the wood, until at last I sank down, utterly exhausted, under a tree.

I know not how the time had passed, but it was already evening, and dark shadows reigned through the forest, when I came again to my recollection. My progress in running so far had passed over like an obscure dream. I recollect only the wind roaring amid the dense canopy of the trees, and that many times I mistook some old moss-grown pollard stem for an officer of the justice, armed and ready to seize upon me!

When I awoke from the swoon and utter stupefaction into which I had fallen, my first impulse was merely to set out again, like a hunted wild beast, and fly, if possible, from my pursuers to the very end of the earth! As soon, however, as I was only past the frontiers of the Prince's dominions, I would certainly be safe from all immediate persecution.

I rose accordingly, but scarcely had I advanced a few steps, when there was a violent rustling in the thicket; and from thence, in a state of the most vehement rage and excitement, sprung the monk, who, no doubt in consequence of the disturbance that I had raised, had contrived to make his escape from the guards and executioners.

In a paroxysm of madness he flew towards me, leaping through the bushes like a tiger, and finally sprung upon my shoulders, clasping his arms about my throat, so that I was almost suffocated. Under any other circumstances, I would have instantly freed myself from such an attack, but I was enfeebled to the last degree by the exertions I had undergone, and all that I could attempt was to render this feebleness subservient to my rescue. I fell down under his weight, and endeavoured to take advantage of that event. I rolled myself on the ground, and grappled with him; but in vain! I could not disengage myself, and my infernal double laughed scornfully. His abominable accents, "He—he—he!—He—he—he!" sounded amid the desolate loneliness of the woods.

During this contest, the moon broke, only for a moment, through the clouds, for the night was gloomy and tempestuous. Then, as her silvery gleam slanted through the dark shade of the pine trees, I beheld, in all its horror, the deadly pale visage of my *second self*, with the same expression which had glared out upon me from the cart in which he had been dragged to execution. "He— he—he!—Broth-er, broth-er!—Ever, ever I am with thee!—Leave thee, leave thee never! Cannot run as thou canst! Must carry— carry me! Come straight from the gallows—They would have nailed me to the wheel—He—he—he!—He—he—he!"

Thus the infernal spectre howled and laughed aloud as we lay on the ground; but ere the fleeting moonbeam had passed away, I was roused once more to furious rage. I sprang up like a bear in the embraces of a boa-constrictor, and ran with my utmost force against trees and fragments of rock, so that if I could not kill him, I might at least wound him in such manner that he would be under the necessity of letting me go. But in vain. He only laughed the more loudly and scornfully; and my personal sufferings were increased tenfold by my endeavours to end them.

I then strove with my whole remaining strength to burst asunder his hands, which were firmly knotted round my throat, but the supernatural energies of the monster threatened me with strangulation. At last, after a furious conflict, he suddenly fell, as if lifeless, on the ground: and though scarcely able to breathe, I had run onwards for some yards, when again he sat upon my shoulders, laughing as before, and stammering out the same horrible words. Of new succeeded the same efforts of despairing rage! Of new I was freed! Then again locked in the embraces of this demoniacal spectre!

After this I lost all consciousness.—I am utterly unable to say distinctly how long I was persecuted by my relentless *double*. It seems to me as if my struggles must have continued at least during a whole month; and that during this long period I neither ate nor drank. I remember only *one* lucid interval. All the rest is utter darkness.

I had just succeeded in throwing off my double, when a clear gleam of sunlight brightened the woods, and with it a pleasant sound of bells rose on mine ear. I distinguished unequivocally the chimes of a convent, which rung for early mass. For a moment I rejoiced; but then the thought came like annihilation upon me— "THOU HAST MURDERED AURELIA!" and once more losing all self-possession and recollection, I fell in despair upon the earth.

viii. *The Devil's Elixir* (II xxii)

[*Medardus recovers his senses in an Italian hospital, then at a Capuchin monastery near Rome. He confesses to his crimes and, as a result of his impassioned public devotions, comes to be regarded as a saint by the populace. However, when he discovers that Aurelia is not in fact dead but is about to take vows and enter a nunnery, his faith is severely tested. At the consecration ceremony, as Medardus struggles to suppress his carnal desires for Aurelia, the mad monk reappears and slays her. Medardus lives out the remainder of his life contemplatively in the Capuchin cloister.*]

When I reflected on my past life, I perceived plainly how, although armed and protected from earliest youth with the best lessons of piety and virtue, I had yet, like a pusillanimous coward, yielded to Satan, whose aim was to foster and cherish the criminal race, from which I was sprung, so that its representatives might still be multiplied, and still fettered by bonds of vice and wickedness upon the earth. My sins were but trifling and venial when I first became acquainted with the choir-master's sister, and first gave way to the impulses of pride and self-confidence. But, alas! I was too careless to remember the doctrine which I had yet often inculcated on others, that *venial* errors, unless immediately corrected, form a sure and solid foundation for sins which are *mortal*. Then the Devil threw that Elixir into my way, which, like a poison working against the soul instead of the body, completed his victory over me. I heeded not the earnest admonitions of the unknown painter, the Abbess, or the Prior.

Aurelia's appearance at the confessional was a decisive effort for my destruction. Then, as the body, under the influence of poison, falls into disease, so my spirit, under the operation of that hellish cordial, was infected and destroyed by sin. How could that votary, the slave of Satan, recognize the true nature of those bonds by which Omnipotence, as a symbol of that eternal love, (whose marriage festival is death,) had joined Aurelia's fate and mine?

Rejoicing in his first victories, Satan then haunted me in the form of an accursed madman, between whose spirit and mine there seemed to be a reciprocal and alternate power of influencing each other. I was obliged to ascribe his apparent death (of which I was in reality guiltless) to myself; and thus became familiarized with the thought of murder. Or was Victorin really killed, and did the Arch-Fiend re-animate his body, (as the vampyres in Hungary rise from the grave,) for his own especial purposes? May it not suffice to say, that this brother, called Victorin, who derived his birth from an accursed and abominable crime, became to me an impersonization of the evil principle, who forced me into hideous guilt, and tormented me with his unrelenting persecution?

Till that very moment when I heard Aurelia pronounce her vows, my heart was not yet pure from sin; not till then had the Evil One lost over me his dominion; but the wonderful inward tranquillity—the cheerfulness as if poured from Heaven into my heart, when she addressed to me her last words, convinced me that her death was the promise of my forgiveness and reconciliation... I sank down into the dust; but how different now were my inward feelings of humility and submission, from that *passionate* self-condemnation, those cruel and violent penances, which I had formerly undergone at the Capuchin Convent!

Now, for the first time, my spirit was enabled to distinguish truth from falsehood, and by the new light, which was then shed around me, every temptation of the devil must, from henceforward, remain vain and ineffectual. It was not Aurelia's death, but the cruel and horrible manner in which it had occurred, by which I had been at first so deeply agitated. But how short was the interval, ere I perceived and recognized in its fullest extent, even in this event, the goodness and mercy of heaven! The martyrdom of the pious, the tried, and absolved bride! Had she then died for my sake? No! It was not till now, after she had been withdrawn from this world, that she appeared to me like a dazzling gleam, sent down from the realms of eternal love, to brighten the path of an unhappy sinner. Aurelia's death was, as she had said before, our marriage festival, the solemnization of that love, which, like a celestial essence, has its throne and dominion above the stars, and admits nought in common with grovelling and perishable earthly pleasures! These thoughts indeed raised me above myself; and accordingly these three days in the Cistercian Convent might truly be called the happiest of my life.

2. Nicol Muschet

i. *The Confession of Nicol Muschet of Boghall* (Edinburgh: Oliver and Boyd, 1818) 12-14.

I met daily with more and more discontent and provocation to leave her [his wife]; and then I deserted her, with a full resolution to go abroad with a comrade, who was then going off; for which I had procured letters of recommendation, with whatever else I needed. And now nothing stopped me, but my not constituting a factor over my fortune; and in order thereto I condescended upon one in whom I confided, who would hardly undertake it, alleging he would be harassed by my spouse pleading an aliment... But not withstanding of that, I could very soon have prevailed upon him, had I not met with James Campbell, some time of Burnbank, and now store-keeper in Edinburgh Castle, who diverted me entirely from that thought, and was the only vicegerent of the devil to prompt me up to be guilty of all the following wickedness; which I greedily went on in, being so far inebriated with these wicked principles, which by degrees (after he understood how my natural temper was to be prevailed upon) he instilled into me. For, till I met with him, who was the only person that ever tainted me with such hellish principles, those who have been conversant with me, both when a boy, and since my arrival to maturer years, can declare, that I was always more ready to suffer injuries than to be any way revengeful; albeit I do not in the least make use of this as an argument, or palliate to my guilt, but rather to magnify it, in so far as I have allowed myself to be so much mastered by that vice, viz. too much simplicity, which, to my sad experience, is a basis to any kind of wickedness. And Burnbank in a little time perfectly well understanding my failing, daily made it his business to assault me by flatteries, whereby afterwards, alas, he entangled me into such gross snares as now I suffer for. For I did not at all think such destructive methods, as he used with me, were for my life; though what I here assert of him does not render him chargeable with my blood; for I acknowledge the justness of my sentence, and my blood to be upon myself: but stepping from time to endless eternity, without the least malice against him, as God is my witness, I confidently and avowedly affirm, he was the only person ever instigated me to do injustice to that woman (whose infirmities, by my oath to God, I was obliged to conceal) and also to debauch me many other ways. And to put such hellish designs as he contrived against her into execution, James Muschet, periwig-maker, and Grissel Bell his spouse, were mostly employed for a piece of money, as afterwards will appear.

ii. *Confession* (35-40)
[*Muschet commissions Burnbank, James Muschet and Grissel Bell to assassinate his wife. After several botched attempts, he resolves to kill her himself.*]

[W]hen she [his wife] came to us, we carried her straight to Mr Lloyd's, where after we had staid a good while, James went off... But (oh! that my head were waters, and mine eyes a fountain of tears, that I might weep day and night, in calling to mind such barbarous cruelty) when she and I staid a good time after him, the devil, that cunning adversary, suggested to me, being now hard-ened and also desperate, by all the foresaid plots failing, that it was but a light thing whether he or I were the executioner: where-upon I yielding to the temptation, did as my indictment bears: and when I returned, thinking James Muschet and his wife would as soon inform of themselves as of me, I called first at their door, and when they came, I told them what I had been at; but what they answered I do not mind: and James went alongst with me to my room; but what my deportment was, or what words passed (my thoughts being so distracted after such wickedness) I have entire-ly forgot.

Because in this preceding declaration, I have given a particular narration of all the circumstances leading to the last and most hor-rid act of this bloody tragedy, wherein others by advice and assis-tance concurred with me, but have rather couched, than particu-larly narrated the barbarous and unnatural murder itself, wherein I alone was the executioner, therefore to satisfy the world as to my impartiality, and to glorify God by taking shame to myself, I shall particularly lay open that black scene of monstrous cruelty with the utmost ingenuity, so far as the perturbation of my mind, amazed upon every remembrance of such unparalleled guilt will allow, which take as follows,

First,—When she and I went out of Mr Lloyd's house, I desired her to go down the Canongate with me; and when she asked on what account, I bade her ask no questions, but go alongst with me; and when we came to the Abbey, she asked, whither I was going? I said, she was not concerned to know, but only she behoved to go with me. And when we were going through St Ann's Yards she wept (oh how does my heart bleed to think upon it!) and prayed that God might forgive me if I was taking her to any mischief, and desired to return, when I swore by all that was good, if she would return I would not stop her, but I was going to Duddingston, and if she would not go with me, she needed never expect to exchange one word with me afterwards; and so we went on, she all the way entreating me to return, which I would not yield unto: for now the devil had got so fast hold of me, being permitted to tempt me to the perpetration of such cruel wickedness, that he would not let me go, albeit my convictions were frequently very strong upon the way, so that sometimes when she was not speaking, I heartily wished she might return, but whenever she spoke, my rebellious obstinate heart, being so far tempted by Satan, would not suffer her. (Oh! that I may be helped suitably to take shame to myself, and give glory to God!) And when we entered the Duke's Walk, she said, that that was not the way to Duddingston. To which I said, I would lead her another way than the road through the middle of the Park, to which she submitted. And when we came to the fatal place, which was near to the east end of the said Walk, (oh unspeakable cruelty!) how I got her down to the ground I do not distinctly recollect, but so far as I remember, it was on pretence of embracing her; then I presented the knife, which when she saw me offer to apply to her throat, she cried out, "And was that your design in bringing me here, to cut my throat?" To which I said, I had brought her there to punish her for so far cheating me, and playing the whore by me. Then she very earnestly obtested me for God's sake to desist; and what she had done amiss before, she would never be guilty of the like in time coming. But notwithstanding of her arguments, which would have pierced the most savage heart, I went on, and designing the knife for her throat, she bowed down her head for defence, when I cut her chin to the bone; and when she got hold of the knife, I so furiously drew it through her hand, that, as I was afterwards informed, her thumb was almost cut off: whereupon she cried out as long as she was able, "My love, my love, do not murder me!" Which doleful cries, with my seeing the blood gushing down, so smote my heart, that if I could, I would have given the whole world to have got it undone: but the cruel murderer of souls suggested to me, that if I should then give over since I began, it would take away my own life by her telling: so with much struggling, by my dragging and throwing her down by the hair of her head, (which, if she had wanted, I am confident I had not got her overcome) notwithstanding of the very earnest and affectionate entreaties which she used so long as she was able, I maliciously went on till I got some strokes upon her throat. "Oh man! it is done now, you need not give me more;" and then her head fell down and she expired. And after she had lain some time dead, I yet fearing she might recover, (Oh, dreadful to mention!) cut her throat almost through, and so left her. And when I came near to the tirlice at the entry of the Duke's Walk at St Ann's Yards, I was so brutally mad (as I was all the time) that I returned to see what case she was in; and when I found no life in her, I went to James Muschet, and from his room to my own as above: and being in such condition, I have entirely forgot how I did, or what I said, but I do not in the least doubt that I did boast of the horrid wickedness. And woe is me that I continued so hardened, not only during the time, by my refusing to hear her pitiful cries and groans (which cries and groans have now a loud voice in my ears), but also after the perpetration, to approve of such cruel barbarity, by my boasting thereof. This, to the utmost of my memory, is the nearest account I can give of that cruel and inhuman murder.

iii. *Confession* (46-50)

As to my misfortunate marriage, I most heartily acknowledge God's divine hand in it, by permitting me (on account of my so much undervaluing that one thing needful, and not only undervaluing it, but greedily going on in the contrary practices, such as drinking, swearing, Sabbath-breaking, &c) to be so far deprived even of my natural senses, as so foolishly to court, upon so short an acquaintance, a person of whose piety and virtue I had so few proofs; and that without so much as in the least consulting or informing my mother (whom in duty I ought to have regarded) and other friends, who might have advised me well; but especially without my asking counsel of the Lord, that the match might be for his glory. And how do I regret my disorderly method of proceeding in it, contrary to the order and decency which Christ has appointed in his church, and the good laws of men have established, by my celebrating it with such a man, and in such a manner, as corroborated and approved of (what I conceive) the sinful superstitions of the church of England, contrary to my baptismal and national vows, and I must acknowledge, to the light of my conscience also...

As to the crime for which I die, I deeply acknowledge, and unfeignedly bewail it. But oh who can sufficiently declare its horrid guilt and dreadful amazing circumstances, which clothe it with the most astonishing and unparalleled aggravations! My heart fails me to think of them, when I remember and consider how exceeding atrocious and heinous the crime is in itself; how contrary to the express letter of God's law, yea, to the very light of nature, and convictions of my own conscience; how extremely opposite to the law of love, as being done to my own spouse, my own flesh, to whom I was under the strictest bonds of nature, and vows to God to defend her from all harm; to the certain destruction of her temporal life, and probable ruin of her immortal soul, she not being allowed time to prepare for death, to pray for pardon, or to repent of sin. There is also a circumstance before the perpetration of the murder, which though it came late to my memory, has very much afflicted my conscience, as being a deep aggravation of my guilt,— upon Sabbath eight days before that fatal act, I was in the Canongate church hearing sermon, where the minister, preaching upon the sixth commandment, did in a very pathetic manner display the exceeding sinfulness of shedding innocent blood; and after sermon a gentleman in whose seat I then sat invited me to Mr Lloyd's house, in which I had never been before that time, which was the very house we carried her to before I perpetrated the horrid wickedness; which concurrence of circumstances, though then not regarded by me, now plainly convinces me that in the righteous judgment of God those very means, which tend to the deterring of others from sin, had the quite contrary effect on me.

iv. *Confession* (55-62)

And now, what shall a poor sinner do, when he sees himself lying under the just sentence of eternal wrath, not only on account of original guilt, but also by reason of the many actual sins he has committed, perhaps against many means and mercies, falling into gross out-breakings (as in my sad and deplorable case); when he sees his sins before him, the justice of God behind pursuing hard, and corruption on every side, and no way to escape? In such a case God must work miracles, and let himself honour upon our sins and corruptions, in blotting them out of the book of his remembrance, and casting them into the depths of the sea of forgetfulness, and that by his infinite free love and rich grace, whereby, "He so loved the world, as to send his only begotten Son to be the propitiation for our sins." Oh how ought we to give glory to the Father, for contriving such a noble device of salvation, to be accomplished by giving his own Son to the death for sinners! And how ought we to ascribe everlasting honour to the Son, in purchasing at so dear a rate, our reconciliation to God, who otherwise were past all hope of recovery! ...

What matter of admiration is it, that ever a holy and just God should have cast his eye in mercy upon me, the chief of sinners, who have made it my business to delight myself in the works of darkness, most part of my short life! But very oft the rudest pieces of clay, that most excellent potter makes vessels of honour, the more to manifest his singular power and art; "For as the heavens are higher than earth, so are his ways higher than our ways, and his thoughts than our thoughts." Well may I say, "his mercies are above all his other works." Oh to have suitable apprehensions of his great mercy, in not cutting me off in the very perpetration of some horrid crimes (which have been very many) but in lengthening out my time, to wait to be gracious, and to work wonderfully in his wise providence upon my soul, in redeeming, regenerating, justifying, sanctifying, and giving me the hope of eternal life through Jesus Christ! What is man, whose breath is in his nostrils, that the God of heaven, whom myriads of angels do serve, should ever have condescended so far as to take notice of him, who so rebelliously forsook his Maker, and brake the covenant! and not only did he condescend to take notice of him, but in such a manner, as, "when he was cast out in the open field, to the loathing of his person, to say unto him, when he was in his blood, Live; yea, to say to him, when he was in his blood, Live."...

I say, in the faith of what I have said, I willingly and cheerfully resign my spirit to Him who gave it, who is one in three and three in one: for dust we are, and to dust we must return: and blessed be God in lovely Jesus, that I am now enabled by faith to look upon all sublunary things as dung in comparison of the excellency of Christ. Oh for tongues of angels, to extol him, never enough to be extolled, who out of mere love did undertake for us poor frail worms, who had ruined ourselves on many accounts, and notwithstanding whereof he extended the bowels of compassion towards us, and that in an eminent manner, by relieving us of all our sins, and nailing him to his cross, and clothing us with his righteousness, that he might present us pure and spotless to the Father. What further shall I say of sweet and lovely Christ? All I can do, is to multiply words without knowledge; for it is impossible any created being can in the least comprehend that boundless ocean of love which he bears to his chosen. Oh for the light of his reconciled countenance to shine upon me! Oh for his favour, for life lies in his favour! All ye hosts of heaven, and inhabitants of the earth, praise and exalt him, and magnify the greatness of the riches of his free grace and pardoning mercy on my behalf.

And now I bid adieu to all earthly comforts and enjoyments; to this vain transitory world, the stage of sin and sorrow: and welcome heaven and eternal enjoyment of God and the Lamb, which, through faith in his blood, I, though the chief of sinners, hope to obtain: Oh that he would enable me to persevere in this faith and hope, and to carry myself, even to my latest breath, with that Christian bravery and resolution that becomes me; being fully persuaded that Death, in his most appalling and dreadful form, is made my friend through the death of my Lord and Saviour Jesus Christ, into whose hands I commit my spirit.

3. S.L. Mitchill

"A Double Consciousness, or a Duality of Person in the same Individual." *Edinburgh Weekly Journal* 31 (1816): 252.

The Medical Repository furnishes the following singular article, communicated by Dr Mitchill to the Rev. Dr Nott, dated January, 1816:—

Where I was employed, early in December, 1815, with several other gentlemen, in doing the duty of a visitor to the United States Military Academy at West-Point, a very extraordinary case of *double consciousness*, in a woman, was related to me by one of the professors. Major Ellicot, who so worthily occupies the mathematical chair in that seminary, vouched for the correctness of the following narrative, the subject of which is related to him by blood, and, at this time, an inhabitant of one of the western counties of Pennsylvania:—

Miss R—— possessed naturally a very good constitution, and arrived to adult age without having it impaired by disease. She possessed an excellent capacity, and had enjoyed fair opportunities to acquire knowledge. Besides the domestic arts and social attainments, she had improved her mind by reading and conversation, and was well versed in penmanship. Her memory was capacious, and stored with a copious stock of ideas.

Unexpectedly, and without any kind of forewarning, she fell into a profound sleep, which continued several hours beyond the ordinary term. On waking, she was discovered to have lost every trait of acquired knowledge. Her memory was *tabula rasa*; all vestiges, both of words and of things, were obliterated and gone. It was found necessary for her to learn every thing again. She even acquired, by new efforts, the arts of spelling, reading, writing, and calculating, and gradually became acquainted with the persons and objects around, like a being for the first time brought into the world. In these exercises she made considerable proficiency.

But, after a few months, another fit of somnolency invaded her. On rousing from it, she found herself restored to the state she was before the first paroxysm; but was wholly ignorant of every event and occurrence that had befallen her afterwards. The former condition of her existence she now calls the *old* state, and the latter the *new* state; and she is as unconscious of her *double* character as two distinct persons are of their respective separate natures.

For example, in her old state she possesses all her original knowledge; in her new state only what she has acquired since. If a gentleman or lady be introduced to her in the *old* state, she will not know that person in the *new* state, and *vice versa*; and so of all other matters. To know them satisfactorily, she must learn them in *both* states.

In the *old* state she possesses fine powers of penmanship; while, in the *new*, she writes a poor and awkward hand, having not had time or means to become expert.

During four years and upwards, she has undergone periodical transitions from one of these states to the other. The alternations are always consequent upon a long and sound sleep. Both the lady and her family are now capable of conducting the affair without embarrassment. By simply knowing whether she is in the *old* or the *new* state, they regulate the intercourse, and govern themselves accordingly. A history of her curious case is drawing up by the Rev. Timothy Aldin, of Meadville.

4. H. Dewar

"Report on a Communication from Dr Dyce of Aberdeen, to the Royal Society of Edinburgh, 'On Uterine Irritation, and its Effects on the Female Constitution.'" *Transactions of the Royal Society of Edinburgh* 9 (1823): 365–79

The communication received from Dr DYCE chiefly consists of a description of a singular affection of the nervous system, and mental powers, to which a girl of sixteen was subject immediately before puberty, and which disappeared when that state was fully established. It exemplifies the powerful influence of the state of the uterus on the mental faculties; but its chief value arises from some curious relation which it presents to the phenomena of the mind, and which claim the attention of the practical metaphysician. The mental symptoms of this affection are among the number of those which are considered as uncommonly difficult of explanation. It is a case of mental disease, attended with some advantageous manifestations of the intellectual powers; and these manifestations disappearing in the same individual in the healthy state. It is an instance of a phenomenon which is sometimes called double consciousness, but is more properly a *divided consciousness*, or *double personality*; exhibiting in some measure two separate and independent trains of thought, and two independent mental capabilities, in the same individual; each train of thought, and each capability, being wholly dissevered from the other, and the two states in which they respectively predominate subject to frequent interchanges and alternations.

The particulars will be most agreeably communicated, in the order of their occurrence which is followed by Dr DYCE,—part of the narrative being given in the words of Mrs L——, in whose house the patient lived as a servant, and the rest in the words of Dr DYCE himself, consisting of the facts which fell under his own observation.

The history of the complaint, while under the eye of this gentleman, extends from the 2d of March 1815, to the 11th of the following June, including a period of more than three months. But the symptoms had made their appearance in the end of the preceding December.

The first symptom was an uncommon propensity to fall asleep in the evenings, for which she was reproved by Mrs L——. This was followed by the habit of *talking* in her sleep on these occasions. She not only uttered such wild incoherent expressions as persons, under the affection of sleep-talking commonly do, but repeated the occurrences of the day. She also sang musical airs, both sacred and profane.

One evening, in the house of an acquaintance of Mrs L——, where she seems to have come for the purpose of seeing her mistress home, she fell asleep in this manner, imagined herself an Episcopal clergyman, went through the ceremony of baptizing three children, and gave an appropriate *extempore* prayer. Her mistress shook her by the shoulders, on which she awoke, and appeared inconscious of every thing except that she had fallen asleep, of which she shewed herself ashamed.

Another evening, having fallen asleep surrounded by some of the inhabitants of the house, she imagined herself to be living with her aunt at Epsom, and going to the races; placed herself on one of the kitchen stools, and rode upon it into the room, with much spirit, and a clattering noise, but without being wakened. Being afterwards severely reprimanded for this exhibition, she continued free from the habit for a week. After that interval, however, it returned in a similar form, with this addition, that, when in this state, she answered questions which were put to her by others. The disease now increased, and came on her at different times of the evening and morning. She sometimes dressed herself and the children while in this state, or, as Mrs L——calls it, "dead asleep," answered questions put to her in such a manner as to shew that she understood the question; but the answers were often, though not always, incongruous. One day, when she was in this state, her fellow-servant was desired to get the key of a closet from her, in order to do the duty which was generally hers, that of setting the breakfast-table. The girl, however, refused to give up the key, and set the breakfast herself with perfect correctness, with her eyes shut. She afterwards woke with the child on her knee, and wondered how she had got on her clothes. If seized in this manner in the house, she was sometimes restored to her senses by being taken out to the cold air, especially when the wind blew in her face. At other times she was seized with this affection while walking out with the children.

In the mean time, a still more singular and interesting symptom began to make its appearance. The circumstances which occurred during the paroxysm were completely forgotten by her when the paroxysm was over, but were perfectly remembered during subsequent paroxysms. Her mistress says, that, when in this stupor on subsequent occasions, she told her what was said to her on the evening on which she baptized the children. It was remarked that, while under the paroxysm, she knew a person better by looking at the shadow than at the body; that is, she perceived those objects best which were presented merely in outline, or were very dimly illuminated. The disease made progress in the interval between its first appearance in December and the beginning of March, though no dates of its different stages are given. From the 2d of March till its disappearance Dr DYCE's account is very circumstantial.

She was brought to him for medical advice by her mother. The mother called these affections *sleepy fits*. The girl herself called them *wanderings*. They sometimes continued for a hour. If they came on when she was in bed, she sometimes rose and tried to raise the sashes of the windows. The eyes were described as half-shut, the pupils dilated, and the cornea covered with a dimness or glaze, resembling those of a person in syncope. She answered many questions correctly, shewing at times scarcely any failure of her mental powers. It was remarked, that she always retained the impression last made on her previous to the fit.

With regard to the case as an object of medical attention, it is sufficient to mention that some foulness of tongue, and other symptoms of torpor or disorder in the alimentary canal, accompanied these mental phenomena, and were treated by Dr DYCE principally with emetics and laxatives, in proportion to their degree.

These symptoms of the paroxysm, as they fell under the Doctor's own eye for the first time, are thus described. "When she was brought to my room she appeared as if in a state of stupor. Her eyes were half-open; but, when desired, she could open them completely. At other times she closed them, as if unconscious of what she did. When desired to look at me, and tell who I was, she gave a vacant kind of stare, and named some other person. When desired to look round, and say where she was, she looked round with some apparent attention; but, though she had been in that room more than once before, she said she was in the New Inn. When desired to turn her eyes to the direct rays of the sun, she readily obeyed, but there was no perceptible contraction of the iris. She saw some object perfectly, for she read quite distinctly a part of the dedication of a book which she could not have seen before, and corrected herself in the pronunciation of the word *conspicuous*, which she had called *conspicious*. Being asked to tell the hour by a watch which was shewn to her, she did not give the proper answer. Pulse 70; extremities rather cold. Being desired to stand up, she did it most readily, but required some time and a little effort to stand firmly, as she staggered at first like a person waked out of sleep. But soon after, she could stand, walk, or dance as well as other people. Being desired to sing, she sang a hymn delightfully; and from a comparison which I (Dr DYCE) had an opportunity of making, it appeared incomparably better sung than she could sing the same tune when well. The same appeared to be the case to persons whose skill in music was much superior to my own."

Her hands were immersed in cold water, in consequence of which she recovered her senses, exactly like a person waked out of a sound sleep, and with the same yawning and stretching. This mode of rousing her had often succeeded in the house where she lived, and was tried now at the suggestion of the person who accompanied her. She now knew the persons and things surrounding her.

The account which she gave of her feelings as connected with her present situation was, that previously to an attack she felt drowsy, with a little pain in the head; then a cloudiness or mistiness came over her eyes; she heard a peculiar noise in her head resembling that of a carriage running, and had a feeling of motion as if she were seated in such a carriage. When this stage supervened, her conceptions of external objects were immediately altered.

Next day (March 5.) while under a fit, she performed in the most correct manner some of her accustomed duties relating to the pantry, and the dinner-table. Dr DYCE went to see her; she gave him a wrong name as formerly; when her mistress desired her to stand straight up, look round, and tell where she was, she recovered instantly; but it was only for a little; she very soon relapsed. When asked to read in an almanac held before her, she did not seem to see it, nor did she notice a stick which was held out to her. Being asked a second time to read, she repeated a portion of Scripture, and did not give a correct answer when asked where she was. Being desired to state what she felt, she put her hand to her forehead, and complained of her head; said, "she saw the mice running through the room." Mrs L—— mentioned that she had said the same thing on many former occasions, even when her eyes were shut; that she also frequently imagined that she was accompanied by a little black dog, which she could not get rid of; did not, in general, express any particular uneasiness from that cause; at times, however, cried in consequence of it, and at other times laughed immoderately. In some of her repeated paroxysms, she insisted that she was going to church to preach. One day, while taking out two infants for an airing, she was seized with one of her fits on the quay, and without hesitation walked along a single plank placed between a vessel and the shore, and even danced on it with the children. Of this circumstance she afterwards, when well, denied all knowledge. This was invariably the case; but with equal regularity she acknowledged and asserted it when under the influence of a paroxysm.

On the following day she had a threatening, which went off without being followed by the usual degree of insensibility. She says she now knows for a quarter of an hour before the attack. This day some local bodily symptoms were added to her usual complaint, which it is unnecessary to particularise, but which were fully accounted for by a horrid transaction which on the following day (the 8th of March), her mother related to Dr DYCE.

Another young woman, a depraved fellow-servant, understanding that she wholly forgot every transaction that occurred during the fit, clandestinely introduced a young man into the house, who treated her with the utmost rudeness, while her fellow-servant stopped her mouth with the bed-clothes, and otherwise overpowered a vigorous resistance which was made by her even during the influence of her complaint. Next day she had not the slightest recollection even of that transaction, nor did any person interested in her welfare know of it for several days, till she was in one of her paroxysms, when she related the whole facts to her mother. Some particulars are given by Dr DYCE clothed in the Latin language, and others were told him which he does not think it necessary at all to detail.

Next Sunday she was taken to church by her mistress, while the paroxysm was on her. She shed tears during the sermon, particularly during an account given of the execution of three young men at Edinburgh, who had described in their dying declarations the dangerous steps with which their career of vice and infamy took its commencement. When she returned home, she recovered in a quarter of an hour, was quite amazed at the question put to her about the church and the sermon, and denied that she had been in any such place; but next night, on being taken ill, she mentioned that she had been at church, repeated the words of the text, and, in Dr DYCE's hearing, gave an accurate account of the tragical narrative of the three young men, by which her feelings had been so powerfully affected. On this occasion, though in Mrs L——'s house, she asserted that she was in her mother's.

Dr DYCE saw her on many subsequent occasions, when similarly affected, and from one fit she recovered in his presence. He said the eyes had now all the vivacity of youth and health. Previously they were like those of a person under amaurosis, or those of a person half-inebriated, and who had never been in that state before. The difference, he says, is not perfectly expressed by either or both of these comparisons, but was very striking to all who saw her...

This case certainly gives an interesting illustration of the obliquities to which the physiology of the nerves, and the exercise of the mental powers are subject.

Somnambulism is in itself a very remarkable phenomenon, not so much from the partiality of the affection of the senses implied in it, for this is sufficiently exemplified in the act of dreaming, in which the imagination alone is active, and is not guided, and but very obscurely influenced, by any of the objects which solicit the external senses. It is well known, however, to those who have studied the history of dreams, that this is not always the case, and that in many instances the manner of dreaming is dictated not only by the scenes in which the individual has been engaged when awake, but by those objects which are at the time presented to his senses, especially to those of touching and hearing. The most remarkable circumstance in somnambulism, is the unequalled accuracy with which a person in that state sometimes conducts his proceedings, an accuracy superior to that of which he is capable when fully awake. A somnambulist has gone out by a window, and walked along the roof of a house, with a degree of security which he never could have enjoyed in the same local situation in his waking hours. Such facts evince a strange mixture of accurate perception and self-management with the absence of general recollection and self-knowledge: and it is remarkable that the accurate perceptions which persons in this situation retain, and which may in some measure be the effect of habit on the faculties, are so completely dissevered from the immediate influence of general sensation, that when the individual is wakened by loud speaking, or by a shock from a by-stander, he sometimes becomes inexpressibly bewildered and unhappy, and does not know where he is. Instances are said to have occurred, in which a somnambulist abruptly wakened while walking out of doors, has, by the unhappy distraction attending the transition, been thrown into a state of permanent insanity.

The influence of association on all out thoughts, on the memory, on the imagination, and even on the freedom and facility of those mental movements which we call exertions of the active powers, is familiarly observed by every person who has paid the least attention to human nature, or to the proceedings of his own mind. We never wonder at our mental acts being varied in their degree of intensity or facility by this all-pervading principle. It is only a greater degree of the same dependence on particular associations that constitutes such anomalies as made their appearance in the history of this poor girl. In other cases, objects are recollected less easily and less vividly in some circumstances than in others. In this case one set of objects was not recollected at all, and could not be in the least degree recognised or brought to mind by any suggested associations, unless they occurred in that train, and while the mind was under that particular diseased habit under which they were generated; and in this case they occurred with readiness and fidelity.

This, indeed, was a case of disease, evidently depending on the state of the brain as connected with the habitudes of the sanguiferous system. In this particular it is to be ranked with the aberrations which constitute many cases of insanity; and it is both curious and humbling to think, that in insanity itself there is scarcely a mental irregularity admitting of description, but what may be shown to be only a greater degree of those mental aberrations, those follies, and those partialities to which the most vigorous and the most correct minds are continually liable.

The strong contrast between the mental states of this person under her fit, and when it was off, is to be classed with a set of facts, of which some other examples have lately come to the public knowledge. One of them was in an apparently simple girl in the neighbourhood of Stirling, who, in her sleep, talked like a profound philosopher, solved geographical problems, and enlarged on the principles of astronomy, detailing the workings of ideas which had been suggested to her mind, by over-hearing the lessons which were given by a tutor to the children of the family in which she lived. The originality of the language which she used, shewed something more than a bare repetition of what she had heard. She explained the alternations of winter and summer, for instance, by saying, that "the earth was set a-gee."

Another case was mentioned in some of the newspapers, two or perhaps three years ago, of a more marked instance of double consciousness. The individual was liable to two states, each of which, if I rightly recollect, continued for two or more years. In the one state, when it first came on, there was an oblivion of all former education, but no deficiency of mental vigour as applied to ideas or pursuits subsequently presenting themselves. It was necessary for this woman to recommence the studies of reading and the art of writing. A separate set of notions, and separate accomplishments were now formed. In one of the states an exquisite talent for music, and some others which implied refinement, were displayed. When another mental revolution arrived, these utterly disappeared, and the individual was reduced to a level with the rest of mankind, displaying a sufficient portion of common sense, but nothing brilliant.

Differences more or less allied to these are produced by a variety of causes.

Sometimes external fortune has an influence of this kind...

Sometimes the state of the brain, as influenced primarily by disease, determines the operation of these mental states.

External applications are well known to possess a similar agency. We all know the influence of opium, and still more familiarly that of inebriating liquors...

The preceding analogies are, I confess, somewhat loose. It would be interesting to have a copious collection of well authenticated facts, and an arrangement given to them fitted to shew the shades of transition by which different mental states graduate into one another.

Appendix C: Contemporary Reviews

1. *Westminster Review*, October (1824): 560-2.

This is a strange tale of Diablerie and Theology. The hero is born in lawful wedlock to a jolly Scotch laird by his outrageous saint of a wife, who is the disciple and admirer of an ultra-calvinist minister, and sits up with him o'nights to discuss the different kinds of faith. The youth becomes one of the elect, and falls in with a strange fellow, who seems to be no other than Satan himself in disguise, who instigates him to push his religious tenets to the most immoral consequences, and then carry them into practice by pistoling a worthy old Gospel preacher, conniving at the execution of a worthy young Gospel preacher for the murder, stabbing his own elder brother, breaking his lawful father's heart, getting rid, it does not appear exactly how, of his mother, revelling in all sorts of excess and atrocity while he possessed the paternal property, and when driven from its enjoyment by the dread of justice, saving its officers trouble by hanging himself upon a hay-stack. All this is represented as having taken place in the lowlands of Scotland, about the commencement of the last century.

There are three good reasons for reading books: first to be instructed by them; secondly to be amused; and thirdly, to review them. The first does not apply at all to the tale before us; as to the second, there are but few whose taste it will suit, and they may be much more highly gratified by many portions of the Newgate Calendar; the third carried us through with that proud consciousness of martyrdom for the public good, to which we are but too much accustomed when labouring in our vocation.

The author has managed the tale very clumsily, having made two distinct narratives of the same events; and, however true it may be in mathematics, it certainly does not always hold in story-telling, that two halves are equal to one whole. The events, up to the flight of the hero from his estate, are first told by the author from tradition, and then by himself. This expedient soon puts an end to all interest about the fate of the elder brother, who is almost the only personage in the book that does not richly merit the gallows here, and perdition hereafter. But soon to put an end to all interest about his best character, is not the best plan for a novelist who has any other object than that of providing materials for a monitory lecture to young writers of fiction. Unless this was the author's design, he must have adopted the plan for the sake of its originality. His ambition is commendable, for that praise has not hitherto been awarded to Scottish novels of the third rate, the class to which this production belongs.

If an author will introduce supernatural beings, he is at least bound to invent plausible motives for their interference in human concerns. The Royal One of the burning lake must have had much less business upon his hands than usual, or have been in a strangely capricious humour, when he became incarnate, and toiled so industriously, merely to get the soul of a raw Dominic Sampson, who was by nature wholly wicked and half-crazy. The devil is very difficult to manage; as much so poetically as theologically. He is sure to be disappointing, wearisome, or disgusting, unless made sublime enough for the reader to tremble at, or grotesque enough for him to laugh at. Our author is neither a Milton nor a Le Sage. His demon is no genius; nor is he.

In the supposed auto-biography of a victim of superstition, to preserve that unity which is essential to the production of a pleasurable impression on the reader, one of two obvious courses must be consistently adhered to. The phantoms of that superstition must either have a real, external being; or they must exist solely in the diseased imagination of the supposed writer. We can readily become, for the time, either believers or philosophers, to relish a good story; but the author must make his election, and adhere to it. The "Justified Sinner" will not allow us to jog on comfortably with him in either character. He is mad enough, for all the arch-fiend's pranks to have been played in his own brain merely: so mad, that we are oft-times convinced they could have no other theatre; and yet, just as we are settling down into this conviction, the most preposterous of his tricks are seriously sworn to by some half-dozen witnesses in their sober senses, on the authority of their own eyes and ears. This inconsistency is as great an annoyance as if the audience were compelled to change their dresses three or four times during a performance, instead of the actors.

It is a still more serious objection, that the author has been unjust to a class of religionists, whose opinions are far from being obsolete, and of whom, though they might have much to answer for, he has given a delineation so grossly overcharged as to make it a hideous caricature. The ultra-calvinists of Scotland did vehemently decry ethical preaching; they did misapply texts of Scripture in a way very inconsistent with the peace of society and the rights of others; they were profoundly ignorant of the science of morals; but neither they nor any other sect, have ever advocated the practice of what they allowed to be vicious, or set themselves in open opposition to what they deemed virtue. The fanatic may think that the purest morals, without faith, will not keep a man out of hell; but he has still (controversy apart) all the reasons for speaking well of morality, and they are neither few nor small, which influence those who expect neither heaven nor hell; and he has all the inducements to its practice which arise from the connection of individual interest with the general good. The most outrageous votary of saving faith, would not brand the character of his own party by recording, that "the true Gospel preachers joined all on one side, and the upholders of pure morality and a blameless life on the other." There is great want of keeping in this and similar language. Men never select such colours for their own portraits; and to make them do so, offends as much against candour as against taste.

There are a few redeeming passages, especially the story of the Auchtermuchty preachment, which is told with some humour; but they only make us regret that the author did not employ himself better than in uselessly and disgustingly abusing his imagination, to invent wicked tricks for a mongrel devil, and blasphemous lubrications for an insane fanatic.

2. *The New Monthly Magazine and Literary Journal*, 12 (1824): 526.

These "Confessions" are, we presume, intended to bring that exaggerated and extravagant style of writing which has lately become too prevalent, into the contempt which it so richly merits. All former horrors are nothing to the ineffable enormities of this justified Sinner, who is a parricide, fratricide, and *clericide*—for we must coin new words to comprehend all his multifarious offences. Nothing more completely ridiculous can well be imagined than the whole of the story. The unfortunate hero is misled by the devil, whom he mistakes for Peter the Great wandering about in Scotland, by whose instigation he is driven to the commission of the most extravagant crimes, under the persuasion at the same time that he is one of the elect. We do not altogether approve of the mode which the author has chosen of attacking the religious prejudices of numbers, who, notwithstanding their speculative opinions, are in no danger of becoming either parricides or fratricides. We must also remark, that in spite of the high seasoning given to these Confessions, they are still singularly dull and revolting, and that it is altogether unfair to treat the reader with two versions of such extraordinary trash as the writer has given us in "the Editor's narrative," and the Confessions themselves. Moreover, though we may be compelled to read as much bad Scotch, as any gentleman on the other side of the Tweed may choose to pour out upon us, yet we do protest most solemnly against the iniquity of bad English, of which the present work furnishes most abundant instances. We account his bad grammar amongst the most crying sins of the miscreant with whose history we are here regaled.

3. *The Examiner*, 1 August (1824): 482-83.

We owe this very singular production, happier possibly in its thought than its execution, to the Ettrick Shepherd. It is an attempt at one of those mystifications in which the Scottish school has been recently so fruitful; and its principal defect is, that with much elaboration in the assumption of disguise, no one can be deceived for a moment. In other respects, the strong hand of Mr. HOGG is often recognisable; and a surprising lack of probability, or even possibility, is accompanied with a portion of mental force and powerful delineation, which denote the conception and the hand of a master.

The idea, considering the country and situation of Mr. HOGG, is a bold one; the more especial and darling doctrines of Calvinism being the objects attacked, and particularly the spiritual fatalism connected with notions of election, reprobation, and faith independent of works. The confessions are presumed to be those of a sombre enthusiast, who is led into the murder of a brother and a mother, under the immediate inspiration of these tenets, operating upon a diseased and melancholy temperament. The result is a practical fanaticism, similar to that of the far-famed cobbler of Messina, who took it into his head that he had a divine commission to put every one out of the way whose existence he deemed injurious to society. We need not say, that Mr. HOGG is borne out by much evidence on record of the baneful tendency of these supralapsarian sentiments, which mislead his hero both negatively and positively;—negatively, in the production of despair; positively, of arrogance, cruelty, and presumption. The mind of the most innocent and harmless of men, COWPER, is distracted with the apprehension of eternal torments on his own

part; while the fanatic of more rigid nerve and firmer organiza-
tion luxuriates in the damnation of every one else, and, satisfied
of the eternal torture of a victim in the next world, feels an irresistible propensity to indulge him with a foretaste in the present.
The latter of these is precisely the "justified sinner" of Mr.
HOGG.

The book opens with the Editor's account of the extraordinary marriage of a Scottish Laird with a babe of grace, spiritu-
ally opposed to him, that a sort of separation takes place from
the wedding-day, which does not however prevent the birth of
two sons, the eldest of whom is taken into the special care of
his open-hearted father, while the latter is reared in all the
gloomy fanaticism of his mother and her bosom friend and
director, a certain fanatical minister. So far plausible: the source
of rancorous religious enmity between the brothers is well
imagined, and the narrative of the murder, as it appeared to
common eyes, interestingly detailed; but when, by a little arti-
ficial contrivance, we get possession of the murderer's confessions, the author flies off in a tangent; for instead of the operation of opinion upon mind and action, we are indulged with a
tale of German *diablerie*, and introduced to a twin-brother of
the Mephistopheles of Faust, one Gil-Martin, which introduction transforms the hero at once into a madman, at the expense
of a great portion of the implied instruction. We may perceive,
indeed, the sort of visions which may colour insanity of a particular description; but that is all. The Elect will observe, that it
is not fair to create a madman, and attribute the effects of delusion to their doctrine; and the Ettrick Shepherd will have nothing to reply, save that persons of their way of thinking are liable
to go mad in the way which he has described; which is not very
wide of the fact; for women have cut their children's throats in
fulfilment of the fiat which ordained their eternal happiness,
and poisoned their husbands because they were not palpably
rejected of God. Unhappily, however, Mr. HOGG is not content either with the internal development of a disastrous principle, or with the introduction of a demon, who, like the unri-
valled demon of GOETHE, is a shadowy personification of the
evil tendencies of our nature. His counterpart, Gil-Martin, is a
very positive personage, and in many respects a mere vulgar
devil, and every way befitting a lunatic, who, being satisfied past
doubt that he is one of the *sealed*, thinks himself clear of sin in
the subsequent murder of his brother. The Scottish Devil, too,

has no atmosphere created for him; and therefore gasps in the ordinary scenes of common life for a more natural element. In short, he is only the exclusive perception of a madman, instead of a being of the poet's mind, created for an object and an end. Mr. HOGG's religious compatriots will discover this, and he will hear of it.

Having discharged our conscience in regard to general plan and adaptation of means to end, we may be allowed to observe, that this fiction has the great merit of fixing attention. Its philosophy, on the other hand, is exceedingly defective; and Mr. HOGG, like many more, stakes himself on the *cheveux de frise* of Calvinism, by combating under the theological disguise of election and reprobation the impregnable doctrine of necessity itself. It is one thing to produce an undeniable generation of events, another to connect it with eternal burning; and we suspect that in reference to the much disputed question of freewill, Mr. HOGG, in his contempt for theology and metaphysics, has never read a syllable on the subject. We gather from him, that every man is the child of his own creation, and may do or say what he pleases. If he can say as much of himself, well; but let him first pause and consider whether he has not more than once favoured himself with an unintended headache after spending the previous evening with Christopher North and Co.? This query reminds us of an anecdote of Foote and Macklin. The latter gave lectures, on the Drama we believe, which the former attended with a view to ridicule. Aware of this intention, Macklin thus addressed the wag: "Clever as you are, Mr. Foote, you do not know what I am going to say." "No," replied Mr Foote; "do you?" This was tart; and yet we suspect that the alleged case of Macklin is essentially that of the whole of us. In a word, until we can create that which governs impulse, we are the creatures of necessity. Mr. Owen has some notions of taking that government upon himself, and when fully established in office, *dele* "necessity" and read "Owen." Will the Ettrick Shepherd, in the plenitude of his free-will, inform us what he intends to think on this subject next year? We are much inclined to believe that even the consequences of the appearance of his own book will render him inadequate to the anticipation. When in this sense man resolves, "the spirits of the wise," as the Royal Hal has it, "sit in the clouds and mock him." Mr. HOGG may be consoled, for although *his* theory was an opposite one, they laughed loudly at Napoleon.

4. *The British Critic*, 12 (1824): 68-80.

Write what he will, there is a diseased and itching peculiarity of style...which, under every disguise, is always sure to betray Mr. Hogg. We had not read twenty pages of this most uncouth and unpleasant volume, before we satisfied ourselves of its parentage: and notwithstanding our usual deep mistrust of internal evidence, we are enough confirmed in our opinion, upon a careful revision of its matter, to treat it as the production of the Ettrick Shepherd.

Out of three hundred and ninety closely printed pages, one hundred and forty-two are occupied by the "Editor's Narrative:" a narrative which we are by no means sure that we wholly understand...A clumsy mixture of the politics of the day is forced into the story...with a view to giving it the circumstantiality of authentic narrative...

In order to make the "Private Memoirs" which are subjoined to this *narrative* in any degree intelligible, it will be necessary to treat them as if they were written in Hebrew, and to begin at the end. When Mr. Hogg has finished his volume, he asks a very *naive* question, which many a reader, we doubt not, will be inclined to reiterate, "*what can this work be?*" And he endeavours to explain its nature by referring to a letter written by himself to that "vast profound" of Scottish lore, Blackwood's Magazine. The letter relates to the grave of a suicide, on a wild height, called Cowan's Croft. Tradition states, that more than a century back, the unhappy wretch whose bones *ought* to moulder in it, hung himself in a singular manner, on a neighbouring haystack. A summer or two back, the grave was opened; the body was found entire; and Mr. Hogg dressed up the facts or the fiction, we know not which, and gave them to the public in the manner which we have described. Another gentleman, the Editor of this volume ("Mungo here, Mungo there," for who can this be, save Mr. Hogg himself?) was attracted by the wildness of the tale, visited the spot, saw the remains of the remains, which he describes with most loathsome circumstantiality, and discovered about them a leathern case containing a printed pamphlet, of which the pages before us are a faithful reprint.

The Suicide, then, was no other than Robert Wringhim Colwan, the Predestinarian and Murderer; and the Memoirs are those of his miserable career. He details his infant training in Hyper-Covenanting-Calvinism, till the stern and ferocious doctrines which he had imbibed, has clutched all the powers of his soul in their unrelenting grasp. A boyhood of petty guile and hypocrisy in trifles prepared him to become a burning light of his sect when he attained to manhood; and we think, it little needed the active and personal co-operation of the Devil himself.—There was no *nodus* which required such cacodoemonical interference, in order to bring the self-justified sinner to the halter which he richly merited, whether adjusted by his own individual hands or those of the public executioner.

Mr. Hogg has probably been reading a German Tale, recently translated into English, under the title of *The Devil's Elixir:* and from this he has no doubt borrowed the machinery of his present volume. The similarity, *mutatis mutandis*, is too striking to be accidental. Each of the heroes of the two narratives is subjected by different means to the same evil influence; each perpetrates most atrocious crimes under this black guidance, and is made to bear the blame of yet more which are committed for him by his diabolical double. The fiend in each assumes another person's likeness: and about each there is an occasional mist and obscurity, which, as it is probable the writer himself has not penetrated, the reader may be excused for leaving as he finds it...

We are unable fully to penetrate the object of the work, but whatever this may be, in its effect we fear it will be mischievous. Mr. Hogg's is not the hand which should approach the abuse of things sacred with raillery; and if his intention be to expose the absurdity of principle and the atrocity of conduct into which the unqualified adoption of the doctrine of absolute election may plunge its followers, we fear he has not succeeded in this attempt without exposing religion itself, in some degree, to the malice of the scoffer. We are far from being among those who hold that Christianity can suffer by a *judicious* ridicule of fanaticism. On the contrary, we think that such a weapon is not only legitimate, but that it possesses a keenness and power which belongs to no other; since there are many things which cannot be attacked seriously without the hazard of bestowing upon them an importance which they little deserve. A laugh raised at the expense of those who profane religion by fantastic and extravagant appendages is widely different from a laugh at religion itself; for inasmuch as the holy truths which we cherish demand our attachment and reverence, in the same proportion do perversions of them call for our indignation and reproof.

In the dexterity or the clumsiness with which this bright but dangerous weapon is employed, lies the distinction between the man of genius and the pretender. Il est vrai qu'il faut prendre garde que les railleries ne soient pas basses et indignes de la verité. Mais à cela près quand on pourra s'en servir avec adresse c'est un devoir que d'en user.[1] The sentiment is that of Tertullian, the words are those of Pascal. We wish that the caution which is conveyed in them had been better known to Mr. Hogg.

1 "One must certainly take care that the raillery is not too low, or untruthful. However, with this in mind, when ridicule can be used effectively, we are duty-bound to avail ourselves of it"—from Blaise Pascal's *Provincial Letters* (1656-7): Letter 11.

Works Cited and Recommended Reading

(Abbreviations: *SSL=Studies in Scottish Literature*; *SLJ=Scottish Literary Journal*)

A. Principal Editions of Hogg's Works

Anecdotes of Scott. Ed. Jill Rubenstein. Edinburgh: Edinburgh UP, 1999.

The Brownie of Bodsbeck. Ed. Douglas S. Mack. Edinburgh: Edinburgh UP, 1976.

Poetic Mirrors. Ed. David Groves. Frankfurt: Peter Lang, 1990.

The Private Memoirs and Confessions of a Justified Sinner. Ed. John Carey. Oxford: Oxford UP, 1969.

Queen Hynde. Ed. Suzanne Gilbert and Douglas S. Mack. Edinburgh: Edinburgh UP, 1998.

A Queer Book. Ed. Peter Garside. Edinburgh: Edinburgh UP, 1995.

Selected Poems and Songs. Ed. David Groves. Edinburgh: Scottish Academic, 1986.

The Shepherds Calendar. Ed. Douglas S. Mack. Edinburgh: Edinburgh UP, 1995.

Tales of the Wars of Montrose. Ed. Gillian Hughes. Edinburgh: Edinburgh UP, 1996.

The Three Perils of Man: War, Women and Witchcraft. Ed. Douglas Gifford. Edinburgh: Canongate, 1996.

The Three Perils of Woman: Or Love, Leasing and Jealousy. Ed. David Groves, Antony Hasler and Douglas S. Mack. Edinburgh: Edinburgh UP, 1995.

B. Studies of *The Confessions*, and Related Works

Anonymous. "The Confessions of an English Glutton." *Blackwood's Edinburgh Magazine* 13 (1823): 86-93.

Bennington, Geoffrey. "Postal politics and the institution of the nation." *Nation and Narration*, ed. Homi K. Bhabha. London and New York: Routledge, 1990. 121-37.

Beveridge, Allan. "The confessions of a justified sinner and the psychopathology of the double." *Psychiatric Bulletin* 15 (1991): 344-5.

———. "James Hogg and Abnormal Psychology: Some Background Notes." *Studies in Hogg and His World* 2 (1991): 91-4.

Bligh, John. "The Doctrinal Premises of Hogg's *Confessions of a Justified Sinner.*" *SSL* 19 (1984): 148-64.

Bloedé, Barbara. "James Hogg's *Private Memoirs and Confessions of a Justified Sinner. Études Anglaises* 26 (1973): 174-86.

——. "*The Confessions of a Justified Sinner:* The Paranoiac Nucleus." Hughes (1984): 15-28.

——. "A Nineteenth-Century Case of Double Personality: A Possible Source for *The Confessions.*" Hughes (1988): 117-27.

Brims, John. "The Covenanting Tradition and Scottish Radicalism in the 1790s." *Covenant, Charter, and Party*, ed. Terry Brotherstone. Aberdeen: Aberdeen UP, 1989.

Calvin, Jean. *Institutes of the Christian Religion.* Tr. John Allen. London: J. Walker et al, 1813.

Campbell, Ian, ed. *Nineteenth-Century Scottish Fiction: Critical Essays.* Manchester: Carcanet, 1979.

Cowan, Ian B. *The Scottish Covenanters 1660-1688.* London: Victor Gollancz, 1976.

Craig, David. *Scottish Literature and the Scottish People 1680-1830.* London: Chatto and Windus, 1961.

Crawford, Robert. *Devolving English Literature.* Oxford: Clarendon, 1992.

Crawford, Thomas. "James Hogg: The Play of Region and Nation." Gifford (1988): 89-105.

Daiches, David. *The Paradox of Scottish Culture.* London: Oxford UP, 1964.

——. *Literature and Gentility in Scotland.* Edinburgh: Edinburgh UP, 1982.

Davie, George. *The Democratic Intellect.* Edinburgh: Edinburgh UP, 1961.

Davis, Leith. *Acts of Union: Scotland and the Literary Negotiation of the British Nation 1707-1830.* Cambridge: Cambridge UP, 1999.

Day, William Patrick. *In the Circles of Fear and Desire: A Study of Gothic Fantasy.* Chicago and London: U of Chicago P, 1985.

Dewar, H. "Report on a Communication from Dr Dyce of Aberdeen, to the Royal Society of Edinburgh, 'On Uterine Irritation, and its Effects on the Female Constitution.'" *Transactions of the Royal Society of Edinburgh* 9 (1823): 365-79.

Eggenschwiler, David. "James Hogg's *Confessions* and the Fall into Division." *SSL* 9 (1972): 26-39.

Fenwick, Julie. "Psychological and Narrative Determinism in James Hogg's *The Private Memoirs and Confessions of a Justified Sinner.*" *SLJ* 15 (1988): 61-9.

Finlay, Richard J. "Keeping the Covenant: Scottish National Identity." *Eighteenth Century Scotland: New Perspectives.* Ed. T.M. Devine and J.R. Young. East Linton: Tuckwell Press, 1999.

Fisher, Edward. *The Marrow of Modern Divinity.* Edinburgh: John Mosman, 1718.

Garden, Mrs. M.G., ed. *Memorials of James Hogg.* Paisley and London: Alexander Gardner, 1885.

Gide, André. "Introduction" to James Hogg, *The Private Memoirs and Confessions of a Justified Sinner.* London: Cresset Press, 1947.

Gifford, Douglas. *James Hogg.* Edinburgh: Ramsay Head, 1976.

———, ed. *The History of Scottish Literature* (vol. 3). Aberdeen: Aberdeen UP, 1988.

Groves, David. "Parallel Narratives in Hogg's *Justified Sinner.*" *SLJ* 9 (1982): 37-44.

———. "Allusions to *Dr. Faustus* in James Hogg's *A Justified Sinner.*" *SSL* 18 (1983): 157-65.

———. *James Hogg: The Growth of a Writer.* Edinburgh: Scottish Academic Press, 1988.

———. "James Hogg as a Romantic Writer." Hughes (1988): 1-9.

———. " 'W—M B—E, A Great Original': William Blake, The Grave, and James Hogg's Confessions." *SLJ* 18 (1991): 27-45.

Haddow, James. *The Antinomianism of the Marrow of Modern Divinity Detected.* Edinburgh: John Mosman, 1721.

Harries, Elizabeth W. "Duplication and Duplicity: James Hogg's *Private Memoirs and Confessions of a Justified Sinner.*" *Wordsworth Circle* 10 (1979): 187-96.

Hoffmann, E.T.A. *The Devil's Elixir.* Edinburgh: Blackwood's, 1824.

Hogg, James. *A Series of Lay Sermons on Good Principles and Good Breeding.* Ed. Gillian Hughes with Douglas S. Mack. Edinburgh: Edinburgh UP, 1997.

Hughes, Gillian, ed. *Papers Given at the First Conference of the James Hogg Society.* Stirling: James Hogg Society, 1984.

———, ed. *Papers Given at the Second James Hogg Society Conference.* Aberdeen: Aberdeen UP, 1988.

Hutton, Clark. "Kierkegaard, Antinomianism, and James Hogg's *Private Memoirs and Confessions of a Justified Sinner.*" *SLJ* 20 (1993): 37-48.

Jones, Douglas. "Double Jeopardy and the Chameleon Art in James Hogg's *Justified Sinner.*" *SSL* 23 (1988): 164-85.

Kearns, Michael S. "Intuition and Narration in James Hogg's *Confessions*." *SSL* 13 (1978): 81-91.

Kelly, Gary. *English Fiction of the Romantic Period 1789-1830*. London and New York: Longman, 1989.

Kiely, Robert. *The Romantic Novel in England*. Cambridge, Mass. and London: Harvard UP, 1972.

Kilgour, Maggie. *The Rise of the Gothic Novel*. London and New York: Routledge, 1995.

Lee, L.L. "The Devil's Figure: James Hogg's *Justified Sinner*." *SSL* 3 (1965-6): 230-9.

Letley, Emma. "Some Literary Uses of Scots in Hogg's *Confessions of a Justified Sinner* and *The Brownie of Bodsbeck*." Hughes (1984) 29-39.

——. "Language and Nineteenth-Century Scottish Fiction." Gifford (1988) 321-36.

Levin, Susan M. *The Romantic Art of Confession*. Columbia, SC: Camden House, 1998.

Mack, Douglas S. "Hogg's Religion and *The Confessions of a Justified Sinner*." *SSL* 7 (1970): 272-5.

——. "The Devil's Pilgrim: a Note on Wringhim's Private Memoirs in James Hogg's *Confessions of a Justified Sinner*." *SLJ* 2 (1975): 36-40.

——. "'The Rage of Fanaticism in Former Days': James Hogg's *Confessions of a Justified Sinner* and the Controversy over *Old Mortality*." Campbell 37-50.

Manning, Susan. *The Puritan-provincial Vision: Scottish and American Literature in the Nineteenth Century*. Cambridge: Cambridge UP, 1990.

Mason, Michael York. "The Three Burials in Hogg's *Justified Sinner*." *SSL* 13 (1978): 15- 23.

Miller, Karl. *Doubles: Studies in Literary History*. Oxford: Oxford UP, 1985.

Mitchill, S.L. "A Double Consciousness, or a Duality of Person in the same Individual." *Edinburgh Weekly Journal* 31 (1816): 252.

Muschet, Nicol. *The Confession of Nicol Muschet of Boghall*. Edinburgh: Oliver and Boyd, 1818.

Noble, Andrew. "John Wilson (Christopher North) and the Tory Hegemony." Gifford (1988): 125-52.

Oakleaf, David. "'Not the Truth': The Doubleness of Hogg's *Confessions* and the Eighteenth-Century Tradition." *SSL* 18 (1983): 59-74.

Pache, Walter. "'Der Ettrickschafer Hoggs.' A Scotsman's Literary Reputation in Germany." *SSL* 8 (1971): 109-17.

Petrie, David. "The Sinner versus the Scholar: two exemplary models of mis-re-membering and mis-taking signs in relation to Hogg's *Justified Sinner*." *Studies in Hogg and His World* 3 (1992): 57-67.

Phillipson, N.T. "Nationalism and Ideology." *Government and Nationalism in Scotland*, ed. J.N. Wolfe. Edinburgh: Edinburgh UP, 1969.

Pittock, Murray G.H. *The Invention of Scotland: The Stuart Myth and the Scottish Identity, 1638 to the Present*. London and New York: Routledge, 1991.

Redekop, Magdelene. "Beyond Closure: Buried Alive with Hogg's *Justified Sinner*." *English Literary History* 52 (1985): 159-84.

Rogers, Philip. "'A name which may serve your turn': James Hogg's Gil-Martin." *SSL* 21 (1986): 89-98.

Schoenfield, Mark L. "Butchering James Hogg: Romantic Identity in the Magazine." *At the Limits of Romanticism: Essays in Cultural, Feminist, and Materialist Criticism*, ed. Mary A. Favret and Nicola J. Watson. Bloomington and Indianapolis, 1994.

Sedgwick, Eve Kosovsky. *Between Men: English Literature and Male Homosocial Desire*. New York: Columbia UP, 1985.

Simpson, Kenneth. *The Protean Scot: The Crisis of Identity in Eighteenth Century Scottish Literature*. Aberdeen: Aberdeen UP, 1988.

Simpson, Louis. *James Hogg: A Critical Study*. Edinburgh and London: Oliver and Boyd, 1962.

Smith, Iain Crichton. "A Work of Genius: James Hogg's *Justified Sinner*." *SSL* 28 (1993): 1-11.

Smith, Nelson C. *James Hogg*. Boston: Twayne, 1980.

Strout, Allan Lang, ed. *The Life and Letters of James Hogg, The Ettrick Shepherd* (vol. 1). Lubbock, Texas: Texas Tech Press, 1946.

Watson, Nicola J. *Revolution and the Form of the British Novel 1790-1825*. Oxford: Clarendon Press, 1994.

Glossary

a'	all	*braw*	fine, splendid
ado	to do	*brikk*	break
ae	one	*brunstane*	brimstone
aff	off	*bum*	buzzing or humming
afore	before		sound
aften	often	*burd*	offspring
ain	own	*burn*	stream
aince	once		
aiths	oaths	*ca'*	call
amang	among	*callant*	young man
an	if	*canna*	cannot
an'	and	*canny*	favourable
ane	one	*carl*	man
aneath	beneath	*cast*	v. to dig, clear out
anent	concerning, about	*cauler*	resh
anither	another	*chafts*	cheeks
atween	between	*chiel*	man
auld	old	*circumfauldit*	encircled, surrounded
aumuses	alms-giving	*clachan*	small village
aw	all	*claes*	clothes
awthegither	altogether	*claithing*	clothing
aye	always, continually	*clapper-clawin*	beating
ayont	beyond, beside	*cloots*	hoofs
		close	narrow passageway
baillie	town magistrate	*cock*	raise
bairns	children	*contrair*	contrary
baith	both	*corbies*	ravens
bane	bone	*corby-craw*	raven
bannet	flat cap	*crap*	crept
bedstrae	bedstraw	*craws*	crows
belang	belong	*creeshy*	fat
bickers	drinking cups	*croon*	bellow, roar
biggings	buildings	*crouping*	croaking
binna	is not	*cuif*	fool
bits	mall		
boardly	burly	*dee*	do
bodle	twopence coin	*dee*	die
body	person	*deil*	devil
Bogle	frightening ghost or	*didna*	did not
	phantom	*dike*	low wall of stones,
bourock	cottage		turf etc.
bouzy	fat	*ding*	beat
bowkail	cabbage	*dinna*	do not
brae	hillside	*disna*	does not
braidside	whole side	*ditit*	daft, foolish
braird	first sprouts of grain	*div*	do

divot	piece of turf, sod	ha'	home
doesnae	does not	hae	have
doiting	stumbling	haena	have not
doitrified	stupefied, dazed	haill/hale	whole
dominie	schoolmaster	halesale	wholesale
donnart	stupid, dull	hame	home
dree	endure, suffer	havers	gossip, trivial talk
dud	sclothes	hay raip	clothes line
dung	struck	het	hot
		heuch	steep bank
een	eyes	hind	farm-servant, plough-
ell	Scots measure of		man
	length	hoad-road	chaos, turmoil
ern	iron	hope	small valley
evite	avoid	houk	dig
		hout na	emphatically not
fa	who	howkin	poking one's nose in
fand	found	howlets	owls
fashed	troubled	hunder	hundred
fat	what		
fawn	fallen	ill-faurd	unpleasant looking
feele	fool	ir	are
fer	far	ither	other
flannens	flannels		
flaring	flattery	jaud	worthless woman
flinders	fragments, pieces	juggs	pillory
flitters	shreds, splinters		
flummery	flattery	kail	cabbage
focks	folks	keek	peep
fou	full (with alcohol)	ken	know
frae	from	ketch	toss
fra-yont	from the other side of	keust	cast
fraze	exaggeration, flattery	kimmers	gossips
		kirk	church
gae	go/gave	kists	chests, trunks for
gaed	went		money
gang	go		
gars	makes, causes	lang	long
gate	way, road	lave	remainder
gaun	going	lay	silence
gayan	very	lead	produce witnesses,
gear	wealth		evidence
ghaists	ghosts	leasing-	
gie	give	making	lying
gin	if	leear	liar
gizened	parched, withered	linn	deep gorge, ravine
gowk	fool, cuckoo	lint-swingling	flax-beating
grit	great	louns	lower class men,
guidit	guided		menials
gull	dupe	lounder	beat harshly

loup	leap	*sidie for sidie*	side by side
		siller	silver
ma	my	*sin*	since
mae/mair	more	*skair*	illuminate
maks	makes	*slough*	outer skin
mall/mell	hammer, mallet	*slumpas*	one lump, together
marches	frontiers, boundaries	*snork*	snort
maugre	despite, notwith-	*speeder*	spider
	standing	*spleuchan*	tobacco pouch
maun	must	*stamack*	stomach
mense	honour, credit	*stanes*	stones
mony	many	*stinted*	stopped
muckil/		*stotts*	bullocks
muckle	large, much	*strodge*	stride
		swee	course, sway
na/nae	no	*swirea*	hollow between hills
neist	next		
		tak	take
o'er	too	*tane*	one
ony	any	*tap*	top
overhie	overtake	*tauld*	told
ower	over	*tawpie*	foolish young woman
		tent	notice
pat	put	*thae*	those
paulies	deformed, sickly lambs	*thrang*	crowd
peeous	pious	*tither*	other
pink	excellent example	*toom*	empty
pirns	spools for thread	*trow*	believe
pit	put	*twa*	two
plack	small copper coin	*tweeled*	twilled (fabric)
poukit	plucked		
		unco	very
raip	rope	*unco-like*	odd, peculiar
reards	roars, makes a noise		
rede	advise	*vera*	very
reid	red		
reistit trams	useless limbs	*wa'*	wall
rin	run	*wab*	web
rowth	plenty	*wad*	would
		wadna	would not
sae	so	*war*	were
sanna	shall not	*waratch*	wretch
sauchless	senseless	*wark*	work
sauf	save	*wasna*	was not
saur o' reek	smell of smoke	*wauken*	waken
scoudered	scorched	*waur*	worse
shakel bane	wrist	*weel*	well
shanned	grimaced	*wha*	who
sib	related to	*whan*	when
sic/sickan	such	*whaten*	what kind of

windlestrae	dried stalk of grass	*yelloch*	yell, shriek
winna	will not	*yerk*	sudden sharp pain
woodriff	woodruff	*ye's*	you shall
wore	proceed cautiously	*yestreen*	yesterday
wrang	wrong	*yon*	that
writer	lawyer	*yoolling*	howling
wynd	narrow alley	*yowes*	ewes